After studying art history in Glasgow, Tom Pugh invented a career as a travelling copywriter and teacher, living and working in London, Sydney and Tokyo before settling in Berlin with his wife and two children. *The Golden Cage* is his second novel.

THE GOLDEN CAGE

TOM PUGH

Published in November 2018 by Crux Publishing Ltd.

ISBN: 978-1-909979-81-9

For Dad

CONTENTS

A Note On The Period ix
Dramatis Personae xii
Chapter 1 1
Chapter 2 8
Chapter 3 15
Chapter 4 25
Chapter 5 36
Chapter 6 42
Chapter 7 53
Chapter 8 61
Chapter 9 74
Chapter 10 81
Chapter 11 91
Chapter 12 98
Chapter 13 110
Chapter 14 118
Chapter 15 124
Chapter 16 129
Chapter 17 140
Chapter 18 149
Chapter 19 158
Chapter 20 167
Chapter 21 175

Chapter 22 181
Chapter 23 186
Chapter 24 195
Chapter 25 203
Chapter 26 209
Chapter 27 217
Chapter 28 228
Chapter 29 236
Chapter 30 242
Chapter 31 248
Chapter 32 263
Chapter 33 268
Chapter 34 273
Chapter 35 279

A NOTE ON THE PERIOD

At the dawn of the fifteenth century, life in western Europe – while often short and unpredictable – was underpinned by a belief system unchanged in a thousand years; a state of affairs which had persisted since Christianity became the state religion of the Roman Empire and set about the systematic destruction of works by pre-Christian writers.

The Church's long monopoly on knowledge was only broken in the first half of the fifteenth century, when the works of Lucretius and Plato were rediscovered (in 1417 and 1438 respectively). The ideas contained in the works of these two authors played a major role in unleashing the astonishing wave of new thinking known as the renaissance (or 're-birth'), leading ultimately to the collapse of the worldview promoted and refined by the Christian Church over the previous millennium.

In *The Devil's Library*, Longstaff, Aurélie and Durant attempt to discover the location of a long-forgotten collection of thousands of the works of antiquity at a time when the first rush of excitement brought about by the (re)discovery of Plato and Lucretius was already congealing – what had briefly been a battle between people who believed in the supremacy of revelation (God's word) versus people who believed in the supremacy of reason (Man's intelligence) had now descended into a battle between two competing interpretations of God's word; the 'Catholic' Christian Church against the various Lutheran or 'Reformed' Christian Churches. The window opened by Plato and Lucretius was being firmly closed by a series of temporal and religious leaders willing to take increasingly violent measures against any threat to their authority.

A brief description of 'the Massacre of Wassy' will help to clarify this: under King Henri II, followers of the reformist church in France (known as Huguenots) faced persecution. After Henri's death, his widow (Catherine de Medici) attempted to end this persecution and create the conditions for peaceful co-existence. The uneasy truce she brokered was torn apart on 1 March 1562 by Francois, Duke of Guise, when he came upon a large congregation of Huguenots in the town of Wassy. Exactly what happened next is disputed but ended in Francois ordering his men to lock a barn which the Huguenots had been using as their church and burn it down, resulting in the deaths of 63 unarmed men, women and children. From this point on, in France at least, there was no longer any room for compromise between the competing versions of Christianity.

Events related in *The Golden Cage* take place in 1565, three years after the Massacre of Wassy and seven after Elizabeth I was crowned Queen of England.

Initially, Catholic Europe appears to have been unconcerned by the sudden appearance of a Protestant monarch on England's throne. Perhaps this was because neither of Elizabeth's two siblings had lasted more than a few years, and even if Elizabeth did prove more resilient than either Edward or Mary, she was still regarded as a mere woman. It was assumed that events would quickly see her cowed, coaxed or married into the true faith.

As months turned into years, however, the rulers of Catholic Europe grew impatient. Singly and together, with varying degrees of enthusiasm, King Philip of Spain, the pope, and the powerful Guise family in France were all increasingly inclined to play an active role in Elizabeth's downfall. This was only partly for reasons of religion; Elizabeth's England was a threat to Spanish shipping in the Atlantic and a thorn in Philip's side as he sought to put down rebellion in the low countries, while for the Guise family, led by Charles, Cardinal of Lorraine, the prize was potentially even greater; his niece – Mary, Queen of Scots – was next in line to the English throne.

Plotters on the continent would also have been encouraged by divisions within the English court. The country had seen four different monarchs in eleven years, during which time the state religion had changed from something of Henry VIII's own invention to something close to Lutheranism under his son Edward VI, then back to Catholicism under 'Bloody' Mary, before Elizabeth picked up where her father had left off with a bespoke form of Protestantism. The short reigns of Edward and Mary meant that these changes had taken place with bewildering speed, with the result that every English man and woman of note had been forced to deny their true beliefs – everyone was a liar, in other words, either now or in the recent past.

In such an environment, it should be no surprise that Elizabeth's court reeked of fear and suspicion. The two principal factions (made up of many smaller cliques) were led by Robert Dudley – the Earl of Leicester and a childhood friend of Elizabeth's who had nonetheless spent his youth soldiering for King Philip of Spain in an attempt to prove his loyalty to her older sister – and William Cecil and Nicholas Bacon – new men and committed Protestants who had nonetheless bent the knee to Mary while many of their co-religionists had gone into self-imposed exile on the continent.

DRAMATIS PERSONAE

Matthew and Aurélie Longstaff, *husband and wife, living at Martlesham in Suffolk*
Gaetan and Laure Durant, *father and daughter, living in Paris*

In England

Sir Nicholas Bacon, *Lord Chancellor of England*
Anne Bacon, *his wife and translator of John Jewel's* Apologie of the Anglican Church
Anthony and Francis Bacon, *their children*
Francis Walsingham, *Member of Parliament for Lyme Regis in Dorset (subsequently principal secretary to Elizabeth I)*
William Cecil (later Lord Burghley), *Elizabeth I's Secretary of State and chief advisor*
Thomas Howard, *Duke of Norfolk*
Robert Dudley, *Earl of Leicester*
John Dee, *mathematician, astrologer and philosopher, suspected of necromancy*

In France

Sir Nicholas Throckmorton, *English ambassador to the French court*
Horatio Palavicino, *English merchant, based in Bordeaux*
Catherine de Medici, *widow of Henri II, French Regent until her son, Charles IX, declared his majority in 1563*
Michel de Nostredame, *physician, astrologer, France's most famous prophet*

The Guise

Charles, *Cardinal of Lorraine*

Francois, *Duke of Guise (deceased)*

Henri (16), *his son and successor to the title*

Mary, Queen of Scots, *Henri's cousin and next in line to the English throne*

The Dowager Duchess of Guise, born Antoinette de Bourbon, *widow of Claude, mother of Francois and Charles*

Chapter 1

Paris, France. January 6th, 1565

In the tavern, no one flinched at the distant crack of musket fire. The sound had become so common, Paris might have been a city in the borderlands between Christendom and the Muselman Empire.

Gaetan Durant looked round at the sorry collection of drinkers – petty criminals, beggars, whores – flotsam and jetsam of this monstrous city. The same faces he saw each time he visited *La Tête du Sarrasin*, but so oddly still tonight they might have been ghosts. It was the sixth of January, twin ceremony of the Twelfth Night and the Feast of Fools. This time last year, soon after Durant had arrived in the capital, there'd been a bonfire at Les Halles, a maypole at Braque's Chapel, a mystery play at the Palais de Justice, all trumpeted by the Provost's soldiers in their suits of fine mauve camlet. This year, the same men were dressed in blood-soaked leather, horns exchanged for swords as they fought to stem the violence. Decent folk huddled beneath their beds, chairs and tables piled against the door, while a few of the indecent, those unwilling to pick a side, huddled together in this tavern.

Durant gestured at the deck of cards, face down on the scarred and pitted table-top. The hilt of a short poniard scraped his ribs beneath the black doublet.

"Where were we, gentlemen?"

Lecornu, to his right, was a thin man with lank hair and a pointed nose, the handkerchief round his neck puffed into some slight approximation of a ruff. His voice was a needling whine.

"The king should be in Paris. He'd know as much, if his father hadn't whelped him on a foreign witch."

Conversation died at the nearest tables. Lecornu looked delighted, as if it were his daring which kept him safe and not the fact of his association with the powerful Guise family. Durant poured himself more wine. The tavern stank worse than a midden. It was freezing outside and roasting in here. The landlord had nailed boards across the narrow windows to keep the firelight from performing its treacherous dance in the windows. Beads of sweat ran down the patrons' necks and the walls were slick beneath the sagging ceiling.

Durant felt an urge to stand, pluck the night cloak from his chair and bid his companions goodnight, an urge which died when he thought of home. Cooped up these last few days, his daughter Laure would not be in a welcoming mood. Durant closed his eyes. He was a trained physician, though he'd never sat for the Doctor's Cap. Already a year in the capital, he had comfortable consulting rooms, reasonable fees – and yet here he sat, partnering with a butcher to make ends meet as a card-sharp.

Durant flicked the cheap, block-printed cards back and forth in his long fingers, making them jump and dance. Manu snorted. There was something that seemed so honest about the butcher's thick beard and leather jerkin, spotted with the blood of his trade. The two of them rarely spoke, an observer would have thought they were rivals. Durant tapped the cards into a tidy pile and dealt. The mark, Lecornu, surveyed his hand with apparent satisfaction. He was a miserable gambler, betting the minimum unless he drew unbeatable cards. Durant and Manu had been working him for an hour already with nothing to show for their efforts but a few shaved coppers. Manu tapped his jaw – time to let the Guise informant win a hand. Not too much; they wanted Lecornu to regret his native caution.

He called after a single round of betting, before he'd even made good on his previous losses. Still, the informer raked the small pile of winnings into his lap with a satisfied smirk.

Durant dealt again. A serving girl walked past their table, face painted to mask a cleft-lip. Lecornu grabbed her by the wrist.

"Your establishment has all the charm of a morgue," he raised his voice, "I thought this was supposed to be a place of entertainment."

The serving girl was only a year or two younger than Durant's daughter. She looked towards the counter. The landlord shrugged, arms folded across his broad chest.

"You heard the man."

She hung her head, face hidden behind long hair as she climbed onto their table. Manu rescued the cards from beneath her feet, Lecornu began a slow clap, the beat taken up at half a dozen tables. The girl lifted her thin arms. The crowd gave a roar of drunken approval when her hips began to move. She started to spin, faster and faster, firelight shone on her bare shoulders, on the un-pleated bodice. Her slender legs flashed beneath the billowing skirts. Her black hair spun in time, eyes closed, the point of her tongue just visible beneath the cleft-lip.

Durant could hear her breathe, hear the scrape of her soft shoes on the table-top, his stomach turned by the scent of lechery. Only the landlord seemed immune, leaning on a cheap bust of St. Giron – his standard perch, from where he told the story of his grandfather several times removed, who'd returned from the Crusades with a severed head, exchanged for the freehold on this tavern.

But Parisians no longer went to war against the Turks. These days, in the dark streets outside, it was Christian against Christian. Rival mobs had been terrorising the provinces for years, killing, looting, raping. Catholic militias devising new tortures for the Calvinist Huguenots, who took their revenge on priests, monks and nuns. The boy-king Charles IX had set off on a two-year tour of the country with his mother Catherine de Medici. They wanted to heal wounds, but the people simply gaped, grumbled at the expense and returned to killing once the Royal Progress had moved on. And the same cancer which had infected the provinces crept slowly through the streets of the capital.

The dancer's feet came together. She threw back her head, dark eyes blazing with pride and defiance.

Footsteps thundered in the street outside, hard enough to shake the timbers. The drinkers fell silent, stared at their cups as boot leather cracked on the frozen cobbles. Who was out there? Lackeys loyal to the Duke of Guise? A mob in service to Montmorency? Would it be *Vive la messe* or *Vive l'Admiral?* Catholic beasts or Huguenot animals?

Five seconds passed. Durant saw Manu bite his lower lip, then raise an eyebrow. There was a knock at the tavern door. Three taps. A pause. Two more. The landlord disappeared behind the curtain, returning with a man in a dun-coloured jerkin.

"The Guise have fled the city!"

Durant glanced at Lecornu. The informant did not seem concerned that his paymasters had given way before their rivals. His beady eyes shifted from man to man, taking careful note of their reactions.

Durant took a long draft of wine, before adding another two coins to the pile. "Lecornu?"

"The Medici witch is to blame." The informant produced a silver coin.

"She's not even in Paris."

Lecornu nodded, as if Durant had proved his point. "This whole Royal Progress is nothing but an excuse for her to go and prostrate herself before her pet sorcerer…"

"For the love of God, Lecornu," interrupted the butcher, "don't get him started on Nostredame again!"

Durant smiled. "I've said it before, Michel de Nostredame is just a harmless old man…"

"Who worships death." Lecornu looked sideways at Durant, before adding one more silver coin to the pile.

Durant raised. He'd seen Manu's signal – Lecornu had taken advantage of the girl's dance to improve his hand with the addition of a card from his sleeve. Two could play at that game.

"So do half the nuns in France."

Lecornu's eyes grew wide. He crossed himself before raising again.

"They say he's constructing a tomb for himself down there. That's what Catherine went to see."

"Gutter-gossip."

"Nostredame did predict the last king's death," Manu attempted to broker a peace; Lecornu was contemptible, but not a man to cross – not with his connections. "I can still remember the words of his prophecy: *The young lion will overcome the older one, On the field of combat in a single battle; He will pierce his eyes through a golden cage, Two wounds made one, then he dies a cruel death.*"

"Overwrought and overwritten," said Durant. "Just an old man desperate to believe he can see the future. Michel has no special powers – trust me, I know the man."

Lecornu gave him a strange look. "So you've said, but Henry was killed in a jousting match against a younger man."

"Pierced in the eye," added Manu, "through the slit of his golden helmet. It took him eleven days to die."

"And both men wore lions on the shields," replied Durant with heavy sarcasm. He looked at Manu with unfeigned disgust. "Not you, too?"

"Nostredame is in league with the Devil," Lecornu stabbed the table-top with a forefinger.

"He's a charlatan," said Durant. "The old are always supplanted by the young and every death is cruel. *I* could write his poems; there's not a man, woman or child in France who'd know the difference."

He placed his cards face up on the table, eyes fixed on Lecornu. The informant stared in disbelief. Durant knew at once he'd been reckless, but the chance had been too good to miss – and Laure would be pleased. He gathered the winnings into his purse and rose, the legs of his chair scraping two straight lines in the saw-dust.

"You're leaving?" said Manu, "with the streets as they are…"

Durant flicked his dark cloak into place. "You heard the man; the Guise have fled." He gestured for the landlord to release him into the cool night air.

"Mind how you go, doctor."

Durant shivered in the icy street. *Mind how you go, doctor.* The simple phrase had long since acquired a bitter edge. The riots had sent a few patients his way – army-surgeon work; a steady stream of labourers and small tradesmen with burns and breaks, stab wounds and dislocated joints – not enough to build the respectable life he'd promised Laure.

Durant pulled the cloak close to hide the collar of his shirt. The street seemed quiet – no heavy tramp of feet or shouted oaths – but still he walked softly, tried to muffle his footsteps. It had taken weeks to learn his way around this labyrinth of alleyways, intersections and cul-de-sacs, like a skein of ravelled thread. Reluctant to head straight home, Durant made for an old tower in what remained of Philip-Augustus's wall, ducked beneath the wooden boards at the entrance and climbed the narrow staircase. He was sweating by the time he reached the top, the sleeping city spread before him, a monstrous giant of chimneys, bridges, squares, spires and bell-towers.

He closed his eyes and remembered the fire which had consumed so many thousands of books, hidden in the forgotten library beneath Naples. Hard to believe only two and half years had passed since he'd fled the smouldering remains with Matthew Longstaff and Aurélie. He smiled at the thought of his two friends; the exiled English soldier and the young Florentine woman who'd been raised and educated by Giacomo Vescosi, regarded by many as Europe's pre-eminent humanist scholar. The three of them had formed a formidable team, defeating the Master of the Sacred Palace and his so-called Hounds of

God, preserving at least one text from the burning library – *On Freedom,* by the Greek philosopher Epicurus. Longstaff and Aurélie had passed it on to their patron, the English Lord Chancellor Sir Nicholas Bacon. Durant had heard nothing of it since, but still remembered the strange sensation of hope which the opening words had inspired in him:

> *What a creature is man. Incomparable in reason, infinite in faculties. What need has he of angels, who can move and feel as angels do? What need of God, who has it within himself to penetrate the deepest mysteries? How perfect he is, the beauty of the world; how short-lived and fearful, the terror of his fellows. Man is dust, made of the four elements of earth, air, fire and water, and animated by the fifth, the quintessence…*

Time for home and bed. Heading back down the stairs, Durant smoothed the front of his black doublet, a fine piece of clothing made from Dutch cloth but threadbare at the collar and cuffs. Laure would have to apply another layer of boot-black. Hopefully, she'd have turned in already. A good night's sleep for them both and tomorrow he'd try to make peace once more. How could he not, after eight years of searching and then the miracle of finding her again?

Durant spun at a sound in the darkness. Pain blossomed – a blood-red rose – a stone against the side of his head. He just had time to see an arm disappearing into shadow, white knuckles, dirt beneath the crooked nails. The image fading as his bones turned to water. His body struck the ground with a muffled thud, his awareness carried off through cracks in the worn flagstones.

Chapter 2

Suffolk, England. February 13th, 1565.

A scream raced through the naked trees. Matthew Longstaff changed direction without thinking, no longer running for the joy of hearing his heart beat after a winter cooped inside. Sparrow ran at his heels. The dog's dark coat was streaked with white these days, but she was still strong, still swift over short distances.

Breath quickening, blood coursing as they sprinted through the beechwood. Longstaff grew angry as he ran, drawn by the cries of pain and fear. This was *his* land, reclaimed after thirty years of exile. A weak sun marked his passage beneath the leafless canopy. He was dressed for comfort and carried no weapon but the short knife in his belt. Leaving his wife asleep beneath the warm covers, he'd risen early to run in the dawn light. And now this.

The screaming stopped. Longstaff crashed into a small clearing, sweat beading in his straw-coloured hair, elbows pumping beneath the heavy shoulders. An eight-point stag lay sprawled in the centre. A man knelt above the beast with a bloody knife in one hand, hacking for the easiest cuts of meat. It was always the same with these bastards: take what they want and leave the rest for scavengers. The man was old, gaunt cheeks hidden beneath a grey beard. The penalty for poaching was death. Sparrow hunkered down at Longstaff's side, teeth bared in a ferocious snarl.

"Get out of here. Go on."

A boy stood perched in a silvery beech, legs planted where a branch forked – the arrow knocked on his bow was pointed at Longstaff's heart.

That arrow – it was a perfect match for the one buried in the stag's throat. Longstaff cursed. He should have known there would be two.

"Get out," the boy's voice was high and clear.

Longstaff raised his hands: "Put the weapon down."

Soon, the lad's thin arms would tire. And then what? Kill a man or let himself be taken? *The penalty for poaching was death.*

Longstaff thought of Aurélie, waiting for him at home. He removed his knife and threw it in the dirt. "Climb down and be on your way. I won't stop you."

A look of contempt twisted the boy's half-formed features.

"Mind, it's only your lives I'm offering." Longstaff's blue eyes were hard and chill as they met the boy's. "The stag belongs to me."

"You're William Longstaff's son?" interrupted the old poacher. He puffed his sunken chest. "I served your father half my life. You're the very spit."

I served your father. Amazing how few of Longstaff's neighbours were willing to make this same admission, even now. Longstaff stared at the poacher's face, lined with the passage of years. It struck no bell of recognition, but that meant nothing – he'd been eight when the king's men took him away from here and sent him into exile. He gestured at the stag.

"My father didn't employ men who'd treat an animal like this."

"My eyes have grown weak," protested the poacher, "and we don't have the luxury of time, the boy and I."

Kneeling beside the stag, Longstaff poured water from his skin, used his palms to sluice the blood away. "Tell the lad to climb down."

The poacher looked up. "Do as he says, Wilf."

The boy took his time lowering the bow. He leapt from branch to branch like a squirrel.

"Where are his parents?"

"Dead."

"I'll warrant you've a rope?"

The poacher unwound a length from his waist.

"What'll you do with us?"

Wilf kept his distance, picking dried sap from his fingertips in a brave show of indifference.

"You didn't see me coming?" said Longstaff.

The boy coloured. "Can't look everywhere at once."

Longstaff nodded. *Too lazy to do his job properly.* "The elm would have given you a better line of sight."

"The branches grow wrong."

"Better than a pine. For climbing."

Wilf rubbed the back of his head. He was younger than Longstaff had thought.

"Pine's all right."

"Wait until you're a stone heavier. Never trust a pine, they keep their deadwood too long." Longstaff supressed a smile. "Find me a branch, Wilf."

"What for?"

"Twice the stag's length, thick enough to bear his weight."

Longstaff trussed the dead animal with the poacher's rope. When the boy dragged a fallen branch into the clearing, he broke off the crown and ran it between the stag's legs.

"I won't have poachers here, so you've a choice. Clear off these lands or hoist up that animal and come with me."

They stared at him. Two sullen faces, one young and one old.

"To what purpose?"

"You were one of my father's woodsmen?"

"Head Woodsman, until he was took away."

"I could use you. The boy, too, despite his wildness. Three square meals a day and a roof over your heads."

What else could he do? See them hanged? Let a man who'd served his father spend his final years living rough? Aurélie would never speak to him again.

Winter had been slow releasing its grip. Only a few days earlier, great drifts of snow had still pressed against the thick, stone walls of the house. Now, as Longstaff led the estate's two newest workers, he felt the sun's warmth on his back, the unmistakable promise of spring. The boy would bring some life to the Martlesham estate and the greybeard must know these lands as well as anyone alive. Aurélie always enjoyed hearing the old folk tales and Longstaff was trying to learn more about the local flora and fauna – both doing what they could to make the place feel like a home. It was harder for Aurélie, born and raised in the Italian city of Florence.

Longstaff walked ahead to the brow of a low hill – his favourite view of the house, nestled among fields just shedding their winter coats of grey frost. During the long decades of exile, he'd imagined it razed to the ground. No other fate had seemed possible. It had taken him twenty-seven years to return and discover the house still stood, and that had only come about by a stroke of good fortune. Sir Nicholas Bacon, Lord Chancellor of England, had sent him south to recover the contents of an ancient library, buried for centuries in secret vaults beneath the city of Naples. Longstaff had failed. The pope's chief censor and spymaster had set the precious scrolls alight, destroying the accumulated knowledge of the Persians, Greeks and Romans in a huge conflagration. Longstaff and Aurélie had only managed to preserve a single manuscript, but that had been enough – just – to persuade Sir Nicholas to keep his part of the bargain. The Lord Chancellor had used his power to erase the stain on Longstaff's name and return the family estate to his possession.

Longstaff moved on, leading the two poachers past wattle and daub outbuildings and Martlesham's small collection of animals. The household would be living on venison for the next few weeks. Longstaff pointed to a shed which doubled as a slaughterhouse.

"My father taught me that every scrap of meat on a stag's body, every ounce of fat, every bone and every hair can be put to good use. I'll be back to check on your work in an hour."

He searched the windows for a glimpse of Aurélie as he approached the house. She'd grown quieter during the winter, less quick to share her thoughts. Of course, she was nothing like the wives of his neighbours. Longstaff had known that when they married – a short ceremony at a church on Thames Street, two days after landing in England. He pushed through the front door, full of the story he was about to tell – threatened by a juvenile in the woods, a chance encounter with a former retainer of his father's…

Aurélie stood waiting at the foot of the stairs. As always, the breath caught in Longstaff's throat; at twenty-five, she was eleven years his junior and the most beautiful woman he'd ever seen. She held a letter in one raised hand. Her cheeks were flushed and the bright blue eyes shone with restless energy.

"It's from Durant's daughter. She says he's disappeared."

Wordlessly, she handed him the letter. When Durant wrote, it was always in Italian, a language the three of them spoke fluently. The daughter preferred French, apparently. It took Longstaff several minutes to decipher her crabbed hand.

Monsieur Longstaff,

We have never met. When my father found me, you and Aurélie had already crossed La Manche and arrived in England.

He described you both as his greatest friends, on other occasions as his only friends. He wrote to you often. You must know that relations between us are strained, despite our joy at being reunited after so many years. So perhaps you won't think it out of character that he has vanished without warning. You are aware, I'm sure, that he freed me from an ill-chosen husband and arranged for the two of us to move to Paris, where we have attempted to make a home together.

I last saw my father two weeks ago tomorrow. The capital is not without its dangers, but I do not believe he is the kind of man who might fall prey to common thieves. Nor, for all his faults, do I believe he is the kind of man to abandon his daughter in straightened circumstances.

He once told me, if anything happened to him, that I should contact you. I am not writing for myself. I fear that something terrible has befallen him. I hope you will not think it forward of me to share these tidings.

Yours in God,
Laure Durant.

A single sheet of paper. Longstaff stared at Aurélie in confusion. "Relations between them are strained? Durant never said."

He barely registered that his wife was packing.

"Perhaps it's a forgery – some kind of trap? We have enemies on the continent. Easier to murder us in France than England."

"Everyone who knew about the Devil's Library is dead, Matthew."

"As far as we know. And there's still a price on my head in Muscovy. This letter seems strange."

"All the more reason to believe it's genuine. A boy arrived from the village at first light. They all know how generously you tip when it's something from France. He left a few minutes ago with a letter for Sir Nicholas."

Longstaff stared at her. "You've written to Bacon already?"

"Who else can provide us with passports?"

"Aurélie…"

"What?"

He gestured helplessly. The room, the house. The fields and forests. He was the master of meadows, pastures, barns. Finally home, a wealthy man with a pantry full of meat and wine. He thought of Wilf and the old poacher, hard at work in the slaughterhouse.

"Who's to say he hasn't just wandered off?"

"Durant? A man who spent eight years searching Europe for his daughter?"

"And eight before that ignoring her! Have you forgotten they're murdering each other in France?"

She knew. She read Durant's letters just as keenly as he did. A vicious civil war was tearing the country apart, while an adolescent king strove to hold the centre. Longstaff held the letter in his fingertips. It seemed a flimsy reason to turn their lives upside down. "What do you think we can achieve?"

"Comfort Durant's daughter. Find out what's happened. What's wrong with you, Matthew?"

He left the room without a word. There were at least a dozen people he'd have to see. "Tomorrow, Aurélie," he shouted back at her. "We're not going anywhere until I've put things in order."

Longstaff sulked for an hour, surrounded by the neat rows of ledgers in his small office. The story of a modest Suffolk estate; records of harvest, rainfall, and livestock, contracts with tenant farmers going back three and four generations. He knew he should make a list of people he needed to talk to, starting with the two he'd employed that morning, but what was the point? Martlesham had survived twenty-seven years without him; it would survive another few weeks while he and Aurélie begged favours from Sir Nicholas Bacon. No doubt, she'd want them to stay there as well.

He was going to bloody kill Durant – assuming the bastard was still alive.

Finally, Longstaff let his eyes fall on the large chest standing in a corner of the room. He muttered a curse before throwing back the lid. For the last two and a half years, his weapons and old travelling clothes had lain abandoned, the long cavalryman's coat, patched and repaired but still serviceable, the padded jerkin – he felt the weight of several small medallions in the silk lining; campaign medals from Metz and Marciano, as well as tokens of friendship and remembrance from fallen comrades. Then his musket, oiled and wrapped in cloth, and the old katzbalger sword. The worn hilt fitted his hand like a glove.

Chapter 3

Longstaff slept badly that night, uncomfortably aware of Aurélie's restless excitement as she lay beside him in the darkness. He wasn't surprised to find himself alone in bed when he woke at dawn.

She'd already packed their breakfast. They could eat on the road, apparently. Longstaff did not comment on her outfit – tight-fitting hose and a tunic which fell to her knees. Nor did he acknowledge her broad grin when she saw him in the cavalryman's coat, Sparrow trotting eagerly at his heels.

"Just like old times."

Their fastest route to the London Road led through the village, blessedly quiet at this time on a Sunday morning. At least they were being spared the weekly trip to church, thought Longstaff, as they rode beneath the tall spire – slender monument to the riches of this land, where chalky clay yielded generous harvests of grain and supported large flocks of sheep.

Longstaff sank lower in the saddle. It wasn't religious sensibility which made him reluctant to worship in the old parish church – in his opinion, one confession was much the same as another when a man needed to pray – but nostalgia. Here, more than anywhere, he missed the sounds and smells of his childhood. The stained-glass windows he remembered had been destroyed, the reliquary smashed, the gleaming chapel plate long since melted down and the frescos replaced with bible verses drawn in thick black paint.

"You're looking forward to being in London again." He had not intended it to sound like an accusation.

"I'm looking forward to seeing Anne and Sir Nicholas. And the boys; Anthony must be nine already, Francis five."

"They're not our friends, Aurélie."

She stared at him. "Anne is the best friend I have in this country. Sir Nicholas would be yours, if you'd let him."

"He forced me to serve him. I could have been killed..."

"He gave you a fair reward. God's teeth, Matthew, we haven't left Suffolk in two years."

They entered a long avenue of elm trees, hundreds of feet high. It would be magnificent in another month with the sun shining down on a canopy of new leaves. Now, thanks to the elm's odd habit of throwing out a strong-side branch, the naked trees seemed oppressive. It was this habit, Longstaff remembered, which made the elm such a popular gallows tree.

Aurélie shivered. "I hate them."

"Magnificent timbering wood."

She laughed at him.

"I'm serious."

"I know."

Longstaff managed a smile.

"Look up," continued Aurélie, "one of the first bright days of the year."

She was right. Even the few travellers they saw on the London Road seemed in good heart – merchants banded together for safety, a group of students and clerics. They passed a stone-cutter and carpenter who'd stopped to exchange rumours of work. The two men stared at Aurélie with frank admiration.

Longstaff warned them off with a look.

"We could cut across country here," he said, "re-join the road further south?"

"I thought you'd never ask."

They galloped at an angle to the road. Longstaff heard Aurélie laugh as he followed over meadows spotted with the first small flowers of spring. He edged alongside, they rode knee to knee for nearly an hour until the open meadows gave way to woods.

"Like old times," smiled Aurélie. "You and I riding together."

"You and I," agreed Longstaff, "Durant and Vescosi."

He bit his lip. Bad enough to mention Durant; what had possessed him to remind her of Giacomo Vescosi? The man who'd raised her and shaped her extraordinary mind lay dead among the ruins of the Devil's Library.

"Do you remember teaching me to shoot?" she said. "That village where I helped the washerwomen?"

"Helped?" he smiled, "that's not how I…"

"Look!" Aurélie pointed at a circle of beech trees on the summit of a distant hill. "Can we camp there tonight?"

Longstaff bowed from the saddle. "As my Lady commands."

The going was hard. Longstaff dismounted, walking Sparrow through the tangle of hazel and hawthorn. The circle at the summit was perfect, except where one of the great trees had been toppled by a storm. Aurélie built a fire where moss had grown across the upper rim of roots to create a natural roof. Longstaff produced bread and cheese from his saddle-bag. They ate side by side, enjoying the sunset with Sparrow dozing nearby in the soft, rabbit-cropped grass.

"The people who planted these tree circles intended them to act as gateways to the next world," said Aurélie.

Longstaff smiled. Out here it was easier to understand her need to learn what she could about her new home. He thought of winter evenings they'd spent in the parlour at Martlesham; the way Aurélie would look up from a book, on the point of sharing some stray thought with him, then check herself and silently return to her reading.

Now, she spoke in the darkness.

"Before Christ came to England, the people here worshipped a god called Woden." Her voice took on a sing-song lilt, weaving through the low crackle of flames, "Woden was hung from a tree, he was pierced with a spear, he was killed and rose again, and when the priests arrived they claimed he was a Devil."

She reached for Longstaff in the darkness, her fingertips slowly tracing the line of his jaw. He sighed, a soft murmur of happiness, as she drew him into her embrace.

*

London's population had doubled twice over in the last fifty years. The very landscape seemed to flow towards the city so that Longstaff felt certain they could have found it blindfold.

It appeared first as a black smudge on the horizon from the hill at Nelly's Hole. The road was bordered by green fields for some time afterwards, but then, by some trick of the light and long before they reached the ancient walls, they found themselves in a labyrinth of tenements, shops, slaughterhouses, churches. Three years earlier these streets had been common ground where old women sold herbs from their tumbledown sheds.

The smell was overwhelming. The horses grew skittish, forcing Longstaff and Aurélie to dismount and lead them through the crowds – preachers and merchants, constables and beggars, lawyers in fur tippets, courtesans with hair piled high. White-chested kites rooted through the piles of refuse in every street. Another two hours passed before Longstaff caught a glimpse of the Thames, looking down the thoroughfare from the market at Leadenhall.

Aurélie's face split into a broad grin when they reached the booksellers' quarter by St. Paul's Cathedral. If the religious wars in Europe were a topic of conversation in Suffolk, they were a visceral reality here. Longstaff heard French, Flemish, Dutch, German and Italian. Men and women who were seen by some as skilled workers and welcome guests, by others as a threat and a cancer; most were refugees from the violence carried out in their homelands by the King of Spain or the Guise in France, by the pope and his Holy Roman Emperor.

Longstaff shook his head. What would his neighbours in Suffolk make of this modern Babel? He could imagine their objections perfectly: *Who are these people? Does anyone know? Under what license do they trade? They might be spies, assassins, crooks, thieves!*

They could say what they liked. Elizabeth was queen in England and she refused to turn her co-religionists away, however much her subjects muttered that the trickle of refugees would soon become a flood.

Aurélie had disappeared into the maze of stalls, leaving Longstaff with Sparrow and the horses. He knew it would be at least an hour before he saw her again. Pushing his way through the jostling crowds of men swapping news and gossip from the continent, he noticed cheaply bound copies of Michel de Nostredame's most recent prognostications. Another trestle had been piled with translations of Petrarch and Marco Polo – it appeared that tales of far off lands were popular among the English dreamers who spent their money here. For a moment, as Longstaff found a place to wait beneath the great pulpit where preachers gave sermons and heralds read proclamations, he felt as if he were at the centre of an enormous, sprawling web of information.

The feeling passed, replaced by a nagging sense that he was being watched. Had he spent too long in the countryside? No one appeared to take more than cursory interest in him. The feeling remained, however, powerful enough that Longstaff greeted Aurélie impatiently when she emerged from the maze of stalls. It was still a long walk to York House on the Strand. They continued west, past the lawyers' Inns around Chancery Lane, then south towards the river. Aurélie quickened her pace, more eager than Longstaff to renew her acquaintance with the Bacons. It was she who knocked at the imposing door, she who gave their names to the servant while Longstaff fussed with the horses.

Sir Nicholas's wife appeared a moment later and wrapped Aurélie in a fierce embrace.

"You must have travelled with the wind," said Anne, "your letter arrived less than an hour ago."

She offered Longstaff her hand. Awkwardly, he inclined his head.

"I'm sorry we gave you so little warning…"

"If you must apologise, do so for having stayed away too long. Your timing is perfect; Nicholas needs cheering up."

"We were sorry to hear he'd fallen from the queen's favour…" murmured Aurélie.

Anne threw up her hands. "He got himself caught between a fool and a rogue. The whole world is obsessed with seeing our queen married – if Elizabeth has a brain in her head, which she assuredly does, she'll avoid the state of matrimony like the plague. Nicholas was denied her presence for a time, but the worst is passed. Not that you'd guess it from the way he carries on."

More servants appeared. They'd taken the bags from the horses and stood awaiting instructions from their mistress. Anne raised her hands in mock horror.

"Tell me you have more baggage, Aurélie! You're to find me as soon as you're settled. We'll see if we can't find you something suitable to wear. Matthew…" she looked him up and down, then shook her head, "you'll just have to stay in your own clothes; Nicholas gets fatter by the day. Well, what are you waiting for? You know the way."

Longstaff was laughing as he followed Aurélie up the stairs. York House was huge; he would have been happy with a simple room, but the Bacons invariably treated their guests to an entire suite. First, a small antechamber hung with yellow damask, then a receiving room with hangings of blue velvet, finally a bedroom – heavy curtains of rose-coloured satin – with adjoining dressing room.

He remained in the receiving room, peering through the windows at Sparrow in the courtyard.

"You didn't tell me Sir Nicholas was in disgrace."

"He isn't anymore," replied Aurélie from the bedroom. He could hear her pouring water into a basin on the dressing table.

"Robert Dudley, your new Earl of Leicester, wants to marry Elizabeth. Sir Nicholas does not regard this as a good idea and hatched a plan to have Dudley married off to Mary Queen of Scots. Dudley found out and went to the queen..."

"Enough," protested Longstaff. "They're mad, all of them!"

Aurélie appeared in the doorway. "Sleep, if you want. I'm going to find Anne; I still haven't congratulated her on her most recent work."

"Remind me?"

"Her translation of John Jewel's *Apologie of the Anglican Church.* I told you." She kissed him on the cheek. "I'll see you at supper."

Longstaff kicked off his boots and stretched full-length on the bed. He thought of Durant. Not for the first time, he wished Laure had included more information in her letter. What had the Frenchman been doing on the day he vanished? What efforts had she made to track him down? Lying in the lap of luxury at York House, Longstaff found it hard to believe that his friend was in any real danger.

He remembered how affectionately Durant had treated Aurélie when the three of them travelled together. In his letters since, the Frenchman always mentioned Laure – she sent her greetings, she was in good health – but rarely revealed anything of substance.

It was dusk when the bell rang for dinner. Longstaff changed in the fading light – he *had* thought to pack a fresh shirt – ran a brush through his straw-coloured hair. There were new candles on the mantel but he left them unlit, reluctant to accept more of Sir Nicholas's hospitality than necessary. A servant led him squinting into the dining room, blinded by the candlelight reflected in a dozen silver plates.

"Matthew!" Sir Nicholas clasped his hand. The Lord Chancellor looked heavier and more careworn than Longstaff remembered, but his smile seemed genuine.

"You remember the boys? Anthony and Francis."

The older boy stood and shook Longstaff's hand, the younger stared at him from between two chairs.

Aurélie came in with Anne through a door in the far wall. Anne and Sir Nicholas took seats at either end of the table. Longstaff sat beside his hostess, opposite Francis and alongside Anthony. Aurélie, diagonally across from him, winked when she caught his eye. The youngest member of the party, in a specially raised chair, made an early attempt to lead the conversation, laying siege to Aurélie with a barrage of terrifyingly precocious questions. Anne was distracted, trying to curb her son's wilder inclinations, so Longstaff turned to Anthony. The boy blushed, breaking eye contact with obvious relief when servants reached between the high-backed chairs to serve an antipasto of meat. Longstaff saw salted anchovies with a sauce of stewed raisins.

"Anne," exclaimed Aurélie with obvious delight, "how thoughtful!"

"We all miss the food of our youth."

Longstaff smiled, only half following the conversation. Sir Nicholas was unusually quiet at his end of the table. On their previous visit, the man had taken obvious pride in making his guests feel at home. Perhaps he was still preoccupied with his recent fall from grace, although Longstaff thought that was unlikely. Sir Nicholas had overcome numerous setbacks on his long rise from 'son of a humble sheep-reeve' to Lord Chancellor of England, leader of the queen's Star Chamber, her spokesman in the House of Lords and chief adviser in affairs of law and order – all posts he continued to fulfil.

Aurélie broke into a peal of laughter. Anthony had said or done something amusing. The boy, on a chair upholstered with extra stuffing, turned pink with pleasure. Longstaff looked over at Francis, already on his second course of roasted meat and vegetables, using a fork after the new continental fashion. Unlike his parents, he held the cutlery in closed fists, sawing at the meat with fierce determination, lifting morsels of food to his mouth as if in mortal fear that a sliver might slip and spoil the table-cloth.

When he and Aurélie were blessed with children, Longstaff hoped they would eat together like this. Aurélie claimed that Anne and Sir Nicholas were so informal at home because they were a widow and widower, both raising children for the second time.

"Lady Anne," said Longstaff, "allow me to compliment your children on their table manners."

She burst out laughing. "We have you to thank for that."

Longstaff smiled in confusion.

"My fault," put in Sir Nicholas, "I told the boys they could eat with us as long as they behaved. It's not often a man of your reputation sits at our table; they're both desperate to hear something of your exploits."

The boys stared at him, eyes wide as saucers, hardly noticing as servants served a final course of cheese, figs and pomegranate. Longstaff didn't want to disappoint, but it was many years since he'd spoken of war in terms of fame and glory.

"Do you two know the soldier's greatest enemy?"

"The French," yelled Francis, drawing a burst of laughter from his father.

Longstaff looked at Anthony, who sat straight as a ramrod, napkin neatly on his lap. He could almost see the wheels turning behind the boy's dark eyes, assessing the likely candidates one by one. Anthony looked up, speaking slowly and carefully.

"I would think, a poor or inexperienced commander?"

"A truly excellent answer."

The boy looked disappointed. "But wrong."

Longstaff laughed. "Right and wrong are luxuries which rarely trouble a common soldier."

"What were *you* going to say," demanded Anthony.

"Lice." Longstaff assumed a solemn expression. "I've fought against the French and I've fought alongside them, too. And soldiers quickly learn what to do with a poor commander, but lice are pitiless – they never tire, give no quarter and resist all blandishment. Away from camp on foraging missions, a wise soldier won't remove his cuirass – not even for a second. Lice are the price we pay for our prudence. Listen closely when you're with soldiers, in the small hours of the night, and you'll hear the rustle of ramrods being pulled from their muskets and slipped beneath plate armour, as men desperately try and scrape the little devils from their fodder."

Both boys had started scratching by the time Longstaff finished. The parents laughed. A moment of levity which Aurélie brought to a swift and savage conclusion.

"You know, don't you," she demanded of Sir Nicholas, "you already know that Durant has disappeared – and you know why."

There was heat in her voice. Longstaff had no idea what she'd seen in Sir Nicholas that he'd missed, but their host's reaction left him in no doubt that she was right.

Chapter 4

"Anne, it's time the children were in bed." Sir Nicholas pushed his plate to one side.

Anne hesitated a moment before rising.

"Anthony, Francis, say goodnight."

They might have begged for one more story, but the atmosphere had changed too quickly.

Aurélie's blue eyes were steady. "You're involved in Durant's disappearance. How?"

"What gave me away?" replied Sir Nicholas.

"In my letter, I said nothing about the reason for our sudden visit. Anne might be too well-mannered to inquire, but I've never known you to exercise that kind of restraint."

Sir Nicholas grunted. "Sharp as a knife. Vescosi always said so. You and Anne are constantly in touch, so I'm sure you know what's been happening here. Leicester – Robert Dudley as was – set a trap for me. I was fat and stupid enough to march straight in."

He gave his round belly a half-hearted pat. Aurélie would not be distracted.

"And?"

He sighed. "Aurélie, my dear, be an angel and pour us wine."

She didn't move. Sir Nicholas rubbed his blue-grey jowls. Longstaff fetched a decanter from the sideboard and filled their glasses.

"I should have sent a warning," continued Sir Nicholas, "to you and the Frenchman both, but I honestly thought it would come to nothing. You have to remember, England is an island – surrounded by enemies and ill-served by two warring factions at court. One is led by Leicester. Since his elevation to the Privy Council, he's proven far more capable than we expected, but he's obsessed with the old codes of death and glory. Given the chance, he'll lead us all to ruin."

Longstaff snorted. He hated these games, had precious little knowledge of the main players and none at all of the smaller men involved or the complex web of feuds and alliances that spanned the country. Frustrated by his ignorance and disgusted by the so-called 'subtle art' of politics, he felt his temper rise. Aurélie kicked him beneath the table.

Sir Nicholas appealed to her directly. "No one loved our late king Henry; he was more monster than man at the end, but many stayed loyal for reasons other than greed or fear. Henry's break with Rome opened a window of opportunity – to rebuild the nation on a reformed Church. When Edward came to the throne, a group of us tried to put this dream into practice. But then the boy died and I had to sit and watch while Bloody Mary undid our work and plunged the country into chaos. God knows what I might have been driven to if it hadn't been for Giacomo Vescosi's wise counsel."

He smiled at Aurélie. "'*To preserve the last remaining scraps of the past and print and distribute new works.*' A noble dream in ignoble times, reason elevated above revelation. Mary would have had me disembowelled if she'd known. Elizabeth is less dogmatic but still, imagine what would happen to me – a man in my position – if it was discovered I was carrying on a clandestine correspondence with a dozen of the most politically suspect men in Europe?"

"Sir Nicholas," interrupted Longstaff, "we've always known you for a plain speaker."

Aurélie narrowed her eyes. "He's trying to tell us that someone's blackmailing him."

A servant knocked. "Sir, the gentleman you were expecting has arrived."

"Try not to let him provoke you." Sir Nicholas rose at a sign of movement in the doorway. "My dear Walsingham. Thank you for coming at such short notice."

The newcomer was in his mid-thirties, slim and pale with a downy little beard on his chin. At first glance, Longstaff could see nothing to account for Sir Nicholas's behaviour – no indication that Francis Walsingham would rise to become one of the most feared men in Europe – except that his dark eyes were wholly devoid of light.

"You've told them?"

"And deny you the pleasure? I'd never presume so far. A drink?"

The bitterness in Sir Nicholas's voice was clear, Walsingham gave no sign of having noticed. He accepted a glass of wine, added water from a jug on the table and pulled two of the high-backed chairs aside to make himself a space.

"You know who William Cecil is, of course."

"Of course," agreed Aurélie. Cecil was the queen's chief counsellor, leader of the faction to which Sir Nicholas belonged.

"A little over a year ago," continued Walsingham, "he commissioned me to create a system of professional intelligencers to replace the Earl of Leicester's network of amateur and unreliable informers. Originally, he intended that we should proceed gradually, but we were overtaken by events when a coded letter was intercepted – a list of questions for an unknown member of the queen's Privy Council. Cecil ordered me to investigate, to identify the traitor on the Council, which is how I came to discover your host's secret connection to Giacomo Vescosi."

"You suspected Sir Nicholas of being a spy?" Longstaff shook his head in disbelief.

"I was duty-bound to demand an explanation," replied Walsingham. "Just as Sir Nicholas was bound – on pain of execution – to answer with the truth. His decision to make a clean breast of his relationship with Vescosi, including your own efforts to find the so-called Devil's Library, allowed me to discount him as a suspect. I continued my search, therefore, slowly chipping away at the list of potential traitors until only a single name remained."

Walsingham hesitated. "If either of you reveal a word of what I'm about to…"

"Just tell them," said Sir Nicholas.

"Very well," Walsingham straightened his robe. "The evidence points to Thomas Howard."

There was a moment of appalled silence. Thomas Howard. The Duke of Norfolk and leader of the northern aristocracy, who ruled as a virtual monarch from his seat at Kenninghall.

Aurélie shook her head. "He's still so young…"

"He's commanded armies," Sir Nicholas shook his head, "negotiated treaties. He's had a place on the Privy Council these last three years. We'd hoped to make him an ally in our struggles with Leicester's faction, but he's always steered his own path. Now we know why."

"He's widely suspected of being a secret Catholic," added Walsingham. "When his wife died two years ago, he became the most eligible bachelor in England and yet he refuses to re-marry. If Elizabeth were to die, he would be the obvious candidate to wed her successor, Mary Queen of Scots, making him king of England and Scotland both."

"None of which adds up to actual evidence against him," said Aurélie.

Walsingham nodded. "Which is why I had to find a way of making sure."

Considering his age, and the company he was in, Walsingham was remarkably self-assured.

"I was briefly at a loss as to how to proceed, before remembering Sir Nicholas's account of your adventures in Italy. The Devil's Library was destroyed. You and Durant failed to preserve even a single document from the conflagration, but imagine for a moment that things had turned out differently – that you *had* managed to save one of those precious books? Why not a forgotten Gospel, in which Christ states unequivocally that St. Peter and his successors represent the ultimate authority on Earth, with exclusive responsibility for interpreting God's word..."

Longstaff was lost. Together with Aurélie and Durant, he had recovered a scroll from the Library, but *On Freedom* – written nearly two thousand years ago by the philosopher Epicurus – was nothing like the text Walsingham described.

Aurélie looked horrified. "Why would you even imagine such a thing? At book like that would render Elizabeth's possession of the English throne illegitimate, destroy the Reformed Churches in Scotland, Flanders and Switzerland. Civil war would break out everywhere."

With a sharp wave of his hand, Walsingham brushed her objections to one side. "You overstate the dangers. Any rational man would dismiss the notion as an absurd fantasy, but the Duke of Norfolk is different. Assuming he is our traitor, we can be certain the rumours of his secret Catholicism are true. Not only that, but he possesses sufficient resources to verify the basic facts of your journey through Italy."

An expression of grudging respect appeared on Aurélie's face. "A believable lie wrapped in a scarcely credible truth."

"Exactly," purred Walsingham.

He looked so pleased with himself. Aurélie stared, as if scales had appeared beneath his lawyer's robes.

"And what? You found someone to whisper in the Duke's ear – tales of a Frenchman who knows the whereabouts of such a Gospel?"

"I did what I judged necessary to unmask a traitor."

Aurélie turned on Sir Nicholas. "And you? You let him blackmail you into using Durant as bait for his absurd trap?"

"If you want someone to blame for your predicament," cut in Walsingham, "then start with your husband. Had he simply returned to Martlesham, I would never have discovered how Sir Nicholas occupied himself during Mary's reign. But erasing the stain on his family name? Rehabilitating a man executed by order of the king? It all leaves a trail."

Sir Nicholas spoke through clenched teeth. "Be good enough to remember where you are. I am perfectly capable of speaking for myself."

Walsingham straightened. "My methods are sound. Durant's disappearance proves it. And now our enemies waste their time searching for a book which doesn't exist while we tighten the noose about their necks. The queen regards Norfolk as one of her oldest and most loyal friends. Without cast-iron proof, we cannot begin proceedings against him."

Longstaff shook his head; it didn't take a genius to see what was coming next. He looked at Sir Nicholas.

"You expect us to help, after what you've done?"

"We expect you to do your duty," interrupted Walsingham. "If the queen is undone, we are lost. The plotters will condemn us all to Hell!"

Sir Nicholas closed his eyes, visibly struggling to master his temper.

"Matthew, I assume you came here hoping I would provide you with a passport to France?"

"That's right."

Sir Nicholas offered him an apologetic smile. "What's done is done. The question now is how we proceed. Our desire is that you continue with your original plans – travel to Paris and assist Laure Durant in the search for her father. Find out who's taken him and why."

"Of course, we'll go." Aurélie glared at Walsingham. "He's left us no choice."

The spymaster ignored her, addressing himself exclusively to Longstaff. "We will provide you with everything you need, but your wife will remain in England. You have my word she will be kept safe, for exactly as long as you act in England's best interests."

*

In their suite of rooms, Longstaff and Aurélie sat opposite one another on the wide bed, thick curtains drawn around the posts to muffle the noise of their raised voices. Walsingham had been adamant. Aurélie was to remain in London, a 'hostage' in the man's own, ill-chosen words. Longstaff had supported his wife's objections and arguments – even adding his own – but hadn't quite managed to suppress a small shiver of relief.

"Be reasonable, Aurélie," he said now, "you can't travel without a passport and Walsingham won't give you one."

"Sir Nicholas…"

"… has a charge of treason hanging over his head."

She shook her head. "Our best friend has been abducted by people who think he knows the location of a lost Gospel in Christ's own hand. It's insane. And you want me to stay here!"

"That's not fair, Aurélie."

"You think I'll be safer," she snarled.

They slept late, as if reluctant to resume the argument. Sir Nicholas had left by the time they came downstairs. They breakfasted alone, in silence, then carried glasses of fresh juice into the gardens behind York House, through the orchard, down to a private dock on the Thames where they leaned side by side against the railing and stared at brick and timber buildings on the opposite bank. The sky was a crisp, pale blue, the water busy with dozens of small craft tracing tangled lines of diamonds on the water's surface. Longstaff heard a distant cry of 'Oars' – some poor soul attempting to flag a passing ferryman.

"I don't think you'll be safer in London," he said. "Not necessarily. Durant might have gone missing in France, but the traitor's here." He toe-punted a stone into the water. "I don't trust Walsingham as far as I can spit. I'm not even sure we can trust Sir Nicholas anymore. That's why I think you should stay, find out what they're planning and make sure we aren't dragged any deeper into this mess. I'll insist that anything I discover in

France, I'll communicate to you and you alone, in a cipher only we understand. Those will be our terms. If they don't agree, we saddle up and ride home to Martlesham."

A servant appeared from among the trees: "Sir Nicholas has returned. He requests that you join him in the study."

"Both of us? Or just him?"

"Ma'am?"

"Never mind," she muttered.

Longstaff followed her into a large, ground-floor study where Sir Nicholas sat waiting for them.

"I saw Walsingham again this morning."

Aurélie grimaced at the mere mention of the man's name.

"Don't underestimate him," cautioned Sir Nicholas. "He may be a dour bastard, but he's clever. Bold when he needs to be with a fine head for detail; it's not a common combination. And Cecil trusts him."

"Then Cecil is as unhinged as the rest of you. A lost Gospel?"

"I didn't think it would work either. But how else do you explain Durant's disappearance?" Sir Nicholas drew a breath. "I'm sorry, Aurélie. I tried, but Walsingham remains inflexible on the point of your staying in England. He has offered one concession, however. Under certain conditions, he's content to let you return home…"

Aurélie looked close to exploding. "Have you lost your mind? Back to Martlesham?"

Longstaff winced. He called it home. For her, the place was always Martlesham.

"Or to remain here at York House, if you prefer," continued Sir Nicholas, "I was intending to contact you anyway with a request that you come and tutor my boys for a season. Your mind is extraordinary, Aurélie, shaped by one of Italy's foremost scholars. Anthony and Francis are still young, of course, but already fiercely curious about the world…" Something in her expression warned him to stop.

"That sounds an ideal solution," ventured Longstaff, grateful despite himself for the effort Sir Nicholas was making.

"Then you stay and play nursemaid to his children," snapped Aurélie.

"Anthony's not that much younger than you were when Giacomo took you in."

"Anne would be pleased," added Sir Nicholas. "We'd count it a great honour if you agreed, and this house is not without attractions." He gestured at the book-lined shelves.

Aurélie clenched her fists in frustration. "If you're so certain Norfolk is a traitor, why not simply have him killed?"

Sir Nicholas looked shocked. "Walsingham used me harshly, too," he said. "He threatened me with the Tower, then put his scheme into action without saying a word. He's still a man of the law, however, as am I. The country is on edge – this is no time to revert to barbarism, even more so if Norfolk does turn out to be a traitor. Can you imagine the outcry if he were murdered? No one has forgotten that the Queen of Scots proclaimed herself England's rightful ruler when Bloody Mary died. Half the country yearns to see her crowned – a Catholic monarch back on England's throne." He shook his head. "If peace holds here, it's only because so many cleave to Elizabeth's compromise between the absolutes of Papism and Lutheranism, but their numbers seem to dwindle by the day. Huguenot refugees are openly abused in the streets. They're our friends, of course, but also free of the ties which bind native Englishmen. Every foreigner is a potential spy, every spy a potential assassin…"

This was too much for Aurélie. "But that's your doing. Each new edict makes it harder for Catholics to maintain a dual loyalty to pope and queen. What better way to guarantee the very outcome you claim to fear?"

"Precisely my point," insisted Sir Nicholas. "Eliminate the threat to Elizabeth and such measures will no longer be necessary!"

"That makes even less sense than Walsingham's plan." Aurélie threw her hands in the air before taking a seat at Sir Nicholas's desk, her back to the two men.

Speaking softly, Sir Nicholas turned to Longstaff. "Your principal contact in France will be our ambassador Sir Nicholas Throckmorton. Catherine de Medici has interrupted the Royal Progress to make a brief return to Paris, but you'll have to hurry if you want to catch him while he's still in the capital. Whatever you discover, he can send us via the diplomatic bag. Walsingham has suggested a code..."

"Whatever I discover, I'll send to Aurélie at this address, in a code only she can understand."

Sir Nicholas stared for several seconds. "He won't like it."

"I'm not asking him to."

Sir Nicholas reached for a box which stood beside his chair: "He sent it for you this morning."

A passport for Longstaff, plus two dozen ecu and a thick sheaf of livres, the principle money of account in France.

"There's more." He showed Longstaff a vial, hidden from Aurélie in the palm of one hand. "Walsingham asked me to stress how vital it is that you avoid falling into enemy hands."

Longstaff tucked the glass tube away in his shirt. The final item in Walsingham's box was a thing of beauty. Even without knowing its purpose, Longstaff felt a small thrill of possession.

"A map of France," said Sir Nicholas, "the most comprehensive ever made."

"You may plot a course by experience," Longstaff read the inscription aloud, *"but only knowledge brings you to a true and fitting destination."*

"Walsingham also offered weapons, but I assume you have your own."

Longstaff did not understand why, but he and Sir Nicholas were suddenly grinning like schoolboys.

"Idiots," Aurélie glared at their host. "Who do *you* think took Durant?"

"Who's our traitor working for, you mean?" Sir Nicholas spread his hands. "English Catholics in exile? Agents of the king of Spain or the pope? If I had to bet, though, I'd lay my money on the Guise; they're fanatics, determined to destroy the Huguenot threat in France. In addition, the Queen of Scots is a member of the family – the Cardinal of Lorraine is her uncle, and the only man who can guarantee Norfolk her hand in marriage in the event of Elizabeth's death."

Sir Nicholas offered his guests a wintry smile. "And then, of course, it's also possible that some combination of these enemies have formed an alliance in common cause against us."

Chapter 5

The whole Bacon family turned out at dawn the following morning to bid Longstaff farewell. The boys stamped their feet in the chill courtyard, Anthony surreptitiously passing Sparrow titbits from the kitchen. Longstaff had thought of leaving the old dog here, but the two of them hadn't spent a day apart since he'd found her as a pup.

Anne took him by surprise, pulling him down and kissing him fiercely on both cheeks.

"Godspeed, Matthew. We'll take good care of Aurélie, never fear."

"Where is she? We'll miss the coach if she doesn't hurry."

Sir Nicholas put a hand on Longstaff's shoulder.

"Throckmorton's a pompous fool. Use him, but don't put your life in his hands. If you need real help, look for a man called Horatio Palavicino at the Hôtel Saint Honoré."

"Who?"

"He's a merchant," Sir Nicholas shrugged, "an adventurer, insufferable under normal circumstances, but trustworthy in a tight corner. I wish I could do more."

Aurélie appeared in the doorway just then. So beautiful, thought Longstaff. He slung his bedroll across one shoulder, sword and musket carefully wrapped at the centre, and his saddle across the other; he would find a horse when he reached Harfleur on the Normandy coast.

The coach for Dover was due to leave from the George Inn in Southwark. It would have been easier to cross the Thames by boat from the private dock at York House, but Longstaff and Aurélie had decided to brave the puddles along the Strand, the great clouds of dust thrown up by chariots, drays and carts. There was something exciting about the noise, a fearful song of wheels, hooves and feet. Coachmen lashed their horses. Drivers yelled curses. For every new building they passed, they saw the ruins of one recently demolished, mourned only by beggars. They were everywhere, heaped together among the piles of rubble; a half-seen, shifting background of grey, greasy rags.

This was King Henry's dissolution of the monasteries. The broken remains of monastic hospitals and alms-houses appeared now in the walls of merchant's homes – rising three and four stories above the ancient vaults – in taverns and pleasure gardens, stable-yards and tight-packed tenements.

Longstaff had seen poverty before but never treated with such indifference, as if the city's gift for spectacle had made men blind. Only a corpse could fail to be excited by this place, and only a monster fail to shudder at its heartlessness.

Crossing the Thames at London Bridge, they found the streets of Southwark no less crowded. Longstaff heard men talking French and remembered what Sir Nicholas had said: *Refugees from religious persecution are openly abused in the streets, as if they were heralds of a civil war. They are our friends, but also strangers, free of the ties of place and history which bind all Englishmen.*

They were also brewers and bookbinders, tailors and embroiderers, gun-makers, dyers and weavers. All struggling to make a living, follow rules which changed with bewildering speed. Elizabeth promised her subjects security, prosperity and a place at God's side in the next life. These gifts were slow in coming and her minsters blamed the delay on contamination from abroad, on the Huguenots who had no parents or grandparents buried in English churchyards. It was the same everywhere; the great men of Christendom seemed to fear any man not trained to know his place from birth.

Aurélie took Longstaff's arm. "The English are unpopular in France, even more so than usual."

He grinned. "You will worry about me, then?"

"Your French is terrible."

"It's fine."

"Not good enough that you can pass for a native."

"My German and Italian are perfect, I can adopt either accent when I speak, pass myself off as Catholic or Huguenot depending on the audience."

The coaching inn appeared in the distance. Aurélie tightened her grip on his arm.

"Do what you can for Laure. Try not to get caught up in the rest of their nonsense."

"She must be out of her mind with worry."

"Probably."

"I'll bring her father home. Don't worry."

He allowed himself to picture the scene. Aurélie snorted.

"What?"

"You're doing it again. Happy ever after, everyone crying tears of happiness." She looked at him. "Durant never told us where she'd been all those years. We have no idea what she's been through."

Longstaff pressed her hand. "You'll see. It'll be fine."

The George was a large, timbered building. Two coaches in the yard, surrounded by a great variety of people – itinerant clergymen, wealthy merchants in velvet hose and buckled shoes, a shuffling chorus of drivers, porters, potboys and whores.

A man stood against the far wall, beyond the traders running their expert hands over barrels, sacks and bales of goods. He was tall, narrow across the shoulders and hips. Longstaff had seen him somewhere before. It was the way he stood, in baggy leggings and a long woollen coat, up on the balls of his feet as if ready to fight or flee.

"I'm sorry," said Aurélie, "I didn't realise I'd be so bad at saying goodbye."

"Hmm?" Longstaff allowed the coachmen to take his saddle and bedroll. Aurélie pulled him aside.

"I have something for you."

A medallion on a thin, silver chain. Longstaff held it in the light. Her profile had been etched on one side – just a simple line drawing and yet the silversmith had clearly been a master. Longstaff could see the wrinkle he loved so well, which appeared at the top of Aurélie's nose whenever she was concentrating.

"I said I was coming with you," she blushed, "I had it made for your birthday. You won't be back in time, better take it now."

She wasn't vain. Commissioning her own portrait was her way of showing how much faith she had in his love. Longstaff reached forward to catch a single tear from her cheek, raised his finger to his lips.

"Be careful. Free us from Walsingham's net if you can but don't take any unnecessary risks."

He wasn't used to seeing her look forlorn. She was young and fearless. Her courage would make her reckless, her otherness paint her as a target. Longstaff felt suddenly afraid. Would he ever see her again? He looked up, but the man in leggings had disappeared.

"France is just a sideshow, the traitor is here in London. Take one of Sir Nicholas's men with you whenever you go into the city."

She rolled her eyes and stuck out her tongue. Longstaff forced himself to smile.

"I'll miss you." He signalled to one of the porters, a coin between his fingers. "See the lady home."

"Matthew..."

He silenced her objection with a kiss. "Humour me, just this once."

Longstaff scooped Sparrow in his arms, lifting the dog ahead of him into the carriage. The road was better than expected, the coach rattled on at pace, from the squalor of London into the open fields beyond – past Blackheath where Wat Tyler and Jack Straw had been deceived and their army of rebellious peasants crushed. Longstaff chuckled as he remembered how Aurélie had raged when he told her about the Peasants' Revolt. An elderly, female passenger, dressed head to toe in black, shifted away from him on the hard bench-seat. Longstaff looked through the window at the Garden of England. This was Walsingham's county – a quilt of tiny fields on either side of the road – inheritance laws that forced ambitious sons up to London, to make their way as clerks and lawyers.

Longstaff thought of the man at the coaching inn. Did he belong to Walsingham? Was Cecil's intelligencer making certain that Longstaff abided by the terms of their agreement? Who else might want to stay informed of his movements? Walsingham's fictitious volume would be a mighty temptation for any man.

At Dover, Longstaff went straight to the docks where a small sloop ferried him to his ship. It was already dark when he climbed aboard, an indignant Sparrow over his shoulders. By moonlight, as the ship dipped and rolled at anchor, it was difficult to tell which of the ghostly figures were sailors and which his fellow passengers. A man appeared from the gloom.

"Matthew Longstaff?"

"Yes."

"The captain bade me give you this."

A single sheet of paper, rolled thin as Longstaff's little finger. He waited for the man to leave before finding a covered lamp and reading the brief message from Walsingham.

> *Sir Nicholas, it appears, favours carrot over stick. His position commands respect; I have found it expedient, therefore, to grant his request and allow your wife to enjoy the comforts of York House for as long as you serve our interests in France. I would not have you journey from us labouring under a false illusion, however; her life is forfeit should you cross us or reveal our purpose to England's enemies.*
>
> *FW*

Longstaff felt a suffocating wave of fury. He crumpled the page, closed his eyes for several seconds before managing to draw breath. He wanted to wring the bastard's neck. Row himself to dry land, return to London and tear the intelligencer limb from limb. But there was still Durant – and what did Walsingham's letter tell Longstaff that he didn't already know? He tore it into a dozen pieces, let them fall overboard and watched as they spiralled slowly onto the water's surface, then retrieved the phial of poison from his jerkin and hurled it after the torn page. One thing at a time – first he had to find out who had taken Durant. Longstaff shook his head in the darkness; first, he had to find his bunk and get some sleep. He led Sparrow below deck. The dog was a poor sailor, letting out a low murmur of complaint with each gentle roll of the ship. She wouldn't sleep on board; Longstaff knew he could count on her to warn him if anyone approached during the night. England would be gone by morning and France already visible on the horizon. For centuries, until the loss of Calais seven years earlier, whoever ruled in England had commanded territories on both sides of the Channel. The Queen of Scots hoped to rectify this anomaly and all of Catholic Europe supported her claim. In their eyes, Elizabeth was illegitimate, a bastard and an abomination. Only chaos in France kept them from attacking. Longstaff shuddered. He'd heard the stories of assassinations, marauding gangs of zealots, contract killings, peasants slowly starving to death on a diet of acorns and brick dust as the struggle for religious freedom descended into a depraved free-for-all. Now, the vagaries of fate – and Walsingham – were conspiring to bring him face to face with the reality.

Chapter 6

DURANT

Lavish praise on kings to make them love you,
Visit you with kindness, not with cruelty.
Who thought he was strong, who could have been weak,
Who chose to kill, when Death spread wide his arms.

Gaetan Durant reached forward to turn the page of a heavy book. His bandaged left hand struck the table. The pain was blinding. He doubled up, knees against his chest and eyes watering. *Careless.* And the fear, always the fear, chasing pain through the hidden corridors of his being, a poison that burned his guts, caused his hands to shake and sweat, made concentration impossible.

He was no stranger to grief. Many years ago, the loss of his wife and parents to plague in just a few short weeks had nearly destroyed him. To survive, he'd become numb; certain that only a fatalist could wring any portion of pleasure from his time on earth. Durant's indifference to life had been a source of secret pride, now exposed as empty delusion. Another layer torn from his self-esteem, more evidence against his supposed intelligence. Grist to fear's mill.

He'd been knocked unconscious on the Feast of Fools – his nocturnal wanderings rudely interrupted after a night at the Moor's Head – and woken many hours later, gagged and trussed on the ice-cold floor of a barn with his night cloak across him like a blanket.

*

The dirt floor was freshly swept, farm equipment stacked and hung from nails in the wall. Scythes, harrows and shears, edged tools which would have made short work of the ropes that held him. He couldn't reach them. His hands had been bound to the axle of a heavy plough. An hour passed before someone came, ample time to flay the skin from both wrists in a vain attempt at escape.

The man, dressed in a farmer's loose smock, set a pail of water beside Durant's head and yanked the gag aside.

"Where's Lecornu?" demanded Durant.

Gilles Lecornu, who'd followed him from the Moor's Head and struck him unconscious. The name translated as 'with horns'. A cuckold. A ridiculous joke of a name. Durant remembered how the man had always introduced himself, an equal stress on each of the three syllables, face blank as he waited for the laughter to die.

"Drink," said the farmer.

"Where am I?"

"Doesn't matter."

"There's been a mistake…"

"Drink. I'm to take the water with me."

He was as good as his word, replacing the gag and disappearing with the pail as soon as Durant had slaked his thirst. He used a chain to fasten the barn's double-doors behind him.

Durant pulled himself up against the plough, relieving the strain on his arms. He was no longer in the city. Through a crack in the doors he could see a blanket of snow. A thin drizzle fell, slowly turning it to muddy slush. He hoped Laure wasn't worrying. There was sufficient money in the house to keep her for several days.

They left him long enough that Durant dropped into a restless sleep. Another stranger greeted him with the dawn – he was being passed from hand to hand like a piece of meat. The newcomer was slight, with a round, open face and what

Durant's father would have called 'smiling gaps' between his teeth. A toothpick hung from a corner of his mouth.

A shadow loomed in the background. If the first man was a fox, then here was a mastiff. Taller than his companion and broad across the shoulders, face hidden beneath a thick, black beard. Both men were wet from the rain, both dressed for the weather in quilted leather jackets. High boots over thick, oiled-wool tights. The fox was bare-headed. The mastiff wore a cap which covered his ears and came down nearly to his eyes. A large knife hung from a girdle round his waist.

"My name is Vincent," the first man spoke pleasant, accent-free French. "I hope you haven't been too uncomfortable."

Durant was unable to reply. After Vincent cut his gag and bonds, the blood returning to his fingers made him wince. Gingerly, he inspected the bruise on the side of his head.

"I'll live."

Vincent nodded. "We have a journey ahead of us."

Durant half rose. "Why am I here?"

The mastiff stepped forward. It was like being hit with a cannon ball. Durant sat down hard, the taste of iron in his mouth.

"Jean-Paul!" Vincent crouched beside Durant. "My companion is a man of few words. He wants you to remain seated while we make our preparations."

Durant spat blood. The blow had been administered as precisely as a blacksmith strikes his anvil, without anger or passion. Jean-Paul removed his cap, wiped rainwater from his broad face with one enormous forearm. Durant flinched. Ugly welts of scar tissue surrounded holes where his ears should have been. They'd been hacked away – as punishment for what crime?

Durant wasn't sure he wanted to know. From his position on the floor, he watched in silence as the farmer drove a horse and cart to the barn doors. A high seat at the front, protected by a canvas awning. A flat bed at the rear, with an iron cage lashed to the boards. The cage was small – four feet by four and half as high as a man. Jean-Paul began to load the cart with fodder, which he covered with a sheet of canvas.

"The cage, as well," said Vincent. "We need to provide our guest with shelter."

Durant shook his head. "I'm not getting in there."

Jean-Paul raised a fist, Durant cringed against the plough. Vincent stepped between them. "Give him time to learn our ways, that's all. It won't take long." He turned to Durant, smiled through the gaps in his teeth.

"Jean-Paul wants to leave you gagged. He wants to tie you flat to the four corners of the cart and cover you with canvas. That way, he suggests, we'd be less likely to attract attention. Inhuman, I know, but he struggles to see that. I've tried to explain. The cage is small, I admit, but at least you won't be bound. You'll be able to see the countryside and breathe the good, fresh air."

The threat of violence lay heavy on the air. With obvious ill-grace, Jean-Paul strapped a square of canvas across the top of the cage. Durant did not fight but nor would he help, forcing them to drag him across the dirt floor and lock him in the cage.

Jean-Paul snapped the reins. Durant was thrown against the bars as the cart rumbled into motion. The weather outside was foul. The light drizzle had become driving rain, cutting visibility to less than a hundred feet. Jean-Paul replaced his cap and buttoned himself into an enormous leather coat. Beside him, Vincent wrapped himself in a cloak. From time to time, as the cart bounced along the rutted track, he removed his toothpick and took long pulls from the wine-skin cradled in his lap.

The scrap of canvas protected Durant from the worst of the rain, but not the bitter cold. They were moving south along a sharp ridge. He saw thick coils of smoke rising from the wooded valley below. Charcoal burners at work even in this miserable weather. Durant imagined the tall, banked fires, men toiling in soot and muck.

He was shivering – his night cloak might have been sufficient for the streets of Paris, hurrying from appointment to appointment, but gave no protection against exposure to this murderous cold – and tormented by thirst as the day wore on. A strange mix of pride and fear stopped him begging for blankets or water. It was impossible to lie flat within the confines of the cage; he kept as low as possible to escape the freezing wind.

They would give him answers soon. They had to.

The sun was hardly visible – a lighter patch of grey in the far west – when Vincent finally looked back. The face he presented was a mask of concern.

"M'sieur, you're freezing! You should have spoken."

He pestered Jean-Paul into turning off the road. It took them a few minutes to build a fire; no mean feat in these conditions. Vincent released Durant, gave him a warm blanket and urged him nearer the flames.

"And drink, for the love of God! What must you think of me?"

Durant lapped at the water, disgusted by a wave of gratitude. He waited for the shivers to subside before attempting to stretch his frozen limbs. Tears appeared in his eyes.

"Sleep now, m'sieur. The weather will be kinder tomorrow."

It was dawn when Jean-Paul shook him roughly back to life. Durant was unbound. Had one of them stayed awake to watch him? Could he simply have walked away during the night? It was still bitterly cold, but dry, the grey of yesterday replaced with a pallid blue. Vincent was nearby, chewing happily on a toothpick. He held a paintbrush in one hand and stood before a strip of canvas. Drops of black paint fell on the grass at his feet.

Durant read the hand-made sign. He was a bandit, apparently, being transported to Lyon on charges of murder and burglary.

"Our disguise," said Vincent. "The roads will get busier."

Durant stared. "Why?"

"Two men travelling with a third locked in a cage. We have to give some explanation."

"What do you want from me?"

"All in good time. But rest assured, my friend, we have instructions to keep you safe."

The sky remained clear throughout the day. Peasants stared at them without curiosity. The road was in good condition and well-travelled. They passed merchants and a noblewoman escorted by four men-at-arms, who read the brief description and turned away indifferently. Vincent bade everyone a cheerful good day. Once, Durant attempted to engage him in conversation. The fox turned and raised a finger to his lips.

"Let's speak no more than necessary." He cast a meaningful glance in Jean-Paul's direction before taking another long pull on his wineskin.

Days began to blur. Fields gave way to pastures. The road passed through a long stretch of forest, with the trees cut well back on either side. They began to climb, first a series of gentle hills, then steeply.

They sat beside the fire each night, eating soldiers' rations of black bread and dried beef. Vincent never offered to share his wineskin, but they travelled with a small keg of fresh water. Jean-Paul passed the evenings whittling small, delicate figures which he abandoned each morning. Durant could not remember hearing him speak. Vincent only spoke to give instructions. Durant followed them in silence. Each day, the people they passed on the road seemed to stare at him more coldly.

He wasn't certain whether it was the fifth or sixth day, when he woke and saw Vincent with the paint brush in his hand.

"What are you doing?"

"Nothing. Lyon is not our true destination, our sign is no longer fit for purpose."

That morning, a prosperous looking farmer slowed his horse and spat through the bars of Durant's cage. In the afternoon, a party of pilgrims crossed themselves at the sight of him. Durant slept badly that night. He was startled into wakefulness at dawn by a truly horrible sound. He rubbed his eyes, trying to bring the world into focus. Jean-Paul stood looking at the latest version of Vincent's sign, head thrown back in laughter. Durant saw a mouthful of rotten teeth, nothing but a jagged stump where his tongue should have been.

The weather was fine that day. Towards noon, Durant's two jailors reined to a halt on the outskirts of a small hamlet.

"Nothing to worry about. The horse is tired."

A peasant drew near, took one look at the sign and ran to fetch his friends. Durant doubted any of them could read, but they had no difficulty understanding whatever symbol or picture Vincent had drawn.

One by one, the peasants took great pleasure in dropping their cloth trousers and urinating on the caged criminal. Durant remained silent, curled in a ball. It was shame that made him bury his face in his hands. He could hear Jean-Paul, attempting to swallow ghastly laughter. Vincent offered him an apologetic shrug when the ordeal finally came to an end, palms up in a gesture of helplessness.

They left the main highway soon afterwards. Their progress slowed, the single horse struggling with his burden along a poorly made track. Trees grew nearer, crowding in on them until the canopies met above their heads.

Vincent roused himself. "This looks a likely spot."

Jean-Paul brought the cart to a halt. Vincent climbed onto the flat-bed and unlocked the cage.

"I apologise, m'sieur. A harmless prank to help pass the time, but perhaps we let it go too far. You weren't in any danger."

Durant crawled out of the cage. He climbed down from the cart, joints cracking along the length of his spine as he walked round to look at the sign.

Vincent had marked it with an 'R' – râpé, rapt, ravissement – and beside the 'R', an 'E': 'enfants'.

"How much more?"

"We arrive at your new home tomorrow. No more games once you start work, I promise."

"Damn you, Vincent. What work? What do you want from me?"

"Obedience, to follow my instructions without question. We don't have time for tricks or sabotage." He handed Durant the wineskin. "You've been chosen to play a role; I need you to embrace the challenge with all your heart and soul."

Durant drank; raw spirits burned the back of his throat. His eyes began to water. "How can I agree when I don't know what you want from me?"

Vincent shook his head. "I said obedience, my friend, not agreement." He looked at Durant's left hand. "We'll take a finger."

Durant stared in confusion.

"The little one. You'll barely notice."

"What?"

Vincent smiled. "My methods are effective. You'll see. Unfortunately, neither Jean-Paul nor I have medical training. Tell us what to do and I promise we'll make the procedure as painless as possible." He nodded at the wineskin. "Drink."

Durant raised the skin to his lips.

"But not too much. You'll want your wits about you." Vincent gestured at Jean-Paul. "You already know how strong he is. You've seen how skilfully he wields a knife. He will not flinch, nor inflict unnecessary pain. Tell us what you need, doctor."

"You're serious?" The question was pointless. Vincent was not acting on a whim. He had planned this and would see it through to the bitter end.

"The more you help, the better it will go. A man of your intelligence; surely you can see that. Tell us what you need."

Durant stared at his left hand. As a doctor, he'd amputated fingers in the past, like lopping off a twig, protecting the branch from the creeping death of gangrene.

Then, it had been a kindness.

Unless the finger was removed, the poison would spread.

Never on a healthy finger.

"I'll need a sharp knife." He hardly recognised his own voice, "a needle and waxed thread, a flat piece of wood, rag strips for binding. And a saw."

Vincent produced a short, serrated knife from his jerkin. He tested the edge on his thumb.

"If you try anything – anything at all – it won't be a finger. I'll take the whole hand. Do you understand?"

They had everything he asked for, further evidence they'd planned this all along. One glance at their rapt expressions and Durant knew there was no sense in begging for mercy. He held out his left arm.

"Make it fast to the board, palm up."

Vincent worked quickly, tying the strips with expert knots. Durant made a fist of his left hand, with all his fingers except the smallest. "Tie the others off to keep them out of the way. One of you will have to hold me."

"Tell us where to cut."

Tears appeared in Durant's eyes. He spoke softly, fearing his voice would break. "Slice a circle round the finger, here. You'll have to stop every few seconds to clean the blood away. Then two straight cuts, flay the skin to the knuckle." Durant swallowed. "I'll probably have passed out by then, which will make your task easier. Bone is easy to cut. Once the finger's off, trim the flaps and sew them back together to make a stump. As neat as you can; too tight and it will itch forever. Too loose and it will snag."

He drew a deep breath before looking at them. "I take it one of you can sew."

Vincent grinned. He was enjoying this. "The equal of any Paris seamstress."

Durant nodded. "You'll need your wineskin. Keep the wound clean." He tried to make himself lie down on the ground. He couldn't. "You'll have to force me."

"Of course," Vincent nodded at Jean-Paul, who crashed a fist against the side of Durant's head.

*

How many days had passed since then? Durant stared at the chain, one end attached to his ankle with an iron shackle, the other fixed by a massive bolt to an oak beam in the centre of the room. The chain had been here when they arrived, a coiled snake alongside two huge packing cases. On that first day, Durant had been too numb to protest when Jean-Paul fastened the shackle. He'd simply cowered, curled in a ball around his missing finger, watching as his two jailors unpacked: a small library of books which they piled up anyhow, then a tangle of alchemical tools – alembics to separate active ingredients from inert matter, aludels to reduce them to ash and dust. Hessian crucibles, retorts and heating mantles – most of which were damaged and looked to have been grabbed at random. Finally, Jean-Paul had smashed the packing cases and used the pieces to board the windows. They'd turned to leave.

"What do you want from me? Tell me, damn it."

"Only that you read, M'sieur, that's all for now."

He'd done as they asked, searching for answers among the books. Searching, above all, for the thread which bound these various works: printed volumes, cheap chapbooks, leather-bound tomes, jumbled together with beautifully illustrated manuscripts – each of these written in a subtly different hand – an odd mixture of sensational prognostications and serious works of natural science. Days passed and still

Durant had no idea of what they were looking for. It might have been anything from the Philosophers' Stone to a cure for plague. Underlined sections in a copy of Augustine's City of God made him think they sought a way to heal the split in Christianity. Then he chanced upon the ravings of a madman: *when I die, be sure and have a scribe at hand. For I have learned to slow the moment of death and will have sufficient time to dictate a report of that which lies beyond.*

Chapter 7

Longstaff reached Paris in six days, on horseback from the port town of Harfleur. He might have managed it quicker, but the animal he'd bought – a chestnut with a steady, pleasing gait – was no longer in the first flush of youth. Like Sparrow, reflected Longstaff ruefully. Like him.

He could have purchased a younger horse, but the stablemaster had claimed this one was battle-trained. Perhaps he'd even told the truth; the horse had served Longstaff well so far, uncomplaining at the long days and nights spent in the open.

March had only just begun, but winter was already in retreat. There was blossom in the orchards of Normandy, adding colour and perfume to Longstaff's journey, which might have been pleasant if not for the gaunt, grey faces of the peasants he passed. Longstaff travelled quietly. Remembering the wise advice of a former mentor – "if you can't think properly, for the love of God at least learn to use your eyes!" – he passed the time picturing the man he'd seen in London, up on the balls of his feet, one shoulder slightly higher than the other. When the distant spires of Paris came into view, he was certain even a glimpse of this shadowy pursuer would set alarm bells ringing.

The road grew busier this close to the capital. Longstaff raised fingertips to his chest where he kept Laure's letter inside his jerkin. Perhaps his old friend had already returned, would welcome him in a few hours' time with wine and a hot meal. Longstaff spat; would no amount of experience ever douse his native optimism? He rode through the Porte S. Denis, along a wide thoroughfare of the same name, while passages of Durant's letters returned to guide his steps:

> *Paris is three towns in one; there's the island on which it was born, which now belongs to the Bishop who sits in Notre Dame, and the University, which commands the left bank and belongs to the rector. Laure and I have made our home on the right bank, which belongs to the Merchant's Provost and is known as the Town. If you and Aurélie should ever visit us, you will arrive in our neighbourhood via the Rue Saint Denis. For safety, we are surrounded here by a wide, deep moat, fast-flowing in the winter spates. At night, all six gates are locked and the Seine barricaded with huge chains so that Parisians may sleep in peace.*
>
> *Our house is close to the great river in an old part of the city, which was hemmed in for many years by a huge, circular wall. Eventually, Paris over-leapt this wall and spread across the plain, but not before the streets within had grown narrow and cavernous, the buildings taller, storey added upon storey like water rising in a reservoir.*

Paris had sounded oddly peaceful in Durant's account. The reality was very different. Longstaff gagged on the stench of piss and rotting vegetables – so much more offensive after the blossom-scented countryside. An open sewer ran down the centre of the road.

An eerie hush hung over the city, despite the clatter of hooves and the jangle of church bells. Shopkeepers along the wide street did not shout their wares but stood in shadow, dealing swiftly with their silent customers. Only the grim soldiers and swaggering lackeys advertised their presence openly. The former stood guard at every crossroads, each group sporting different livery as if the vast metropolis had become a series of rival states. The latter announced their mercenary status with naked daggers pushed through iron rings on their belts. Most wore black woollen leggings pushed into high-heeled boots and revealed their temporary allegiances with brightly-coloured ribbons.

To a man who could read them, these badges and ribbons revealed how power ebbed and flowed in this city. A stranger was at a disadvantage. Longstaff dismounted, trying to make himself as inconspicuous as possible, leading the horse until the Rue S. Denis struck a great east-west road running parallel to the Seine. A stable-yard dominated one corner of the crossroads. Longstaff had arrived, more or less. Durant's home was somewhere in the densely knotted maze of streets between this thoroughfare and the river, heading east towards the tall spire of Notre Dame.

The stable-yard seemed as good a place as any to lodge the horse. A gaily painted sign reminded Longstaff he hadn't eaten in hours. He handed the stable-master coins from Walsingham's purse, nodding and blankly smiling when the man replied with a volley of unintelligible slang. He didn't ask for directions. There would be time enough to eat when he located Laure. He turned on his heel, bedroll and saddle slung across one shoulder. The houses appeared to lean against each other, gables on the lower storeys with carvings in the shape of griffins, eagles, serpents.

Longstaff turned left and right. A band of barefoot children ran past. They looked feral but were neither desperate nor courageous enough to take on a full-grown man and dog. Longstaff reached a winding street of two-storey houses with open workshops on the ground floor. The artisan's quarter. He was getting close. Feeling more confident, he stopped to check his route, speaking slow French to a pewterer sat idly at his workbench, and hiding his true nationality in a broad Italian accent. He had no idea whether the tradesman was taken in by the charade – Longstaff hardly looked Italian, with his blue eyes and straw-coloured hair. He held up a coin. The pewterer drew a rough charcoal map on a scrap of cloth. More twists and turns, along Rue des Ecrivains, left onto Rue Marivaulx, where he saw a red and white striped pole – blood and bandages – above a simple sign: 'Gaetan Durant, Chirurgien'.

Surgeon? Years ago, Durant had studied Medicine in Montpellier. He'd put his studies aside when his daughter disappeared and never had the chance to sit for his cap.

Naturally, he couldn't claim to be a physician, but 'surgeon'? He might have set his sights a little higher.

The sign hung from the wall of a small house – exposed timbers and a rounded doorway, upper storey jutting out and casting the street into shadow. A bell rang when Longstaff pushed through the unlocked door into a ground floor consulting room. Two heavy wooden chairs on either side of a desk, glass jars on a series of shelves, squares of lighter wood where pieces of furniture had recently stood.

"You came."

Longstaff turned. She leaned in the doorway, left shoulder hidden behind the frame. Even in that dim light, Longstaff had no doubt she was Durant's daughter. She had his pale complexion and high cheekbones, the same dark eyes smudged with sleeplessness. She was dressed in skirts of striped tiretaine, white knit-stockings and wooden houseshoes. No sign of jewellery, not even the small crucifix all French women wore.

Longstaff smiled. "You're just as he described."

"A girl of twelve?"

"I still can't believe he found you."

"A true miracle."

Longstaff flinched, shocked by the bitterness in her voice.

"You'd better come up."

He climbed the narrow staircase after her, Sparrow's claws scratching the wooden boards behind him. Light from a single window illuminated the living quarters. A pail of fresh water. A rickety dining table. Pots and pans hanging from hooks on the walls. Beside a heavy chest, in one corner of the room, Longstaff saw a pile of straw shaped to form a mattress and covered with a sheet. Laure sat at the table, tracing patterns on the surface with a fingertip. Her eyes watered. A moment ago, they'd been clear and hard. Longstaff wasn't sure what to say.

"He would never have abandoned you. You know how long he searched…"

She rubbed a tear away with the heel of one hand.

"You must be hungry."

The knife beat a violent tattoo on the chopping board, rising in volume whenever Longstaff attempted to restart their conversation. Sparrow, who'd fallen asleep in a single beam of late afternoon sun, stirred uneasily but did not wake. Laure set two plates of bread and vegetables on the table, took a seat and waited with obvious impatience for him to join her.

"You intend to look for him?"

"To find him" said Longstaff firmly. "You must have some idea of what happened?"

She nodded at the large wooden chest. "Nothing's missing. There were riots in the city shortly before he disappeared. Paying customers for the first time in months…"

"Your father is one of the most gifted healers I've ever met."

"And one of the least diplomatic." She shrugged. "He'd been working flat out for days. It did him good; he almost looked happy when he left."

"To go where?"

"To celebrate. To drink. To get away from me for an evening."

Longstaff frowned, not sure he'd followed correctly, though Laure's French was mercifully free of slang.

"I don't understand."

"Nor did he. When my father found me, he expected a grateful, broken child he could devote himself to healing."

Durant had never explained where Laure had been in the years before he found her, and Longstaff had never asked, preferring to imagine the two of them building a future together, not raking over the coals of the past.

"Did he have..." the word escaped him for a moment.

"Enemies?"

It was the same word. Longstaff coloured slightly. "My French used to be better."

"You used to know my father better, if you need to ask that question."

"Someone in particular?"

"He was always starting fights. One day, he'd curse the king for leaving Paris, the next he'd denounce the Guise as warmongers. Another day it might have been the Huguenots, or people profiteering from the violence."

"Quite a list."

"His patients were the sort who couldn't afford any better. He was good with them. He could have built up a practice…"

They both heard it at the same time. The past tense. Laure clapped a hand to her mouth. Anger rose in a rash above the neckline of her striped dress.

"The tavern he went to," said Longstaff. "Can you tell me how to find it?"

"For all the good it will do you."

"I have to start somewhere." He nodded at his few possessions – sword, rifle, saddlebag – dumped in a pile beside his sleeping dog.

"I'll be back for them later."

"You can stay here. There's another room."

She led Longstaff to a narrow door he'd mistaken for a cupboard. The space beyond was cold – the small window was missing a pane of glass – and bare except for a second straw-pallet. Laure spoke to his back, giving him directions to a tavern called La Tête du Sarrasin - *the Moor's Head.*

"Mind where you walk," she finished. "We're not far from the Court of Miracles."

"The what?"

"Where the thieves and beggars go at night. Where cripples throw away their crutches, legless men rise to their feet and the blind recover their sight. That's why they call it the Court of Miracles." She gave him a half-smile. "They don't like strangers. The last troop of provost sergeants who ventured in were never seen again."

"Give the dog some food when she wakes…"

Longstaff looked out of the window. *How in God's name?*

The clothes were different. The man was no longer clean-shaven, but his shoulders were the same, an identical line running to the slim hips. Longstaff stepped slowly away from the window.

"What is it?"

"I'll be back."

He ran downstairs, steadied himself with a breath then crashed into the street. Empty. Longstaff thought he saw a flash of colour at the far end. Brown perhaps, but the light was poor. He sprinted in pursuit, emerged onto a busier street choked with carts and pedestrians, in time to see a man in brown vault over a handcart, knock a serving girl to the ground. Bystanders formed a knot. Longstaff crashed into them, stumbled to one knee, broke free of grasping hands, then followed his quarry into an alleyway. A stitch began its painful work. Too long a winter, too many hours spent curled beneath the furs. The leather soles of his boots too loud on uneven cobblestones. He'd lost his rhythm, didn't know these rutted streets. Around him, a thousand church bells began to ring the hour.

He ran through the warren of winding alleys, a rising mound of tight-packed homes, past a strip of cottage gardens running to a filthy canal. He sprinted over a narrow footbridge. The passage on the far side was deserted by the time Longstaff reached it. He bent double, elbows on his thighs as he spat, then hurried into swallowing rows of cheap tenements. Left and right, guessing at random. He slowed eventually, taking breaths, walking until the roar in his ears faded and the stitch died to a dull ache.

He was lost in Paris, with sunset only minutes away. He remembered Laure's warning about the Court of Miracles. Running, he'd had the lowering sun in his eyes; now he bent his steps eastward until he came to a square he recognised. A group of lackeys at the fountain, sharing a wineskin and dressed in shirts of fine cambric linen. He could find his way back from here but saw no need to hurry. A hard knot of anger had formed at his failure to catch the man who'd shadowed him from London. *Or was his imagination playing tricks on him?* Longstaff only knew he was in the wrong frame of mind to spend an evening with Laure. But the right frame of mind for a tavern? If he'd understood Laure's directions, the Moor's Head was only a short walk from here.

Chapter 8

A sign hung over the door from two slight chains. A severed head – brown skin, hooked nose, long black moustache – in a brown oval that might have been a sack or a puddle. Only four tables were occupied inside. Three men at a gaming table, not playing. Four women with heavily painted faces, laughing together over a bowl of gruel. A larger group of stone masons, covered in dust. A trio of men at a table in the corner, two with tell-tale iron rings on their belts identifying them as mercenaries, all three sporting home-made badges on the right shoulder: yellow and red stripes quartered by a cross. Some kind of bird in each of the four quadrants

The tavern's patrons ignored Longstaff as he nodded to the heavyset landlord, then sat at a table as far from the open fire as possible. The woman who waited on him had large, tired eyes and a cleft-lip.

"Wine. A jug of your best."

He could picture Durant here. The sweating walls and chipped tables. The place stank of cheap wine and broken dreams, the women just attractive enough, the patrons just well enough dressed to keep the last embers of hope alive. Hint of secrets and the outside chance of a quick profit. Longstaff knew the gamblers were his likeliest source of information, the people Durant would have spent his time with. A tailor and his apprentice – judging by the elaborate needlework on their tunics – and a butcher in his mid-thirties. This last was the cardsharp, decided Longstaff. Every tavern had its expert on separating the unwary from their money – young noblemen, merchant's sons looking for excitement, drunken labourers on payday. The tailors would be his helpers, hard men despite their elaborate costumes, there to make up the numbers and take home the scraps.

Longstaff gave a grunt of pleasure when his wine came. The girl smiled. He reached out to touch her sleeve.

"Sit down a moment."

He saw the look of surprise. "You must be my teacher tonight," Longstaff pulled her onto his lap, speaking in loud, broken French.

"How do you call this in your language?" He pointed at a small cask of wine on the distant counter.

She lowered her eyes. "Tonnelet."

"And the man beside it, scowling at me?"

"Le propriétaire."

Longstaff persisted with his game while the tavern slowly filled around them.

"I'm looking for someone," he said, as soon as he felt confident the other customers had lost interest. Quickly, he described the way Durant swept his hair back from the high forehead, the flat grey eyes. "He always used to dress in black. Good quality doublet and hose."

The girl looked away. It was clear she knew exactly who he meant.

"Gaetan Durant is a friend of mine. When did you last see him?"

She pulled away, knocking the table as she rose. Wine from Longstaff's cup splashed his boots. A genuine mistake, judging by the girl's terrified expression.

"M'sieur, I'm so sorry."

She was on her knees by the time the landlord appeared, dabbing at the spots with the hem of her skirt. He grabbed her shoulder, shoving her towards the serving counter. "Fetch a cloth."

The man turned to Longstaff. "Allow me to fetch you another, M'sieur."

Longstaff smiled, to show his mood had not been spoiled by the girl's mistake. He had no desire to cause her trouble. "Kind of you."

The two of them fussed. Longstaff made no objection when the girl departed with her employer. He took a long drink from the replenished cup, clasped his hands behind his head and let his chin fall forwards.

Aurélie's medallion nestled in the open collar of his shirt, at an angle which allowed him to see the blurred outline of landlord and serving girl in the polished silver. The former was staring straight at him, head cocked to one side as the girl stood on tip-toe, whispering in his ear. Longstaff looked up – the two conspirators sprang apart – he faked a yawn and rose to his feet, strolling to the gaming table.

"If you're looking for a fourth, I'll take a seat."

The butcher wore a leather jerkin, stained and spotted with the blood of his trade, a sheathed knife tucked in his belt. He stopped shuffling a deck of block-printed cards and studied Longstaff for a long moment.

"We're playing doublets."

"Deal me in."

"You'll find us a fair game. No hidden cards or mirrors." The man smiled, letting his eyes rest for a moment on Longstaff's medallion.

"New to Paris?"

Longstaff shook a few coins from his purse onto the table. "Passing through."

"Dangerous times for travelling."

"I don't take sides."

From the corner of his eye, Longstaff saw the landlord approach the three men in matching, homemade insignia. He threw down his cards with a show of disgust.

The butcher laughed, scraping a small pile of coins towards him. "Do you want to continue?"

"We've only just begun," Longstaff pushed more coins into the centre of the table. He didn't care whether he won or lost, only that playing earned him the right to stay.

"I'd hoped to meet an old friend here. Man with a Bordeaux accent, though it was in Montpellier I met him first. He was studying…"

"Only fools study," interrupted the butcher, "but then, the south is said to be thick with them."

The two tailors chuckled. "I've been there," said the older one. "My brother fell in love with a Provençale. A good man, my brother, with a fine business. He saw this girl – beautiful, you have to give them that – couldn't get her out of his head. Sent me south to treat for her hand and paid a fair wage for the job, too, but her father wouldn't hear of it. A man from Paris! Wanted to give me a whipping just for asking."

"That's why I've never been," the butcher stared hard at Longstaff, "ask the wrong questions, you'll be lucky to get out alive."

The tailor continued talking, apparently oblivious. "I heard later, the girl's father said the same thing whenever a suitor called. A man from Marseille! A man from Lyon! In the end he married the girl to his own brother. Their children were soft in the head."

The butcher lay down his cards. He'd won again. Longstaff shook more coins from his purse. He tried to concentrate, watching for tells the way Durant had taught him. His best efforts made no difference to the result.

There was a lull between hands, while the older of the two tailors went to relieve himself in the gutter outside. The butcher spoke to the man's apprentice. "Go tell the girl to bring some food. And more wine."

The apprentice stood without a word. The room had grown crowded while they played and he had to force a path to the counter. The two mercenaries in matching insignia had disappeared. Their weasel-faced companion sat alone. Despite the press of people, no one seemed eager to join him.

The butcher spoke without moving his lips. "Toward Les Halles, an overhanging staircase at the top of a long rise, opposite a statue of Saint Agnes. Meet me at midnight. Don't answer now. Don't even fucking nod. Keep your mouth shut and watch you're not followed."

He struck the palm of one hand against the table top. Coins rattled in time to the beat. "A song."

The landlord produced a lute from behind the counter. A man with broken teeth hurried to take it. He matched the butcher's beat for a moment, drumming his fingers on the instrument before starting to play. A jaunty song, unfamiliar to Longstaff but obviously well-known to the patrons who laughed at the conclusion of each bawdy verse.

The tailors returned. The serving girl arrived with a platter of bread and cheese. The minstrel completed his song, swept the worn cap from his head, thrusting it at people before they'd finished clapping. Many threw in a copper, Longstaff included. The landlord stood with the lute in one hand and a jug of wine in the other. The musician hesitated, eyes flicking back and forth. Eventually, he exchanged his meagre earnings for the jug and retired to a corner of the room.

Longstaff looked back at the gamblers with a laugh. The two tailors sat with their arms crossed.

"Game's over for tonight."

The older man looked at the butcher. "You'll be satisfied with what you've had of him, as well, if you've any sense."

"Have I done something to offend?" said Longstaff.

"Game's over, that's all."

"You're refusing me the chance to make good on my losses?"

No one replied. Longstaff was briefly tempted to make an issue of it, push the tailor to explain himself. He rose to his feet, thinking of his midnight rendezvous, and drained his cup at a single swallow. The serving girl arrived at his elbow. Longstaff paid for the wine and tipped her generously. People at nearby tables were shouting to make themselves heard. The girl spoke so softly that Longstaff nearly missed her words: *take care in the street.*

She was gone before he could react. Longstaff gave the card-players a curt nod and pushed his way to the door. For a moment, the air seemed fresh after the tavern's fug. He felt briefly lightheaded before the Seine's fetid stink arrived to help him find his bearings.

'Take care in the street.' 'Watch you're not followed.' Where was the danger? What had he done to draw it his way?

Longstaff stepped away from the tavern into darkness. A few lights still burned in the jutting, first floor windows, turning the way below into an inky black tunnel. He could barely see the hand in front of his face. Couldn't hear anything. The two mercenaries – if they were waiting somewhere near – would have seen him framed in the open doorway. Longstaff eased a knife into his palm as he neared the corner, held his breath, anticipating an attack which never came. It was too early to make for Les Halles and his rendezvous with the butcher. He did not want to lead anyone to Laure. Nor could he walk the streets at random, with the Court of Miracles lurking somewhere within this maze. Longstaff watched for signs he was encroaching on forbidden territory. The few people still about carried torches, shallow pools of light in the sleeping city. Longstaff tried to avoid them as he paced the tortuous lines of la Plâtrerie, la Verrerie, la Tixanderie, snaking back and forth across the neighbourhood. Half an hour had passed before he was certain. They were behind, following in his wake with the ease of men born to these streets. If they were the two he'd seen in the tavern, they were armed with sword and hammer – against his single knife. He had to lose them somehow. Longstaff began to weave from side to side, as if the wine he'd drunk had made him unsteady. He led the mercenaries in a wide circle, then stopped – hands on hips – when he struck Rue de la Plâtrerie for the second time.

Durant would have managed it with greater flare. Longstaff turned and retraced his steps, a dumb-show to make them think he was lost, looking for his way – to force them deeper into hiding, make them wait a beat longer before resuming their pursuit, earn himself precious extra seconds…

He'd walked this street just a few minutes earlier, seen the chair propped against the wall of a house, the grinning gargoyle above. Years of swinging the long bidenhänder war-sword had made Longstaff's arms massively strong. He pulled himself up, disappearing into the shadow of a jutting loggia as his pursuers turned the corner. They hurried past, stopped at the far end of the street, looked left and right before retracing their steps, poking into every nook and shadow, among the barrels of water before each house. *Please God, don't let them look up*. He was deep in shadow, they'd have to light a torch to find him. Longstaff closed his eyes when they were directly below, fearful the whites would give him away.

"Where's the bastard gone?"

"He can't have just disappeared."

"Can't have reached the end of the street that quickly."

The voices grew quieter. Longstaff felt safe in the darkness. A false sense of security which might cost him his life. The person living here might have heard him climb, might be about to draw the curtain…

"Maybe he's staying here? One of these buildings."

The mercenaries walked back and forth, searching for him in the street below.

"What now?"

"We have to tell him."

"Tell him what?"

"We know the street. It's better than nothing. We'll get some street-children here before dawn, have them watch until he shows up."

The second man spat a muttered curse. "He'll have our heads."

They drifted away, leather soles rapping an angry beat on the cobblestones. Wary of a trap, Longstaff counted slowly to a hundred. If he didn't move soon, he would miss his rendezvous with the butcher. How much time had he wasted already? How long until midnight? He only had the vaguest idea of where to find the statue.

Longstaff crept through shadow to the end of the street, straightened at the corner and walked casually towards the river, turned the next corner and crouched in darkness. The street remained silent. No one approached. Nothing but the sound of his own beating heart. Church bells tolled the hour. Eleven already; Longstaff rose to his feet and hurried in the direction of Les Halles.

The butcher had chosen a wise location for their rendezvous. The houses here had been built back to front, with only windowless gable-ends facing the street. There were no hidden spaces from which to observe the wide street and anyone standing beside the statue at the top of the rise could see for several hundred yards in both directions. Or could have done in daylight. Longstaff waited in a deep pool of shadow until he saw a flash of clothing – apron and red hose hidden beneath a dark cape. The butcher turned at the brow of the hill.

Longstaff walked forward, hands empty at his sides, and took a seat at the saint's feet.

The butcher remained standing. "You weren't followed?"

"I was. Not anymore. Who are they?"

"Who are you?"

"Gaetan Durant is my friend."

"I liked him, too. Night after night those bastards sit there, making sure no one says a word about what happened," he looked round. "Right here, perhaps."

"They killed him, you think?"

"Durant was always shooting his mouth. Maybe it was something he said. Lecornu followed Durant one night and I've never seen him since." He paused. "No sign of a body, though."

For the first time, Longstaff found himself hoping that Walsingham was right. It was too wretched, imagining Durant had lost his life in an act of random violence. He remembered the badge the three men had worn.

The butcher froze. "I thought I heard…"

"Stay where you are," Longstaff continued talking. He took one step back, away from the butcher. Another careful step, a hand on his chin as if lost in thought. The spy broke. Longstaff cut off his escape. The man screamed. Longstaff drove a fist into his gut, knocked him to his knees and choked him into silence.

"Lecornu!"

The butcher acted before Longstaff could stop him, sliding his knife between two ribs with the neat precision of his trade.

"What in God's name…" Longstaff stepped back. The corpse fell in a bloody heap. The butcher stared at him with wild eyes.

"His life or mine. I had no choice."

Further down the hill, a light flared on the side of a building. Somewhere, a bell began to toll.

"You fool! He might have told me where to find Durant."

Longstaff shook his head in disgust, though he could not blame the butcher. If was no easy thing, to kill a man in cold blood. Better to act at once, before the calls of creed and conscience began their work.

The butcher cleaned his blade on the dead man's tunic. Longstaff hunkered beside him. Shouts interrupted his study of the homemade badge.

The butcher flinched, "We'll be caught like rats."

"Wait," snapped Longstaff, but the man was already sprinting, footsteps merging with the sound of heavy chains, wound from their drums and drawn across the streets. Lecornu's scream or some other disturbance? It hardly mattered. The noise would shake the good folk of Paris from their beds. Already, the first would be leaning from their windows, lighting torches mounted on the sides of their houses. Longstaff started to run, not trying to catch the butcher, thinking only of reaching Laure's home, safety, just a few streets from here. He'd mapped the route in his head before the butcher arrived. He was out of breath by the time he reached the Rue Marivaulx. Approaching torches lit the surgeon's sign as Longstaff shut the door behind him, leaned against the solid planks of oak.

The ground-floor consulting room was dark. At the top of the staircase, Longstaff saw a light beneath the door. Laure must have closed the curtains with care; he'd seen nothing from the street outside. He found her asleep at the table, head turned sideways on her arm, gallon bottle of wine at her elbow.

"Hello?"

Her head jerked up. Despite the chill, her cheeks were flushed. She'd opened the collar of her blouse and loosened the bodice below.

"There was no need to wait up."

"You took off like a scalded cat."

She poured two cups of wine, pushed one across the table. Longstaff drained half at a single swallow.

"I saw someone I recognised in the street outside." He held out his cup for a refill – the tension of the last few hours had made him thirsty. He'd left her without a word of warning and not returned for hours. He was still out of breath, still seeing images of Lecornu's corpse in his mind's eye. He sat down opposite Durant's daughter and braced himself for the inevitable questions.

"Did you catch him?" She spoke as if they answer were a matter of complete indifference.

"No."

Her eyes were red with drink. "Next time, perhaps."

Longstaff waited.

Laure drank another cup of wine. "I've been thinking about my childhood."

"What?" He shook his head, uncertain how to interpret this sudden change of subject.

"The days before my mother died. The home I grew up in, playing hide and seek among the rows of vines. Then he took me away, set himself up in Montpellier and devoted himself to medicine. What should I have done? Alone. Lucky if I heard two words from him in a fortnight. No companions beyond an old woman he found to feed me. He promised to teach me letters, but somehow there was never time. I was always too young, too needy. When you're twelve, he said. The year I turned twelve, he forgot my birthday."

She took her cup of wine and stood before the darkened window. "Did he ever tell you what happened to our family home?"

Longstaff shook his head.

"I've thought of it every day since he found me, but never found the courage to ask. He was always so cross, so disappointed." She faced him, eyes ablaze with drink and anger. "He won't tell me what happened to my childhood home. I'm damned if I'll give him the satisfaction of asking."

Longstaff didn't know what to say. He had no idea what it meant, that they'd stayed silent on this topic. Not just for a day or a week, but for more than two years. Laure laughed at his confusion. "He never even told you where I'd been all that time?"

Helplessly, Longstaff shook his head. "He was happy just to have you back."

"I ran away with a travelling barber-surgeon." She stared at him. "Laugh, Matthew Longstaff. This is funny. My father was studying to become a physician at one of Europe's most prestigious faculties, and I ran away with a barber-surgeon. Seduced him. In the back of his wagon beneath the striped awning. Then said I'd cry rape unless he took me away with him. Poor man. He was terrified my father would realise what we were plotting." She sighed. "No chance of that. The barber-surgeon was a good man. We might have made one another happy."

Laure moved to stand behind Longstaff, one hand lightly on his shoulder. He could hear the drink in her voice, laced with bitterness.

"What happened?"

"He caught a fever from one of his patients and died."

"And still you stayed away?"

"I sold his instruments. The horse and cart fetched a good price. I thought I was free. By the time I realised how stupid I'd been, I was trapped more securely than ever."

A slow shudder seemed to run the length of her body. Her hand moved from his shoulder to his chest.

"Laure…"

"I'm lonely, Matthew."

Aurélie's medallion grew warm against his chest. Laure tried to pull him to his feet.

"I'm married."

"But still a man."

He turned, lifting the portrait so she could see. "This is the woman I love."

He was shocked by the look of hatred on Laure's face.

"I know all about her."

Longstaff slipped off the chair, stepping beyond Laure's reach. "I'd like to be your friend…"

Anger blossomed in her cheeks. "This is the mighty warrior he never stopped talking about?"

"Don't talk like that."

"Why not," Laure took a mighty swig from the bottle, "how many times have I listened to him talk about you and your perfect wife. I've earned the right."

She slumped down on the straw-pallet, one hand on the neck of the wine bottle. "Love has nothing to do with what I'm offering."

Longstaff sat at the table with his back to her, ignoring a volley of slurred insults. He did not look round until she began to snore. It had been a long day, he could barely muster the energy to direct a few well-chosen curses in the direction of his missing friend.

Chapter 9

The dawn bells started singly – a scattered ringing at first – then gathered in density until the noise rose in a solid mass from every belfry in the city.

Laure must have grown used to it. When Longstaff peered into the main chamber from his garret room, after his eyes had adjusted to the gloom, he saw her still fast asleep on the straw-pallet. He slipped across the room in stocking'd feet, boots in one hand – he told himself it wasn't cowardice but consideration for her feelings. She'd be ashamed. Best if they had some time to recover their poise. Longstaff made the father responsible for his own embarrassment. Durant had spent so many years searching for Laure. How could he have allowed such a long-held dream to descend into such a poisonous reality?

Laure would see his sword, musket and saddle when she woke and know he hadn't left for good. Longstaff dropped a hand on Sparrow's broad head as the two of them snuck down the staircase. It was still quiet when they reached the crossroads at rue S. Denis, where Longstaff completed a rudimentary toilette at the fountain. He needed information, and the two names he'd been given in London belonged to men of wealth and high status. Sir Nicholas Throckmorton and Horatio Palavicino. The former was Queen Elizabeth's ambassador to the court of King Charles of France. Pompous and rigid, a pedant and stickler for protocol, according to Sir Nicholas. The same man had described Palavicino as an adventurer, insufferable under normal circumstances, but trustworthy in a pinch.

It was still too early for social calls. Longstaff stamped the streets of Paris, keeping a wary look out for the man who'd pursued him from London, the two who'd stalked him the previous evening. His fond hopes of reaching the city and completing his task with no one any the wiser had proven ludicrously optimistic. The townsfolk stared straight through him; he knew how he must look – unshaven, in hard-worn leather jerkin and boots. A civil war simmered beneath the surface of this city and mercenaries were two a penny. Reaching the Seine, Longstaff spent several minutes staring at the sluggish water. A group of washerwomen worked beneath him on the riverbank, singing and shouting and pounding at piles of sheets and linens. Longstaff realised he could understand most of what they said. His ear was improving, long dormant knowledge of the language slowly coming back to life.

He retrieved a shard of charcoal from a pile of cinders. From his jerkin, he withdrew the scrap of cloth with the pewterer's crude map of Laure's neighbourhood. On the reverse side, in broad strokes, he made a sketch of the insignia worn by Lecornu and the two mercenaries.

Throckmorton or Palavicino? Pompous or insufferable? On a balance of probabilities, insufferable struck Longstaff as the lesser of two evils and Palavicino would be easier to reach at his *Hôtel* off the Place de Grève.

The square was one, vast building site, the air thick with stone dust, great clouds vibrating to the ring of masons' hammers. The Maison aux Pilliers had been torn down thirty years' earlier and a new city hall, intended to become the largest in Christendom, was slowly being raised in its place.

Non-stop work over a period of decades had not interfered with the square's most hallowed purpose, however. Longstaff saw the enormous pillory at once. A steep flight of steps up to a platform at the top of a cube of masonry, ten feet high and hollow inside. There was no one on the platform at this hour of the morning, but the recent unrest had no doubt produced a backlog of criminals. An offender would soon find himself tied to the plain, oak wheel, forced to his knees with hands behind his back, exposed to all four corners of the square by a hidden crankshaft.

Already, a fair number of Parisians were strolling in anticipation, recalling performances they'd witnessed in the past. Longstaff hurried past as the first cider and barley-beer vendors wheeled their barrows into the square. The Hôtel Saint Honoré was on the far side. He paused at the foot of a wide flight of stairs, looked through souterrain windows at a swarm of servants in the kitchens.

Longstaff had no idea whether Palavicino was a temporary guest or had reached an accommodation with the owners to maintain a permanent suite of rooms. He might have inquired if he hadn't been so intimidated by the sheer opulence of the place, staring like a peasant at the hall's high-vaulted ceiling. A servant hurried forward.

"I'm here to see Horatio Palavicino," Longstaff snapped.

The man looked him up and down, before glancing at Sparrow. "What name shall I say?"

"Tell him a friend of Nicholas Bacon."

The servant gestured towards a dark corner. Longstaff nodded. He had no desire to mingle with the men assembled here. Black-robed clerics gossiping in small groups. Merchant princes in velvet surcoats conducting business at half a dozen tables.

A boy appeared, still in livery but clearly inferior in rank to the previous servant.

"M'sieur." He gave a short bow before leading Longstaff across the marble floor – Sparrow's claws clicked like dice in an ivory cup – up a staircase to rooms on the first floor. The boy knocked, then stepped aside so Longstaff could enter.

The room was warm. A man in his early thirties sat beside a fire, tall and well-made with thick black hair, dressed in hose and a white silk shirt, open at the collar.

Longstaff stood to attention. "My name is Matthew Longstaff. I was given your name by Sir Nicholas Bacon."

An amused expression softened Palavicino's hawkish features. "I know who you are. And why you're here."

Despite his Italianate name, he spoke with the slow, confident drawl of an English aristocrat. "You'll join me for breakfast, of course."

I know who you are. How long had Walsingham and Sir Nicholas been plotting? Longstaff's stomach didn't care, grumbling at the sight and smell of the food on a low table beside the fire. Pancakes, bacon and beef, fruit, eggs, fish, cheese and bread. Fresh milk and ale to drink.

"I always find," continued the merchant, "the most comfortable way of being an Englishman in France is conforming to their stereotypes. With the funds to do so properly, of course." He gestured at the chair opposite his own. "What are you waiting for?"

Palavicino maintained a courteous silence while Longstaff ate, picking at morsels from his own plate and tossing scraps for Sparrow, who'd made herself comfortable beside the fire. The dog drew nearer their host, even submitting with apparent pleasure when Palavicino scratched the top of her head. Longstaff squinted in surprise. She was usually warier of strangers.

"A fine animal. Wish I'd seen her in her prime."

Longstaff grimaced. It was increasingly impossible to ignore the white hairs, advancing like an army across the dog's black coat.

Still quick, still strong, he told himself. Longstaff withdrew the scrap of cloth from his pocket and passed it over. "I'm looking for someone, abducted from a Paris tavern in January. The men responsible wore this badge."

"You don't recognise it?"

"I'm a stranger here. The stripes were red and yellow."

"The colours of Lorraine. In the middle we have the cross of Anjou. The eaglets represent three territories in the Holy Roman Empire, which lie between the Rhine and the Moselle.

You've made one small mistake; I imagine there were only seven stripes on the original you saw?"

"It's possible."

"I don't mean to criticise. You've a fine hand." Palavicino smiled. "Seven – to represent each of the sovereign houses from which the family claims descent – Hungary, Naples, Jerusalem, Aragon, Guelders, Jülich and Bar."

"Then it is the Guise."

"Officially, the family are outraged a group of street thugs have appropriated their badge and motto: *one for all, and all for one.* But yes, it's reasonable to conclude the Guise family were behind your friend's disappearance. You seem disappointed."

"I fought against Duke Francois of Guise at the siege of Metz." Longstaff shrugged, unsure of how to explain. He'd been twenty-five, a humble soldier in the Holy Roman Emperor's army of a hundred and twenty thousand. They'd expected to take the city in hours, but Duke Francois, who'd led the defence, had wasted no time in removing civilians from the city, razing the suburbs and building high ramparts from the rubble. The man's leadership had been inspired, holding out for months with only six thousand men and a handful of guns, but that wasn't why Longstaff remembered him with admiration; when his own commanders had finally conceded defeat, long after the weather had turned and sickness swept the camp, carrying off sixty thousand in less than a month, they'd abandoned the dead and dying to their fate. It had been the enemy, the Duke of Guise, who'd organised treatment for the stricken men. Longstaff had never heard of anything like it, before or since.

"The Duke is an honourable man."

"The Duke of Guise is a boy," replied Palavicino. He stared at Longstaff. "Where have you been, man? Duke Francois was assassinated two years ago. His son wears the title now."

"I didn't know."

Palavicino tossed the scrap of cloth on the fire. "Your investigations would appear to support Walsingham's theory."

"You know about him?"

"Cecil's up and coming man?" Palavicino nodded. "I know he thinks the Duke of Norfolk is a traitor. I admit, I find it hard to believe."

Longstaff grimaced. "That's why I'm here. He and Sir Nicholas need irrefutable proof before they can take their suspicions to the queen. And I need to find Durant. Assuming it was the Guise, where would they have taken him?"

"To the book, I imagine."

It took Longstaff a moment to understand. "The lost Gospel? It doesn't exist, a figment of Walsingham's over-heated imagination."

"But will your friend be able to persuade them of that? Will he want to? Imagine how desperate they are to believe it does exist – absolute proof that all Huguenots will spend eternity in the fires of Hell. It would settle this country's religious wars at a stroke and put the Queen of Scots on England's throne."

"Mary of Guise, as was."

"There you are. What would you do in Durant's place? Tell the truth or spin a tale? They'll kill him either way."

"Play for time. Durant is resourceful…"

Palavicino snorted.

"I asked you where?" said Longstaff.

"How in God's name should I know, though they're unlikely to have him in Paris for fear of the connection becoming public. The family is protective of its honour to an almost insane degree."

Palavicino fed Sparrow another sliver of bacon. "Catherine de Medici leaves tomorrow to re-join her son on his Royal Progress around the country." He misunderstood the expression on Longstaff's face. "Don't tell me you haven't heard of it? The poor lady would be devastated after the trouble she's taken – the pageantry, the feasts, the performances. Everyone has their favourite. I'm partial to the enchanted castle outside Rouen, six maidens held captive by devils and giants, the four Marshals of

France riding to their rescue. A mock battle before our heroes overcome their foes and free the distressed damsels. Catherine's way, you see. She hopes to make her nobles forget their religious differences in an ocean of pleasure. She hadn't reckoned on how jealous her Parisians would become. They forced her back, demanding ingenious spectacles of their own!" He paused to smile at his own eloquence.

"What does any of this have to do with me?"

"Tonight, before she leaves, Catherine will host an entertainment for her loyal subjects in the capital. The present head of the House of Guise will be there. Throckmorton, too – you'll want to communicate what you've learned and he has the most reliable couriers."

Palavicino donned a jacket, made of rings of steel so fine it was scarcely thicker than velvet, before completing his outfit with a grey and silver doublet.

"Are you coming?"

"Where?"

"My tailor, of course. I'd lend you clothes of my own, but you've the shoulders of an ox."

Chapter 10

AURÉLIE

Aurélie woke, wrapped in silk sheets beneath a heavy quilt, the early morning sun glowing gold against the curtains. She was tempted to stay in bed where it was warm, but the lure of the city was too great. She could hear it, lapping against the walls of York House, full of life and energy even at this hour.

The air was cold. Thank God for the thick carpets, strewn with lavender and basil. Her footsteps stirred the scents into life as she walked to the dressing table and pulled a brush through tangled hair. Her face was tanned from the days spent outdoors at Martlesham, blue eyes still smudged with sleep. Her fair hair had drawn attention in Florence. Here, it was her golden complexion that marked her out as different. Aurélie smiled at her reflection, lips parted to reveal even teeth.

Sir Nicholas had been as good as his word, engaging her as tutor to his sons. It was thanks to their good offices that he was finally allowing her to leave the house. Not that her confinement had been onerous. The Lord Chancellor's London residence was enormous, with gardens stretching from the Strand to the Thames. Sir Nicholas had given her free run of the library. Anne treated her as a long-lost sister. The house itself welcomed a constant stream of visitors, including many of the kingdom's most distinguished men and women.

In the looking glass, Aurélie saw the blush rise in her cheeks. She knew she should be furious. Walsingham had used them as bait. Sir Nicholas had acted as the man's willing accomplice in this game of politics, keeping her cooped up here; for her safety, he claimed – and because of the assurances he'd given her husband.

Aurélie thought of Matthew, the fear she'd seen in his eyes when he boarded the coach. And here she sat, making herself pretty in a looking glass. She shook her head. It wasn't like her to behave so agreeably.

Aurélie scrubbed her face and armpits with cold water from the basin. Anne had lent her a blue, damask dress; she made a deliberately poor job of tying the laces before setting out to negotiate the endless corridors. At a turn in the stairs, she caught sight of the two boys. Anthony and Francis knelt with their hands wrapped around the bannister, faces shining with excitement.

That raised a smile, still visible when she joined her hostess downstairs.

"You look flushed." Anne rose to greet her. "Step into my parlour, dear. Let me retie your laces."

Aurélie laughed. Anne always referred to this room as her parlour. Attractive self-deprecation in a woman of so many accomplishments. True, her work table and writing instruments were hidden from view in a small ante-room, but the parlour itself left no doubt that Anne was a woman to be reckoned with. Books lined the walls, her own translations prominently on display in place of the usual staid examples of needlework and embroidery. There had been no one like Anne in Suffolk, another woman Aurélie could talk to, the way educated men talked among themselves.

"There, let me look at you."

Anne raised a hand to her own elaborate curls as she assessed Aurélie's appearance. It was one of her maxims that men would only allow her to think for herself as long as she remained beyond reproach in all other respects.

"Sit down, Aurélie. I can't offer you any food, I'm afraid. The boys have prepared a picnic. It's a surprise. You're not to say I told." She smiled. "It's remarkable how they've taken to you. Anthony waged a perfect war against his last tutor and Francis always follows where his brother leads."

"They're a credit to you, Anne. And a pleasure to teach."

"High time you and Matthew began a family of your own."

Aurélie broke eye contact. Anne looked mortified. "I'm sorry. That was thoughtless of me..."

"There's still time."

"Of course. That's not what I meant at all. You came to visit friends and here we've separated you from your husband and placed you under virtual house arrest." She leaned forward to cover Aurélie's hand with her own. "You've been kind, not holding it against us. I can only imagine how worried you are."

"About Durant, mostly. Matthew can take care of himself."

Aurélie smiled. The flaws in her husband's character – those small frustrations that arise in any near relationship – had faded from memory in the last few days.

The boys appeared in the doorway. Anthony had a covered basket on one arm. "Ready?"

"One moment, young man," interrupted Anne. She took him by the forearm, turned him so he faced the large tapestry. "What do you see?"

Anthony rolled his eyes. "The trial of Orestes."

"What was his crime?"

Anthony flushed. "He murdered his mother. It was the first criminal trial with a prosecution and a defence. It was how the Athenians freed themselves from barbarity; the foundation stone of their achievements."

Anne smiled. "They freed themselves by placing responsibility for justice in Athena's hands. Goddess of Wisdom." Anne looked at him. "For the purposes of this outing, Aurélie is Athena. Her word is final. Do you understand?"

"Yes, mother."

Aurélie pressed her friend's hand. "There's nothing to worry about."

"Beyond reproach," murmured Anne.

Francis stamped his feet, a young colt waiting to be given his head. "This way. Follow me. Put your cloak on. It will be cold on the river."

"Shhh," hissed Anthony, holding the garden door for Aurélie.

The sky was a brilliant blue. New leaves were beginning to appear on the trees, daffodils appeared in clusters on the lawn. Anthony took her hand as they walked along the path. Aurélie could see his breath. She pulled the woollen cloak tight about her shoulders. Francis had run on ahead, down to the private wharf where their bodyguard waited patiently.

"Mistress Longstaff." The former soldier touched a knuckle to his forehead. He had that quiet air of competence which Aurélie admired in Matthew. She suspected the two men would have liked each other.

"Hello, William."

"Mind where you step."

Aurélie grinned as she boarded the small boat, amused at how they all insisted on behaving as if she were a lady. Anthony settled a blanket over her knees.

"Where to, young master?" asked William.

"Whitehall Stairs. No hurry."

The boy uncovered his basket with a conjurer's flourish, revealing a picnic of hard-boiled eggs, grilled chicken breasts and bread. The tide was with them, William only had to flick the oars to steer a course around the punts, wherries and sailing boats. Aurélie trailed her fingers in the cold water. She was enjoying her role as tutor, forming the boys' minds via the same practice of question and answer which Giacomo Vescosi had used to educate her in Florence. She smiled as she imagined his outrage – he would have been appalled to know how much she shaped her lessons to fit the orthodoxies of this time and place. She knew the story of Orestes better than Anne did, but could not share her true observations with Anthony and Francis.

They were being raised to venerate the rule of law. What would they think if they knew that Orestes's lawyer had secured an acquittal for his client on a false technicality, claiming that '*the mother is no parent of that which is called her child, but only nurse of the new-planted seed that grows*'?

Despite having killed his mother, in other words, Orestes was innocent of the specific charge – murdering someone of his own blood. A terrible argument, but one cleverly designed to appeal to the judge in this instance, who'd had no mother of her own having emerged full grown from Zeus' head.

The rule of law as it worked in practice, thought Aurélie; lawyers said whatever was necessary to win their cases – and with each half-truth and gentle lie, the state acquired a little more control over the individual. The execution of justice was a sacred duty, and also power in its purest form…

William navigated a bend in the river. "Fine view of the palace from here."

Francis looked round. "Where Father presented me to Queen Elizabeth."

"She called him Hamlet," put in Anthony.

Francis blushed. "Because our name is Bacon."

"Because you're the runt of the litter!"

The older brother laughed at his joke. Francis lashed out at him. The boat rocked wildly. Aurélie employed her best schoolmistress voice. "If the queen has given you a nickname, it means she holds you in great affection. I'll wager she does not call your father 'Sir Nicholas'.

Anthony rolled his eyes. "Mother says she calls him *far too often*."

William roared with laughter. Anthony looked panic-stricken. "You won't tell him I said that?"

"Don't worry, young master, your secret's safe with me." William nodded ahead. "Whitehall stairs. Just as you commanded."

Two soldiers, stationed on the wharf, lowered their pikes when they saw the Lord Chancellor's crest and helped the small party disembark.

"We'll be back in two hours," William slipped them a couple of coins. Anthony and Francis had already gone ahead. The queen was still at Oatlands, not due back in London for another few weeks. As Aurélie watched her two charges scramble through the deserted gardens, she was struck by just how high Sir Nicholas had risen. The boys showed her the bowling green and the cock fighting pit. Anthony dragged them all to the tiltyard. Aurélie enjoyed his disappointment when they found the place empty. She'd always suspected he was less bookish than he pretended, in deference to his parents' interests and preferences.

"Perhaps, if we wait. Someone may come."

Anthony shook his head. "It's not why we're here. This way."

Aurélie exchanged glances with William. The former soldier smiled; boys and their schemes. They followed Anthony to a low door in the outer wall.

"Short-cut," he shifted his weight from foot to foot while the guard fumbled for his keys, then led them down a narrow alley east of the Palace. The first thing Aurélie noticed was the smell – a man hurried past with a pomade at his nose – then the smoke, as they passed a series of butchers' yards, where men hacked haunches into steaming slabs of beef.

"Where are we going, Anthony?"

They emerged into a river of people, moving north-east towards a sea of canvas tents on St. James's fields. William placed a hand Anthony's shoulder.

"Hold on, lad. A visit to the gypsy fair was never part of my instructions."

"Please, William. Just a few minutes."

Aurélie hid a smile. Francis lined up alongside his brother. The younger Bacon would happily have followed Anthony into Hell.

"No," William shook his head. "Places like this attract every kind of villain. Your mother would have my guts."

"What could possibly happen, with you here to protect us?"

Aurélie burst out laughing. "The boy has a point, William. It's early; the place won't draw a real crowd for hours."

Francis nodded furiously. William tousled his hair.

"We'll have a look, but everyone stays together."

"What do you lack? What is it you buy?" the cries went up as they walked among the tables loaded with thimbles, rattles, haberdashery, good luck charms, pomades, maps of sleep and death. There were puppies and birds for sale. A bear roared in the distance. Anthony looked at William.

"Not today, young master."

The press of people grew as they penetrated deeper into the maze of tables and awnings. Aurélie led her charges to a makeshift cook-shop. They found space on a bench, ordered a jug of mulled wine and watched a troop of performers stroll by: a bearded lady, an acrobat who led a dog with two heads, three men carrying a stuffed and mummified Mameluke, fresh from Egypt. A puppet-master began assembling his box on the far side of the thoroughfare.

Aurélie found the visitors no less interesting than the performers. The poor in their greasy rags, shying clear of the wealthy in scented doublets and velvet hose. Gowned priests, lawyers from Westminster Hall. Every item of clothing told a story. As did the way that people walked, how they carried themselves, concealing their flaws and drawing attention to their virtues.

Francis plucked at her cloak. "Can we watch the puppet show?"

William shrugged, leaving the decision to her.

"Very well. But stay where we can see you."

Anthony took Francis by the hand. The two boys dodged among the passers-by. Aurélie could still see the backs of their heads. She might have joined them in front of the small puppet theatre but they looked so absorbed, so content in their own world, she felt a strange reluctance to intrude.

"Will you be with us long, miss?" said William

"Tired of my company already?"

The former soldier sipped easily at his wine. "You're good for the boys. Anthony, in particular. He comes to me for sword practice."

Aurélie smiled. "That makes us colleagues."

"Hardly..."

William rose to his feet. The crowd had appeared from nowhere, noise of their approach masked by the din of rattles and drums. A great tidal wave that surged up the thoroughfare.

Aurélie had only looked away for a moment. The two small heads were nowhere in sight. She had a sudden vision of Francis, tiny fingers slipping from his brother's grasp. *Oh God, Anthony, don't let go of him.*

Where was William? Already wading into the crowd, working fists and elbows. Where had it come from? This crowd. This trickle that had become a river in full spate. She caught a glimpse of Anthony's face, saw him lifted from his feet and swept away in the great press of bodies. Where was Francis? Aurélie plunged into the wave of men and women, stink of sweat, grease, anger and excitement. The noise was deafening, even above the terrified beating of her heart. It was hopeless. The only option was to bend, stay upright, pray she didn't fall. Anthony was clever. He would do the same, wait his chance.

Aurélie never thought of calling for help. She was concentrating too hard, whipped along on the crest of tangled limbs and tensed muscles, no idea of where they went or why. She sensed no anger in the crowd, only a deafening excitement. People roared and shouted, all sense crushed from the words.

The crowd's momentum was suddenly checked, a wave crashing into a sea wall. People fell. If they were lucky, friends helped them up. Aurélie shook her shoulders, jack-knifing her body to win a few extra inches of space.

"Hats off."

Within seconds, a thousand voices were calling out.

"Down in front."

Aurélie knew these cries from the theatre. As people complied, she saw the Eleanor Cross and shook her head in disbelief. On a normal day, she could have walked from here to York House in quarter of an hour.

Another row of spectators doffed their hats and hunkered down. Sixty yards away, Aurélie saw a scaffold above the sea of heads. Two uniformed men used their horses to beat the spectators back and clear a narrow path to the scaffold steps, the platform decorated with a wooden block and basket. Figures mounted the steps. They looked like toys from where Aurélie stood, identifiable by their costumes rather than their features. The judge, two priests, the executioner with his sword. The condemned man, dressed in a white linen gown.

Aurélie closed her eyes. Had William reached the boys and spirited them away? She looked left and right. No sign of them, or of any way out. People began to shout. Someone launched a cabbage at the platform. The priests rushed the final offices. The condemned man stood. Aurélie was too far away. She could not see what he looked like, whether he'd been beaten, whether he prayed or cursed. He placed his head on the block. The executioner removed it with a single blow. As one, the crowd gave a low groan of excitement, then quickly lost interest as the executioner and judge performed the ritual exchanges. The axeman's assistants mopping up. Gaps appeared around Aurélie; she could move her elbows, then turn in whole circles. Where were they? She was desperate to find them, desperate to find they'd been spared this horrible spectacle, moving forward as the crowd thinned, drawn by the mad notion that the scaffold itself would offer a perfect view. She was halfway there when she heard her name.

Aurélie pushed past stragglers, her knees weak with relief. They'd been closer than her, seats in the stalls rather than the circle. William held Francis. The boy looked tiny, arms flung about the soldier's neck. Anthony stood beside them, one hand on his brother's back, eyes still fixed on the scaffold.

"Are you all right?"

Francis turned at the sound of her voice, climbing like a monkey from William's arms to hers.

"They're fine."

"Who was he?" demanded Francis. He sounded hysterical. Aurélie had no idea what to say. Anthony bent down to retrieve a crushed lily from the ground.

"A traitor," he said.

"The martyr's flower."

"Exactly." Anthony held it up for his brother to see. "This is what father works so hard to prevent. There are people who wish us ill, who spread false ideas in this country by secret means. When we are insufficiently vigilant, tragedies like this are the result. But the queen's intelligencers grow more skilful every day. They watch the foreigners, stop up the routes by which infection enters. It's just a matter of time. Soon, it won't be necessary to execute Englishmen for sedition anymore."

The breath stopped in Aurélie's throat. She wanted to grab the boy by his shoulders and shake him.

"Something terrible happened here today, Anthony." She gestured at the scaffold. "This is evidence of failure, not success."

He turned to her, pale but composed. "With all due respect, Aurélie, I would not expect you to understand."

Chapter 11

AURÉLIE

In silence, they made their way back to York House. It was easier to walk than return for the boat. Anthony's comment had effectively destroyed any chance they had of keeping the adventure to themselves. Anne's smile faded at once. The front of Aurélie's dress was covered in mud. Anthony's clothes were torn. More than anything, it was the pinched expressions of shock and guilt on their faces. Francis had not cried when he and his brother were first swept up in the crowd. He had not cried when the axe fell, but this silence was too much for him. At the sight of his mother, he promptly burst into tears.

Anthony took a step forward.

"We were caught in a crowd of people. Rather stupidly, as it happens. By the time any of us knew it was an execution, we were trapped. There was no way to get out again until the crowd had dispersed. I made sure that Francis looked away, but he's still very young. I think it's possible he may have nightmares."

"You were at Eleanor's Cross?"

Aurélie recognised the look in Anne's eye. She knew what was coming and could feel her own anger rise to meet it. She took a breath, made one last attempt to stave off the inevitable.

"The boys are fine…"

"You'd let a child speak for you?" demanded Anne.

"He spoke for himself. Well and bravely."

Anthony flashed her a smile. Aurélie still could not look him in the eye.

"It really is my fault, mother," said the boy. "If I hadn't insisted on going to the fair, none of it would have happened."

There was no spite in what Anthony said. Aurélie knew he was genuinely trying to help and yet the result was disastrous.

"You took them to the gypsy fair?" Anne's eyes were ablaze. "I trusted you with my children."

Aurélie remembered the way Anthony had spoken to her. She'd never asked to be a nursemaid and she was damned if she'd be treated like one. "If your children have nightmares, it's none of my doing."

Anne's eyes grew wide. "How dare you speak to me like that."

"Oh? How should I speak to my jailor?"

Francis, sensibly, began crying again. Anne raised her voice. "There will be no lessons this afternoon. Aurélie, when my husband returns from Westminster, I shall tell him to find you in the library."

Dismissed. Aurélie turned on her heel, stalked away from them all. For all his muscles, William hadn't said a word. Even when they could no longer see her, she made certain they could still hear, slamming the library door behind her.

*

Aurélie stood at the high, tilted table. The book in front of her acted as a balm, slowing her pulse, pushing the two insults to one side. She'd been wrong about Anthony – his mind was far from unformed – but now was not the time to untangle how much of her anger sprang from shock, how much from guilt, how much from a genuine sense of injustice. For the moment, all she wanted was to lose herself in words, slip away from this golden cage for an hour or two.

She was reading Aquinas, and when she grew weary of his endless misogyny – strange how she could read and admire a man who would describe her as *vir occasionatus,* a defective or mutilated man – she could fetch another tome from the shelves. Sir Nicholas's library was a treasure chest. He'd allowed her free access on the day Matthew left, at the same time as he'd snatched her freedom of movement. Even then, her role in this house had been hopelessly confused. She remembered her host's eyes, the sadness in his voice as he requested she remain within the walls of York House. She'd been torn between anger and gratitude, had masked this conflict beneath a display of good manners, complimenting him on the astounding variety of his collection. She still remembered his reply.

"Eventually, I intend to donate these books to my old college at Cambridge, where they can serve the greatest number of people. For the present, I find I can't bear to part with them. Read them, Aurélie, and salve an old man's conscience."

She glanced around the room. One day, she would have a place like this – an uncompromisingly perfect reflection of her temperament, tastes and history. Sir Nicholas maintained two desks; he was more scrupulous than most in trying to keep his public and private interests separate. On the desk where he attended to the queen's business, his personal motto was picked out in gold lettering: *safety in moderation.* On his private desk, each of the six drawer-fronts was carved with a different device, representing Norfolk, Essex, London, Middlesex, Somerset and Dorset – the six shires where he'd acquired holdings in the course of his long career. On the surface lay manuscript copies of works by Leonard Digges and Thomas Blundeville, scientists to whom Sir Nicholas acted as patron. The bookshelves were decorated with an unusual motif – three cranes in flight – reference to a Cambridge tavern where the great Reformist and Humanist thinkers of their day had gathered to exchange ideas. Sir Nicholas had joined them as an undergraduate, the happiest days of his life he often claimed, when he'd briefly believed the two schools might merge and usher in a new and glorious future.

A servant entered with bread and a bowl of soup. Aurélie was still banished from the rest of the house. She carried on reading – letters sent to Sir Nicholas from Constantinople by the famous merchant adventurer Anthony Jenkinson. Everyone in London knew the name. With no contacts, no previous knowledge of the people or their languages, he had convinced the Ottoman Empire that England was a worthy trading partner. Now he wrote to Sir Nicholas begging for the crown's support, requesting that an English ambassador be sent to Constantinople, someone with the authority to hold Suleiman the Magnificent to his promises. For a moment, Aurélie allowed herself to dream of a new life in a far-away land. She stared at Jenkinson's sketches of a lost script he'd seen in the East – on tombs, monuments, steles and ruins. What secrets might be revealed if someone managed to decipher these strange, angular marks?

For as long as Aurélie remained lost in thought, she was invulnerable. She ate carefully, hand cupped beneath her chin to prevent crumbs falling on the pages, never looking up until Sir Nicholas entered. He carried a taper in one hand, made a slow circuit of the room, lighting candles.

"I have been forbearing..."

The fall of the executioner's axe swept through Aurélie's mind, along with Anthony's reaction. "And I have treated you with all the courtesy due a generous host," she interrupted, "even acting as unpaid tutor to your children, despite the fact you conspired to send my husband into danger. Tell me again, Sir Nicholas, which of us has been forbearing?"

"From now on," he replied, "you'll remain in this house."

Her head snapped up. "You're being absurd."

"And you're being stupid. Today, it was chance that might have carried you away. And tomorrow? Walsingham has dropped you in it up to your pretty neck. I won't have you or the children put needlessly in danger."

She saw his anger.

"What am I to you," she demanded. "Friend, hostage, honoured guest? Or just a nuisance? Am I your children's tutor or a fellow scholar? How can any person play so many roles and not make mistakes?"

"I appreciate your position here is complicated…"

"My husband is in danger. One of my closest friends has disappeared. Now you want to shut me up in this house?"

"If you were in Walsingham's keeping, as he wanted, do you think your accommodation would be as comfortable? Would he make the same effort to respect your freedoms? I gave my children into your care today, as your husband gave you into mine."

"He did no such thing. Don't confuse me with one of your English ladies, brought up only as far as my knees."

She was losing her temper, could hear her native accent threatening to overwhelm the brittle English words. She pointed at the shelves. "Where is the manuscript I rescued from the Devil's Library?"

He appeared to flinch. Aurélie took a step closer.

"*On Freedom.* The only known work in existence by Epicurus. Where is it, Sir Nicholas? And the rest? My former guardian devoted his life to building a network of scholars across Europe, who risk their lives to preserve what little remains of the past from the book-burners in Rome. I brought you a list of safe-houses, sympathisers, donors, printers, distributors. Giacomo Vescosi's dying wish was that you continue his work. What have you done with it all? Are you my friend, Sir Nicholas, or my enemy?"

"I am Queen Elizabeth's servant!" He took a deep breath. "You're right. I haven't tended Vescosi's legacy with as much devotion as I might have done, but I have my reasons and I stand by them!"

Aurélie gazed past him. *Epicurus's book.* She'd read it non-stop on the journey to England, had known it nearly by heart. The words had faded with time, but not the startling beauty of the ideas: *And I insist on the testimony of the senses, against all other claims of authority. And I will work by the light of this testimony towards an understanding of the hidden structure of things.*

She folded her arms across her chest. “Why are you keeping it secret?”

“The ideas are too explosive, Aurélie. People aren’t yet ready to take responsibility for their own lives in the way Epicurus proposes. Why do you think most are so happy to give their consciences into the hands of priests?”

“Epicurus moulders in a cupboard because *you* have decided that people can’t be trusted?”

“I need a drink.”

Sir Nicholas poured wine from a decanter on the sideboard. He looked smaller – the anger had leaked away, leaving weariness in its place. “There were those of us who hoped Elizabeth would become queen, but no one ever thought it would happen. As Lord Chancellor, one of my duties is to speak for her in parliament. Do you know what she had me say in my very first speech?” He closed his eyes: “’Inform the House I will never be governed by my will or whim to such an extent that I impose chains upon my subjects or give them cause to engage in riot or disorder.’ To my knowledge, it’s the first time that any monarch – anywhere – has acknowledged limits on the divine right of kings. Do you understand?”

“Pour me a drink.”

He handed her a full glass.

“I joined Giacomo Vescosi’s network during Bloody Mary’s reign, when it looked as if my public career was finished. I took comfort in his tales of a magical library containing the sum of human knowledge. But it’s gone, burned to ashes by your own report. Queen Elizabeth sits on the throne of England, surrounded by enemies on every side. Keeping her safe is the task which occupies me now.”

He slumped into a chair. Aurélie re-filled his glass.

“Walsingham’s scheme won’t keep Elizabeth safe,” she spoke gently, as if the two of them were old friends.

"He's a fanatic," said Sir Nicholas, "who genuinely believes that all Catholics are predestined to burn in Hell. But that doesn't mean he's wrong about the Duke of Norfolk. Honestly, I don't know whether to admire him or loathe him."

He smiled at her. "Tell me, Aurélie, how can we improve your situation here?"

"In Florence," she said, "I was beaten as a witch and nearly burned at the stake. I fought the Master of the Sacred Palace and won. Matthew only agreed to leave me here because we're threatened by plots hatched in this city. Stop treating me like a child and let me help you."

Chapter 12

A thousand torches lit the Palais de Justice. Longstaff hesitated at the entrance to the great hall, letting the crowds rush past like an invading army, charging up the steps, rushing along the interior walls, swirling around the seven huge pillars.

"Why here?" he muttered, meaning 'why me?'.

His companion shouted to make himself heard.

"First residence of the Kings of France. Catherine's no fool – she may have left her son in the provinces, but she wants all Paris to know she represents him tonight."

Palavicino had done his best to explain. As an Italian, a woman and a regent, Catherine lacked the authority to stop France from destroying itself in civil war. That's why she'd had her son crowned before he reached his majority and taken him on a tour of France, the greatest Royal Progress ever undertaken, intended to last two years and involving more than ten thousand courtiers, cooks, servants, grooms, masons, carpenters...

The Queen Mother's flare for theatricals was a welcome distraction in the provinces, but Paris had reacted like a spurned lover, forcing her to abandon her son for several weeks to soothe the troubled capital.

The entrance to the ancient palace was guarded by two stone lions, heads bowed as a demonstration of Might's humility at the feet of Lady Justice. Longstaff felt a stab of sympathy as he passed, dragging his feet like a child. He, too, wanted to sneak away, tail between his legs. He was not a courtier, despite Palavicino's efforts to prettify him.

Insufferable. The word described Palavicino perfectly. Longstaff and the merchant were dressed alike, but the latter looked dashing in his suit of clothes, while Longstaff worried his own broad shoulders and callused hands made a mockery of the beribboned doublet and silk sleeves that fell to his fingertips.

And yet he hadn't rebelled, not even when Palavicino suggested he have his hair soaped and perfumed. All day, he'd found it oddly impossible to fault the logic behind any of the merchant's suggestions. Naturally, he wanted to see the new Duke of Guise with his own eyes, and, of course, he could hardly attend this event in his own hard-worn clothes. When the tailor had finally finished his prodding and poking, and Palavicino reminded Longstaff that Sir Nicholas Throckmorton would be at the Palais de Justice, it had seemed reasonable to return to the Hôtel Saint Honoré and accept the merchant's offer of stationary and the time required to compose an encrypted letter to Aurélie.

Longstaff felt the paper beneath his doublet. He'd worked on it throughout the afternoon. Then the tailor had arrived for a second fitting; by the time the man left, it was already too late to return to Laure and explain what was happening.

Longstaff stepped on the merchant's heels, their progress interrupted by a knot of brightly dressed guests, all marvelling at the chandeliers above. Thousands of candles hung from the vaulted ceiling, coaxing rainbows from the stained-glass windows. The merchant's smile never wavered as he poured forth an endless list of names and gossip. Longstaff could have listened for a century and still barely scratched the surface of the various intrigues and machinations surrounding him in this vast room, the high politics and low feuds tearing France apart. He plucked a sweetmeat from a passing platter; pork in cider, beef in radish sauce, sliced tongue and a seemingly endless array of sugary confections. He ate with his mouth closed. The guests around him, in their elegant silks, all smiled with upper and lower lips just touching at the centre; this was how Catherine smiled, to conceal her ruined teeth, and it had quickly become the fashion at court.

"That's her," said Palavicino, "the looks of an Italian matron, the bearing of a Queen of France."

Longstaff craned his neck. At one end of the hall a platform of gold brocade had been erected on a giant slab of polished marble, where the infamous Catherine de Medici sat in state.

Her face did not appear to have been painted, in contrast to many of the men and women present. She was dressed in black, dark hair set with sparkling stones. A female dwarf sat beside her in a miniature version of the same high-backed throne, making it difficult to judge Catherine's height or figure.

"The Queen Mother believes that dwarves are a source of good luck," said Palavicino.

Longstaff nodded. A green parrot walked back and forth along one arm of Catherine's throne, while a long-tailed monkey perched on a carving of her personal device – a broken lance above the words *'Lacrymae hinc, hinc dolor'*.

"From this come my tears and my pain," translated the English merchant. "You must know the story. Catherine's husband, King Henri II of France, lost his life in a jousting accident seven years ago. She's worn mourning ever since. A shame, when you think that her previous device was a rainbow. She claims she begged him not to fight that day; her favourite soothsayer had predicted the accident years earlier."

The band struck up. Drums and horns to quieten the crowd while servants cleared a space before the platform. Longstaff felt Palavicino take hold of his elbow, dragging him backwards into the crowd. He was reaching for a dagger when the horns died, but it was excitement he could hear in Palavicino's voice, not fear: "Hurry, man."

A liveried servant stood beside one of the seven massive columns. Money changed hands, too quickly for Longstaff to see how much.

"Come on," Palavicino placed a well-shod foot in the servant's hands, clasped to make a thief's ladder. Longstaff stared.

"Monsieur Palavicino has reserved an excellent position for you, sir."

Up he went, stepping on the servant's head to reach a gap in the masonry above a seated sage cast in marble. Across the bobbing heads, a river of white entered through a doorway on the far side of the hall, accompanied by a splendid cacophony – full orchestra of flutes and rebecs. A collective sigh rose from the crowd, parting to form an impromptu dancefloor. Women dressed in flowing silks. At least eighty, according to Longstaff's hurried estimate.

"All high-born maidens of France," said Palavicino. "Sir William Cecil would bite his arm off for a group of intelligencers half so effective. Catherine uses them to learn the secrets of her *grands seigneurs.*"

They began to move, a variation on an old dance with new steps that would have caused a scandal in England, before the musicians moved seamlessly to a more decorous melody. The maidens lowered their eyes and the greatest men of the capital stepped forward while Catherine de Medici sat perfectly still, her black dress a stark but regal counterpoint to the whirling, white-clad maidens.

"Oh-ho," murmured Palavicino.

At the same moment, a frown appeared on Catherine's brow.

A young man, in burgundy hose and black doublet, walked among the dancers with such steady purpose the musicians lost their beat. A piper made himself blush with an unexpected trill. The young man smiled. He was very tall, pale with strawberry blond hair and broad across the shoulders. With a slight bow, he extended a hand to one of the maidens. An older courtier looked livid but retreated wordlessly into the crowd. An enemy for life, thought Longstaff.

"Who is he?"

"Your new Duke of Guise."

The musicians struck up again. The great crowd watched in silence as Henri of Guise and his chosen partner danced alone in the huge space.

"Elegant," said Palavicino cheerfully, "thinks himself a tragic hero. When his father was murdered, he took a solemn oath to pursue revenge against all Huguenots, *'without truce or respite, to be God's exterminating angel on earth until the very last heretic has been cut off'*."

"*He's* supposed to have arranged Durant's abduction?" said Longstaff

"Not him," replied Palavicino. "Pay attention, Longstaff."

While all eyes had been on the boy, a man in cardinal's robes had joined Catherine de Medici on the platform. That wasn't all; the mood had shifted in the great hall, subtly but decisively. Catherine's guard stood less easily, eyes trained on a collection of new arrivals – lackeys sporting earrings, artfully curled moustaches, rapiers with elaborately decorated hand-guards. Longstaff's own suit of clothes were a model of restraint by comparison.

"Charles, Cardinal of Lorraine," said Palavicino, "true head of the House of Guise."

The newcomer had the same penetrating blue eyes as his brother and nephew, but not their fair colouring. The music drew to a close, followed by a wave of muffled gasps as people saw him. Cardinal Charles raised his hands for silence. He spoke for nearly an hour without losing the attention of his audience, quoting poets and statesmen in French, Italian and Latin, managing to appear both humble and learned whilst simultaneously lavishing praise on his hostess. Finally, the cardinal clapped his gloved hands. Servants streamed towards the platform.

"The Queen Mother's presence consoles us for the absence of our monarch, but it does not make us forget him. We think of him on his tour of our great and sadly divided land, bringing understanding and love where before there was hate. We cannot achieve what he can. We would not presume to offer him counsel or advice. Humbly, we only beg that his mother take these few comforts to him that he may dine at ease and wake refreshed from each night's sleep."

The cardinal described each item as it was set down before the platform: "Two chandeliers from Venice, a dining service, three golden lamps finished with precious jewels, a marble bust of Marcus Aurelius brought back from my own recent trip to Rome."

Palavicino grinned. "He can't risk an open break with Catherine; he needs her to legitimise his position, just as she needs his money and men. Come on, Longstaff, time to mingle."

They descended from their high perch and began to cross the hall. "Watch them," whispered Palavicino – his smile remained in place throughout the low monologue – "Catherine is our sun, of course, and Charles our bruised and angry Mars. Planets, nonetheless, which march in step; one can't move without the other being forced to keep pace. And each planet has its many moons, dancing in tandem. See the fabulously ugly man standing before the platform, a hand on the hilt of his sword? Gaspard de Saulx, devoted to her Majesty."

The sword was enormous, the man himself as unattractive as described, though dressed in a suit of modest grey. He was obviously ill at ease, eyes shifting back and forth between the cardinal and a second man.

"Jean Rastignac," said Palavicino, "the cardinal's principle satellite and head of his personal guard."

Rastignac stood with one hip jutting towards the Queen Mother. The basics of his costume were almost elegant – just as the man himself could almost be considered handsome – but rendered grotesque by the exaggerated ruff and codpiece. Rastignac was more than a simple bodyguard; he was also here to display the essential brutality which lurked beneath a thin veneer of civility, to intimidate and create an aura of invulnerability around his master.

"They say he and the cardinal are half-brothers," continued Palavicino. "Rastignac's a bastard, schooled in the martial arts, as deadly as he's loyal."

The cardinal leaned across the Queen Mother, whispering in a way that made the hair rise on the back of Longstaff's neck. Catherine shook him off, lifting her voice so that it carried across the hall.

"But, my dear cardinal, I've always believed magic to be immensely powerful. It must be, mustn't it? Or the Church wouldn't be so anxious to keep it from the common folk?"

Palavicino waited for the buzz of conversation to resume before continuing his commentary.

"The man applauding with such vigour is Cosimo Ruggieri, a Florentine magician Catherine keeps to tell her fortune and scare her enemies."

"The cardinal looks like he's bitten a lemon," said Longstaff.

"There was a time people thought him a moderate. It was Duke Francois, his assassinated brother whom you esteem so well, who refused even to speak with Huguenots. Charles spent several years negotiating in apparent good faith. He was in Italy when he heard of Francois's assassination, suckling at the vengeful breast of Mother Church."

Palavicino paused a moment, staring at the cardinal.

"Normally, he wouldn't suffer Ruggieri to appear in his presence. You should have seen his reaction when Catherine and the young king paid a private visit to Nostredame, early in the course of their Royal Progress…"

"I've heard of him."

Palavicino did not look impressed. "Every man, woman and dog in Christendom has heard of Nostredame. Catherine trusts him completely, ever since he predicted the time and manner of her husband's death."

Palavicino ushered Longstaff through a low, interior door, into a chamber that seemed given over to pleasures of the table. The press of people grew greater, red-faced and sweating, lit by the flames of huge fires. Decanters of wine passed from hand to hand.

"Are you hungry?" said Palavicino. "They're serving cibreo tonight, a Florentine favourite of Catherine's, made from gizzards, testicles, offal and cockerels' coxcombs."

They did not linger. The merchant drew Longstaff deeper into the labyrinth of interconnected rooms. In one, a dozen men had organised themselves in a disorderly queue. A woman sat at a table, dipping her breasts into goblets of wine and offering them to the eager gentlemen. Longstaff looked away.

"A pretty enough sight," said Palavicino, "but not what we've come to see."

Longstaff dropped back a little, chilled by the amusement in Palavicino's voice. A blast of fresh air struck them as they stepped onto a terrace, down a flight of steps into torchlit gardens where Catherine had created a wonderland. Longstaff looked for the glass in his hand, but not a drop of wine had passed his lips. Not yet; though he felt certain he'd need a drink after this. Dwarfs and giants strolled side by side among huge, pink birds. Ponies had been painted with black and white stripes. Longstaff saw highland cattle with their shaggy coats woven into plaits and finished with colourful ribbons. Somewhere in the darkness, he heard the roar of bears.

"Impressed?"

The merchant's manner was beginning to grate.

"A tradition started by the ancient kings of Mesopotamia," said Longstaff, "who received foreign beasts as tribute and created elaborate gardens to house them. 'Paradeisoi', in their own language, which some scholars claim would later serve at a literary model for the Garden of Eden."

Longstaff hadn't spent all this time with Aurélie without learning a thing or two. He made a show of straightening his doublet. "What are we doing here, Horatio?"

"He's coming now," the merchant nodded at the terrace. "Remember, he knows nothing about the Duke of Norfolk – only that Walsingham suspects a traitor on the queen's Privy Council."

A shadow jogged stiffly down the steps and hurried in their direction.

"Allow me to introduce her majesty's ambassador to the French Court, Sir Nicholas Throckmorton."

The newcomer led them deeper into shadow. Longstaff only had time to register that he was tall and slim with iron grey hair.

"Did you see?" said Palavicino. "Quite an entrance the boy and his uncle made."

"A petty show of strength," Throckmorton's voice was sharp with impatience. "The cardinal has been on a charm offensive for months, claiming he regrets his former hostility towards the Queen Mother. Brought about by the loss of his brother apparently; it temporarily unmoored him."

"Do you believe him?"

The ambassador snorted. "What do you want, Horatio?"

"To present Matthew Longstaff. I'm sure Walsingham has told you all about him. I've just been introducing him to the Guise."

Blood drained from Throckmorton's face.

"From a distance," Palavicino laughed softly, "acquainting him with their appearance only. It seems they've fallen for Walsingham's ruse. The Frenchman was abducted by men wearing the Guise badge."

Throckmorton scowled at Longstaff. "Their official badge?"

Longstaff described Durant's abductors.

"I know the group," said Throckmorton. "They're not above acting on their own initiative; brawling, intimidation, extortion. Your friend's probably lying in a ditch somewhere."

"It wasn't a random attack," interjected Palavicino. "We think one member of the group observed Durant over a period of time, then recruited two more to carry out the abduction. The three of them have since taken steps to intimidate witnesses. Someone must have passed his name to the family."

Longstaff withdrew the letter from his doublet, marked for Aurélie Longstaff, care of Sir Nicholas Bacon. "It's all in here, for the next London-bound bag."

The ambassador took it with obvious reluctance. "You're not going back?"

"My task is to find Durant."

Throckmorton crossed his arms. Longstaff had a strong impression the man was torn between conflicting inclinations.

"Durant is a friend of mine," he added, "his daughter has asked me to help. There's no reason anyone should suspect that my search is anything other than a personal matter."

"Rubbish. Fall into their power, Longstaff, and they'll use you to stir up a world of trouble for us."

"We've been over this," said Palavicino. "The cardinal is actively colluding with King Philip of Spain. We know he's attempting to have Elizabeth excommunicated – at a stroke that will change her murder from an act of regicide to an act of piety. And we know a member of the queen's Privy Council is helping him. You agreed, we have to do everything we can to stop him."

Throckmorton spat. "If the Guise discover an English spy in their midst…"

"But you do have spies," interrupted Palavicino. "Dozens of them, including one living on the Guise family estate at Joinville."

Longstaff struggled to keep his expression neutral. Palavicino hadn't said anything about a spy. 'Insufferable' did not do the man justice.

Throckmorton still held Longstaff's coded letter at arm's length. He glanced at it now, his cheeks dark with suppressed rage. "I want it known I disapprove of this enterprise in the strongest possible terms."

Longstaff resisted an urge to shake the man. He'd been manipulated, separated from his wife, thrown in harm's way. He took a step towards the ambassador.

"I don't know anything for certain," said Throckmorton. "You wouldn't believe the rumours which come out of Joinville. The cardinal's mother runs the place as her personal fiefdom. They say she's a witch, that she sleeps beside her son's open coffin."

Palavicino snorted.

"Of course, it's nonsense," muttered Throckmorton. He took a breath. "My source informs me that a mysterious guest currently resides within the walls of Joinville, under lock and key. No one sees him but his jailor. No one knows his name or why he's there."

"Durant," said Longstaff.

"It could be," acknowledged the ambassador, "I hope to God Sir Nicholas Bacon knows what he's doing." He tucked Longstaff's letter away in the folds of his doublet. "Do you have a plan of the estate?"

"I've been there," interjected Palavicino. "I can give our friend the information he needs."

Longstaff thought of Charles, Cardinal of Lorrain, and his nephew Henri. The two most senior members of the Guise family were here, only a few hundred paces away. He felt a terrible urge to carry them both into a dark corner. Five minutes alone with them and he'd know for certain where Durant was being held.

Throckmorton appeared to read his mind.

"Sir Nicholas Bacon told me you were discreet. You're not to approach the cardinal or his nephew under any circumstances. Leave Paris at once, tonight if you can. When you reach Joinville, you're to reconnoitre only. For God's sake don't go blundering in there with your sword drawn."

"He's not a complete fool," said Palavicino.

"Get him out of here, Horatio," Throckmorton turned on his heel, leaving them alone.

"That went well," muttered Longstaff.

"Don't take it personally. The man has a demanding mistress."

"Elizabeth?"

"Catherine." Palavicino smiled; he seemed to be enjoying himself. "I think he fears for his sanity if he ever gets too caught up in her games. Her husband left her with three small boys and a divided kingdom. There's no one she can trust and so she lies – even when she tells the truth – and casts a spell of madness. Throckmorton's right about one thing; Catherine's hatred of the Guise is all that keeps the English safe at night – give her a reason to trust them and we're finished."

Palavicino steered Longstaff around the ancient stone walls, through alternating patches of revelry and darkness, pursued by sounds of laughter from within.

"The Queen Mother leaves Paris tomorrow. Throckmorton is obliged to travel with her. I'll go, too, to keep him company before returning to my headquarters in Bordeaux. That's where we'll be, respectively, should you need us again."

They were both strangers – Palavicino and Throckmorton. Longstaff hated having to rely on them. The merchant seemed likable enough, content with himself and happy to take the world as he found it, but what did any of that prove in the great scheme of things?

"Hurry," urged Palavicino. "We have a busy night ahead, my friend, if we're to see you safely away in the morning."

Chapter 13

Before he could set off for Joinville, Longstaff had to take leave of Laure. He returned to her small home on the Rue Marivaulx an hour before dawn. She was awake, still dressed and pale as a ghost. She seemed to look right through him.

"You're all right."

Longstaff cursed himself for being so stupid. He had disappeared just as her father had, sending no word of his whereabouts.

"I'm sorry. That was thoughtless."

Laure jerked to her feet, turning away from him. "You must be hungry."

"I don't have much time."

"You have to eat." She prepared eggs with dill and lemongrass, served on slices of thick-cut bread. There was an awkwardness to the way she moved, an embarrassed vulnerability that reminded Longstaff of his missing friend.

"I don't normally drink like that," she said. "You came all this way to help my father. I hope I did nothing to offend you."

It wasn't a question. Longstaff's eyes widened in surprise. Had she forgotten? Or was this her way of burying the past?

He smiled. "I've seen your father do the same – seek a moment's relief in wine. What's the point of parents, if we can't make them responsible for our own occasional weaknesses."

She gave him an uncertain smile. "The apple never falls far from the tree?"

"I'm sorry," said Longstaff, "that wasn't what I meant."

She was twenty-one years' old. Two nights ago, she might have been twice that age. Now she could pass for a child.

Longstaff finished his mouthful. "What happened between the two of you?"

She was silent for a long time. Collecting her thoughts or hoping he'd forget his question? Longstaff wasn't sure.

"I'm not the first child to run away from home," she began haltingly, "of course I wanted him to notice – that was the point – but I hardly thought he would. I never believed he'd destroy his whole life, give up his dream, spend all those years looking for me. I was angry when I left, but I never wanted that for him." She shook her head. "If he'd found me happy, he might have been able to forgive me, but I was a mess. The man I took up with, after the barber-surgeon; he wasn't a kind man. My father claimed it was his duty to rescue me and Duty's a cruel mistress. It's not his fault we're trapped now – a cage of our own devising and we can't find the way out."

Longstaff did not know what to say. Her pride seemed to prevent her from asking questions, though he could see how much she wanted answers. Would she find comfort in knowing the man who'd orchestrated Durant's abduction was dead? It wasn't safe to mention the involvement of the Guise – the less she knew about that the better. Naturally, the same went for Walsingham.

"I'm sure your father did not leave you by choice. I can't tell you more, but I promise I'll do everything in my power to bring him home safely."

She wouldn't look him in the eye. Longstaff had no idea whether his short speech had reassured her. She offered no clues, no tearful pleas or words of bitter recrimination. She only stooped and rested her head against Sparrow's warm coat for a moment while Longstaff buckled the old katzbalger sword around his waist.

*

He followed the Seine out of Paris – after a brief stop to collect his horse from the stable-yard on the Rue S. Denis – and struck a cluster of villages beyond the southern wall, all making a good living from their position on the river's banks. Villagers poled themselves back and forth on skiffs, servicing an endless succession of flat-bottomed cargo boats, collecting tolls on behalf of absent landowners, selling supplies, providing pilots for the various reefs and shoals. The road itself was dusty, crowded with merchants banded together for safety, pilgrims engaged in fierce displays of piety, ampoules of holy water in their hats, badges on their cloaks or hammered onto walking sticks – St. Peter's keys, St. James's shell, St. Veronica's veil. Longstaff stayed in near identical inns on the first five nights of his journey to Joinville, was given the same thin stew to eat, eavesdropped on the same muttered conversations, paid the same inflated prices even when the rooms were taken and he was forced to sleep on the taproom floor, wrapped in his long, cavalryman's coat.

By the time he reached the market town of Romily-sur-Seine, he'd had enough. Standing beside the river, where it made its great southward curve towards the city of Troyes, he stared at the road and knew he'd rather take his chances in open country. He turned east, following an old footpath between two fields. For the first time in days, Sparrow loped ahead. Longstaff shifted in the saddle, stretching his arms and rolling his shoulders. He hadn't realised how tense his fellow travellers had been.

Cutting across country would reduce the absolute distance to Joinville but these meandering paths – working their way around woodlands, patiently following every rise or dip in the land – would probably add time, particularly when Longstaff considered how much more likely he was to lose his way. Speed and safety carried their own dangers, however. Lolling along the highway, part of an endless shuffling crowd, the road ahead no different from the road already travelled, negotiating each evening with rapacious innkeepers; it was both exhausting and boring – enough to make him dull, lazy, impatient and foolish.

At noon, Longstaff stopped to let the horse graze and share a simple meal with Sparrow. Looking back across the tilled fields, he saw church spires in the distance and one great watermill visible through a fold in the landscape. Ahead, there was nothing but woodland. Longstaff flipped open his saddlebag and found the small bottle of brandy Palavicino had given him, a perfect complement to his newly buoyant mood. His eye fell on a thin roll of paper, carefully wrapped in leather.

Walsingham's map. Perhaps he'd be able to find the most direct route after all. There was Romily-sur-Seine, written in tiny letters. Longstaff followed the line of the Seine as it wove its way south and east – and there was Joinville. On the map it was hardly further than the length of his thumb.

Longstaff felt the pale sun on his shoulders as he stared, waiting for a story to emerge from among the lines and symbols. Nothing happened. No hills came into view, no tree lines or distinctive crags, no creeks or rock formations. No names, except of towns and cities, written in the same neat and tidy script, no sense of a journey made and told and repeated over generations, until each landmark had a life of its own. Longstaff looked up, at the fields ready for sowing, trees thickening into forest, tracks running parallel to streams, following the path of least resistance through the gently rolling landscape. Walsingham's map was a record of place, he realised, stripped of life and history.

Deliberately, he returned the document to his pack. It was time to move on, heading east with the sun on his back, making for a tendril of smoke glimpsed from the summit of a low hill. He struck an old drovers' road soon afterwards. The smoke came from a wooden shack beside a stream; part farmhouse, part watermill, part inn. A man appeared while Longstaff tethered the horse.

"Bed for the night?"

"And a hot meal," Longstaff turned with a smile, "fresh hay and water for the animal."

"I'll send the boy. Come in, make yourself comfortable."

Longstaff dipped his head on the way inside. The ancient doorway was carved with acorns. How many people would still recognise this as a charm against lightning? He ran his fingers across the smooth surface, just as Aurélie would have done. The single ground-floor room was filled with the smells of home. The landlord, his wife and three children sat down to eat with Longstaff. The room was warm, the food hot and filling.

In the morning, Longstaff asked about the road to Joinville. It didn't feel like a risk – he'd said nothing about himself and the landlord was hardly in a position to start sending messengers.

"Fastest way's a track through the deepwood."

"Safe?"

The man shrugged, extending an arm to demonstrate the wide curve of a stream. Longstaff's route would take him via King's Oak, Witch's Creek, a clearing called Maiden's Blood – all the information he needed, everything he'd searched for in vain on Walsingham's clever drawing. One of the boys led the horse out with a bundle of fresh hay strapped across the withers. The landlord's wife appeared and passed him up a package of bread, cheese and salted fish.

A dead pigeon marked the deepwood's border, wings fanned on either side of a burst of breast feathers. A fox, most likely. A falcon would have crushed the breastbone, a sparrowhawk just nipped it out. Longstaff felt excitement as he walked among the trees. It was noticeably colder, the branches above so tightly woven he could scarcely see the sky, even this early in the year. There was precious little deepwood left in England, none at all in Suffolk. More in France, he knew, but this was the first he'd seen since landing at Harfleur. It was all disappearing – as people demanded grazing land for their livestock, bigger fields for their crops, more wood for their homes and ships, charcoal for smelting iron-ore in ever greater quantities – but Europe had once been covered in forests like these; close-packed, dark, silent and unbroken for hundreds of miles in every direction.

Worked by herds of auroch and swarms of giant boar more than by men. People said the auroch were gone and Longstaff didn't relish the prospect of meeting a boar. Who knew what other dangers lurked among these ancient trees? He tried to concentrate, sharpen his senses – if was for just that reason he'd left the road – but felt as if he were walking on sacred ground, past a greater variety of trees and plants than he could name.

Longstaff kept on through the day, hardly aware of his surroundings until he came to a stream where the water ran black with the coming of night. After making a small fire, he lay with linked fingers behind his head, Aurélie's medallion balanced on his lips. The grass was soft beneath his shoulders, one side of his body warm while the cool night air raised goose-bumps on the other.

By noon the following day, the undergrowth had thinned enough that Longstaff was able to ride again. He saw signs of small-scale logging and charcoal burning, as more and more sunlight fell through an irregular canopy of branches. It was nearly dusk when he reached a cluster of three stout buildings overlooking a meadow with their backs to the forest. Two small children fell silent as he approached. A man appeared in the doorway of one of the houses, wiping his hands on a piece of cloth.

Longstaff raised his empty palms. "A good day to you, neighbour."

He remembered to exaggerate his German accent; if Parisians treated Englishmen with suspicion, he hardly dared think what the folk out here would make of him.

"We don't get many visitors by way of the deepwood."

The man was short and well-timbered, bull-necked and bearded. A second man appeared, almost identical to the first, the same even features set in a round face beneath dark, close-cropped hair. Both were dressed in leather jerkins and stiff linen breeches. Brothers, guessed Longstaff as he dismounted.

A third man appeared, the physical opposite of his neighbours – tall and fair, clean-shaven and long-haired – a dozen tin badges had been hammered to the doorframe above his head. Catholics, then. Longstaff attempted a smile; as good a time as any to rehearse the performance he intended to give at Joinville.

"I've been travelling for weeks," he said, "all the way from the land of the Magyars and this is the first time I've lost my way. Doesn't it always happen when the end's in sight?" He smiled at them again, each in turn.

"A crusader?" The younger of the two brothers took a step forward.

The fair-haired man folded his arms. There was a glimmer of angry intelligence in his eyes. "Where are you headed?"

"Joinville. I've done my time on the borders of Christendom and would serve the family again, if they'll have me."

"You've served the Guise before?"

"At Metz," Longstaff nodded, "under Duke Francois."

The brothers crossed themselves.

Longstaff stared at the taller man, pressing his advantage. "Twelve years, I shed blood for the true faith; what do I find when I come home? Cobblers and coiners claiming to know the will of God, priests murdered, holy relics burned. That's why I seek the Guise." Longstaff dropped a hand to the hilt of his sword, beginning to enjoy his performance. "Or perhaps I've mistaken friends for adversaries?"

"No!" said the younger brother. "We're with you. We fight…"

"Shut up, Benoit!" The fair-haired man turned to Longstaff. "It's growing late. You'll stay, of course."

At his signal, a woman emerged from the dark interior of his home.

"This is my wife. You've already met her brothers."

Longstaff's first instinct was to ride on - he could not put his finger on it, something was wrong here – but Sparrow had already made friends with the two children and staying would give him the opportunity to refine his impersonation of a German mercenary.

"Matthias Lammermeier," he introduced himself, using the name of the merchant who'd given him sanctuary in Lübeck after his father's execution. "Thank you. I'd be delighted."

Chapter 14

AURÉLIE

Her Royal Highness, Queen Elizabeth of England, had returned to London from her winter lodgings at Oatlands in Surrey. It was her practice to change residence every few months, partly for reasons of hygiene, partly so she could be seen by as many of her subjects as possible. Thousands had turned out yesterday for a glimpse of the Royal Carriage. Today, a selection of the better sort had been invited to gaze on her at Whitehall.

Faithfully, Aurélie had promised she would do nothing to draw unwanted attention, even padding the waist of her plain dress and strapping her breasts. She stood mute – eyes wide, mouth agape – listening as Anne explained her presence to an acquaintance.

"She's Italian, acting as governess to young Francis. Children pick up languages so fast at his age. She has a fair hand with the boy, we thought it would do no harm to bring her."

"Very kind of you. But wise?"

"As my husband likes to say, how are we to show our neighbours the error of their ways, when so few are exposed to the glories of our English court?"

Anne bade her acquaintance farewell, then led Aurélie and the two boys further into the maze. It was not designed to confuse – the pebbled paths between the hedges were too wide for that, the design a simple one, leading only to the centre. Aurélie could hardly believe how the place had been transformed since she'd been here with Anthony and Francis. The hedges were a rich green, with no chinks of light in their foliage. The borders had been planted with a wild profusion of flowers. *Greenhouses.* It was the only explanation. They could not possibly have shipped so many. The extravagance was extraordinary, even to one who'd been raised in Medici Florence. Part of Aurélie was appalled – a sudden cold snap and every one of these plants would die – and part of her was enchanted to find such a riot of colour after the sterile winter months.

Aurélie and Francis were dawdling. Anne put a hand on Anthony's shoulder, pausing so the two of them could catch up. The two women were back on good terms. Aurélie had been worried – she'd spoken hard words – but Sir Nicholas had come to her rescue: "Have you forgiven Anne for her part in the disagreement?"

"Of course." Aurélie had been shocked. "She was worried about her children. It's no wonder she spoke as she did."

"And do you think Anne lacks the same ability to put herself in another's place?"

The man wasn't stupid. Aurélie had to give him that. His sons took after him in that respect. She smiled at Anthony, the perfect gentleman in miniature. They had never talked about what passed between them in the shadow of Eleanor's Cross. He treated her with the same affection as previously and, in her daily lessons, Aurélie tried to suggest the folly of believing that any single doctrine, no matter how enforced, could ever lead to a universally happy society.

Anne looked the three of them over, before raising a hand to check her own elaborate curls. Aurélie realised why as soon as they rounded the next corner.

The centre of the maze. A huge pebbled square about a smooth lawn, with pure white fountains at each of the four corners. The falling water wove itself around music played by a small orchestra. No one danced. It was too cold to sit and picnic on the perfect lawn. All eyes were fixed on the figure who commanded a raised platform in the centre, covered in cloth of lawn.

Queen Elizabeth of England. Dressed in white, she shone in the sunlight. Jewels sparkled. Her auburn hair, which fell in thick locks to her shoulders, glowed against the white furs. Hard to believe she was beset on all sides by enemies. France. Spain. Scotland and Ireland. Catholics across the continent were taught by their kings and bishops to pray for her death each night, asking God that Mary, Queen of Scots might unify the thrones of England and Scotland in the one true faith.

But then, reflected Aurélie, wasn't that the point of this display? Elizabeth the Indomitable. Immovable. The sun around which this island nation revolved. Few of her subjects dared leave the path, content with a turn about the square before they hurried home to tell their friends and neighbours what they'd seen.

Only the truly mighty strolled on the grass. Dressed in silks of gold, red, silver and pink, they were on display just as much as their queen. From Aurélie's observations it appeared Elizabeth favoured two distinct types: the respectable and reliable, and the glamorous and amusing. The latter were more numerous, strutting about in exaggerated codpieces, earrings poking through their curled hair. Aurélie smiled when she saw Sir Nicholas among these butterflies. Her host was decidedly a member of the sober type. He stood on the lawn in conversation with Anne's brother-in-law, William Cecil. Known as the Queen's Mind, this was the ring-master, the friend and ally who kept his hands clean while Sir Nicholas and Walsingham did the dirty work. Both men were dressed in muted colours. They looked tired; slow and heavy among the bright courtiers.

Anne leaned close. "Norfolk wears an emerald green doublet." She spoke softly, not looking at the man she described.

Aurélie stared. This was the spy on the queen's Privy Council. England's only Duke, who had fallen for Walsingham's baited trap. He was beautifully dressed and bore himself well enough, but the eyes were small and too round, as if startled by sudden light. She judged him a bluff and hearty type, after the

English manner. Hard to believe he possessed the murky depths of a conspirator.

Aurélie pinched her cheeks and wiped one greasy palm across her forehead. By design, she had made herself look sweaty and unimportant, and knew how deceptive appearances could be. Young as he was, the Duke of Norfolk had already commanded armies and negotiated treaties with the Scots. Cecil had secured him a place on the Privy Council three years earlier, hoping to make him an ally in his endless battles against the queen's favourite, the Earl of Leicester.

To Cecil's chagrin, Norfolk had quickly demonstrated his independence.

Anne hissed at her. "For Heaven's sake, keep walking."

Norfolk and Elizabeth had been friends since childhood. Aurélie remembered what Sir Nicholas had told her: "Norfolk's wife died two years ago. He's the most eligible bachelor in England, yet he hesitates to take a new wife. If Elizabeth were to die, he would be the perfect husband for her successor, Mary Queen of Scots. Elizabeth's death would make him King."

The pathway was crowded, the lawn studded with men and women who put the flowers to shame, and still a newcomer caught Aurélie's eye. Mid-thirties, she judged, with the first touches of grey at his temples. So handsome it made her smile. He sported long moustaches and seemed to have thrown off the awkwardness so many Englishmen cultivated. His sky-blue doublet was studded with pearls and cut to reveal the lines of a martial figure. The man had a word for everyone he passed but did not stop until he reached the platform where he made a deep bow before his queen.

A smile lit Elizabeth's face. Aurélie was too distant to hear what they said. She looked down at her own plain gown, prompted by a sudden notion that it wasn't Elizabeth on display, but her, and everyone else here – unwitting players in an entertainment for this couple.

"Who is he?"

"The Earl of Leicester," whispered Anne, "Robert Dudley, as was."

Aurélie blinked. Cecil's great rival on the Privy Council. The man at the heart of every rumour in London: he had murdered his wife; he was about to wed the queen; he was betrothed to Mary Queen of Scots.

Elizabeth referred to him as 'Two Eyes'. His enemies called him 'gypsy'. He was the man who'd caused Sir Nicholas's recent fall from favour, the man whose network of intelligencers Walsingham hoped to supplant. Like Norfolk, he was also a childhood friend of the queen's.

Anne was doing her best to keep them moving – a single slow circuit around the lawn – but Aurélie paused and looked again. No painter could have executed a better image of strength, prosperity, happiness.

Aurélie stared at Norfolk's glowing face. The Duke looked round, as if sensing her scrutiny. She felt a sudden terror that he'd seen through her disguise. She wanted to hide. She couldn't look away, but then he laughed at something his companion said, the humble nursemaid apparently forgotten. Aurélie looked again and saw a tragedy – not just Norfolk, but also Leicester. The crypto-Catholic Lord of the North and the Reckless Adventurer. The two most powerful men in the country – along with William Cecil. Leicester's father had been executed for conspiring against Elizabeth's sister, Bloody Mary, and Norfolk's had been beheaded by order of King Henry VIII. The same mad king who'd had executed his own wife, depriving Elizabeth of her mother.

Was it treachery or fear which bred so many orphans? So much blood, thought Aurélie, so much pain hidden beneath these smiling masks. She looked down at Anthony and Francis. How many more would there be?

"You look pale, Aurélie. Are you well?"

"I'm fine."

Sir Nicholas had finally noticed them. He crossed from grass to path as if it were the easiest thing in the world. Another deception, along with his hearty greeting and apologies to his family that he'd left them so soon after arriving. And then, in an undertone to Aurélie, "have you seen enough?"

More than enough. She nodded.

Clapping his fat hands, Sir Nicholas raised his voice.

"High time you were all heading back to York House. The young men can only stand so much excitement!"

He winked at Anthony, ruffled Francis' hair, already ushering them out of the garden and into the maze.

"I'll follow as soon as I can."

Chapter 15

DURANT

I accept no testimony, but that
Of my senses, by and through whose light
Mankind may pierce the veil, exalt the mind,
Vanquish a baser tyranny than death.

Bone-weary, Gaetan Durant shifted on the cot. He'd been working day and night, frantically composing, editing, flipping back and forth through the library of books in search of adequate models, and still they were never satisfied. He'd completed nearly half the one hundred four-line poems they wanted. No wonder his brain ached. Thank God the old fraud hadn't picked a more complicated form.

Durant had boasted to Lecornu of being able to compose prophesies as convincing as those of the famous fortune-teller, Nostredame, but it had still come as a surprise to discover it was true. He had proceeded methodically. *First,* forget the real Nostredame, whom he'd known and admired in Montpellier. *Second,* exaggerate. The prophet's own sentences overflowed with extremes. Pain rendered as agony, death as eternal damnation, wine as a torrent of blood. Step three had been more complicated. Nostredame's critics claimed his quatrains were nebulous, open to endless different interpretations. In fact, Durant's close reading had revealed a consistent philosophy: there is no loyalty that cannot be overcome by greed, no heroism that won't be undone by malice. No good that will not fall victim to evil.

And then, the final element in this bitter mix, to season the whole with fleeting glimpses of shadowy figures, plots and conspiracies, imply knowledge of a dark purpose that lurks beneath the surface of this chaotic world. Durant was convinced it was this final element, more than any other, which accounted for the startling popularity of the prophet's work.

He wanted to pace but the shackle tore at the skin round his ankle. No doubt his old friend Longstaff would simply have yanked the chain free and used the trailing end to beat his captors to death, but Durant wasn't made of the same stuff.

The chain was short. He couldn't reach the door or the stone fireplace with its stub of melted candle, only the narrow cot which stood against a wall and the long table on the far side of the beam.

Durant shuffled back and forth beneath the bundles of herbs they'd hung from the rafters. Thyme, parsley, some dried lavender. All harmless. All part of Vincent's attempt to make the place look like an alchemist's cave. Durant might have found it funny under other circumstances.

He sat down: *pick up the quill, go on writing the four-line prophesies.* He hadn't realised how much he'd come to rely on his daily excursions into this fantasy realm. Was it more than that? Starved of human contact, was he, too, starting to believe in divine inspiration? Nostredame had written about a world soul, apprehending past and future within an eternal present. What flaw, wondered Durant, had seduced the old man into believing such self-important nonsense? As he became more and more absorbed in the creation of his forgeries, Durant was barely aware of a growing sense of superiority. Nostredame was wrong. Chaos was not the illusion, but the reality. There was no dark conspiracy or hidden order. On the contrary, that was precisely Man's purpose on Earth – to develop his powers sufficiently that he might finally vanquish chaos and bring about the longed-for age of reason.

There was no mirror in the room. Durant ran his fingers down the sharp, vertical lines of his face, nails catching in the thin beard, trying to make a mirror of his fingertips. It was

Laure's face which swam into view. His pale complexion and high cheekbones, but her mother's eyes. Her mother's smile.

Durant had not mourned when his wife died. Sickened by the robed priests and their tales of suffering, he'd turned his back on the consolations of faith, taken his five-year old daughter to Montpellier and enrolled at the medical faculty, determined to penetrate the secrets of nature and discover a cure for the plague.

Those months after his wife's death; that was when fear and humility might have served Durant, as a counterpoint to the unholy arrogance of his ambitions. Nostredame, who'd been one of his tutors at the university, had tried to tell him as much, but Durant hadn't been ready to listen. Not then.

"Am I interrupting?"

Durant flinched. He hadn't heard the door open and yet there was Vincent, leaning against the frame with a wineskin in one hand, eyes flicking from the shackle around Durant's ankle to the bolt in the central beam, making sure neither had been tampered with.

"Time for the correspondence."

The same procedure they followed each evening. Vincent dropped a pile of letters on the table, already sorted by order of importance, then took the chair opposite, picked up the poems Durant had produced during day and started reading. On his side of the table, Durant began dealing with the post. The first correspondent was Swiss, but Durant kept to the florid French he'd become so familiar with. It was spring; he advised the man to open a vein, vomit, purge his body of ill humours. Bathe more regularly and cut down on red meat. The tone came naturally – thin-skinned, peremptory. Not the kind of man to suffer fools gladly.

The letters seeking medical advice were the easiest. The others required more time. A priest who wanted to know the location of a lost relic, an advisor to the Duke of Florence who sought advance knowledge of plots against his master…

Vincent interrupted him, tapping the latest batch of four-line poems into a neat pile. "I believe the pupil is beginning to surpass the master. The beat is more percussive, the allusions more poetic, the sensibility more sublime."

He offered his wineskin across the table. Durant nearly choked on the rough spirits. The heavy chain shifted like a giant serpent on the floor.

"How is your finger?"

"Healing."

Vincent poured again. The temptation to drink was strong, to treat this man as a companion and relieve the awful loneliness. Durant shook his head.

"One more won't hurt. You've done well, doctor. One would almost think you'd found your true calling. You could set yourself up as his rival, when we're done here."

Durant's hands began to shake. "When we're done?"

"That's right," said Vincent, "you've never asked – what will happen to you once your task is complete."

Durant's task. One hundred four-line prophesies to stir a nation into action. Vincent had taken a perverse pleasure in explaining his master's aims. The Guise had been plotting for years. The pope was preparing a Bull to excommunicate the English Queen. The King of Spain was mustering an army. Now, the Cardinal of Lorraine needed to rouse the people of France and put pressure on the French crown to join this unholy enterprise. Durant cast an involuntary glance at his left hand.

"I do your bidding because the alternative is pain and dismemberment, but I'm not a fool. Your master would be mad to let me live. I know too much."

"In France, you're a problem," Vincent waved the wineskin in agreement, "but say you were to go abroad... You're obviously a gifted healer."

Durant shook his head. "I can patch a wound, tell bloody flux from a case of dropsy."

"You could become a first-rate physician," said Vincent.

"There was a time I thought so, too," a bitter smile twisted Durant's lips: *I dragged my infant daughter from her home, her mother in the ground less than a week. Pride and grief chained me to my studies. Laure never settled in Montpellier. Her anger became a reason to avoid her. Whole weeks went by without us speaking. And for what? So I could listen to those high and mighty doctors in their pulpits, reading from books written hundreds of years earlier?*

Durant remembered his frustration, how he'd longed to shake the complacent bastards, for as long as it took to make them see the world as it truly was. Doctors harmed as often as they healed, but it didn't have to be that way. Before Laure had disappeared, he thought he'd seen an alternative. He looked up.

"My daughter, too?"

"If that's what you want."

For a moment, Durant allowed himself to indulge the fantasy. He remembered the running battles through the streets of Paris, so that even dishonest men feared to show a light in their windows after dark. Paris, where he'd made such a poor job of ingratiating himself with his fellow professionals. He'd blamed their malice for the failure of his practice, but his heart had never been in it. Not then.

"There are other centres of learning." Vincent rose. "Far from here, where no one can make trouble for my master."

"You'd never allow it," said Durant, "not really."

"Why else would I make the offer? You're already doing everything I want," Vincent paused in the doorway. "There is just one thing I'd ask in return, though. The prophesies you've produced so far are admirable, but a touch morbid. How about a ray of hope, in return for the prospect of a new life in a far-away land?"

Chapter 16

The taller man was Jules, the two brothers Tomas and Benoit. The woman blushed whenever Longstaff looked at her. She had changed for the evening meal; not the sort of thing Longstaff would normally notice but the dress was striking, made from emerald green silk. She kept grabbing handfuls of the skirts when she moved, to keep the hem from trailing.

A rough-hewn table dominated the single room, a flight of stairs in one corner, another curtained off. Two beautifully made armchairs stood on either side of the fireplace. The older child placed three candles at regular intervals along the table and lit them with a taper from the fire. Longstaff wrinkled his nose, expecting the acrid tang of cheap tallow. The scent of good beeswax reached him instead.

The brothers removed their boots in the doorway, replacing them with lambs-wool slippers. Jules stood silent while his wife ladled thick soup into silver bowls, then clasped his hands and led the family in prayer.

"Lord, we give thee thanks for our daily bread, enough that we may share our bounty with a traveller from a distant land. We beseech thee, make us strong enough to resist the depredations of our enemies, who work in league with Satan. O Lord, only with your help can we drive them from our poor beleaguered land."

Longstaff thought of Durant, held captive only a few miles from here. That was his hope, anyway, but surely it had been too long – the Cardinal of Lorraine had had months to discover that Durant knew nothing about a lost Gospel – and yet Longstaff had no choice but to continue his search, hoping against hope that his friend had convinced his jailors to keep him alive.

"Amen," chorused the extended family of foresters.

The spoons they used were silver. The chairs were a mixture, some as rough-hewn as the table, others would not have looked out of place at York House. The food was delicious; no wonder the people here looked so healthy. Longstaff remembered the gaunt faces he'd seen on his journey from Harfleur to Paris, the constant stream of beggars he'd passed on the road to Romily.

Thomas leaned forward. The older brother ate from a silver bowl but spilt food into the dense curls of his beard. "Tell us more about the old Duke of Guise."

"Francois? He was your neighbour," said Longstaff.

"You said you served under him at Metz. We weren't fortunate enough to know him at such close quarters."

Longstaff nodded. His theatrical gifts were limited, but his admiration for the deceased duke was genuine. "Francois knew the name of every man under his command. He understood the importance of infantry and artillery, as well as cavalry. No detail was too small. A lesser general could not have held Metz for so many months, but the Duke thought of everything – equipment, munitions, victuals, discipline."

"He wasn't a clerk," said Jules.

"I've never known a more chivalrous man," agreed Longstaff. "Midway through the siege, a slave fled the Emperor's army. He belonged to the Commander of Cavalry, who petitioned the Duke for the return of his property…"

"What did Francois do?" Benoit leaned forward in his chair.

"He returned the horse as a mark of courtesy but not the slave, whom he said had become free on reaching the privileged soil of this glorious kingdom of France."

The three of them sighed at this latest proof of their hero's grace.

"It was Francois who showed us the way," said Jules. "At Wassy."

Longstaff strugged to control his expression. The mercy which Francois had shown at Metz had been in short supply later in his career, when he'd ordered the massacre of unarmed Huguenots at Wassy, women and children among them.

Jules drained his wine, wiped his mouth with the back of one hand.

Longstaff turned to the man's wife. "The food is wonderful, Madam. I can't remember the last time I ate so well."

She blushed again, raising a hand to check her coif was still in place.

"We don't get much news here, sir. Won't you tell us something of the Holy Land."

Longstaff smiled. "I wish I could. One day, God-willing, we'll retake those sun-baked plains from the infidels."

"Amen."

One of the children added more wood to the fire. The temperature had climbed steadily during the meal, Longstaff loosened his shirt collar.

"Do you have dealings with the family at Joinville?"

"We support their aims," said Thomas in an oddly flat tone. Benoit broke into a peal of laughter. Jules smiled.

"The Duke's son can't be much more than a child," persisted Longstaff, "and his uncle, the Cardinal of Lorraine, has his religious duties. Who runs the household at Joinville?"

"The cardinal's mother will receive you."

"A true noblewoman," added Thomas, "the dowager duchess was a Bourbon, before she married into the Guise family."

The youngest child was staring at Aurélie's medallion.

"Who's that?" she demanded.

"An image of Our Lord's mother," said Longstaff, looking down at the glittering portrait, "I prayed to her once and was spared when I should have died. I wear it to remind me that I'm pledged to fight for her, and those who support her, for as long as I have strength in my arms."

Benoit struck the table with a fist, staring at Jules. "That settles it, does it not?"

Thomas also looked at his brother-in-law. "Well, Jules?"

The taller man remained still for several moments, long hair falling in curtains on either side of his face.

"Very well," he said at last. "We can't leave him here. It won't hurt to have someone remind them at Joinville that there are Frenchmen who still fight."

"Assuming he wants to come," added Thomas.

"Where?" Longstaff feared he already knew. He thought of the woman's costly dress, the silver plate, the quality of the food and wine.

Jules walked to the room's hidden corner, pulled back the curtain to reveal a bed. "Sleep now," he said, "we leave in three hours."

"To do God's work," added Benoit, so emphatically that further questions seemed impossible.

Longstaff lay behind the curtain, listening to the woman usher her children upstairs to their sleeping quarters on the first floor. During his walk through the deepwood he'd half-forgotten the war that raged among the people of this land. He wanted to leave, but knew he stood no chance of reaching the horse unobserved. He had no doubt he could kill these three men, but then what? Make a widow of the woman and orphan the children after they'd invited him into their home?

No hurry. Later, he would find a moment to slip away. Longstaff closed his eyes, breathing the forest smells made sharp by a light dew, calling on the soldier's knack of sleeping without sleeping, mind at rest but senses still reaching out. One by one, he pictured the three men, their height and weight, what he'd been able to glean of their characters. He tensed and relaxed his muscles, reminding himself of what was required to swing a sword, to stand like a rock or sway like a dancer. He knew instinctively when the three hours were past – the door opened a moment later. Longstaff remained where he was until the scent of candlewax reached him. The three men looked ghoulish by the light of a single flame. Each wore a heavy jerkin sewn with Catholic charms. The table had been cleared, the wine bottle replaced with one of spirits. Jules poured generous measures into four crystal tumblers.

"It's time."

Benoit threw open a chest to reveal a motley collection of weapons. Jules chose an old sword and tucked a pistol in his belt. The brothers opted for a hammer and scythe respectively.

"Take your pick," invited Thomas.

Longstaff saw a mace and half a dozen daggers, a flash of gold beneath – rings and bracelets, mounted enamels set with precious stones. Plunder, like the silver plate and silk dress. As often as he reminded himself this was none of his business, he could not stop an image rising in his mind; some poor family of Huguenots, asleep in their beds with no idea that this might be their last night on earth.

Longstaff shook his head. "I have my own weapons."

His hosts knelt before the fireplace. At first, Longstaff thought they intended to pray. One by one they gathered handfuls of ashes which they rubbed across their heads and into their dark beards. Jules bound his long hair with a lady's ring taken from the chest.

The older child appeared at the top of the stairs, rubbing her eyes.

"Where are you going?"

"We'll be back in the morning," replied her father. "Go back to bed now. Pray for papa and your uncles."

The girl looked at Longstaff. "And him?"

"Why not?"

The horses were already saddled, Longstaff's animal and three more. Even by moonlight they looked quick and strong. Mounted on the lead horse, Jules turned to survey his motley crew.

"Ready?"

"As we'll ever be."

They rode hard for a stretch, Sparrow loping gamely alongside, almost invisible against the black meadows. Longstaff stayed close to his hosts – they knew these paths, he didn't – and breathed a sigh of thanks when the road finally widened. His relief was short-lived. Up ahead, he saw orbs of light in the darkness. Torches. Four more men waiting at a crossroads, hair and beards grey with ashes, clothes sewn with catholic trinkets. The men were armed with swords, daggers, long-picked staves and cudgels. Longstaff kept his face carefully neutral.

The new men muttered oaths at the sight of him. One of them spurred a heavy grey horse against his chestnut.

"Who's this?"

"A good man," replied Thomas. "I vouch for him."

Longstaff could hear Sparrow panting beside him, blown from the long run. He reached down. Obediently she raised her paws. He took her beneath the shoulders and hauled her up across the saddle, a prodigious display of strength.

The man grunted. Thomas passed Longstaff an unlit torch. More were being handed out. As Longstaff rode, his mind's eye filled with images of a former life, the daily foraging expeditions that were the lot of every soldier, roaming from village to village, stealing every movable object – when there was anything to steal – threshing and grinding when there wasn't. Now, he pictured another farmhouse somewhere ahead in the darkness, about to be preyed on by these night-riders. Could he stand by in silence? Against seven men, the odds were long on surviving a direct confrontation.

Steel-shod hooves clattered against cobbles. One man remained behind to tend the horses. Longstaff signed for Sparrow to stay, before following the rest towards a fine home. Not a farmhouse, as he'd expected. They were on the outskirts on a small, unwalled town. The sturdy front door yielded at the second charge. Longstaff followed the night-riders inside, past a brass plaque on the door frame: *Pierre Legris, Lawyer.*

A large ground-floor room, abandoned in a hurry. Longstaff saw a rag-doll peep from beneath an armchair. There were notches in the central beam, made to mark the growth of children. He moved as if his limbs were attached to strings, at the command of a puppet-master, fingers on the hilt of his old katzbalger sword, resolved to die before he let these men harm women or children.

Jules stood over an open sack, looking at a pile of heavy clubs.

"We agreed," he spat. "Which of you sent them this warning?"

Longstaff felt a wave of relief. He imagined the absent lawyer finding the clubs. Pierre Legris might have hesitated a moment, exchanged a silent look with his wife as they absorbed the meaning of this sinister message, then a flurry of terrified activity: round up the children, get away, gone in such a hurry that the clubs were left strewn across the floor.

Thomas returned from the dining room. "Stripped. Plate's all gone. Even the fucking glassware."

Jules raised a torch above his head. "We didn't come for plunder."

He was only half right, reckoned Longstaff. For men such as these, profit was no less important than the purity of their Catholic nation.

Benoit crashed down the stairs. "They've taken the jewellery and clothes."

"We're here," shouted Jules, "to drive out these heretic scum, not get rich at their expense. Make sure they can't come back."

They worked quickly, yanking open chests, pawing through the contents before adding them to a growing pile in the centre of the room. A pyre, Longstaff realised. He smiled. Let these idiots burn the house to the ground. Time for him to slip away. At least one of the night-riders had felt sufficient compassion to warn the family. Longstaff's eye fell on the sack of cudgels, discarded in a corner, forgotten amidst the family's fevered packing.

Really?

Longstaff looked at the grim faces of his companions, their ashen hair decked with religious symbols. Which of them would have sent a warning?

A single musket shot cracked like thunder. A shout reached them from outside: "You're surrounded. Go ahead and light your fire. None of you will leave alive."

Two of the riders turned on Longstaff. He dropped a hand to the hilt of his sword.

"Well?" came the shout from outside.

Jules stood in the doorway. "I know that voice."

One of the men – Longstaff didn't know his name, had barely registered his existence until this moment – tried to run. Eyes wide with panic, he pushed past Jules, sprinting into the dark night.

"Wait!"

The remaining night-riders stood in silence, listening to the shouts of triumph outside, the screams of their companion and the distant whisper of blades hacking meat. Longstaff thought of the French word for a butcher's chopping block: *massacre.*

"Two dead already," shouted the voice. "We know what you've done. All of you. It ends tonight."

Longstaff looked around. The riders stood transfixed. He put his shoulder to the door frame and peered out at a line of torches in the earth.

"Benoit," he snapped. "Run to the back. See if we're surrounded."

The young man hesitated but no one countermanded the order. They were all in shock. Benoit returned a moment later, face drained of blood.

"They're everywhere."

Longstaff nodded. "They'll be standing in a ring, far enough from the flames to protect their night vision. They want us lit up by the torches, where they can cut us down." He looked at Jules. "Can we count on help arriving?"

"No one in these parts will stir before daybreak."

Longstaff looked at each of them in turn. "I'm not the traitor. I don't know you. I don't even know where we are. I didn't get you into this. As God is my witness, I'm your only chance of getting out."

Slowly, six pairs of eyes focused on him.

He looked at Jules. "You know the man. Get him talking."

The forester seemed about to protest, then thought better of it. He nodded and licked dry lips.

"I'm sure Legris doesn't want his house burned down," he shouted. "And you don't want the blood of seven God-fearing men on your hands."

Longstaff ran to the back door. "Are the beds still made? Fetch me the sheets."

He bound them into a rope, tied one end to the back door and used his tinderbox to light the pyre, watching the flames grow as he re-joined the huddle of men. He'd left his own musket strapped across the horse's rump, but four of the men had pistols.

"We go together, hard and fast. Through the front door…"

"You're mad."

"It's the only way. Forget the horses..."

"Easy for you to say."

Longstaff did not reply. No point wasting time. He snapped orders at the men; he hadn't been a soldier for nothing and wasn't surprised to see them nod, faint hope raising arms against despair.

"There can't be that many. They'll be spread thin. You men with pistols, take up positions by the west window. Fire on my command. Then we go. It's night. There's deep cover only a few hundred yards away."

"One for all and all for one," Benoit quoted the Guise family motto.

"Run in silence," interrupted Longstaff. "Stay close until we reach the torches, then scream yourselves hoarse. Spread out.

Give yourselves room to swing a sword but don't go looking for trouble."

Enough. He didn't want to give them any more time to think. He could hear the fire crackling at their backs.

"Stand."

Longstaff yanked at the sheet-rope. The back door flew open.

"Fire," he roared.

Four shots cracked in the night.

"Now," he shouted. "Go!"

They ran in step. Twenty long strides to the torches. Longstaff flinched in anticipation, heard the crack of musket fire, felt a ball brush his sleeve. Benoit screamed. The men scattered, yelling in fear and anger. Longstaff took another four strides, eyes closed to protect his night vision. He had to get past the line of torches. Another volley of shots. He threw himself down. Were the musketeers reloading? Had they thrown their guns aside and drawn swords? He heard fighting to his right and sprinted left. A shape loomed ahead, steel flashed in the moonlight. Longstaff stepped inside a clumsy stroke, felt his knee connect with a man's chest, scrambled to his feet. Where were the horses?

Sparrow. Longstaff would recognise her bark anywhere. He ran towards the sound. The horses strained at their ropes, eyes wild with panic, hooves striking sparks on the cobblestones. All except for Longstaff's animal, standing with his ears pricked.

Longstaff was alone. No sign of either besiegers or the men he'd used to cover his own escape. He couldn't hear anything but the screams of horses as he spurred his own mount into a gallop, Sparrow bounding at his side.

They left the road soon afterwards, picking their way through heavy undergrowth. Sparrow's eyes were still sharp. Longstaff let her take the lead, following with the big horse. Hours passed before they finally stumbled across the entrance to a deep holloway. The whole region was riddled with them

– forgotten roads sunk deep in the soft chalk landscape, worn by feet, hooves and cartwheels over a period of centuries. Longstaff led the animals inside, pushing past sprays of cranesbill and hart's tongue, and cursing himself for a fool. He shouldn't have been anywhere near those people. Angrily, he hacked nettles and briars aside, then made himself a bed beneath the trailing plants.

Chapter 17

AURÉLIE

Aurélie sat in her room at York House, reading a book taken from Sir Nicholas's library. She was finding it difficult to concentrate – too much time spent cooped within these four walls – and started with relief when Anne knocked at her door.

"I'm not interrupting?"

"Not at all. Come in."

"Walsingham is waiting for you outside."

Anne looked her young friend up and down, nodding her approval of the damask gown. "Beyond reproach," she smiled. "You have to go, Aurélie. I'm afraid you have no choice."

Walsingham did not speak when Aurélie joined him in the closed carriage. He merely nodded, the gesture almost lost in the shadowy interior. Aurélie began to unfasten the thick leather flap on one of the windows.

"Leave it. This isn't a pleasure trip."

She fell back in her seat as the driver navigated his way past carts and drays.

"Where are we going?"

Walsingham looked at her with ill-concealed dislike. "I can only conclude you've all taken leave of your senses. What in God's name possessed you to visit Whitehall?"

"You were there?"

A quick shake of the head. "I know how to keep a low profile. But there are people who act as my eyes and ears. I may be new to this business, but I learn fast." He leaned forward. "I will not allow your foolishness to jeopardise our enterprise."

His look was eloquent; she was a woman, a foreigner, incapable of understanding what was at stake. She wondered for a moment if he was capable of acting on his implied threat – to have her killed if Matthew failed in France.

"I saw the Duke of Norfolk at Whitehall. He and the queen have been friends since childhood."

"And?"

"Just that."

He rolled his eyes. "You *saw* him? That may have been enough for you – the rest of us are obliged to seek actual evidence."

"I have to remind myself," retorted Aurélie, "by evidence, you mean Durant's abduction."

She listened to the sounds outside, the shopkeepers' cries of '*What do you lack?*', the rapid tap of cobblers' hammers. She caught the scent of baking. It seemed to go on for ever. Again and again, the same smells and sounds. Walsingham unfastened the leather flap.

"Are you driving us in circles?"

Over his shoulder, Aurélie saw a brothel. They were in Clerkenwell, on Turnmill Lane. There was the nunnery. Abandoned now, but the sight still sent a shiver down her spine. All those women, locked away their whole lives.

The driver leaned down. "I swear the bloody street's bewitched. Never in the same place twice. Don't worry, I'll have you there in a minute."

Walsingham left the flap open. He looked vulnerable in the sunlight, still a young man with the cares of state already chiselling away at him. He did not appear to relish her scrutiny.

"I don't like this any more than you. When Cecil asked me to create a network of intelligencers, to replace Leicester's, the original intention was that it should happen gradually, but we've been improvising ever since that cursed letter turned up. As soon as the evidence started pointing at the Duke of Norfolk, Cecil was forced to disown me. He can't have anything to do with investigating someone so powerful. He's been clear – I'm a dead man if I get this wrong."

The appeal in his voice caught Aurélie off guard. She broke eye contact. Was this the true Walsingham or simply more deception? She thought again of the party at Whitehall – Norfolk, Leicester, the queen herself – so many damaged orphans hiding their pain beneath such bright masks.

Walsingham turned back to the window.

"We've passed this way twice already, you fool."

"Yet here we are, sir."

The driver turned into a narrow cul-de-sac, scratching his head in apparent confusion. Their destination lay at the far end, four storeys fashioned from huge blocks of stone, several long windows. The house was a miniature castle. Walsingham led Aurélie down a path lined with bindweed and ragwort. The arched door opened before they had a chance to knock.

"Good morning, Dr. Dee. This is the young lady I told you about."

The name was familiar to Aurélie. Everyone in London had heard of Dr. Dee. A man of great learning to some. To others he was a necromancer in league with the Devil. Many of a religious bent wanted him hung and done with it, but the number of people who came to consult him, including not a few of power and influence, were legion.

"Come in, Aurélie Longstaff."

He was in his late thirties or early forties, dressed in a black cloth gown.

"I'm afraid Mrs. Dee is away from home."

He ushered them into a small parlour, pointing to cups on the low table. "Help yourselves. An herbal infusion of my own creation."

Dee kept his eyes on Aurélie. They were slightly too large for his face. His mouth was invisible beneath a dark beard, which spilled over the small ruff. Aurélie wasn't accustomed to such close scrutiny. She had the impression he was weighing her.

"She doesn't know why she's here?"

Walsingham cleared his throat. "We have received a letter from your husband."

She turned on him. "Intercepting my post?"

"People come to me with their problems and puzzles," interrupted Dee, "a book they're worried might be heretical, a code they can't decipher. Generally speaking I'm equal to the task, but this is not a code in the usual sense of the word."

Aurélie looked at Walsingham. A small smile of victory on her lips as she pictured him trying, and failing, to make sense of Matthew's letter.

"Where is it?"

Two sheets of good quality paper. Aurélie realised both men were staring, expecting her to decode it at once. She shook her head, determined to make Walsingham sweat for his high-handed behaviour.

"If you'd managed to decipher the letter's contents, would you even have told me that Matthew had written?"

"A fair question." Dee nodded.

Walsingham drew himself up to his full height. "I disapprove of this arrangement. I never pretended otherwise."

"And yet you did agree." She turned to Dee. "I require peace and quiet."

Walsingham stamped to the window, exasperated. Dee winked at Aurélie as he led her up a flight of stairs.

'My workshop," he announced with a flourish, showing her into a large room on the first floor. Three of the walls were covered with bookshelves. Along the fourth, beneath the window, Aurélie saw a table covered with manuscripts in various states of disrepair, alongside an array of tools, scraps of leather and cloth.

A book lay perched on the arm of a comfortable chair. While Dee cleared a space at his table, Aurélie picked it up and flicked to the frontispiece. An old man scrutinised the night sky. An astrologer, surrounded by the tools of his trade – maps, globes, compasses…

"Michel de Nostredame," said Dee. "His almanacs are sold at half the city's bookshops. He's clever; see how he depicts himself alone in his study at night, mind open to the messages inscribed on the stars. Look closer, at the laurel crown and the sky-blue stone he wears on his finger. Natural instinct and poetic furor," Dee sounded amused. "My own labours in the field attract less attention. People crave sensation. Few are interested in understanding the science which underlies true divination."

"I've rarely seen so many books in one place."

"I collect them, as Walsingham collects people. I apologise for my part in his deception. I only needed a glance at your letter to know that deciphering it lay beyond my powers. I'm not a magician," he twinkled. "Take as long as you need."

Aurélie did not move until she heard the click of the latch. *Matthew.* She sat at the long table, overcome with sudden impatience, not yet reading, only seeking the phrases by which he let her know he was safe and that he loved her; details she would omit from the plain version demanded by Walsingham.

It took her less than ten minutes. Dee was right; this wasn't a code, but rather the continuation of a conversation between two lovers. Reference to the colour red meant loss or grief. White was a mirror – truth being the opposite of whatever Matthew wrote. The most startling revelation appeared in a single sentence, made up of apparently unconnected words until Aurélie traced Fibonnaci's Golden Spiral on the surface of the page:

> *Durant removed by men loyal to the Griffin. Will seek him at the family seat.*

Aurélie and Longstaff had spent an enjoyable hour dreaming up codenames for half the princes in Europe. Philip, King of Spain, was *Centaur.* Catherine de Medici was *Mermaid. Griffin* was the name they had assigned Charles, Cardinal of Lorraine and Head of the House of Guise. Aurélie frowned. She'd been hoping to discover that Durant had left Paris in pursuit of a woman or to escape gambling debts. If the Guise had abducted him, it looked more and more as if Walsingham was right. The Duke of Norfolk had been seduced by the false whispers of a lost Gospel and had passed on Durant's name to his co-religionists in France.

Aurélie rested a hand on the letter, feeling Matthew near. He was heading into the heart of Guise territory. Exactly the news Walsingham was hoping for. Aurélie decided to make the intelligencer wait a little longer. The garden at the back of the house sloped down to the river Fleet. What more could she learn about the infamous Doctor Dee?

He was a skilled bookbinder, judging from the tools on his worktable, and an astrologer by his own account. Walsingham held him for a code-breaker and his collection of books suggested a scholar. Aurélie reckoned there must be at least five hundred volumes on his shelves, stacked with their spines upward to protect the pages from dust. She spent several minutes reading the titles, many of which she knew from Vescosi's library in Florence, and others which her former guardian would have paid any price to own.

Aurélie lingered at one particular shelf, devoted to English history. The Historia Regum Britanniae, and manuscripts by Nennius, Geoffrey of Monmouth, Bernard Ripley.

"Aurélie?"

Dee stood in the doorway. Obviously, he knew how to move about his own house without making a sound.

*

"Well?"

Aurélie took a breath. "Matthew believes Durant was abducted by men working for the House of Guise."

She saw the look of triumph on Walsingham's face.

"It's hardly a cause for celebration."

He clasped his hands. "You're right. It confirms our worst fears; a spy on the queen's Privy Council, passing secrets to her most determined enemies." He looked at Aurélie. "Perhaps that explains my apparent pleasure. Fighting an invisible enemy is a thankless task. Now we can finally flush Norfolk into the open and crush him."

Dee shook his head. "You have no proof of anything."

"He's right," said Aurélie. "All you have is a single letter, requesting certain pieces of information which only a member of the Privy Council could know. It bears neither the name of the sender, nor the intended recipient. Durant's disappearance may have convinced *you* that Norfolk is the guilty party …"

"And Durant's abduction by the Guise?" Walsingham sounded indignant.

"Circumstantial at best. The queen has known Norfolk since she was a child. You need more if she's going to overlook a lifetime's loyal service." Aurélie shook her head. "You need something in Norfolk's own hand."

Walsingham scowled at her. "Then we keep digging and watching. Elizabeth is far too trusting. This is our best opportunity to show her how deceitful these people are." He stood. "I'll leave you the carriage. You can find your own way back to York House?"

"Of course."

"Dee, you'll lend me a horse."

"*A* horse, he says, as if I have more than one." The astrologer sighed extravagantly, but Walsingham seemed oblivious to humour.

"You're being childish. A boy will return it within the hour."

He left the house with barely a word of farewell. Aurélie caught Dee's eye. The astrologer's laughter was infectious. "There's a man who takes his duty seriously!"

"I should be going as well." She did not rise. "You have a remarkable collection of books."

"So you said. From you, I take it as a genuine compliment."

"Me?"

"You studied under Giacomo Vescosi. His death was a sad loss for Europe's small community of genuine scholars."

Aurélie waved the condolences aside. "Not even Sir Nicholas possesses so many works of English history."

"I found most of them myself, rotting at the back of despoiled churches and monasteries."

"Where Matthew and I live," said Aurélie, "there's a hovel nearby. An ancient woman lives there who tells stories of the old England, handed down across the generations, of how this country was before the Conqueror came..."

Dee nodded. "William the Conqueror knew the English would give him no peace for as long as they knew who they were. That's why he ordered everything destroyed – books, works of art, meeting halls, even itinerant storytellers. Only a very few works survived, hidden in monastery libraries where they lay gathering dust until King Henry VIII began his war with Rome. Henry ordered the monasteries destroyed, the relics sold off and our literary treasures burned."

He poured her a cup of his herbal concoction. "Bernard Ripley says the isles of Albion and Ireland should be called Brutanicae, not Britanicae, because they were discovered and conquered by Brutus, descendant of the demi-god Aeneas and through him Venus and Jupiter. The line continues to Arthur, first true King of Britain. A divine line, according to Ripley, by which mankind progresses through the ages toward a glorious destiny. At its height, the Roman civilisation surpassed everything that had gone before; in truth, it was just a stepping stone. London is the new Rome."

Aurélie raised an eyebrow. "It's a theory, I suppose."

He smiled at her. "Many of the books I discovered were so damaged I had to teach myself the bookbinder's art. The power to peer backwards is no less valuable than the power to see ahead."

Aurélie snorted. "There is no such power, unless you mean conjecture based on reasoned analysis of past and present events."

"When we observe the movements of the stars and planets," quoted Dee, *"we see the higher, inward purpose of the Gods."*

"Cicero," Aurélie identified the quote. "He may have said it; that doesn't make him right."

Dee looked at her with new respect. "There are so few people with whom I can discuss my work…"

Aurélie smiled. "Your work as a bookbinder, code-breaker, fortune-teller?"

"My work as a keeper of secrets, too shocking for vulgar eyes."

He spoke with such droll exaggeration that Aurélie laughed. Later, she cursed herself for thinking she had his measure.

Dee walked her to the waiting coach. "I hope you'll come again. At present, even in this new Eden, people like you remain a rarity."

He kissed her hand before helping her up the step. Aurélie looked back at him through the open window.

"Giacomo Vescosi believed that life was a tapestry. He collected all sorts of things from the Roman past; reliefs, glassware, half-ruined statues. He was looking for the dropped stitches, hoping they might shine new light on the uncertain ways of the present."

Dee shook his head. "Life is a river, not a tapestry, and there are no flaws in water."

Chapter 18

As much as possible, on the last leg of his journey to Joinville, Longstaff was careful to avoid people. With renewed enthusiasm, he returned to Walsingham's map, wringing what meaning he could from the strange hieroglyphs. He was the middle part of a caravan; Sparrow led, the horse brought up the rear, all three of them learning the peculiar ways of these woods, riddled with tracks and old holloways, the gentle hum of nature a constant counterpoint to the small sounds of their passage.

On the evening before the battlements of Joinville finally came into view, Longstaff made for higher ground. Partly, he wanted to take his bearings. Partly, he wanted the pleasure of gazing at a distant horizon. Ancient hands had raised a standing-stone at the summit. After seeing to the animals, Longstaff used it as a back-rest, feeling the sun's stored warmth through his jerkin. The evening was so mild, he saw no need to build a fire, just helped himself to rye bread with hunks of cheese. He cleaned and oiled his musket, took a stone from his pocket and whet the edge of his katzbalger sword. A thrush began to sing. Then a nightingale. A moment's brief discord before the first fell silent. Longstaff stared up at the cloudless sky and felt a moment's strange vertigo. He remembered, on a similarly clear night, Durant telling him that God wasn't cruel. On the contrary, He had given mankind the ability to build a world free from injustice and ill-fortune. Could He be blamed if we'd wasted so many centuries pursuing other goals? Durant claimed things would be different one day, when man learned to comprehend the hidden structures of this world and make it paradise.

As if to prove the Frenchman's point, a flock of migrating birds swooped overhead, forming and reforming their strange patterns. One day, we'll know why; that's what Durant would have said. Aurélie would have quoted the various theories offered by ancient authorities. Longstaff only worried they'd both be punished for such hubris. He removed the chain from around his neck, staring at Aurélie's profile until a thin strip of cloud covered the moon's face. At least she was safe under Sir Nicholas Bacon's protection in London.

*

The forest had been cleared in a wide ring around the fortified palace at Joinville. Longstaff walked the treeline for several hundred yards before climbing into the high canopy of a holm oak for a better view. Built on the spur of a hill, overlooking a small market town on a bend of the river Marne, the sheer scale of the place took him by surprise. He stared at the huge walls, which Horatio Palavicino had told him dated back to before the first Crusade; maybe so, but they'd been reinforced since then with towers at regular intervals and sloping bulwarks designed to withstand modern artillery.

Longstaff counted two gates. The only other break in the walls was a low, grated archway through which a small stream ran, wending its way down the hillside before joining the river below. Beyond the walls, and the tiny figures marching back and forth, were a series of buildings – stables, storage barns, barracks, a smithy – set beneath magnificent gardens which climbed the spur, up to the palace proper. Longstaff could just make out a series of doors opening onto a buttressed terrace from the ground floor gallery. According to Palavicino, the extended Guise family had their living quarters on the upper floors.

Where would they keep a prisoner? The palace was built on rock, which meant no cellars. Longstaff assessed it with a soldier's eye. The Guise did not lack for enemies. How many soldiers did they keep within the walls? He ripped a strip of bark from the tree, idly tearing it to pieces until his fingers were sticky with sap. With luck, he might be able to sneak in by night, but his half-formed notion of conducting a silent search, perhaps leaving a single guard with a bump on the head while he and Durant made their escape, was revealed as an empty dream. What had seemed so possible last night, beneath the many-starred sky, looked a different proposition now. There were simply too many places they might be keeping Durant. He would have to try a different approach – the sort of charade his friend enjoyed. Fraud, deception and artifice.

At least the horse looked right, and Sparrow could be trusted not to fluff her lines. Longstaff was Matthias Lammermeier, soldier of God. Men on either side of the road fell silent as he passed, looking up from their work in the hop gardens and fish ponds. Longstaff kept his face impassive, they could not know how his heart raced as he approached the heavy gates. Another group, in Guise livery, were putting a string of horses through their paces. Longstaff nodded left and right. These people would be more difficult to fool than a troop of vigilante peasants. He remembered something Durant had told him once: don't worry how people see you, the trick's in how you see them – not through your own eyes but those of the man whose identity you've assumed.

Longstaff squinted into the pale sun. The walls bristled with soldiers. Sparrow lowered her chest nearly to the ground, baring teeth grown blunt with age.

"Who are you?"

"Mattias Lammermeier," Longstaff adopted his German accent: "Seeking service."

"Who speaks for you?"

"I've lived in the lands of the Magyars for the last ten years, fighting on the borders of Christendom."

A new face appeared on the wall, made up of a series of flat planes; flat nose, flat cheeks and jaw.

"Where are you from?" he asked in German

"A day's journey from Strasbourg," Longstaff replied in the same language, as boldly as he knew how.

"That's not what your accent says."

Longstaff forced a laugh. "I spent the last decade serving under a man raised in Lübeck."

"Max Weber? Don't tell me that old bastard's still alive?"

A trap? Longstaff had no idea. He shook his head. "Max Meyer."

"Never heard of him."

The face disappeared. Longstaff heard a series of muffled shouts before the gates swung open. He nudged his horse forward. A long wooden barracks to his left, stables and a stone granary on raised pylons to his right, on opposite sides of a wide, cobbled yard. Beyond that, a dozen more buildings. The place resembled a small town.

The same German soldier appeared as Longstaff dismounted. He introduced himself a second time, hoping he cut a believable figure in his jerkin and long, cavalryman's coat.

"Rudi Vischer," replied the German, in buff leather coat trimmed with gold braid, "Captain of the Guard."

There were soldiers everywhere. Real soldiers, nothing like the idiots he'd ridden with a few nights earlier, or the lackeys who clogged the streets of Paris. Looking at the familiar uniforms, Longstaff repressed an odd sense of having come home. Some of the men were local, from Chaumont, eastern Champagne and other borderlands where the Kingdom of France met the Duchy of Lorraine, but Longstaff also recognised colours and accents from Normandy and Picardy, Italy, Germany and Scotland. He identified arquebusiers, faces pitted with gunpowder specks, Swiss reiseläufer, and pikemen.

"My God," he said, "you must have upwards of fifty men here!"

Vischer grinned. "You don't know the half of it. We've a company of Bretons on manoeuvres, bombardiers in the town, and a troop of *arme blanche* up at the palace."

Longstaff did the calculations. To sustain a force of so many men, the Guise would need half a ton of un-milled flour each day and a hundred gallons of fresh water. For each horse, twelve pounds of grain and a similar quantity of hay. It was an impressive display of military reach.

"What for?" he asked.

"Anything and everything," laughed Vischer, "that's all."

There was no need for Longstaff to say more. He waited while Vischer looked him over, aware he bore the tell-tale marks of a true soldier, for those who knew how to look. The constant fear of death bred a peculiar quality of stillness. The sounds and smells came back to Longstaff as he endured Vischer's scrutiny. The fluttering pennants, men praying and drinking until trumpets gave the order to raise pikes and march into the first volleys of musket fire. Adrenaline and fear. A thousand men welded into a single, lethal force. Long wooden pike-shafts splintering as the two sides came together. Men shutting their eyes to avoid being blinded. Bodies on the ground. The stronger side edging forward across a carpet of the dead. And then the aftermath, which always claimed more lives than the battle itself as men drifted though the cannon smoke like ghosts.

It wasn't something that could be told, and it wasn't something that could be concealed from those who'd heard the same screams and waded through the same bloody chaos.

Vischer gave a slow nod. "It's no fucking sinecure. There's a nasty little war on here – brother against brother – not like anything you'll have seen before."

A group of soldiers had formed a loose ring around the two of them.

"A chance is all I ask," said Longstaff. "You won't regret it."

Rudi Vischer took several backward steps and drew his sword.

"Not up to me, my friend. The family decide – though a recommendation never hurts. Just need to make sure you're what you claim, that's all."

"Now?"

"Unless you have something better to do?"

Longstaff hunkered down beside Sparrow, telling her what was about to happen, then ushering her out of the ring of spectators. This was not a fight to the death, not unless the German had somehow seen through his lies. It was a test of skill; every company of fighting men was jealous of its reputation, newcomers never welcomed until they'd shown themselves worthy.

Longstaff stretched neck and shoulder muscles, then swung the *katzbalger* through a series of wide arcs. *Still quick, still strong*. It had been several months since he'd practiced with the sword, years since he'd drawn it in anger.

"Shields?"

"Not today."

The prospect of a fight had given the watching soldiers new energy. Several laughed. All began to stamp their feet, setting up a dull tattoo. Vischer attacked, forcing Longstaff back with a series of heavy blows. The clash of steel produced a roar from the crowd. Longstaff defended with a series of classic strokes, determined to give a good account of himself without embarrassing Vischer, until suddenly the German thrust at his stomach, nearly gutting him. Longstaff turned the longer sword aside, felt the tip of Vischer's sword nick his cheek.

Longstaff stepped back. *What kind of game was this?* He countered with a controlled stroke from right to left. Vischer swatted the blade aside.

Longstaff flexed his shoulders. *Time to find out how good this bastard really is.* He swung in a wide arc – sword-arm moving with the old fluency. The German countered easily, then charged, knocking Longstaff to the floor. He rolled to his right as Vischer's sword sent up a shower of sparks. Longstaff ducked beneath the whistling blade, then countered with a wild swipe of his own. Why was Vischer provoking him like this? It made no sense; Longstaff could neither win, nor be the first to yield. Those were the rules. And yet they were fighting near their limit, no longer themselves, and the contest became genuinely dangerous.

Vischer attacked. Longstaff shifted his weight and countered with a broad, backhand stroke. Vischer parried high. Longstaff lunged, left hand dipping so fast Vischer missed the flash of steel, until he felt the dagger's sharp blade against his throat.

"Enough?" demanded Longstaff through gritted teeth.

Both men were winded, both sweating. A broad grin split Rudi Vischer's face. The men watching broke into spontaneous applause.

"Can't have them thinking I'm soft on a fellow countryman. You do our homeland proud."

"I take it then, I've earned an audience with your mistress?"

Vischer nodded. "Your animals will be taken care of. I'll need your weapons."

Longstaff flipped his sword, handing it hilt first to Vischer, along with the dagger he'd produced from his jerkin.

"How many more?"

Longstaff smiled. "Two."

"You'll get them back."

Vischer whistled, a high note which startled birds from the eaves of nearby outbuildings. Longstaff watched them dart back and forth as a boy took his horse, then ordered Sparrow to stay and walked after the German, climbing past stables and workshops, over a humped wooden bridge. The stream was a clever innovation, providing water for the gardens and fountains. It wasn't strictly necessary – Longstaff noticed at least three well-heads. He shaded his eyes to follow its twisting path, small tributaries running towards various outbuildings, before it disappeared through the low arch at the base of the eastern wall. The sloping lawns were magnificent, the flowers not yet in bloom. Longstaff guessed they'd be red and yellow, the colours of Lorraine, of the banners on either side of the huge palace doors – the Guise battle standard which had been bastardised by those thugs in Paris.

There were people everywhere, all appeared well-fed, despite the poor harvests of the previous few years. Longstaff could not imagine the cost of running such a vast estate; more like the palace at the heart of a feudal kingdom than a country retreat. He saw one man leave the main path and follow the stream's winding course across the lawns to a windowless out-building, set apart from the others. Longstaff could not immediately guess its purpose; neither stables, nor workshop nor barn. Certainly not a guesthouse. Perhaps a storeroom of some kind. The man himself carried a single bowl of gruel on a tray.

He saw no more. A valet awaited them at the entrance to the great hall.

"Potential recruit," announced Vischer, "begging an audience at her Grace's earliest convenience."

Longstaff had expected a long delay before the dowager duchess received him, but the valet signalled they should follow him up the marble staircase. Longstaff and Vischer replaced their boots with soft slippers from a cupboard before hurrying in the servant's wake. Longstaff craned his neck to study the ceiling fresco; one arm extended from a cloud, monstrous fingers gripping a sword above the words *fecit potentiam in braccio suo.*

Longstaff was no scholar, but he recognised this quote from the Bible: *he hath showed strength with his arm.*

"Quite something, no?" said Vischer as they followed the servant along a seemingly endless corridor. "You should see the chapel; the family were great crusaders. One of them was the first king of Jerusalem. Any number of relics from the Holy Land – St. Joseph's belt, Geoffrey de Joinville's shield. Jeanne d'Arc stayed here just days after God spoke to her. Here we are."

The servant left them in a small ante-chamber. Fine tapestries lined the walls, more frescoes on the ceiling to commemorate Guise achievements of the past. Vischer indicated a full-length mirror. "You might want to see to your appearance."

Longstaff brushed dust from his collar and smoothed his thick hair to one side; he was looking for a job as a soldier, not a courtier. He raised two fingers to the shallow cut on his cheek.

"Is there a physician, anyone who could provide me with a swab of iodine?"

"On his way."

Longstaff grunted.

"One of them, anyway," added Vischer.

"How many are there?"

"Two, and a surgeon; four valets, an apothecary, nine stable hands, three musicians, a pastry cook, a sauce-maker and a sauce-maker's assistant."

"The Guise don't believe in half-measures?"

"Treat them as royalty and you won't go far wrong. When you see her Grace, stress your service against the infidels. The family takes great pride in its connections to the Holy Land."

"You're not staying?"

"Big strong man like you?" Vischer clapped him on the shoulder. "You'll be fine. I'll find you later, we can swap campfire stories."

Chapter 19

Longstaff was disappointed when the physician arrived. Ridiculous, of course, but he'd hoped Durant might appear in the doorway. This member of the medical profession was older, plumper, unable to silence a constant stream of complaints at the interruption to his normal routine. Still, he did a good enough job of cleaning and swabbing the shallow cut. Longstaff looked in the mirror once the man had left. The iodine had left a large purple stain across one side of his face.

"M'sieur Lammermeier?"

A small boy, dressed in silk, stood in the doorway.

"Her Grace will see you now."

"Already?"

A good sign, thought Longstaff. Perhaps the dowager duchess saw this meeting as a mere formality. He followed the boy along the corridor, the squealing laughter of children briefly audible as they passed one door. The Guise family creche. While the men and women of the family went out into the world, the children remained here, raised beneath the matriarch's stern eye. Belatedly, Longstaff realised the boy was no servant.

"I'm honoured," he said, "to have someone of rank come and fetch me."

The boy – he couldn't have been more than nine – glanced back over his shoulder. "My father is Rene D'Elbeuf."

"Do you like it here? I hope to find a place at Joinville myself, you see."

"You could not hope to find a better position anywhere in Christendom," replied the boy with great solemnity.

"Thank you, my Lord," Longstaff bowed, only half in jest, "you've given me great reassurance."

The light in his eye woke an answering twinkle in the boy, who raised a finger to his lips after checking they were alone in the corridor. "Look here."

He opened the next door, gesturing for Longstaff to peer inside. The room was empty. The curtains had been drawn, it took a moment for his eyes to adjust. The first thing he saw was a coffin.

"Hers," whispered the boy. "She spends an hour here each day, contemplating her death."

A chair stood beside the coffin. Longstaff saw a sewing case next to a neat bundle of clothes. "And works while she contemplates?"

"For the poor, to be given out when she dies so they can attend her funeral in respectable clothes."

Longstaff supressed a shudder; this was the atmosphere in which Duke Francois had been raised. And his brother, Cardinal Charles, Chief Inquisitor in France. This is where the family hatched their schemes. For the first time, Longstaff felt a tremor of disquiet. He closed the door.

"Lead on," he said, "we don't want to keep her waiting."

The last door. The boy opened it without knocking. On the far side of the room, windows reached from the floor nearly to the ceiling. Longstaff blinked in the sudden onslaught of daylight.

"Thank you, Rene," the voice was a whisper, dry and thin as parchment. "You may leave us now."

The duchess sat in a straight-backed chair, ancient hands crossed on the head of a walking stick. Alone except for an equally aged Sparrowhawk which peered at Longstaff from a perch beside the chair.

Antoinette de Bourbon, Duchess of Guise, widow of Claude and mother of Francois and Charles. Shrunken by age, but the eyes were still sharp and bright, unflinching in the presence of a soldier. Longstaff knew immediately there was little point in mimicking the manners of a courtier. This woman had no interest in his gentility; she only wanted to know that he would give his life to defend her family's interests.

He bowed, taking in the black stockings clocked with silver thread. Two rosaries hung from the waist of her black satin dress, the collar held in place by an amber broach in the shape of a cross.

"Thank you for seeing me, your Grace. My name is Mattias Lammermeier."

"Monsieur Vischer delivered you personally, and sent for a physician to attend you?"

"He did, your Grace."

"Then you've impressed him. The man is generally a fine judge of character. Not infallible, though."

"Which of us is, your Grace?"

"You come from Strasbourg?"

"From near there. Originally."

"And you served against the Ottomans, though no one here can vouch for you."

"I served under Max Meyer. One of your men has heard of him."

What had possessed him to say that? He felt at once he'd made a mistake.

"You have no letter of introduction," she persisted.

"I did not know I'd need one. I spent more than ten years fighting on the borders of Christendom, engaged in constant skirmishes with the Turk. Not many survive so long. It is God's work, hard work, with precious little opportunity for advancement or enrichment."

"So, you've come to us in search of an easier life."

She was inviting him to repeat himself. He forced himself to answer in short, simple sentences. He was a soldier, made taciturn by a life of action, uncomfortable talking about himself; the things he'd seen and done.

"I served under your son, your Grace, at the siege of Metz."

"And?"

"I would serve a family which shares my anger at the slights and insults directed against the Church."

Longstaff saw her nostrils flare. She'd sensed something. He stood at attention, eyes fixed ahead. The silence stretched.

"No," she said at last. "Not anger. Your motives are more complicated."

The statement was not framed as a question. Longstaff sensed he should drop to one knee, pledge undying loyalty to the Guise and their cause. He remained on his feet; on behalf of the man whose identify he had invented, who did not exist in this world.

"I have pinned my hopes on finding a place in your service. I believe your family offers the best hope of destroying the Huguenot heresy. And, yes, I'm also seeking a measure of security. I have little to show for a lifetime of sacrifice."

She was going to turn him down. He'd said the wrong thing, or the right thing in the wrong way. He had no talent for dissembling.

"I am sorry for your troubles, but your journey has been in vain."

"Your Grace…"

"We cannot provide employment for every masterless soldier who knocks. God willing, there will come a time when we no longer need the ones we have."

"If I've offended…"

"I am a charitable woman, Monsieur Lammermeier." Her smile resembled a sliver of ice. "I do not provide for the poor out of pity, however, but only because God commands it. In my experience, decisions born of pity rarely turn out well. If I wrong you, you have my apologies." She sighed. "The old are often wrong, led astray by a lifetime's useless knowledge. When it comes to my family, however, I've learned to listen to my heart, and my heart speaks against you. Return to the kitchens. The steward will see you have sufficient food for the next leg of your journey."

She glanced at the window. "It's still early. I don't believe we're under any obligation to offer you lodging for the night."

Longstaff had been dismissed. A servant waited for him in the corridor, a question in his eyes.

For one wild moment, Longstaff thought of lying. Would she check? How long would it take him to find Durant? A day? Two at the most.

She wouldn't have to check. Somehow, Longstaff felt certain, she would simply know.

"The family has no need of my services."

The servant lifted his chin, the better to peer down his nose at the rejected suitor. Longstaff felt a hot flush of anger as the man led him through the bowels of the house, avoiding the grand staircase and delivering him directly to the kitchens. He waited, conscious that his cheeks were burning, while a maid found him a jug of barley beer and a trencher of meat. She showed him to the door, where his boots were already waiting. Longstaff followed a sunken path round the side of the palace, only re-joining the main approach some way below the gardens.

He walked across the humped bridge, glancing at the windowless outbuilding he'd noticed earlier; he wasn't looking forward to collecting his horse, the soldiers in front of the barracks all watching him leave, knowing his offer to join them had been declined.

The wide courtyard was almost deserted. Except for an odd triumvirate in the very centre; Sparrow and Vischer, waiting for him on either side of the saddled horse, Longstaff's musket and bedroll already strapped across his rump.

The German mercenary returned his katzbalger sword and knives.

"I'm sorry…"

"No need," Longstaff cut him off. "The Duchess makes her own decisions, she made that clear."

"Where will you go?"

"Wherever they're hiring."

The German mercenary seemed genuinely upset. He had accepted Longstaff at face value, in a way his mistress had not. "You came all this way. Your heart was set on serving the Guise…"

"Pity won't fill an empty stomach," snapped Longstaff, swinging into the saddle.

"I can't make out what she was thinking, that's all."

The gates of Joinville closed behind him. What had he learned? What could he salvage? That low outbuilding? The Guise may, or may not, be holding Durant there. Joinville was filled with experienced soldiers, but not impregnable. The walls were vulnerable in several places, not least where the stream flowed through that low arch.

Longstaff did not look back until he reached the treeline. Even then, he stayed on the road for a while, until he was certain no one followed, then slowly retraced his steps to the same oak tree. His anger grew less in the forest's dark embrace, the stream's twisting course still in his mind and the entrance to an old, forgotten holloway. The light was already fading, too late to find it now. He took care of the animals first, then climbed into the branches of the oak, counting torches on the distant battlements while he dined on Guise food and drink. He conjured with impressions of the fortified palace, the locations of the various buildings, the way the birds had flown from the eaves of the stables, startled by the sound of swordplay, swooping over the walls in search of food and fodder for their nests. Dimly, he remembered a story his first commander had told about a Viking queen. He spat, as if to expel the idea. There had to be a better way.

A jackdaw croaked to greet the dawn. Longstaff woke among fluttering starlings, still cradled in the oak's wide branches. He was frozen stiff and soaked in cold dew. He stretched, stiff bones cracking loud enough to startle the birds into silence, and listened for what their song usually hid; a swift rustle in the grass, the sigh of leaves caressed by a soft breeze. The rising sun burned fog from the hollows, lifted dew from the turf, revealed a brilliant blue sky, smoke curling from chimneys in the distant market town to merge with a few white clouds.

As he stared at the high walls, Longstaff saw flocks of tiny birds fly up, circle the palace before swooping in his direction, bringing with them the same dark notion of the night before. The birds of Joinville, who made their home in the eaves of barracks and stables and flew beyond the walls each day to forage among the trees.

Longstaff slid to the forest floor, ignoring an attack of pins and needles, certain he remembered stowing a packet of seed at the bottom of his saddlebag. And a length of twine. He hadn't worked this trick in years and hoped he hadn't lost the knack. It didn't take long to find a cleft stick. He tore a strip of bread from the remains of his trencher, rolled it in a ball between his fingers, moistened with spit and scattered with a pinch of seeds.

Longstaff lay perfectly still, staring at the baited stick, one end of the twine in his fingers. A small bird settled in place a few moments later. Longstaff drew on the twine, attempting to close the cleft on the bird's legs. His fingers twitched, the bird took fright, disappearing in a sudden flutter of wings.

Longstaff was finally successful at the third attempt. He hurried forward, took the bird carefully in cupped hands and placed it in his emptied saddlebag, then repeated the exercise throughout the morning and into the afternoon. It was exhausting work, moving regularly, lying in darkness, concentrating on a single spot until his eyes hurt and his shoulders ached. For every bird he caught, at least twenty fled the trap, but he kept going until the supply of seed was exhausted. Eleven birds in total. A tiny number. Longstaff rubbed his eyes. He didn't know whether to be pleased or disappointed.

He had no time for the luxury of reflection. There was too much to do. Yesterday, he'd stumbled on the holloway by chance. Now, it took him more than an hour to find the entrance. He scrambled down beneath the covering foliage.

No idea whether this had been a drovers' road, market path or pilgrims' way. All that mattered was that after centuries of use – while cartwheels, hooves and feet wore away at the surface, digging ruts in the exposed stone, which turned to waterways in heavy rain and cut the path still deeper – this old holloway had been forgotten.

Even at midday it was dark, the sun's light kept out by a thick roof of brambles and roots. Longstaff hacked a path through a field of chest-high nettles, feeling as if he were a thousand miles beneath the Earth's surface. He thought of Walsingham's map; the land wasn't flat as it appeared there, but folded and furrowed, raised by man's industry and lowered by his habits. A stray beam of sunlight lit the high walls for a moment, illuminating roots turned half to stone among the strata. Longstaff pushed on, slowly finding a rhythm, a sense of order among the chaos. His progress became smoother, until the way ahead was suddenly barred by piles of rubble. Probably dumped during the construction of Joinville. Longstaff climbed the tumble of stones and poked a small peephole in the matted floor above.

Damn! Dead ahead, he saw a guard spit from his sentry post on the high walls, still thirty paces away. The stream was to the left, zig-zagging its way towards the Marne. And there was the low arch, secured with five thick bars.

Longstaff retraced his steps, taking care to mark and smooth his passage. It was nearly dusk by the time he returned to his camp beside the tall oak. His saddlebag was where he'd left it, a box of leather stiff with ancient horse sweat. Longstaff had feared the birds might die of fright during the afternoon, but the darkness inside seemed to have soothed their fears. He lay on the ground, listening to their soft chirruping and listing everything he currently lacked; sufficient food for an extended reconnaissance, any real evidence that Durant was in that outbuilding, or within the walls of Joinville at all.

And what *did* he have? Just a single, wildly reckless notion for how to breach the walls and rescue his friend – assuming the bastard was even there – and bring an end to this whole, ridiculous escapade.

Chapter 20

AURÉLIE

Out of breath, dashing headlong down the Strand, Aurélie was determined to reach York House in time for the boys' bedtime story. She had fallen into the habit of visiting Dee's house in Clerkenwell twice a week – his books, and his company, were a welcome distraction from Matthew's continued silence.

Today, she had stayed longer than intended. Why were so many learned men obsessed with secrets? The more time she spent with Dee, the more she learned of his fevered ambitions, the more she thought it was because some part of him still retained a sense of how ridiculous his notions would sound if uttered in public.

Aurélie thought of Sir Nicholas, and his reluctance to print and distribute *On Freedom* by Epicurus. Fear or ambition? In Dee's case, it was definitely a case of the latter. For all his charm, there was darkness in the doctor. He had devoted his life to unravelling the mysteries of nature – his books were wild in comparison with the rows of well-behaved children on the shelves at York House, full of blood and magic – but that wasn't enough to satisfy him. It was his yearning to serve as the nation's high priest which made him dangerous. Never thinking it might be her, Aurélie pitied whichever poor soul would be foolish enough to come between Dee and his ambitions.

The boys were already dressed for bed when she entered their room, a nest of nooks and crannies, furnished with a child-sized table and chairs, a miniature castle and wheeled wooden animals.

"We were starting to worry," said Anthony.

"Not me," said Francis.

Aurélie stood for a moment, seeking inspiration in the events of her day while the boys climbed into bed.

Anthony broke the silence. "Any news of Matthew?"

Aurélie forced a smile. "Have you said your prayers?"

"Downstairs with mama and papa. Can we have a story about intelligencers?"

Aurélie saw the look of alarm on Francis' face. The younger brother disliked stories in which people pretended to be something they weren't. Aurélie kicked off her shoes and made herself comfortable between the two of them. Francis wriggled close. Aurélie experienced a familiar sense of well-being. She was still young; it would happen for her and Matthew. In recent days, she'd kept thinking of her husband's gentleness, his stubborn refusal to see that he was not typical, that other men were incompetent, paralysed by fear, venal. He'd enjoy seeing her now, though he'd be outraged if he knew the kind of stories she told the boys.

Aurélie was strict during the day, conscientiously observing the curriculum stipulated by Sir Nicholas and Anne. In the evenings, however, hidden in the fantastical garb of fairy-tale and legend, she gave herself greater licence.

"Herakles…"

"We know the story of Herakles," objected Anthony.

"A version of it," she replied, "the one they tell children."

"Go on," urged Francis."

"Herakles was one of the happiest men alive, in love with his family and so proud of his powerful body that he earned his living by performing feats of strength."

She reached out and felt Anthony's slim bicep. The boy giggled.

"Until, one terrible day, when he was tricked into thinking that his wife and children were serpents sent to kill him."

She spared them the lurid descriptions of crumpled bodies and bloodshot eyes. A shaft of moonlight shone through the window, casting ghostly shadows across the room as Aurélie spun her tale of crime and atonement, giving faithful versions of the tasks Herakles had to overcome in his quest for redemption.

"But he hadn't done anything wrong," objected Anthony, "he was tricked."

"If he hadn't taken such pride in his body," said Aurélie, "he might have cultivated his mind enough to see the trick."

When she resumed, Aurélie gave the tale a new ending, taking inspiration from her own journey to the Devil's Library.

"Herakles journeyed deep into the earth's heart. It was hot in the tunnels. Alone, weak from his exertions, he followed the path of an underground river, so hot that steam rose from its surface. He crossed an ancient bridge into a labyrinth and wandered for hours before he found the centre, empty but for an old mirror. Herakles brushed a thick layer of dust from its surface. Instead of his reflection, he saw his wife and children playing together in a grove of olive trees. He called, but they couldn't hear..."

"Yes they could," said Francis. Anthony had already dropped off. The younger brother sounded anxious, kept from the brink of sleep by his concern for Herakles.

Aurélie pressed her cheek against his, breathing in as he breathed out.

"They couldn't. Not until a wise man appeared and asked a series of questions. He wouldn't grant Herakles permission to re-join his family until he was certain it was what he really wanted."

Francis smiled. He closed his eyes and snuggled close.

"Aurélie," he murmured, "how can Herakles be a hero, after what he did?"

"He isn't, my sweet. The hero is the man who followed behind with a stylus and tablet, who wrote the story down to help others avoid the same mistakes."

The boy was asleep. Aurélie kissed his eyelids. She thought of Dee, who'd lurked at the edges of her story and would no doubt have claimed the role of wise man for himself.

The common folk of London would more likely have seen him as the trickster, and there was also justice in that view. Aurélie shook her head as she remembered his crude jingoism, his desire to fashion a glorious future for England by spinning an absurd fantasy from the threads of an invented past. For all his claims to the contrary, he was no true scholar; he did not have the patience to learn from the past or from the proud and ancient cultures of the East. He preferred a blank canvas – England after Henry VIII's Dissolution of the Monasteries – on which he could daub his own fevered imaginings.

Aurélie lay awhile between the two warm bodies, thinking of the letters which the adventurer Anthony Jenkinson had sent her host, his crude sketches of a strange language that no one had been able to read in over a thousand years. With a sigh, she extricated herself from the tangle of childish limbs and tiptoed from the room. Sir Nicholas stood waiting for her on the landing.

"The boys?"

"Asleep. Did you want to see me?" She thought she detected a new light in the heavy-lidded eyes.

"If you wouldn't mind. In my study?"

He poured them both wine before settling in his favourite chair. "I saw him again today. The Duke of Norfolk. Every damned day I see his face and force myself to smile as if he weren't the vilest traitor on God's earth." Sir Nicholas's lip curled in disgust. "When Walsingham first told me that Norfolk might be disloyal, I prayed he was wrong, that his loathing for Catholics had warped his judgement. I prayed the traitor would be someone else. Even the Earl of Leicester would have been better – he has his hangers-on, but none who'd stick by him through a charge of treason."

"Norfolk's different?"

Sir Nicholas shifted in his chair. Aurélie heard the wood groan beneath his weight.

"He *is* a Catholic, however much he tries to hide it, with power enough to raise the North."

Sir Nicholas began to extemporise as if he were in a court of law. "Word reaches the Duke of Norfolk. A book has been discovered, a fifth Gospel written in Christ's own hand, in which he gives Peter and his successors inalienable rights over doctrine, and which was last heard of in the possession of a Frenchman named Gaetan Durant. For weeks, nothing happens. I assume, naturally, that Norfolk is innocent…"

"Or possessed of an ounce of common sense," interrupted Aurélie. "Only a fool would believe in the existence of such a book."

Sir Nicholas shook his head. "A heretic would believe."

"A Catholic," Aurélie corrected him.

"Or a traitor, if it makes you happier."

"None of this makes me happy. The threads of faith and treason have become so tangled on this island it's a wonder anyone still knows up from down."

Sir Nicholas fixed her with a look. "I was hoping for something more constructive."

"Sorry. Go on."

"Imagine my concern, therefore, when you and Matthew arrive with a letter from the Frenchman's daughter. Naturally, Matthew travels to Paris to discover what has become of his friend. From him, I learn that Gaetan Durant has been abducted by men in service to the Guise."

"That's your story?"

"You disapprove?"

"You have no evidence linking Norfolk to Durant's disappearance. He's the queen's friend. She won't disregard a lifetime's loyal service on the strength of a possible coincidence."

Sir Nicholas permitted himself a small smile. "I agree. Without proof, we'd be mad to raise our heads above the parapet."

Aurélie saw something in his expression. Her eyes grew wide. "You have it!"

"Breathe a word…"

"I don't want to know." She looked at him. "Something in Norfolk's own hand?"

Sir Nicholas nodded. "Proving his complicity beyond all reasonable doubt. He writes to his masters in France that he's established an illegal printing press in London, as per their instructions, and is ready to begin distribution as soon as he receives a copy of the fifth Gospel. We still need to proceed cautiously. Elizabeth will be embarrassed; we'll need to mitigate that as much as we can."

Aurélie stared at him. "You want to reveal this to her in public?"

"I was sceptical at first, but Walsingham is right; it will be good for her. Elizabeth is maddeningly difficult when it comes to her protection…"

Aurélie took a deep breath. "You're moving too fast. At least wait until Matthew returns."

"I know the queen," Sir Nicholas nodded to himself, "if we don't go public, she'll find a way to sweep this whole mess under the carpet. I thought Walsingham might argue for a delay, try and turn Norfolk or feed him false information, but he's just as eager to bring this to a head."

"You trust him?"

"The man's obsessed. He's using his own servants as agents and his own money to pay them. His ability to spot connections in an avalanche of information is extraordinary."

"His star is rising…" began Aurélie.

"As mine wanes, you mean?" Sir Nicholas shrugged. "Nothing lasts forever, least of all a monarch's favour. Who knows what Elizabeth really thinks. That's one advantage she has over her father; the demands of his gender forced him into constant action while she enjoys the liberty to prevaricate. A freedom she's predisposed to indulge. That's why we have to trumpet Norfolk's treachery from every bell-tower in the land."

"I don't understand."

Sir Nicholas smiled. "The queen's own words: *I do not wish to make windows of men's souls.* This is our chance to show her how wrong she is."

Aurélie's stomach turned. She'd heard arguments like this before and knew where they led.

"During her sister's reign, Elizabeth herself paid lip-service to the Roman faith. How can she deny her subjects the same protection?"

"Too late for that. If Spain invades, we need to know who we can trust. The time has passed when it was still possible to be both an Englishman and a Catholic. Cecil understands; that's why he had Walsingham create his network of intelligencers. You've seen them on the streets of London. Dutchmen, Germans, Huguenots from France…"

"Refugees from religious persecution."

"God knows how many spies lurk among their ranks. Even the best intentioned bring dangerous ideas."

Aurélie felt as if the breath had been driven from her lungs. "You mean me. People like me, who've given up everything."

"Try and understand. We've all placed our lives in Elizabeth's hands, a woman, who refuses to let us protect her adequately." He looked at Aurélie. "There is nothing we wouldn't do to keep her safe – nothing we haven't already done."

Sir Nicholas heaved himself to his feet, fetching down an ornate silver plate from one of the shelves. In the flickering candlelight, Aurélie saw a young couple embossed in the centre, seated in imperial majesty: *Francis and Mary, by the grace of God, King and Queen of France, Scotland, England and Ireland.*

"A gift from Walsingham," said Sir Nicholas, "the plate Throckmorton was given to eat from at a banquet to celebrate

Francis' coronation as King of France in '59. Can you imagine!" He shook his head, more exhausted than angry. "When Francis died a year later, it brought us breathing space, but Mary has never seen fit to renounce her claim."

An inscription ran around the plate's edge: *Gaul and warlike Britain were in perpetual hostility – at that time they fought amongst themselves with equal hatred – now the Gauls and distant Britons are in a single territory – Mary's dowry gathers them together in one empire – because of this you will keep your weapons under a French peace – your forefathers could not achieve this for a thousand years.*

"Philip of Spain believes England belongs to him, by virtue of his marriage to Bloody Mary," continued Sir Nicholas. "The French claim sovereignty through the Queen of Scots. As we speak, the pope is composing a Bull of Excommunication against Elizabeth – they mean to make her murder an act of piety in the eyes of Catholics. Wherever we turn, we find ourselves trapped. England lies exposed, a patient on the operating table, worked on with scalpels from without, eaten by cancer from within..." He paused to catch his breath, "and so we act. Not in secret, but as men bound by the laws of this land. Norfolk is a spy, no more or less, and when the executioner severs his head it will be as a traitor, not a heretic whom the Romans can claim for a martyr."

Aurélie sat in silence. There was nothing left to say.

"Of course," added Sir Nicholas, "there's always a danger the messenger will be shot. It's hardly without precedent, but at least that will be an end to it."

Chapter 21

In the version Longstaff had heard, the Viking queen's name was Olga. When her husband was murdered by the Derevlians, she raised an army and laid siege to their city of Iskorosten. The inhabitants begged for mercy. Olga offered surprisingly generous terms. She didn't ask for honey or furs – the usual stuff of tribute – but only birds; three pigeons and three sparrows from each household. The birds were duly caught, caged and lowered from the high walls. Olga thanked the townsfolk, then had her men tie burning rags to the birds and release them. The panicked animals returned to their nests in the city, setting every house on fire. A great wind blew the flames into an inferno. The citizens came pouring through the ruined gates, and the Viking queen had them slaughtered.

A few years later, the Orthodox Church made Olga a saint. Longstaff knew he would not be forgiven so easily if he copied her ploy, either in this life or the next. He did not want anyone to die. He only needed a distraction. What damage could eleven birds do? With barely a breath of wind in the air? He could not be certain if all of them nested in the stables - or, indeed, if any of them did – but there were plenty of men behind the walls, more than enough to prevent any fires from spiralling out of control.

Why then, did he feel so uneasy as he carefully removed the birds from his saddlebag, smeared them one by one with melted wax and wood shavings before returning them to darkness? Poor creatures, but what choice did he have? Durant in danger, possibly dead already. A spy on Queen Elizabeth's Privy Council. Aurélie held under house arrest as surety that he'd strain every sinew in pursuit of Walsingham's elusive proof.

At dusk, when the first flares of torchlight appeared on the distant walls, Longstaff returned to the holloway, Sparrow at his heels and the saddlebag slung over his shoulder. He'd thought the dog might come with him but she sat on her haunches, barely visible in the darkness, and refused to budge.

Alone, Longstaff descended into the deep-harrowed holloway. It was slow going; invisible brambles tore at his clothes and skin. Longstaff bit his lip, oppressed by the need for silence. The slightest sound would carry on a night like this. A whole lifetime seemed to pass before he reached the tumble of stones, covered in moss and lichen, turf and bramble above. A painstaking climb with the bag slung across his shoulders until at last he pushed headfirst through the thick undergrowth.

His jerkin and trousers were dark brown. He was filthy. Invisible. He took a deep breath, toes probing for dry branches which might snap, rabbit holes which might send him sprawling and set the birds free in a great chirrup of outrage. He reached the lee of the walls, hunkered down beside the small stream where the wall was just a single layer of rough-hewn stone, as thick as his arm was long. The five iron bars were fixed in crumbling mortar, worn by the never-ending passage of water. Would they give? They were set a foot apart. He only had to remove one.

Longstaff prepared his tinder box and matches. For good measure, he sprinkled each bird with a few drops of lamp oil before setting his fires and releasing them into the night sky. Up they went, desperate to escape the flames. One by one they disappeared behind the walls. *Making for their nests as their distant forebears had done in Dereva?* Then, the birds had numbered in their thousands. Longstaff had eleven. He pictured small baskets of dried twigs tucked among wooden rafters and crossed himself for the first time in years. Not so much a prayer as an attempt to ward off evil; the baser man, the animal rising up and taking hold of his better self. The stable roof was tiled, the tiles held in place with little strips of lead.

Longstaff imagined the flames growing in secret, feeding on the tinder-dry beams beneath, before erupting with enough force to send tiles shooting into the air. He counted to one hundred before stepping into the stream, sword drawn, one heavy boot placed against the central bar.

The wait seemed endless, each second wrapped in ice as water soaked his boots, driving daggers of cold into his flesh. His shoulders dropped in disappointment. Had the birds died before reaching their nests? Had the flames failed to catch?

A roar of warning sounded inside the walls. Longstaff reacted too slowly. He waited, foot drawn back, palms braced on either side of the arch. Another roar. A crash. The bar held firm, a shock ran through Longstaff's body. Now, he could hear rising pandemonium. All eyes on the flames. The men would have been drilled for just such an event. Fetching buckets, forming a chain.

The chapel bell began to toll. Longstaff kicked again. Adrenaline built with each successive failure. *Come on.* Six strong kicks and the bar gave way. Longstaff splashed forward, scraping his head on the arched roof. Had anyone noticed the small, winged carriers of fire, or connected the flames with a possible assault on Joinville? Sheathing his sword, Longstaff strode towards the courtyard. As if he belonged. No one paid him any attention. A man staggered back from the blaze, flesh scored by drops of molten lead. The fire's snap and crackle stripped his scream of power. Grooms led horses from the stables, the men and women throwing water on the flames seemed cast in ghostly, silent shadow. New flames surged through gaps in the tiles, drawing light from the cobbled yard, making a corridor of darkness for Longstaff to walk through.

Fires had broken out in the barracks, as well as the stables. Appalled at what he'd unleashed, Longstaff didn't slow until he was over the humpback bridge, deep in the swallowing darkness of the lawns beyond. He checked himself, a single, calming breath before approaching the lonely outhouse. A man stood guard, eyes fixed on the distant stables. Longstaff heard a crash, men pulling down buildings to create a firebreak. The guard flinched. Longstaff knew him – the jailor he'd seen with a bowl of gruel.

"We have to move the prisoner. Take me to him."

The man had his key in the lock. "Wait. I don't know you..."

Longstaff had him by the throat, crushed the windpipe until the body went limp. He turned the key, kicked the door open with a heel and dragged the man inside.

A single corridor, half a dozen low doors on either side.

"Durant?"

One by one, Longstaff tried the doors – all empty save the last. He fumbled with the keys, trying three before he found the right one. "Durant?"

He could just make out a silhouette, a man lying curled in a corner. Too short and shapeless. Longstaff shook him roughly by the shoulder.

"Where are the other prisoners?"

The man was old. His eyes snapped open, showing none of the confusion that usually accompanied such a rude awakening.

"There's no one here but me."

His dark robe stank, as if his captors had not allowed him to wash in weeks.

"Who is it you're looking for?"

Not you. Longstaff was about to turn on his heel. Everything – the lies, the fire –had been for nothing. The prospect of failure made him answer.

"Gaetan Durant."

The old man blinked. "I haven't heard that name in years."

The noise from outside rose in volume – bells, barked orders, panicked screams. There was no time.

"Take me with you." The prisoner seemed to sense Longstaff's reluctance. "Gaetan isn't here, but we can still get away before they realise what you've done."

"If you slow me..." Longstaff did not complete his sentence. The threat was hollow, born of frustration. "Do exactly as I say. Stay close."

The old man kept one hand on Longstaff's shoulder as they hurried past the unconscious jailor. The shouts grew louder at the door. Longstaff peered out, as a plume of smoke billowed from an upstairs window of the main building. At least one of the birds had preferred the company of gentle folk to horses and soldiers. There were women and children up there. Longstaff cursed; there was nothing he could do for them. And the men below would know they were under attack now, if they hadn't realised it already.

"Don't run," he hissed. "Keep your head down. If anyone stops us, I do the talking."

He led the way, striding across the lawn as if he had every right to be there. He could tell them he was moving the prisoner. He should have brought the jailor's keys. A dozen men ran across the bridge. Longstaff emerged from darkness a moment later, leading his charge in the opposite direction. He stepped aside to let a second troop run past.

"Well," he demanded, "are the fires out?"

None of the men stopped. "Not yet," shouted one, "nearly."

A bend in the path revealed the glow of sullen flame, plumes of black smoke rising from the outbuildings, blinding the firefighters, obscuring the moon above. Longstaff heard people panting nearby, a hacking cough. He cut away from the path, leading the old man behind the barracks, picking up the stream's path once more. He pushed the prisoner ahead of him into the ice-cold water, certain they must be challenged at the low archway. Nothing. They splashed the last few yards. The old man had a paunch on him, his filthy robe snagged on the iron bars. Longstaff pushed from behind, heard the man groan in pain as he scraped through.

"Come on," he urged. *Thirty paces to the holloway.* He'd taken a careful bearing before releasing the birds. Their luck held. If any men were still on the wall, none looked down. Longstaff turned and offered a hand to the prisoner. The fire's glow could not reach them here. There was no longer any need to worry about noise.

"Come on!"

Sparrow sat on her haunches at the entrance. The prisoner shied away from the big dog, Longstaff dropped to his knees and hugged her fiercely. He was parched and badly in need of sleep. He hadn't dared hope his plan would run so smoothly, except it had yielded a stranger instead of the hoped-for friend.

They ran through the trees, back to the tall holm oak. The horse was there, along with Longstaff's coat and other possessions. He hardly paused to wet his lips before climbing the tree; he couldn't leave without taking one last look – smoke, greyed by moonlight against the black sky. He breathed a silent prayer of thanks; the fire-fighters had kept the flames from spreading.

Longstaff heard Sparrow growl. The dog crouched low to the ground, hair up along the length of her coat. Longstaff scanned the trees; there was no way the men at Joinville could have organised so quickly.

"Is someone there?"

No reply, and no time to linger. The sun would rise in less than an hour. He dropped to the forest floor and climbed into the saddle, pulling the prisoner up behind him. There would be time for questions later.

The old man wrapped his arms round Longstaff's waist.

"Head west," he said. "They'll look for us on the road to Paris. Head for Orléans. I have friends there who can help."

Chapter 22

DURANT

Only a God could so misapprehend Man,
Foresee him set aside strength, renounce the spoils
Of conquest. Embrace emptiness; it takes,
Divinity to spring the devil-formed trap.

Gaetan Durant lay back, staring up at the cabin's pitched roof. Birdsong reached him here in the mornings and evenings, but it was quiet now. They'd taken the last of the quatrains yesterday – one hundred four-line poems – the moment of truth had finally arrived. Would Vincent keep his promise, let him leave France and start again?

Durant still had no clear idea of where they were. A small cabin at the edge of a high meadow. Steep hills to the south, thick forest dropping to a wide valley on the north, east and west. Vincent's mute companion disappeared once a week, leaving before dawn, returning with provisions at nightfall, which meant there had to be a town somewhere within a single day's ride.

Durant climbed to his feet. At least the work had kept his cabin fever at bay. What would it be? Freedom or execution? If it was the latter, he'd already decided on his last request: *Remove the manacle. Let me walk across the meadow, feel the sun on my face once more.* Would his voice hold steady? Would he beg? Why didn't they come and put him out of his misery?

Vincent and Jean-Paul spent their nights in a nearby storehouse just a stone's throw away. Durant had retained an image of the low-slung building, raised above the ground on stone pylons. His cabin had been built after a different fashion.

Durant's eyes strayed to the loose floorboard he'd teased up one night, fighting the spikes of fear which came with every creak and groan. Unlike the storehouse, the cabin sat directly on hard earth. Durant had hollowed out a space beneath. His hiding place. A tiny act of defiance against his captors, only there was nothing to hide. Not even a fork in the cabin, let alone a knife. They made him eat with his hands.

He looked at the four wooden cups lined up on the table. Two were already empty. He filled them all from the pail they brought each morning. The rest he kept for his ablutions. *Why didn't they come?* There was still Nostredame's correspondence; perhaps they weren't finished with him after all?

Durant straightened his doublet, little better than a rag by now. The collar and cuffs of his shirt were black, patches of sweat formed solid crusts beneath his arms.

Footsteps. Durant felt sick when Vincent appeared, fox-like eyes inspecting the bolt in the central beam, checking Durant hadn't tampered with it during the day. He picked a splinter from the doorframe, studied it a moment before putting it to work as a toothpick.

"You look nervous, my friend."

Durant said nothing. Vincent tossed him a wineskin. "Drink. You've earned it."

Durant tried to concentrate on the toothpick; such a stupid habit given the gaps between Vincent's teeth. "I'm not thirsty."

Vincent took a seat, filled the two empty cups from his wineskin. "You must be worried about your daughter. Is there anything we can do for her? Does she have enough money?"

The table was narrow. Did Vincent keep the keys on his person, wondered Durant? One quick punch. Do it now, while Jean-Paul was away. Durant raised the cup to his lips. As fast as he was, he knew Vincent was faster. Durant kept his eyes closed as the spirits burned away the taste of failure.

"I've done everything you asked. You said I could leave, that Laure and I could start again in a new country."

"About that," Vincent gestured for him to sit, "we need to talk. I have no intention of going back on my word, but it seems we're not yet able to dispense with your services."

They still needed him. Durant suppressed a sigh of relief. He'd never felt so tired. He was alive. He had no idea for how much longer, or what they wanted from him now. When had life become so precious? Was it the thought of seeing Laure again? Of resuming his career as a healer?

"What do you want me to do?"

"Not much, not in comparison with what you've already done. Another dozen quatrains, composed for an audience of one."

"Who?"

"You're more than capable of rising to the challenge. I have no doubt of that," Vincent smiled, "Nostredame himself couldn't have produced your most recent creations – for all his faults, the old bastard would never have anything to do with the apocalypse."

He drained his cup, then made for the door. "Sleep well tonight. You'll need your wits about you in the morning."

Durant gripped the table. "Wait. There's something I want in return."

Vincent turned. "Anything. For a friend."

"Let me out. Just for an hour. Take this damned manacle off and let me walk in the meadow."

Vincent raised an eyebrow.

"Please. I'll go mad otherwise."

"I'll think about it. Until tomorrow, doctor."

*

The old bastard would never have anything to do with the Apocalypse. Durant gagged, surprised by a sudden swell of nausea. He knocked over piles of books, looking for Nostredame's journals. There. Six identical notebooks, bound in calfskin, the prophet's private thoughts and observations over a period of decades. Durant had used the journal sparingly during the last few weeks. They contained no shortage of rich material, but also too much of the real Michel de Nostredame. After reading these pages, Durant invariably crammed too much in the next quatrain, struck a note of human complexity when mystical ambiguity was the effect he wanted. He flicked through the pages of the most recent volume until he found the passage he was looking for:

> *Just as the great cartographers of our time are giving form to this world, so it will be possible to map the next. I am nothing more than a conduit to the truth, granted the ability to channel the celestial music even when its meaning remains obscure. To fulfil my purpose, I must retire from this world of corruption and strife, hide from the incessant demands upon my time. I will take refuge within a deep mausoleum, filled with books, a writing case, candles, ink, and paper. I will bolt the doors, and in the months that remain to me, between my death to the world and my actual demise, I shall be vouchsafed a vision of what lies on the other side of life. I shall write it down in a book, and man shall have victory even over the universal victor.*

Durant stared through the narrow window, lost in thought for several minutes before turning to the first of the six volumes. He was immediately struck by the difference in tone.

> *Victims of this plague stare vacantly into space. When they are forced to walk, they do so with jangling strides, rarely looking left or right. In the worst affected villages, no one remains to dig graves; the bodies are stacked in ricks. Where possible, however, the dead are buried in pits. Many of these are insufficiently deep, with the result that, as the corpses swell, the topmost are pushed to the surface. Tribes of feral dogs infest the region and feed on the corpses. The rich diet makes their coats sleek and glossy. They grow fat and tempting in a time of hunger. There is no one left to bring in the harvest. Crowds of ragged people swarm in the soup shops, wasted to skin and bone. Men feed on dogs, and dogs feed on men.*

Nostredame's first wife and two children had been claimed by plague. When they had known each other in Montpellier, Durant remembered behaving as if their experiences were equivalent despite the fact that his own daughter had survived. Nostredame had been too kind to correct him. Durant re-read the passage with a growing sense of dread. Each of the adjectives – sleek, ragged, glossy, and that final, mirrored sentence – pierced him to the heart. Nostredame had tried to simply observe, tried to separate what he saw from what he felt and understand how the plague worked. Those words of description, swelling in the second part of the passage, were his fate, the first steps – taken in heroic seriousness – on a road which ultimately led to the florid language of his mad prophesies.

Durant sat down, overcome by a wave of horror as he realised what he'd done. Vincent had been right. Despite Nostredame's frequent allusions to God, the old man had never once predicted the end of the world. On the contrary, he presented the future as endless. Bleak, admittedly, but never fixed in absolute terms.

In his forgeries, however, Durant had described the End of Days as imminent and inevitable, with the English queen cast in the role of anti-Christ. God's wrath would only be averted if every righteous Frenchman worked to bring about her death.

Durant lay awake long into the night, attempting to persuade himself that his rhymed predictions were ambiguous, open to a range of interpretations. Then he would remember a particular word or phrase he'd used. Self-loathing rose like acid in his guts when he thought of the passages in Nostredame's early journals. Dispassionate observation descending into second-rate poetry – less an attempt to render the reality of what he'd seen than a distraction from the pain of standing witness. It was Nostredame's own innate goodness which had propelled him into the disorientating realms of vision and dreamscape.

Durant may have mimicked the old man's style, but the forgeries he'd produced were empty of heart or soul.

Chapter 23

Longstaff forced the pace along a clear track. It hadn't rained in days, the ground was firm, though a good tracker would have no difficulty following the marks of their passage. He'd closed the jailhouse door behind him, he was almost certain. How long had the jailor remained unconscious? How long before the prisoner had been missed?

There was no point being optimistic, they were on his trail already. He had attacked the Guise family home, set fires, endangered lives and freed a prisoner. They could not know for certain that the old man's rescuer and the unemployed soldier of the previous day were one and the same person, but they surely wouldn't discount the possibility. Longstaff cracked the reins, maintaining cavalry pace – walk a mile, canter one, gallop three, canter one, then walk again – for as long as he dared across a series of meadows. The horse held up well. Poor Sparrow no longer had the strength for days like this, but she remained willing. Longstaff changed direction a dozen times, attempting to confuse pursuit, but always keeping to a broadly westerly heading.

Why Orléans? The man behind him was silent, only groaning softly with each change of pace or direction. Never complaining, even when he began to lose consciousness. Longstaff felt the man's head nod against his back – still nearly two hours until sunset, but the horse was struggling, too – he turned off the track, heading through a wide strip of trees, the ground relatively clear beneath the horse's hooves, then entering the deepwood beyond.

It took time to find an adequate campsite. A small clearing where drinking water bubbled from a tumble of rocks. Just a patch of wet, marshy ground. Longstaff slid down from the saddle, the stranger attempted to follow. He was at least thirty years older and God alone knew when he'd last ridden a horse. Longstaff caught him, laid him gently on the soft earth.

The prisoner hardly stirred, only turned on his side, knees up against his chest like a child, and began to snore.

"You and me both," muttered Longstaff. He forced himself to see to the animals, then covered the sleeping man with his bedroll. It was still light when he sought his own rest, stretching full-length on the ground, saddle for a pillow and his coat for a blanket.

He woke before dawn with his arms around Sparrow, fingers woven in the dog's thick coat. The man beside him still slept. Longstaff's first thoughts were of food. He raided a nearby bird's nest, built a low, covered fire and set to work on breakfast. The smell woke his companion. Longstaff had a hundred questions, but forced himself to be patient a while longer, first offering the man water and food. The prisoner's appetite was prodigious; it seemed a fair bet he'd make a full recovery from the trials of his captivity.

"Gaetan Durant," Longstaff reminded him. "You said you knew him."

"I haven't heard that name in over ten years. What made you think he'd be at Joinville?"

"I'll ask the questions."

"Durant was a pupil of mine," the old man shifted, trying to make himself comfortable. "And a friend. For a time, I was quite carried away by his idealism."

"An idealist?" Longstaff bit back a laugh. "Are we talking about the same man? Always dresses in black. Never smiles. Drinks too much. Starts fights he leaves other people to finish."

The old man shrugged. "He grew bitter. That's what happens to idealists. And then, of course, his daughter disappeared. He'd already broken with me, but I still heard of it. A sweet child, and he'd already lost so much. He might have made a wonderful physician."

Longstaff stared at him. "Who are you?"

The man plucked a leaf from his hair, then puffed out his chest with mock self-importance. "Michel de Nostredame."

"The prophet?" Longstaff rocked back on his haunches, regarding the man. "I carried one of your rose pills for years. Durant claimed he used to help you make them." He began to recite: "An ounce of sawdust from a fresh, green Cypress tree; six ounces of Iris of Florence…" He stumbled; the conversation had taken place years earlier, almost a different life.

"Three ounces of cloves," continued Nostredame, "three drams of tiger lily; six of lignaloes. The ingredients are ground into a powder, then mixed with the petals of three hundred roses, but mind they must be picked before dawn. Shape the paste into lozenges no bigger than a thumbnail, dry thoroughly and store in a sealed place. In case of plague, keep one on the tongue at all times."

"Durant always said they were useless."

Nostredame gave a low, throaty chuckle. "I imagine he was even less polite when it came to my prognostications."

"Do you know where he is?"

"I have absolutely no idea." The old man repeated his original question. "Why were you looking for him at Joinville?"

"He disappeared from Paris several weeks ago, taken by men working for the Guise family. I heard rumours of a prisoner held at the palace…"

"… and put two and two together."

"Charles of Guise, Cardinal of Lorraine, has been led to believe that Durant knows the location of a particular book; one they'd do anything to find."

"Led to believe?"

"The book doesn't exist. It's a fiction, designed to smoke out a traitor. What did the family want with you?"

"The cardinal hoped I might help him gain influence over Catherine de Medici."

"Did you?"

"Help them?" Nostredame sounded offended. "Of course not."

"You seem remarkably healthy. I can't see a mark on you."

The astrologer shrugged. "I imagine people are talking about my disappearance – the famous prognosticator who vanished in a puff of smoke."

It wasn't a boast. Nostredame sounded weary of his fame.

"How long have you been their captive?"

"Several months. You're a foreigner, of course, that's why you haven't heard."

"Men like the cardinal don't issue empty threats."

Something was wrong with the story. Two men, who had once been close friends, both abducted by the Guise to participate in entirely separate plots against the English Crown?

"Did you ever hear your jailors talk about the Duke of Norfolk?"

Nostredame shook his head.

"Or a lost Gospel," continued Longstaff, "written by Christ and demonstrating beyond doubt that St. Peter and his successors should have exclusive responsibility for interpreting God's word?"

"A what? No one would ever believe in such a thing?"

Longstaff spat in frustration. "Catholics would, according to certain men in London."

Nostredame raised both eyebrows, which was all the answer Longstaff needed. Westminster was a nest of fools as much as vipers. What if Walsingham was wrong about Norfolk? He'd been so certain, so pleased with himself, but what if his loathing for Catholics had made him see what he wanted; where another player in the game had created only empty spectacle? But then, why *had* Durant been abducted? It made no sense.

"What…"

Longstaff heard the low thrum of cord released from tension. Pain blossomed in his shoulder. The whistling sound of an arrow came next. Nostredame's face disappeared, replaced by a canopy of trees as Longstaff was knocked flat. He heard the soft rasp of another arrow drawn from its quiver, forced himself to sit, bit his lip to keep from crying out. His musket was on the far side of the campfire. With the arrow in his shoulder, he couldn't even throw a knife. A man appeared from the trees, sword at his side, dressed in a long, oiled coat with the hood pulled low over his eyes. He took two steps into the clearing, preceded by an arrow aimed unwaveringly at Sparrow.

"A longbow?" muttered Longstaff.

"They still find favour with a certain breed of huntsman. Your animal's dead if she moves."

He appeared to have identified Sparrow as the only remaining threat. With justification, reflected Longstaff – Nostredame was an old man.

The bowman pushed back his hood. Longstaff recognised him then. He'd seen him before, among the booksellers of St. Paul's, at the coaching inn in Southwark, loitering in the rue de Marivaulx in Paris. Here among the trees, Longstaff realised he was seeing him in his true element for the first time.

"You spied me twice among the bricks and mortar," the man spoke English with a west country accent, "but never a glimpse of me in the green. I've been on your trail for weeks, close enough to smell you most of the time." He gave a short, sharp laugh.

"Who are you?"

Longstaff's voice was rough with pain and anger. Why was Nostredame trying to stop him standing?

"Out of my way, old man."

"Your wound," replied the astrologer in French, "you could die."

Longstaff knocked his hand away. Nostredame broke eye contact first, shuffling reluctantly to one side.

"You, too, Sparrow."

The dog settled on her belly, teeth bared and shoulder muscles bunched.

"You made it too easy," continued the stranger. "A trail of destruction in your wake even a child could follow. The dog might have given me away, but you were always in too much of a hurry to pay attention."

Longstaff thought of the words which had been running through his mind for weeks: *get it done, get it finished, get back home to Aurélie.* Why was he still alive? Why hadn't the man finished him with the first arrow?

"Who are you working for? Norfolk?"

"Give it up," said the bowman. "We know Walsingham's paying you to frame him?"

Frame Norfolk? Longstaff shook his head in confusion. "What are you talking about? Walsingham sent me here to find proof against Norfolk, not manufacture it."

The bowman ignored him. "You," he ordered Nostredame. "Open his saddlebags and shake out the contents."

There wasn't much of interest. Walsingham's leather-bound map raised a brief spark of curiosity. The assassin swung his bow, aiming at Longstaff's heart.

"At least let the old man go."

"My orders are to find out whether the book really exists, then kill you and get home with no one the wiser." The bowman shrugged, "that means your new friend has to die."

Longstaff closed his eyes. An image of Aurélie formed in the darkness, he staggered to his feet. "At least tell me who you're working for."

"For all the good it will do you, the Earl of Leicester commands my loyalty. Goodbye, Matthew Longstaff," his fingers tightened on the string.

"Wait!" Nostredame stepped between the two men, hands clasped in supplication. "Don't kill me. I won't breathe a word. I'll disappear. No one will ever hear from me again. I swear."

He spoke with unsettling urgency, shuffling forward with tiny steps. His face appeared to crumple as he switched to his native language, the deep voice filling with passion, like sails before the wind, sentences rolling to the rhythm of his odd, archaic French. He spoke faster and faster until Longstaff could no longer follow the words. Was he pleading, cursing, declaiming?

The assassin appeared to shake himself from a state of trance. His eyes grew wide, lips curved in a snarl. The bow shifted, seeking the prophet, intending to end his chilling rant.

Sparrow sprang at the assassin.

Too slow.

The assassin brought his bow to bear, released in the same smooth action. The arrow pierced Sparrow's chest. The assassin staggered as the dog's body struck him. He twisted to push Sparrow aside, reaching for his sword.

Too slow.

Longstaff had a dagger in one hand. His knees shook from blood loss. He fell, burying his blade in the bowman's chest, driving it home with the weight of his own body.

Too weak to roll away, he lay with his head to one side, staring at Sparrow beside him in a growing pool of blood. His vision blurred when Nostredame pushed him clear of the corpse. Longstaff gasped as the Frenchman pulled at the laces of his jerkin. Daylight faded to shades of red, then black.

He came to on a bed of grass with the sun's warmth in his bones. Someone held a water skin to his lips. Longstaff choked weakly on the sweet liquid.

He should be dead. The man had been a stone-cold killer. How had Nostredame managed to distract him?

Longstaff felt a whisper of breeze across his bare chest. The astrologer had removed his clothing to treat the wound.

"You took it out?"

"The arrowhead passed clean through your shoulder. Easy, once I'd broken the shaft. Stopping the blood was more of a challenge."

Longstaff looked down at a cool compress of green leaves, poking out from beneath strips of torn cloth. He felt a sudden wave of dizziness.

"What have you given me?"

"Something for the pain."

"Help me sit."

Something for the pain. Something that seemed to have cauterized his feelings, he thought, staring at the man he'd killed. Sparrow lay in a shallow grave nearby.

"You've been unconscious for several hours," Nostredame gestured at Sparrow. "I assumed you wouldn't want to leave her for scavengers. The ground is hard, the earth shot through with ancient roots. I've done what I could," he looked as his own gnarled hands, "you're in no fit state to wield a shovel."

"And him?" Longstaff gestured at Leicester's assassin.

"I'm an old man plagued with dropsy. Not a bloody saint."

Tentatively – fearful of the pain – Longstaff attempted to lift his right arm.

"Careful," said Nostredame. "It won't heal if you tear the stitches."

Longstaff ran his hand along Sparrow's back. She'd been a pup when he rescued her from a life in the bearpits. He wanted to weep, but the tears refused to flow. What had Nostredame given him? Sparrow's thick coat, smooth in one direction. Sharp grey bristles pricked his palm in the other. She'd run at his side across the frozen wastes of Livonia and made the old house at Martlesham feel like home. Sparrow and Aurélie. One was dead and the other held in her gilded cage in London. Longstaff was lost in France and Martlesham lay empty again.

Slowly, using his feet, Longstaff filled in Sparrow's grave, shooing Nostredame away when he offered to help.

"Check the corpse for anything we can use."

"I found his horse and pack while you slept. We have sufficient provisions for the next few days."

The assassin had spoken English, Longstaff remembered. "How much did you understand of what he said?"

The astrologer shrugged.

"Did you hear him say 'Leicester'?" persisted Longstaff

"That's the name I heard."

What in God's name did it mean?

"Great men plot against one another," added Nostredame. "It's the way of the world."

"Not this time." Longstaff shook his head. "If the Earl of Leicester believes my wife is part of a conspiracy to frame the Duke of Norfolk, then her life is in danger. Not only hers. I have to get this information to England."

How? He was in no fit state to ride that far. He needed Throckmorton or Palavicino, but both men had followed the Queen Mother south to meet the Royal Progress.

"We'll reach Orléans in a day or two," said Nostredame. "Believe me, I need to contact the Queen Mother no less urgently than you need to contact your wife. My friend in the city has connections all over Europe, including London. There's no faster way."

Chapter 24

DURANT

Ice-cold, bathed in sweat. Body arch'd in pain.
He held a cup to her lips and watched,
Afraid to touch. As wine traced
A bloody path along her sunken cheek.

Gaetan Durant set the bucket down in a narrow shaft of sunlight. He'd become clumsier since the loss of his finger, with a constant tingling where there should have been absence. He'd heard men talk about this ghostly sensation; until now, he'd never really understood.

Nostredame's copy of Ibn Sīnā's *The Book of Healing* lay open on the table behind him. Durant did not believe the Persian's advice would work, but the phantom itching was driving him mad. He'd reached the point where he was willing to try anything.

He bent over the bucket – right hand held above eye level where he couldn't see it – concentrating only on the reflection in the still water. He moved his fingers, one by one, from thumb to pinkie, then repeated the procedure with his left hand, which he kept tucked behind his back while his eyes remained glued on the motionless reflection…

Two loud knocks at the door. It was only mid-morning. Durant straightened without answering. Vincent came in first, Jean Paul at his heels with a pile of correspondence. The seals were already broken, envelopes ripped open, the contents perused and separated into piles. Today, tomorrow, next week. A never-ending stream of letters to persuade the world Nostredame still lived. Jean-Paul cleared a space in the middle of the table, between the row of cups at one end, the jumble of quills, ink and paper at the other. Vincent began reading the topmost sheet, covered in Durant's neat hand-writing. The page below was blank.

Durant wet his lips. "I'll get to work at once."

"The correspondence can wait."

Vincent crumpled the sheet and threw it in the empty fireplace. "You completed a hundred perfect quatrains in a matter of weeks. Now you're producing rubbish at the rate of one a day. What's wrong?"

Durant nodded. "Writing for the masses is one thing…"

"She's just a woman."

"She's Catherine de Medici."

"Just a woman, soft in the head when it comes to her children. The English threaten, the Guise offer salvation. How hard can it be?"

A steady drip of doom-laden prognostications, designed to force her into action.

Durant cleared his throat. "The mob is the mob. It will stoop to meet its destiny whatever I write."

"Don't tell me you've grown a conscience?"

"I want to live."

"We've talked about this. A fresh start in a far-away land, remember?"

Durant grabbed one of the wooden cups, drained the contents in an attempt to steady his nerves. He did it without thinking; it was the first time his brain had compensated for the missing finger. He looked down at Nostredame's copy of the *Book of Healing*.

"You make it sound like a fairytale."

The fox laughed – Durant still thought of his two jailors as fox and mastiff – and took a seat at the table, apparently unconcerned when Durant elected to remain standing.

"I like you, doctor, but I need these prophesies. If necessary, I will dismember you piece by piece, but I would rather find a civilised solution. You spent eight years of your life searching for your daughter. Don't you want to see her again?"

For a moment, Durant wondered what might have happened if Laure had been happy when he found her, with a brood of grandchildren ready to be dandled on his knee. Instead she'd been married to sadist.

"Laure is a survivor," he said. "She'll probably be better off without me."

He felt a small surge of satisfaction as he saw Vincent's jaw tighten, then hurried to soothe his jailor's temper. "I'm sorry. I want to help."

Vincent did not look convinced. He rose, gesturing for Jean-Paul to open the door: "Time begins to press, my friend. Be careful not to try my patience too far."

The door swung closed. Durant released a long-held breath. He wanted to pace, but the chain's weight had become so much a part of him he simply sank into a chair. Vincent had been lying. There was no point in hoping otherwise; Durant had long since decided he would never give them what they wanted.

He picked up a quill, decorated a fresh sheet of paper with a few dozen words and twice as many crossings out. This was for show. The fruits of a frustrating day's labour, which he put to one side. He sat very still for several minutes, listening, trying to imagine what Vincent and Jean-Paul were doing out there.

The Cardinal of Lorraine needed the support of the French crown to guarantee the success of his enterprise against the English. Durant would not give the man any more ammunition to use in his attempts to start a war. He remembered listening to Longstaff's descriptions of the horrors he'd seen, stepping from grass onto the bodies of fallen soldiers, entrails hanging out, skulls smashed, fingers twitching at the end of severed arms: "the feeling of triumph, every step across that grisly carpet, a step closer to victory."

He would not give them what they wanted, and yet he could not stop himself from writing. After so many weeks, his very blood seemed to beat to the simple rhythm of a four-line quatrain. The certainty of approaching death. Tiny letters. As small as he could make them, on both sides of the page. He lived in fear that Vincent would notice the diminishing supply of paper.

He wrote verses forgiving Laure and asking her to forgive him in turn – tentative attempts to mine the pure stuff of love from the accumulated miseries of experience – and verses inspired by Longstaff and Aurélie which dwelt on the consolations of friendship. Perhaps that was natural, with death so near at hand. He bade farewell to his long-dead wife. Normally, when he thought of her, it was as he'd seen her last, drawn in the heavy lines of death. Now, he was a granted a vision from before the plague. Her beauty, that glow of happiness when she'd realised she was pregnant, the first precious swell of her belly. He worked on, trying to capture the sound of her laughter.

Durant wrote for hours, composing, editing, revising. Verses in which he exalted arrogance as the worst of all man's failings – his way of apologising to Michel de Nostredame for having simultaneously stolen his name and poisoned his purpose.

He still had over an hour to himself, assuming Vincent kept to his usual routine. Durant set the quill aside, reading as the ink dried on the page. New quatrains, written for all the people he loved as acts of atonement for his many different crimes. Then, hurried by a strange sense of foreboding, he lay full length on the floor.

Listening.

The sound of laughter reached him from the direction of the storehouse. Nothing untoward. He crawled to the loose floorboard, teased it up and added his day's work to the thin pile of papers below. Enough to satisfy Vincent, if the fox only knew of their existence.

Footsteps. Vincent was early. Durant took his seat in front of the page he'd prepared that morning, drumming his fingers as if in search of inspiration. Vincent gave a jaunty knock before entering. He appeared to be in excellent spirits, whistling a thin tune through the gaps in his teeth.

"Getting on?"

Durant grimaced.

Vincent looked down at the ink-splattered page. "I've been thinking about what you said. Sunshine on your face. A bit of fresh air."

Durant eyed him warily.

"Don't look at me like that!"

Vincent laughed as he produced the key to Durant's shackle. "Perhaps it will inspire you."

Durant was halfway to the door, before he realised Vincent wasn't following.

"Hay-fever, but you go on ahead." He made himself comfortable at the table. "Don't worry. Jean-Paul will keep an eye on you."

The mastiff stepped aside, allowing Durant into the late afternoon sunshine. He turned in a slow circle, taking in the storehouse where Vincent and Jean-Paul lived, and the wooded valley beyond. He walked around the cabin with its steeply pitched roof. The chimney stack was taller than he'd expected, to prevent stray sparks from drifting into the thatch below. And then a wide meadow, dotted with wildflower. The thick grass rose above his ankles. Every step stirred a dozen scents. The meadow ended in a steep escarpment, bearded by a tangle of briars and brambles. There could be no escape in this direction and Jean-Paul seemed content to let him wander. The sharp tang of peppermint carried on the breeze. Once, Durant had gathered peppermint with Nostredame to create infusions against digestive problems. Elder had a similar effect. Wild herbs grew everywhere along the boundary of the meadow. Purslane, which helped break fevers. Thyme produced an ointment effective against pustules when mixed with fat. Myrtle soothed rashes. What else? An odd smile appeared on Durant's face when he saw the small, bell-shaped flowers, a dull purple, tinged green at the edges. Words ran through his head, strung together like a children's rhyme: *divale, dwale, banewort, devil's herb, beautiful death.*

Jean-Paul was still some way off. Durant stared across the meadow, past the cabin, at the narrow path which disappeared into the woods beyond. He closed his eyes, head tilted towards the sun. He wished Longstaff and Aurélie could read the verses he'd written for them. Nostredame, too. And Laure, for whom he'd crossed the length and breadth of a continent. A matter of bone and muscle only. It had been a penance; he'd been no better than the professional flagellants one saw on the pilgrim trails, never truly believing he'd find her again and never truly opening his heart to her when the miracle did occur. Laure would never read his verses. It would have to be enough that he'd written them. His way of saying goodbye.

Durant wanted to live. More now than at any time since his wife had died. Part of him yearned to give Vincent the quatrains, see if the fox would keep his word and let him start again in a far-off country, but he refused to play any further part in the Cardinal of Lorraine's attempts to start a war. Durant smiled; he had poured his heart and soul into these last prophesies and tonight he would destroy them. Once they were gone, he would follow them into oblivion.

Durant turned. He tripped, giving a strangled cry as he fell on the bell-shaped flowers. Then up on his elbows, frantically digging in the earth. He needed the root. Had it now, tucked deep in his shirt before rolling over on his back. Jean-Paul stood wordlessly above.

"Rabbit hole," announced Durant. He made a show of examining his ankle, before climbing to his feet. "Don't worry. No harm done."

He could feel the belladonna plant beneath the waistband of his hose. His filth encrusted clothes were perfect camouflage.

He would prepare the draft tonight and make his own decision on when and how he left this world.

*

Vincent plucked the toothpick from his lips, pointed it at Durant with a broad smile on his face.

"Superb. Why didn't you show me these before?"

Durant blinked owlishly, eyes still adjusting to the gloomy interior. "What?" He stared at the dislodged floorboard as Vincent pumped his lifeless hand.

"It was a struggle at first, to read such tiny writing. You were clever about the paper. It was the ink that gave you away."

"They're mine," said Durant.

"Her majesty will be enchanted, once the verses are properly edited and transcribed of course." He held a flimsy page in his fingers. "Royalty is royalty. They won't read a thing unless it appears on leaves of finest velum, bound in leather, set with precious stones and clasps of gold and silver. Not even when it comes from the renowned Michel de Nostredame." He clapped Durant on the back. "I do believe we're done here."

Vincent looked over Durant's shoulder at Jean-Paul. "You'll leave with these at dawn."

Bonelessly, Durant sank into a chair and poured himself a generous measure of raw spirits from Vincent's wineskin.

"Go ahead," said his tormentor. "You've earned it."

Durant closed his eyes. "A last drink for the condemned man?"

"Not quite yet. We have to wait for instructions. My master may still have further use for you."

"The correspondence?"

Vincent poured for himself. "If that's what he wants."

"And if there's nothing more for me to do?"

"A second chance, in a far-off land?" Vincent gave him a pitying look. "You and I are men of the world, doctor. I hope we can agree the time for useful fantasies is at an end."

Chapter 25

Even with two horses, it took another three days to reach the gates of Orléans. The slow pace was murder for Longstaff, thinking of the predators circling nearer and nearer his wife. He pinched the soft flesh on the inside of his forearm – patience! It wasn't only his wound which held them back; the Guise would have men scouring the country by now and Leicester's man had delayed them sufficiently that the danger was as likely to be found ahead as behind.

They kept to the woods as much as possible, so dense in places they were forced to walk the horses. Nostredame's limp grew progressively worse. The old man collected a selection of plants each evening for the pain he never complained about. They made a fine pair, thought Longstaff – jaw clenched on a piece of wood to keep from crying out while Nostredame's rough fingers checked his own wound for signs of corruption – one old, the other infirm.

His inspection finished, Nostredame made himself comfortable on the far side of their campfire, cross-legged, eyes closed. So still he might have been dead. The same strange ritual he performed every evening. Longstaff looked for Sparrow, wanting to bury his fingers in the dog's thick fur. Instead, he wrapped them tight around the medallion Aurélie had given him.

The desperate act of a man with nowhere left to turn. Was he doing the right thing, creeping through these forests with an aging charlatan, making for a city where he knew no one?

So many questions. Leicester's assassin had set Longstaff an impossible riddle. Was Norfolk really a traitor, working together with Catholic Europe towards the destruction of his sovereign? Was Walsingham an honest intelligencer or a religious bigot obsessed with destroying an imagined threat to the reformist cause? Where did one end and the next begin? Could Sir Nicholas be relied upon to know? What if Walsingham's belief in Norfolk's guilt was genuine, but misplaced?

Longstaff spat a curse. These so-called great men, bewitched by the same spells they'd cast to trap their enemies, like children, playing games to obscure the fact they no longer knew what was real and what was make-believe. He had to get a letter to Aurélie. She had to tell Sir Nicholas and Walsingham what he'd learned of Leicester's involvement, then go into hiding until he could return to England and protect her. She was a pawn; always the first piece sacrificed when the game was joined in earnest.

Longstaff began to pace, back and forth across the clearing – if he started now, how long to reach the coast, how long to find a boat? He could imagine Aurélie's reaction when he appeared on the doorstep, without Durant, bearing information he could just as easily have sent. She would not thank him for his concern. Instead, she'd blame him for turning his back on their mutual friend, jeopardising the unmasking of a dangerous spy, all from a misguided sense that she was unable to take care of herself.

The astrologer shook himself free of whatever waking dream consumed him each evening.

"We'll be in Orléans tomorrow."

"You said that yesterday."

"That was before I'd mastered the secrets of your remarkable map. I have the way of it now, for good or ill."

"What's that supposed to mean?"

"The urge to produce a document of such precision must come, at least in part, from a desire to undermine the importance of lived experience. Your map leads to a place without room for memory or hearsay."

Longstaff spat in frustration.

"I'm speaking metaphorically, of course," continued Nostredame. "It's become a habit over the last two decades. In the short term, your map will lead us to Orléans, sometime tomorrow afternoon, from which city you will be able to send your letter to England, and I mine to Catherine de Medici."

Longstaff resumed pacing. "I saw her in Paris three weeks ago."

"She should never have come to see me last year, interrupting the Royal Progress and drawing attention to our relationship, but she insisted, no doubt misunderstanding my protestations as the false modesty of a courtier. I urged her to come with as little fanfare as possible. She brought her son," Nostredame shook his head. "King Charles IX arrived on the biggest horse I've ever seen. He wore a purple cloak with silver ribbons, an amethyst in one ear and a sapphire in the other, but let him play, if he must. The poor boy's not long for this world."

Longstaff rolled his eyes. "You're sure of that, I suppose."

"Catherine will live to see each of her sons crowned, and she has one more after Charles." The prophet sighed. "No doubt the Cardinal of Lorraine heard about her visit to my home; I was abducted by his men only a few days later. If I *had* agreed to his demands, the Queen Mother would be his by now. We'll know more tomorrow. Jean de Tournier is one of the best-connected men in the country."

"Your mysterious friend in Orléans?"

"He comes from a good family, unlike the majority of my publishers. Who knows, he may have some idea of where we can start looking for Durant." The dark eyes sought Longstaff's. "It was my growing reputation as a prognosticator which caused the break between us."

"He told me you saved Bordeaux from plague by closing the public wells, insisting people drank running water and preventing other physicians from bleeding their patients."

"I did all of those things," Nostredame nodded, "whether they made a difference, or the disease simply burned itself out, who knows? No doubt your friend went on to explain how I disowned these methods in order to qualify as a physician?"

Longstaff remembered the exact words Durant had used: "It was that compromise, made so many years ago, which lies at the root of his ridiculous career as a fortune teller."

Nostredame burst out laughing. "That's him, the very spit. He said as much to me during one of our last conversations, before his daughter disappeared: divination is no better than revelation. *The only way to know God is through observation and the patient accumulation of knowledge.* He spoke with such certainty, as if it were self-evident that Mankind can be perfected. As if I, in my attempts at poetry, were betraying this truth." He shook his head. "My ancestors were Jewish merchants, middle-men who facilitated the trade between Moors and Christians, which means I know something of all three religions. It doesn't matter whose learned men you interrogate, Longstaff, or whose history you study. We all walk in circles, each generation remaking the world to suit its own needs and prejudices. One generation learns to manipulate clay and concludes that we were formed from earth. Another develops hydraulic engineering and explains mankind in terms of the four humours. Ingenious men closer to our own time invented clockwork mechanisms, and now the human body becomes a machine, our organs and muscles only cogs and gears. I know you doubt my ability to see into the future, but one thing is certain; the men who follow us will look back at our clockwork model with contempt. The men who follow them will do the same, infinite layers of ignorance piled one atop the next.

"Durant believes a road stands ready-paved before us – all we have to do is start walking and it will lead us to perfection. But there is no road, leading from the past, through the present and into the future. There are only layers, the bones of each successive generation piled in great heaps. Those scraps of depth and texture we cling to with such tenacity – that sense of movement through the ages – are vastly outweighed by the endless repetitions. It wasn't only the Israelites who wandered in the desert. It's all of us, walking blindfold through this world."

Longstaff dreamed of an enormous net that night, drawing tighter and tighter about him. They'd seen no sign of pursuit since fleeing Joinville, but he was under no illusion the Guise had given up. Descriptions of Nostredame would have been circulated, perhaps of him as well, rewards for their capture cried in every town and village in Champagne.

Assuming Nostredame was right about their location, they would soon be among people again. Longstaff passed a pot of boiling water to the astrologer, a sliver of soap from his pack, and a sharp knife.

"Hair and beard," he said. "No arguments."

Longstaff finished the job himself, cropping the grey hair as neatly as possible. Nostredame looked years younger, slighter, and oddly vulnerable.

"How long had you worn that beard?"

"Thirty years, give or take. I feel naked."

"Your jaw's too pale. It's too early in the year for walnuts..."

Longstaff hacked at a young oak, mixing sap with ashes from the fire to form a paste.

"Rub it in."

Nostredame's skin took on a uniform grey tone, so that he looked like a man recovering after a long illness.

The map brought them to the forest's edge shortly after noon. In the distance, beyond a ring of farm land, they saw the walls of Orléans with the wide Loire sparkling beyond.

"Take off your robe," said Longstaff, "do what you can to remove the worst of the stains."

The astrologer grumbled but did as he was told. While he worked on making his robe more respectable, Longstaff removed the saddle from the horse they'd taken from Leicester's man. He took off his jerkin, wrapped it in his cavalryman's coat and bound both across the animal's naked back.

Nostredame presented himself for Longstaff's inspection. The improvement to his robe was minimal but would have to do. Longstaff belted his own sword around the old man's waist, then insisted they swap footwear – his leather boots for the astrologer's closed sandals.

"Mount up," he said. "I'm your servant."

"Whatever you say."

Nostredame set off at a walk. Longstaff followed on foot, in his shirt-sleeves, leading the second animal by the bridle.

"Tell me more about this publisher."

"Jean? Sharp as a pin. His family made their fortune in wine and he ploughed his share of the inheritance into books..."

The road was quiet. People at work in the fields on either side or tending the fish ponds closer to the walls. No one paid any attention to the two travellers. Nostredame talked on, appearing to take no notice of their surroundings. Longstaff suspected the soldiers on the walls would be more alert; it was possible the Guise had anticipated they would make for Orléans. He altered his stride, dropping his shoulders and swinging his arms more vigorously than usual. The way a man walked gave him away as much as his face, more so from a distance. A master of disguise might hoodwink his own mother up close, but unless he changed the way he moved, she would know him at a hundred yards.

"…and almanacs, of course. There's no shame in that. In many respects, I take as much pride in my almanacs as in the prophesies themselves; they help my readers manage their lives. I always include a calendar, weather forecasts, all the major fairs listed by region…"

Chapter 26

The North Gate was open. Nostredame talked on as they passed beneath the arch, whether because he thought it would make them less conspicuous or for the pleasure of hearing his own voice, Longstaff wasn't sure.

The guards, in pale blue doublets trimmed with silver ribbon, gave them a cursory glance but made no move to stop them, preferring to remain in the shade of the customs house. Longstaff in his role as attendant hurried forward to clear a path through the newsmongers, leading his master along the wide thoroughfare which ran towards the river, finally emerging in front of the university. Longstaff paused to stare at the law students running back and forth in their long robes.

"Impressive, no?" murmured Nostredame. "The city stands at the Loire's most northerly point, thus its closest point to Paris. You have to travel a long way before reaching the next bridge. Having become rich on tolls and taxes, Orléans invests its wealth in learning."

Longstaff followed him across the square and into a side street on the far side. He shifted uneasily while Nostredame rapped knuckles against a wooden door, tall and wide enough to admit a carriage and horses. A servant appeared. Nostredame stepped past him into a central courtyard. Longstaff saw a two-storey house at the far end, stables on the left and a huge, open-plan workshop in a remise on the right.

"Jean," shouted Nostredame.

The man was in his early thirties, in scarlet hose and a fine linen shirt, covered in ink stains with the cuffs rolled up above his elbows. His long hair was tied at the base of his neck with a scrap of ribbon.

"Help you, m'sieur?"

"Lost the use of your eyes, man? It's me."

Jean de Tourniers squinted. The light of recognition dawned. "Michel? God's blood, what have you done to yourself?"

"We seek your hospitality, Jean. And your assistance."

"Of course, whatever you need." The publisher wiped his hands on a rag, then kissed his most profitable client on both cheeks.

"You look terrible. The mountain air was less effective than you'd hoped? At least your hands have healed, it seems."

"My hands?"

"Forgive me. I'm forgetting my manners. Come in, bring your friend…"

"Matthew Longstaff, this is Jean de Tourniers."

"An honour to meet you, m'sieur."

Inside the house, the publisher led them to his study on the upper floor. Serried ranks of ledgers covered the walls, alongside books bound in fine, hand-tooled leather. Piles of chapbooks were stacked neatly in a corner. De Tournier ushered his guests into two comfortable chairs on either side of an unlit fire. Nostredame unbuckled Longstaff's belt, letting the sword fall to the floor as he sank into the deep cushions. Longstaff paused for a moment to stare through the single window.

"The university puts butter on my bread," said the publisher, dragging a heavy chair from his desk to the fireplace. "The view helps me keep that in mind whenever I'm working on another of their wretched law books."

He put a hand on Nostredame's shoulder. "I'm glad to see the pain has receded. Allow me to express my admiration; to have produced such astonishing work, given the circumstances – nothing short of miraculous."

A frown creased Nostredame's brow. He leaned forward in his chair. "You don't seem very surprised to see me, Jean?"

"I know how impatient you are to have your most recent verses printed and distributed. Naturally, I assume you've come to check on my progress."

"Has my disappearance aroused so little notice?"

"Forgive me," de Tournier faltered, "I don't understand."

"I was abducted and have been held captive for several months."

"It's not three weeks since I received your latest collection of quatrains."

Longstaff saw an expression of panic on the prophet's face.

Crossing to his fine knee-hole desk, de Tournier began rifling through packets of correspondence. "The proofs went to the printers a week ago. I must say, I was hurt you refused to give me a march on my competitors. The race is well and truly on, but it's wonderful work, Michel. I devoured it in a single sitting. Such strength in the line, such delicacy in the sentiment. Even considered purely as poetry, I believe it merits comparison with Labe or Villon."

Nostredame was flushed. His brow had darkened and a vein at his temple began to throb. The publisher fell silent, wordlessly handing him the sheaf of papers.

"I have not written a word in months," Nostredame's voice rose an octave. "Has no one noticed? Has the world gone mad?"

Longstaff met de Tournier's eye while the prophet read. Both men looked away in embarrassment.

"You honestly believe that I composed these verses?"

"Why would I doubt it?"

"Foresee him set aside strength," quoted Nostredame, *"renounce the spoils/Of conquest. Embrace emptiness; it takes,/ Divinity to spring this devil-formed trap."*

"Granted, you're not usually so erratic in your use of punctuation, but the rhythm, the tension, the tenor of the words…"

"'The Moors know him as Masi al Dijar, the Imposter/We know him by the name of Antichrist'. When have you ever known me invoke the End of Days? This isn't even my handwriting."

"But you explained! The joints had swelled in your hands and knees to the point you couldn't walk or lift a pen. You were in such a fever of composition; it became easier to dictate than write and you employed a clerk for the purpose."

The publisher crossed to a sideboard, poured himself wine from a crystal decanter and drained it at a single swallow. He appeared to remember his manners, returning to the fireplace with glasses for Nostredame and Longstaff.

"This isn't a joke?"

The prophet shook his head. His fury seemed to have robbed him of the power of speech.

"You've had problems with dropsy before," said the publisher. "It seemed plausible."

"We have to recall the proofs at once."

"Too late," the publisher gave a sad shake of his head.

"This is about more than your profits," shouted Nostredame. "About more than my pride, if it comes to that. These verses were composed for a very specific purpose."

"It's not my pocket I'm worried about," said de Tournier. "You gave the instructions yourself: no restrictions at all on who can print and distribute, so long as you're credited as the author. The book is coming off the presses as we speak. Hundreds of booksellers across France have already invested in publicity, paper, ink. It's set to be the publishing sensation of the decade," he began to pace, "in a week, your name will be on the lips of every man and woman in France."

"I didn't write these verses, Jean."

"I believe you, Michel. But if they fooled me, no one else is likely to spot the fraud."

"Who?" the prophet ground his teeth. "What bastard can have done this?"

"Isn't it obvious?"

Both men turned to stare at Longstaff. He dropped a hand over the side of the chair, expecting to find Sparrow's warm coat. He knew what must have happened, felt as if he'd known for days – just a question of the final pieces falling into place.

"Durant," he said. "What other explanation is there? They must be holding him somewhere, forcing him to produce work in your style." He turned to the publisher. "The letters you received from Nostredame. Did they have a return address?"

"A whole series of them," he turned to his client, "you travelled north from Salon, hoping the exercise and a change of air would do you good. The most recent return address is a coaching inn in the Ardèche, on the outskirts of La cité des Montlaur. You've been there for some time."

Longstaff took a long draft of wine, allowing himself a moment to savour the vintage. Finally, he knew where to look for Durant. His friend was alive or had been only few days earlier. Surely, they wouldn't kill him now. A man able to imitate the famous prophet would be much too valuable.

Reluctant to accept his poetry could be reproduced so easily, it had taken Nostredame a moment to digest the truth of Longstaff's words. Now his understanding seemed to leap ahead of Longstaff's.

"If Gaetan was abducted for the purposes of forgery, then what of your own mission? Is the Duke of Norfolk innocent, after all?"

He was right, Longstaff realised. This changed everything, upended all Walsingham's assumptions.

"That's not all," Nostredame slumped in the chair, loose pages on his lap. "The cardinal did not abduct Durant on a whim. From what I've read, he has a very specific purpose in mind; he means to start a war. Durant may have captured my style, but he has corrupted my intent beyond recognition," he scowled at de Tournier before continuing, "the stupid bastard has filled his work with references to the End of Days, as if any failure to heed his warning will lead directly to Armageddon. It's clever; there's nothing which calls for a holy war explicitly, but endless references to a fork in the road; one future in which Catholic princes lead France to glory, another in which the land is laid waste and Satan reigns for a thousand years. He writes that the enemy is separated from us by blood, flesh and water – blood and flesh are a reference to the protestant rejection of the miracle of transubstantiation, water to the English Channel. He describes a tyrant with both male and female reproductive organs – that calumny has been spread widely enough that people in France will soon think of Elizabeth."

He looked at Longstaff. "It's subtle enough. On their own, the verses are unlikely to provoke anything more than tap-room gossip. Should Catherine de Medici announce her intention to join forces with Philip, however, and the pope give his blessing to their great enterprise, everything Durant has written will appear in a new light. Frenchmen will puff out their chests, march to their deaths convinced they've been chosen to restore God's kingdom on earth.

"Catherine is the final piece, "he continued, "because she controls the king. If she joins with the Guise and Philip of Spain… You don't need to be a prophet to know what happens next."

"The combined might of France and Spain," said Longstaff, "the whole thing sold as a holy crusade against heresy. England won't stand a chance."

"I have to reach Catherine," said Nostredame. "We can stop this, as soon as she sees how the Guise have manipulated her faith in my powers."

"They'll be watching," interrupted the publisher, "Guarding against just such an eventuality."

"They aren't the only power in the land, Jean. Can we impose on you for ink and paper? I expect M'sieur Longstaff is impatient to begin work on his own letter."

"Help yourself." Jean le Tournier gestured at his desk. "You must be starving, the pair of you. I'll tell the cook to prepare something. I won't be long."

Longstaff and Nostredame sat across from one another at the publisher's desk. Longstaff had spent the previous three days silently composing his letter to Aurélie. He had already decided on the form of words he would use, how to encode the various pieces of sensitive information. It was the work of a moment to incorporate these latest revelations. A great enterprise, launched against England's Protestant monarch by the combined Catholic powers; it was the stuff of nightmares, though Walsingham had alluded to just such a threat. Longstaff remembered lying with Aurélie in the guest room at York House, choosing a codeword which neither had expected to need. He did not read through his work. Perhaps he'd misspelled a word or two; it did not matter. He knew with certainty that Aurélie would understand everything, that no one else could make sense of it at all. He folded the page, melted a nub of wax and sealed the makeshift envelope with Aurélie's medallion. He drew a fingertip across her profile, shallow in the still warm wax. A sudden wave of longing forced him to his feet. He crossed to the window, the wide square strangely quiet for the time of day.

"Finished," said Nostredame, "I've set out the facts of my incarceration at Joinville. Now all that remains is to impose on our host for the use of two reliable messengers." For the first time, he allowed himself a drink. "Jean always did keep a good cellar. Hardly surprising given the family history. Where can he be with that food?"

Looking at the two letters, side by side on the desk, Longstaff felt a heavy burden lift from his shoulders. The slow pace of the previous days had been torture. Distantly, he heard the clatter of hooves and allowed himself to imagine a messenger was already saddling his horse. The wound in his shoulder began to throb; he'd been pushing himself too hard. He'd killed a man, set a fire that might have killed many more, lost Sparrow and barely given himself a second to think about any of these events. He needed a day to recover his strength, then he'd head south to La cité des Montlaur and Durant. The advantage was his now, and he meant to make it count.

The door opened. Both men looked round, expecting to see de Tournier or a servant backing into the room with a tray.

The last thing they expected was Rudi Vischer's grinning face. At a signal from Joinville's captain of the guard, men in Guise livery stormed the room with their swords drawn.

Chapter 27

Longstaff was forced to his knees. He did not resist as the soldiers took his jerkin and boots, ripped his shirt as they searched for the knife strapped to his chest. Only a few days earlier Rudi Vischer had been his ally, but there was no sign of affection or pity in the soldier's expression now. He spat in Longstaff's face, eyes sparkling with triumphant malice.

"Bind their hands."

His men were only marginally less brutal with Nostredame. Longstaff used a shoulder to wipe the spittle away.

"It was nothing personal."

Vischer reddened with anger. "The Duchess came within an inch of roasting me alive. I grovelled in the dirt for a chance to prove my loyalty. Find the prisoner, she told me. Do you want to know what else she said?"

Vischer drew near. Longstaff sensed he would not like the answer.

"Find out who took him and why, by whatever means necessary," Vischer smiled. "Believe me, my friend. I mean to obey."

Nostredame caught sight of de Tournier, lurking in the corridor. "What have you done?"

"They arrived yesterday," the publisher spoke as if this were all the explanation he needed.

A bull-necked soldier steered Longstaff out of the room, treading on his heels, forcing him through a narrow door on the ground-floor, down a twisting staircase of undressed stone to the cellars. The soldier did not bother lighting a torch. Longstaff felt the man's rancid breath on the back of his neck. He put one shoulder against the rough wall, navigating each uneven step in darkness, round half a dozen turns until light returned. Torches had been set in wall-mounted sconces. The soldier shoved Longstaff further into the maze, to the last of a series of interconnected rooms. A heavy door lay open. Longstaff scraped his head on the lintel, reopening an old graze. Two men in Guise livery were still at work inside, removing dust-covered bottles and throwing the shelves into an adjoining room. Iron manacles were fixed to Longstaff's wrists, a length of chain run through a bracket on the wall, so short he was forced to stand. The soldier kicked his legs away to make sure. Pain roared through Longstaff's shoulder, bringing tears to his eyes. Please God, let the stitches hold. As if that was the worst of his problems. Did he only imagine it, or could he feel blood leaking from the wound?

They left him in darkness. Longstaff had no idea how many hours passed before the same two soldiers returned with a lit brazier that gave off coils of ugly black smoke and a laden trestle table. Longstaff's flesh cringed as he looked at the items on display – choke pear, knee-splitter, Heretic's Fork.

The brazier caused the temperature in the room to rise, fouling the damp air. When Vischer entered several minutes later, he wore a posey of flowers in his collar. The same, thick-set soldier accompanied him, wearing a leather apron over his uniform.

"Comfortable?" inquired Vischer.

Longstaff said nothing.

"You know what strappado is, I assume," continued the German. "Typically, that's where we'd begin – tie your arms behind your back, pass a rope through an iron ring in the ceiling, then suspend you a few inches above the ground – looking at the wound in your shoulder, I have a feeling that would be too much, too soon."

Vischer smiled. "In some respects, you're fortunate my mistress thought to include a professional investigator as part of the party. Amateurs tend to make a mess of these things, always breaching that strange line where pain becomes pleasure. I'm sure you've seen it happen, tortured men demanding more and worse, almost as if they thought they were in a whorehouse."

Slowly, he unfastened the thin chain that hung from Longstaff's neck, taking a brief look at Aurélie's image before placing it on the brazier. He perched on the edge of the table, one knee across the other. "I'm curious, did you really fight the infidels or was that another of your lies?"

"Does it matter?"

"Yes."

"The fire," said Longstaff. "At Joinville. Was anyone hurt?"

The smoke was making him dizzy; he stumbled over the hard, German consonants.

"I should have known," Vischer shook his head. "You and I are not even countrymen."

Longstaff looked up from Aurélie's medallion. "For what it's worth, I'm sorry."

The investigator blew on the coals until they glowed. Longstaff coughed as the smoke grew thicker. Vischer unhooked a leather flask from his belt and held it to Longstaff's lips.

"Go on," said the mercenary, "you must be parched."

Longstaff drained the contents and coughed again. He turned his head before spitting on the stone floor, to avoid provoking his captor more than necessary.

"Let's start with your real name and country, shall we?"

Longstaff shook his head.

"I understand," said Vischer, "you want to test me."

He retrieved Longstaff's chain from the brazier, the cool ends in his fingertips. The medallion itself shone a dull orange.

Longstaff shied away. Vischer pressed a filthy thumb against the wound in his shoulder, causing him to buck in agony.

"Hold still," whispered the mercenary. "Lower your head. It will go worse if you fight."

Vischer hung the chain about his neck. Only the ends rested against Longstaff's skin. Still, he could feel the flesh blistering along his collarbones. He ground his teeth, determined to hold this position for as long as necessary.

"Stand up straight," said Vischer.

Longstaff gave the tiniest shake of his head, felt flashes of pain on either side of his chest.

"Stand up, you bastard!" Vischer jammed the heel of one hand against Longstaff's brow with such brute force his head was thrown against the wall. Unconsciousness claimed him; blessed relief from the searing pain.

The darkness was not quite absolute. A torch had been left burning in a neighbouring room, a line of golden light shimmered beneath the door jamb. Slowly, shapes swam into focus. For several minutes, Longstaff stared at his own stockinged feet. Then at the beads of sweat running down the walls.

How badly had they hurt him? He had flopped forward when he lost consciousness; the medallion had not had time to embed itself in his flesh, he saw lines of puckered flesh over each of his collarbones, joining at his sternum in an ugly pink circle, Aurélie's profile just visible among the livid ridges. His fingertips found a lump the size of an egg on the back of his head, but it seemed the stitches in his shoulder had held. Nothing life-threatening.

Over the next few hours, soldiers in Guise livery turned the damp cellar into a bona fide chamber of torture. Longstaff watched in horror as they brought in pitchers of water and a selection of wedges and mallets. One man fixed an iron ring in the ceiling, as if Vischer had decided to risk the strappado, after all.

Longstaff leant against the wall, trying to relieve the pressure on his legs and shoulder simultaneously. He closed his eyes and slowed his breathing, knowing he would need his strength for Vischer's next visit.

The German mercenary treated him with the contempt all soldiers reserved for spies, but if he was still angry over the way he'd been tricked at Joinville, he gave no sign after that first visit. Nor did he appear to take pleasure in inflicting pain but went about his work with calm professionalism.

Longstaff rarely struggled against his bonds, except to try and win a few moments of relief for his shoulder. Nor did he attempt to reason with his tormentor. Her Grace, the Dowager Duchess of Joinville, may have been leagues away, but Longstaff could sense her presence; it was her iron will that animated Vischer and his comrades, her orders they treated as holy writ. It was her face Longstaff saw when Vischer questioned him, her clean hands, scrubbed each morning by a maidservant. Her fury at having been crossed.

"Talk," whispered Vischer, "your friend the fortune-teller has told us everything. The publisher, too." The mercenary rubbed thumb and forefinger together. "You'll talk in the end. Why make it hard on yourself?"

Longstaff shook his head, braced for the next lightning strike of pain. He had to stay focussed. He wasn't a fool. Of course he would tell them everything, but at a pace of his own choosing. Too much, too soon, and Vischer might grow lazy, hurt him for the sake of it. He had to keep the man honest, keep testing his professional expertise. But not too much. Too much and he risked provoking an outburst of frustrated bloodlust.

Longstaff slumped, exhausted, when Vischer left. Alone in the darkness, he could not help thinking of Walsingham's phial of poison, flung into the Channel on the crossing from England. The days of fear and darkness were taking their toll as much as the pain. He'd lost all track of time. His flesh shrank from the damp walls of the chamber. He flinched at every sound, whether the tiny patter of rat's feet or the distant barking of a dog. Something had changed in the house; Longstaff was deaf and dumb down here in its bowels, but he'd learned its moods. A strange hush had descended in the previous few hours, as if the building itself were holding its breath. The man who brought Longstaff his daily gruel and a cup of tepid water did not pause to taunt him in the normal way. His movements were more precise, whereas usually it was a matter of indifference to him whether a portion of the gruel slopped over the sides of the bowl.

Longstaff had been down here too long. The sound he dreaded most, of footsteps in the adjoining room, had become the one he most looked forward to; he had nothing left to tell his captors, no way of satisfying them except with agony. He had revealed everything he knew, about Walsingham and the imaginary Gospel, about Sir Nicholas Bacon's involvement, the appearance of Leicester's assassin in the woods west of Joinville. He'd told Vischer about his childhood, his father's execution, his childhood spent on the Baltic Coast, and the years fighting for the mercenary general Il Medeghino in Italy. There was nothing left – even Aurélie had been laid bare for the mercenary's inspection. Longstaff took another nervous inventory of his injuries. The mercenary had refrained from breaking any major bones. Longstaff still had both eyes; he might lose the hearing in one ear, having been held under water too long, but the other still worked. Nothing troubled him as much as his thirst. Perhaps Vischer lacked the authority to inflict permanent damage. Or was it another of his tricks?

Vischer was a soldier. A man who understood the limits of human endurance, a skilled interrogator, who would know – please God – when his victim had nothing left to give.

Footsteps. Longstaff struggled to stand up straight, manacled hands at his sides. A soldier on parade as the door swung open. He squinted against the sudden flood of light, heard a muffled curse. It wasn't Vischer's voice.

"My God, Longstaff, what have they done to you?"

Nostredame.

"If I'd known you were coming, I'd have cleaned up."

The prophet was escorted by two soldiers. One released Longstaff from his manacles while Nostredame swept various, hideous instruments from the trestle table.

"Bring him here."

The soldiers lifted Longstaff onto the table.

"He needs fresh air," said Nostredame.

"No chance," the soldier dashed Longstaff's sudden hope of a miraculous reversal in their circumstances.

"What's happening?" he asked.

"Vischer has given me permission to treat your injuries."

"No sport to be had in executing a corpse?"

Nostredame offered a grim smile. "His orders were to keep you whole. The injuries he's inflicted are superficial. The problem is the wound in your shoulder. Can't you smell it?"

Longstaff knew better than to risk shaking his head. "Can't smell a damn thing down here. I'm glad to see you've fared better."

The old man shrugged. "There's nothing they don't already know about me."

"Nothing they don't know about me, either," said Longstaff. "Not anymore."

Nostredame rapped out a series of commands. He wanted fresh water, fresh linens, medical equipment and a series of potions and lotions. One soldier left the chamber, the other began to sweep the flagstones.

"Don't worry," said Nostredame, "it's not for your benefit."

He seemed to forget Longstaff's presence then, except in so far as his body presented a series of problems he needed to solve. The Englishman was washed from head to toe in fresh water. Nostredame cut his hair and beard – a precaution against lice, reminding Longstaff of the story he'd told Anthony Bacon just a few short weeks ago in London. His fingers were reset and splinted, a poultice applied to the back of his head, an ugly yellow salve to his burns, all before the prophet examined the principal source of concern.

"This may hurt a bit."

The words came out automatically, as if addressed to a normal patient rather than a man who'd been repeatedly tortured over a period of days. Longstaff opened his mouth to laugh. Nostredame thrust a piece of leather between his teeth. "Bite on this."

Longstaff heard the scrape of scissors, one blade against the other. He had no idea whether Nostredame was cutting cloth or dead flesh. The pain came later, as he listened to the old man offering up a silent prayer of thanks.

Longstaff was still unbound the next time he regained his senses. Very carefully, he sat up on the table; someone had put him in a fresh shirt and his own trousers, brushed and smoked since he'd seen them last. His wound had been re-dressed and bandaged. There was still pain, but localised, reduced to a dull thud rather than a constant roar that ran through his whole body and robbed him of the ability to concentrate. He knew at once that Nostredame must have given him something. The room had been swept and sluiced with water. The flagstones still gleamed at the edges, though they'd had time to dry in the centre. Four torches burned in the room, one on each wall, together with long sticks of incense.

Nostredame sat at a table set with fruit and a jug of weak ale.

"Come and eat," he indicated the chair opposite, "we don't have much time before the cardinal arrives."

Longstaff rubbed bloodshot eyes. "He's here?"

"I haven't seen him. My quarters are more comfortable than yours, but I'm still kept under guard, only allowed out to exercise my skills as a healer. The cardinal has not deigned to visit; more interested in you, it seems."

Fearful of aggravating his wound, Longstaff used his left hand to lift the beer. Two broken fingers stuck straight out from the glass. His head was pounding, and the few pieces of fruit he managed sat heavy in his shrunken stomach.

"Jean sold us out," said Nostredame.

"You don't say."

"For a patent – exclusive bookseller to the House of Guise. And because he didn't want to miss out on the profits from my latest, sensational work."

Soldiers appeared. Nostredame rose at their signal, dropping a light hand on Longstaff's shoulder before he left.

"I'm sorry," he said. "Coming here was my idea."

Longstaff looked straight ahead, unable to suppress a shudder as the soldiers re-fastened the manacle around his ankle. They were kinder this time, running out a sufficient length of chain so he could remain sitting.

Charles, Cardinal of Lorraine, was forced to stoop as he came in through the low door. Hairs rose on the back of Longstaff's neck. Previously, he'd only seen the man from a distance. The cardinal was no longer dressed in his fine robes of office, nor was he surrounded by the usual cortege of hangers-on, but still seemed perfectly at ease. He walked across the room with no hint of fastidiousness, a pair of wooden overshoes his only concession to the surroundings.

"Matthew Longstaff, I believe?"

Longstaff said nothing. The cardinal took a seat, fingers laced beneath his chin.

"My brother, Francois, was murdered near here, did you know? Cut down by a Huguenot assassin. Odd, don't you think?"

"What?"

"That God should have brought me back here, at the start of our great enterprise."

"The start of a war."

The cardinal spoke firmly, but with no trace of impatience. "The war's been raging for years already. My intention is to end it."

Longstaff shook his head. "Tens of thousands will die. Men with families and lives of their own, who only want to be left in peace."

"Your Queen Elizabeth has no heirs. Even if she isn't carried off by disease or chance, how much longer do you think the English will suffer themselves to be ruled by a woman? War against England will reunify France, remove Elizabeth from the throne and see her replaced with a Catholic monarch – my niece, as it happens. England's support for the rebellion in the Netherlands will evaporate. The Huguenot cause will wither and die, reduced to an easily contained rump in Switzerland, and life will return to its proper rhythms."

He treated Longstaff to a mocking smile. "Don't you want to know how I can be so certain of the future? It's certainly not from listening to Nostredame. Originally, before word reached me of a man who claimed he could imitate the astrologer with perfect felicity, my intention was merely to silence Nostredame. I asked him to pen a few verses but didn't press when he refused. I wouldn't have used them anyway. He knows Catherine, you see, and might have found a way to let her know he was writing under duress."

Longstaff was painfully aware of how closely those bright eyes were watching him.

"It's you, Matthew Longstaff," continued the cardinal, "you're the reason I feel so sure of success. Your arrival here is proof that God continues to smile on the true Church. I have no idea whether or not the Duke of Norfolk is Catholic – he's entirely loyal to your heretic queen, as far as I'm aware – the rumour of a lost Gospel never even reached me until today. The reason I had Durant abducted is quite unrelated to the games your statesmen are playing and yet his disappearance was treated in England as evidence that the Duke of Norfolk is a traitor. And who does Sir Nicholas Bacon chose to send to conduct his investigations in France? You, Matthew Longstaff. Surely even you can see; a stroke of fortune like that can only be God's work. An unmistakable sign that our enterprise has His blessing."

"What are you talking about?" Longstaff's hands began to shake, not from anger, but from the effort of supporting himself at the table. Exhaustion was slowly reclaiming him, drawing dark curtains across his eyes.

"You've gone quite pale," observed the cardinal. "I have no desire to overtax your strength. Rest, Longstaff, gather your powers. You still have a vital role to play."

The cardinal was already at the door. "I sent your letter, by the way. I thought you'd want to know. Not the one Nostredame wrote to Catherine, of course; that one I burned. But yours, to your beloved wife, carrying news that the Earl of Leicester tried to have you killed. It will help our cause admirably – sowing and deepening the divisions among Elizabeth's chief advisors."

The guards did not chain him by the wrists again. Longstaff lay on the hard floor, eyes closed, the darkness tinged a dull red by the torchlight, happy in the knowledge that his captors believed they knew everything. His torments were over for the moment. Men moved round him, though none tried to rouse him until Nostredame reappeared.

"Can you move?"

Longstaff kept his eyes closed while Nostredame gave him water and changed the dressing on his shoulder.

"Thank you."

"For what?" the prophet sounded furious, "I feel like a farmer, fattening a prize animal for slaughter. What did he want?"

The cardinal? Aurélie would have called him a man without a soul. Right now, Longstaff would have given his own just to hear her voice.

"For a man of God," he said, "the cardinal seems a poor Christian."

Longstaff did not hear the astrologer's reply. He'd fallen asleep again, a deep, dreamless sleep under the influence of whatever sleeping draft Nostredame had mixed with the water.

Chapter 28

DURANT

Love of the son, that his life be spared,
Clasp'd jewelled hands around the sea God's staff,
Made war on those who called her Serpent's slave.
Or were destroyed, abandoned, forgotten…

Nothing as dangerous as hope. Nothing as likely to make a man snatch defeat from the jaws of victory. Gaetan Durant stared at the two wooden cups, lined up on the table in front of him. When Vincent visited in the evenings, he always took the cup on the right and left the other for Durant.

Nearly always.

Durant resisted the urge to pull one cup closer, push the other further away. He removed his doublet and placed it on the table beside him over a pile of torn paper.

Come. Now. Before Jean-Paul returns. Vincent's partner had left this morning before dawn, for his weekly visit to the nearest town. He usually returned an hour or two after sunset.

Durant was committed. He'd deliberately finished the last of his water ration just a few minutes earlier. He could still lick the inside of the cup, of course. But then what? The dose was insufficient to kill. He'd ground the belladonna root into a fine powder, left it to dry throughout the morning, then mixed it with sap from the same plant and smeared the sticky paste inside one cup, into tiny scratches he'd made with his fingernails. It would be several minutes before Vincent's eyes grew accustomed to the dim light in the cabin. There was almost nothing to see. But the taste? The stuff Vincent drank was rot-gut, powerful enough to hide most sins.

Durant sat quietly, a length of chain piled in his lap and his eyes on the shackle around his ankle. He'd fashioned cloth pads from the hem of his doublet, but the skin above and below the heavy iron ring was a mess of bloody scabs.

Vincent appeared in the doorway. "Contemplating your past? Or your future?"

His eyes traced their usual pattern – Durant, shackle, bolt, fireplace, window – he spat his toothpick on the floor, then padded into the room on silent feet. He was an animal. A predator who would amputate a finger just to make a point. Durant felt a sudden spike of terror. Of all the half-baked plans…

Vincent was too strong, too quick. Why hadn't Durant just prepared a lethal draft, as he'd first intended? He could have made himself comfortable on the floor, his face in the solitary patch of sunlight. For centuries, belladonna had been used to relieve pain. Symptoms varied from person to person, but Durant was a skilled herbalist; no reason his death couldn't have been accompanied by gentle visions of a better world.

Now, if he failed, there would be no quick and merciful death. Only bloody agony over a period of days and weeks.

He forced himself to smile. Moving with care, he lifted his doublet and revealed the pile of torn paper below.

"Nostredame's correspondence."

Vincent smiled, as if this tiny act of defiance made perfect sense. "Don't worry," he said. "Letters go missing all the time. The world is an imperfect place."

He used his thumb to knock the plug from the wineskin, poured generous measures into the two cups. "After all these weeks together, I feel oddly moved by your predicament. I wanted you to know, in the letter I sent with your verses, I advised my master you should be kept alive."

He took the cup on the left, spinning the liquid in lazy circles. Durant raised his own cup in a bitter toast. The liquor burned his throat.

"You have valuable skills," added Vincent before drinking. "That's what I wrote, though it's only half the story."

He frowned, turned his head and spat on the floor. Durant held his breath.

"I'm disappointed in you, doctor," said Vincent. "I can't abide a dirty cup."

He produced a rag from his shirt, wiping his cup clean before pouring again. "Cleanliness is next to Godliness."

Durant put his own cup to bloodless lips and drained the contents.

Vincent took a good, long swallow before pulling his chair closer, forcing Durant to meet his eyes.

"Don't tell me you're not curious. I won't believe it. How often does it happen that men like you and I have the chance to shape history?"

Durant said nothing. He was struggling to control his expression. How much of the toxin had trickled down Vincent's throat? How much had been absorbed into the soft membranes of his mouth?

"You're quiet. I understand the waiting must be hard, but Jean-Paul will be back soon. We'll know then, one way or the other."

Durant watched him closely. In all the weeks he'd known him, Vincent had never shown any ill-effects from the spirits he drank so freely.

"You think I'm a monster. What kind of man could want to start a war, play a part in so much death and misery?" He laughed. "They're peasants, they'll die anyway. Carried off by plague or musket ball? What's the difference?"

Durant held out his cup for more. He might have imagined it; a slight tremor as Vincent poured.

"The verses you wrote, doctor. Men will run into the English guns with your words on their lips. Doesn't the thought stir you at all?"

Vincent loosened his collar, then sat back in his chair with an odd smile. "The evenings are growing warmer. Your verses will infect the people like a summer fever." His pupils had grown huge. He blinked, as if forcing himself to concentrate. "Water."

Durant gripped a handful of chain and swung at Vincent's head. Too soon. The fox half-ducked the blow, pushed himself away from the table. His chair fell with a crash. If he escaped beyond the chain's reach…

Durant threw himself across the table, wrapped his arms round Vincent's legs. The fox collapsed. Durant on top of him, held by the chain as Vincent tried to crawl away. He saw the knife at Vincent's side, fingers fumbled at the unfamiliar sheath. The fox was trying to turn. Durant plunged the blade between his shoulder blades, struck ribs, stabbed and stabbed again.

It was still light. Still time before Jean-Paul returned. Durant searched for the key. Nothing in Vincent's belt or around his neck. He ripped open the man's shirt. Nothing. He lashed out in fury, struck Vincent so hard the eyes rolled up until only the whites showed. He searched again, with the same miserable result. An hour. One solitary hour to get free of here. Durant used Vincent's shirt to wipe the warm blood from his hands and face. He picked up the knife and started digging at the bolt in the central beam.

A nightingale began to sing. *Free as a bird.* Hidden in the gathering dusk. Durant's mind was playing tricks. He thought he heard hoofbeats. He couldn't hear a thing above the frantic chiselling, hacking, sawing. Where was the damn key? How far would he get hauling this length of chain? Durant blinked sweat from his eyes. *Focus on the task at hand.* He thought of Longstaff's advice. *Empty your mind of everything but the fight. Fight to win. If you fight for any other reason, you will die.*

Durant fought the wood. He pushed the point of Vincent's knife as far as it would go, twisted with all his strength, bored holes around the bolt. One at a time. The wood was dry, the steel was strong.

Time was short. He heaved on the chain. The bolt held firm. Too soon. One more hole in the beam. He pulled, felt the bolt move, sharp metal grooves tear at the dry wood. Then it came, sent him flying back across the room. He gathered the chain in his arms and staggered outside, lips pressed tight against euphoria. A stiff wind set his clothes fluttering. The sun was a great ball of fire disappearing in the west. It would be dark in another few minutes. Durant hurried to the storehouse, past the fire-pit where his two jailors cooked their meals, where they took turns watching him through the night, one pair of eyes always fixed on his cabin door.

Two straw pallets inside. Vincent's leather bag at the foot of one. Durant dumped the contents on the floor – spare items of clothing, a needle and thread, tinderbox, a purse full of coins. Their store of food was stacked inside the door beside a small water-butt. A supply of ink and paper on a shelf above. And there, hanging on a nail. The key. Durant's fingers closing on it when he heard a horse above the whistling wind.

Jean-Paul. Even with Vincent's knife, Durant knew he was no match for the mastiff. He lacked the courage even for a surprise attack. He'd seen no musket or pistol in the storehouse; it was too dark to find one now. Durant put the key in his mouth, gathered the chain into his arms, link by link, and slipped out of the storehouse. He lay in darkness, in the shadow of the low building, watching Jean-Paul ride into view and giving silent thanks his jailors had never provided him with clean linen. His clothes were the colour of mud, his feet were black and his hands still covered in blood.

How long until the mastiff realised something was wrong? Durant slipped the key in the shackle's lock. Jean-Paul reined the horse to a halt, eyes on the open cabin door.

Durant turned the key. The shackle opened with a sigh, masked by the wind and the noise of Jean-Paul's dismount. The mastiff approached the cabin warily, hand on the hilt of his sword, then rushed inside when he saw his friend. He never looked back or he would have seen Durant running. The noise he made was inhuman.

Durant swung the door shut, rammed the deadbolt home.

What now?

Jean-Paul crashed against the door, knocking Durant off balance. The walls shook as he charged again. Durant struggled for breath, flinching at the stream of mangled oaths. He knew the cabin. The windows were barred, the door reinforced. The walls were made of seasoned timber. Vincent had chosen his prison well, but it would not hold Jean-Paul. Not for long.

Durant ran through the darkness. The sun had disappeared, the moon not yet risen. He dropped to his knees in the storehouse, fingers scrabbling through Vincent's possessions, searching by touch for the tinderbox, heart racing in wild counterpoint to Jean-Paul's attempts at escape.

Boom.

Durant shuddered. He clasped the tinderbox in one hand, half a dozen tapers in the other. Steady, now. He cupped his hands against the wind. The flame caught at once.

Death by burning, flesh black as coal at the centre of a bonfire. Durant had seen men burned at the stake, seen them struggle at the top of tall pyres, fat and blood drip from the roasting bodies. He flung taper after burning taper into the thatch.

Durant stood waiting for the first flames to appear. It didn't take long. He imagined Jean-Paul looking up, the sudden terror as he made sense of this new sound – the snap and crackle of fire. The mastiff threw himself against the door with redoubled strength. The cabin shook. Durant crouched on the threshold, Vincent's knife in one hand, ready to lunge if the timbers blew apart. The fire spread like plague, whipped into an inferno by the wind. Step by slow step, Durant was forced back by the heat. When he drew breath, stabbing pains ran the length of his throat; the air already robbed of its life-giving qualities. His hair began to singe.

Jean-Paul's efforts to escape became weaker. The man was evil, a sadist, but no one deserved to die like this. Durant hoped the thick coils of smoke claimed him before the flames.

The roof caved in several minutes later. Durant crouched lower, knuckles white on the knife, terrified of what might emerge from the breach. A blistered monster, more dead than alive, come to smother him in a final, charred embrace.

He must have slept. He woke on the grass, knife still clasped in one hand. Low flames danced across the black remains of the cabin. Durant scrambled to his feet, but there was no sign of movement. No sign of life. He averted his eyes, stumbled bleary-eyed towards the storehouse. *What now?* Strip naked. He drank from the water-butt, scrubbed at his body with a sliver of soap from among Vincent's possessions. How long before people arrived to investigate the thick column of smoke? Durant found a shirt, a pair of woollen tights and Vincent's good cloak. No shoes or boots, but there was money. He could buy what he needed as soon as he reached a town.

He found Jean-Paul's horse grazing in the meadow, saddlebags still strapped to its rump. Durant fumbled at the clasps. Food. A good cheese, cured meat. A letter addressed to Vincent. Durant broke the seal and read with growing dread.

Vincent,

It seems we have further need of your charge after all.

In a previous letter, I referred to the man called Longstaff. Already recognised in Italy as an enemy of the Roman Church, he was recently seen in Paris with the English ambassador and is a known associate of at least one member of the heretic queen's Privy Council.

We have him in our power and propose to stage an entertainment. An assassination, accompanied by sundry effects. Longstaff will play the role of villain, sent by England to murder France's foremost astrologer.

To maximise our advantage, I require six further quatrains from our mutual friend, in which Nostredame appears to foretell the time and manner of his own demise. At whose hand, by whose order, and to what foul purpose. The time has come to craft a legend.

Apply yourself to this task with your habitual zeal and resourcefulness, and continue in the affections of...

C

Chapter 29

Longstaff drifted in and out of darkness on the first two days of their journey from Orléans, heading south and west along the Loire in a flat-bottomed boat. Then, sometime during the second night, he was moved to a carriage, the footwell between the benches covered by a trestle and topped with a straw-pallet, making a bed long and wide enough to accommodate him. At dawn, he propped himself on one elbow, staring glumly across a landscape of endless fields.

He could not see enough to know how many people rode alongside. From their formation, he judged it must be at least sixteen. The flanks were guarded by Rudi Vischer and six of his men, professionals who carried short, double-edged swords and long pistols in the manner of light cavalry, any trace of Guise colours removed from their hard-wearing boots and jerkins.

The men nearer the carriage were mounted on finer animals, wore velvet hose and doublets slashed to reveal brightly coloured silks in the lining. The cardinal's swaggering lackeys – grim-faced beneath the ribbons and jewels, naked blades in iron rings on their belts. Unlike the soldiers, whose practical garments drew attention to Guise virtues, these men were dressed to highlight the terrible fate which awaited any man or woman foolish enough to cross the family.

Longstaff recognised their leader from the Queen Mother's ball at the Palais de Justice in Paris – Jean Rastignac, himself a bastard clipping from the family tree. The big, cold-eyed killer rode shoulder to shoulder with his master, the two of them on a pair of matched, white stallions. The cardinal had set aside his robes of office in favour of a suit of dark cloth. Rastignac wore his distinctive codpiece and ruff, but there was nothing decorative about the great-sword tied slantways across his back, nor the wheel-lock musket hanging from his saddle.

Longstaff's arm began to ache from the effort of supporting his weight. A water-skin lay beside him on the makeshift bed. He took a long drink, before falling back on the pallet, lulled to sleep by the steady drumroll of hooves on hardpacked earth.

He did not wake again until the carriage stopped, sun framed in the right-hand window, huge and orange as it prepared to dip below the horizon. He opened the door and climbed down, putting one hand against the woodwork to steady himself. The doors of the carriage were plain, no sign anywhere that it belonged to such an illustrious figure.

Nostredame climbed down from the bench-seat.

"How do you feel?"

"Stiff. Sore. Better."

Even in the failing light, it was clear to Longstaff that he wasn't the only one affected by the trials of the previous weeks. The fortune-teller looked grey, gaunt under the week-old beard, with dark rings beneath his eyes.

The soldiers made camp, established a perimeter, set guards and saw to the animals. The lackeys prepared the evening meal, laughing and joking among themselves beside a fresh-kindled fire. They were loud and coarse, and appeared to share a fondness for boasting of the poor regard in which they held their own lives. In a hundred different ways, however – the way they moved, the shape of their hands and shoulders, the quality of their weapons and the fact of who they served – it was clear these were no mere roaring boys. Every one of them a skilled and merciless killer.

Rastignac and the cardinal emerged from a nearby stand of trees, the former carrying a short-handled shovel and enclosed chair with a hole in the seat.

"There he is," the cardinal seemed to be enjoying himself, "the agent of my destiny! Have you worked it out yet, Longstaff? Men will talk of you in the same breath as Brutus and Cassius."

He laughed at Longstaff's expression. "Too perfect. That you, of all people, should fall into my hands."

Rastignac exchanged his shovel for a chain; one end went round Longstaff's ankle, the other round Nostredame's. He drove a heavy metal spike through a link in the middle to make them fast. Given time, Longstaff could have worked it free, but not in silence. Not surrounded by sixteen fighting men.

Once again, Nostredame retreated into his own private world, staring into the campfire with glazed eyes. Longstaff did not manage to exchange a few words with him until the small convoy stopped at noon the following day, when the astrologer applied another thick layer of salve to the burns on his neck and chest.

"How does it feel?"

"Does it matter?" said Longstaff, provoked by the prophet's air of calm, "they're going to kill us."

Nostredame offered Longstaff one of his infuriating smiles. "Am I right in thinking you've never seen the orient?"

"What?"

"It's written in your destiny," said the astrologer. "On your body, actually; the nest of moles on your chest. No chance of you dying before you've been east of the Bosphorus."

Longstaff just stared.

Nostredame approached the cardinal. "I wonder whether I might ride in the carriage this afternoon."

He held up both hands, wincing in pain as he tried and failed to straighten crooked fingers. "Two and a half days on that bench-seat have triggered an attack of dropsy."

The Cardinal of Lorraine shook his head.

"I can ride," interrupted Longstaff. "Let the old man go in the carriage, if he wants."

He was glad when the cardinal agreed, though it meant riding with his hands bound to the saddle. Longstaff tried to concentrate on the sun's warmth, the sound of birdsong and the glorious fresh air. He refused to believe this was resignation, more a realistic assessment of his position. He was gathering his strength, certain he'd need it soon.

Why hadn't the cardinal simply killed him? Nostredame, too. They weren't heading back to Joinville, their route was south and west, moving fast. Longstaff stared at the cardinal's straight back. The man was clever and vain, that much had been clear at the Queen Mother's ball in Paris. Above all, he was arrogant, convinced that his own interests and those of France were the same.

Longstaff watched, half-hypnotised by the cardinal's precise gestures. Rastignac leaned close to his master, interrupting with a question, prompting another low volley of instructions. Longstaff became convinced they were plotting his death, a pair of calculating impresarios, excited by their own native flare for a well-judged entertainment.

His blood ran cold, as piece after piece of the cardinal's plan seemed to fall into place. The eager veneration accorded to Nostredame in his native land, above all by the Queen Mother. Longstaff's own presence in France on the orders of men close to Queen Elizabeth. The cardinal knew everything. He knew about Longstaff's meeting with the English ambassador Throckmorton and the merchant Palavicino, about his presence at the Palais de Justice on the evening before Catherine de Medici left Paris. He knew that Longstaff's wife was currently lodged with England's Lord Chancellor, that the two of them had once served a clandestine group of scholars, regarded as heretics and traitors by the Roman Catholic Church. It was more than enough to convince most Frenchman that Longstaff was an assassin, sent by Queen Elizabeth to kill Nostredame. Didn't the prophet's latest verses identify Elizabeth as the Antichrist? Of course, she'd want him dead.

Rastignac hauled on the lead rope. Hands bound, Longstaff nearly fell as his horse skittered level with the cardinal's mount.

"Leave us, Jean."

The lackey passed the rope to his employer, then wheeled and joined the press of men about the carriage.

"Rastignac grew up in this part of France," said the cardinal, "he assures me you'll reach your destination tomorrow."

The rope lay loose across the neck of his horse. The arrogant bastard hadn't even bothered to take hold of it. For a moment, Longstaff felt tempted to spur for the treeline. How far would he get before the soldiers ran him down?

"We've given the location considerable thought," continued the cardinal. "We need privacy, of course, but a ready audience near at hand. People who'll talk, with access to a printing press. And not too far from the Royal Progress, currently strung out along the road between Périgueux and Bordeaux. That's where I'm heading," he smiled, "I mean to give myself the pleasure of seeing Catherine's face when she learns her precious fortune-teller has been murdered."

The cardinal raised a hand, bringing the convoy to a halt.

"Get Nostredame. I want them both to hear this."

Vischer pulled the astrologer from the carriage and escorted him forward.

"Catherine de Medici is expecting me," said the cardinal, "which means it's time to say farewell."

He paused, as if expecting a reaction. Nostredame remained silent.

"I hope to arrive before she receives your final quatrains, in which you predict the time and manner of your own death." The cardinal forced a laugh. "You and Durant are the poets, of course, but I did take the liberty of offering some suggestions: *But though my life's thread be cut / With English steel, still I will remain. / To guide the fleur de Llys, protect it from / the perfidious plots of the Rose.* What do you think?"

"As you said," replied Nostredame, "you're no poet."

The cardinal smiled. "If you truly possessed the gifts you claim, you'd have divined my intentions by now. You should be grateful, you know – I'll see you remembered as a martyr, have your body paraded round France as a holy relic. Not many charlatans can look forward to such an afterlife."

He looked at Rudi Vischer.

"Your men will come with me. You're to remain with my irregular bodyguard, under Rastignac's command. When it's done, return to Joinville and tell my mother what you've seen."

Vischer saluted. "As you command, your Eminence."

Finally, the cardinal gazed with obvious affection at his lackeys.

"You know what to do?"

The men grinned.

"Until we meet again," he wheeled his horse before galloping away, Vischer's five men whipping their mounts to keep pace with him.

"Still think we're getting out of this?" muttered Longstaff.

Nostredame paid him no attention. Possibly, he hadn't heard over the shouts and whoops of Rastignac's men. The reduced party moved on. The trees grew closer, in eloquent echo of Longstaff's own lowering mood. Great oaks, hazel and hawthorn, their trailing boughs entwined, rough ragged moss spread everywhere. A single idea dominated Longstaff's thoughts – at the very moment when Aurélie learned of his death, she would hear him described as a murderer. Longstaff pictured her, a lock of hair tucked behind one ear, her delicate wrists, the skin so translucent he could trace the blue veins beneath. He thought of the spirit which animated her, the effort she'd made to conceal how ill at ease she felt at Martlesham. An act of love – hers for him – when he'd always thought that he was the provider. Walls and a roof were easy, an excuse for avoiding the harder task of allowing her to think what she wanted, say what she wanted, go where she wanted. Aurélie had let him believe a fantasy. For love? What did stone walls and a roof have to do with love, if she was unhappy there?

Chapter 30

AURÉLIE

Aurélie hurried through Holborn. On Turnmill Lane, just before the infamous brothel, she saw a wine merchant forced to consume his own wares, gallon by gallon. From the shouts, he'd been caught adding beetroot and pine resin to cheap German wine, passing it off as Cretan retsina. Aurélie pushed through the press of men and women. One smashed open a new keg, men fell to their knees, lapped wine straight from the gutter. Aurélie did not stop to watch.

A messenger had arrived at York House that morning. At last, another letter had come from Matthew. Dee and Walsingham were waiting for her at the house in Clerkenwell. Aurelie had planted a loud kiss on the young messenger's forehead and laughed to see him blush, thrown a cloak over her light dress, only stopping to say goodbye to Anthony and Francis.

"No lessons today. I'll be back in time for your story this evening."

"On you honour?"

"Cross my heart."

She smiled as she cut through Jerusalem Passage – it held no terrors for her, hadn't she once walked the streets of Florence disguised as a serving girl, with contraband documents in her skirts? – then circled St. James's Church on her way to the Close. The entrance to the cul-de-sac still had a habit of taking her by surprise.

The door swung open the moment she knocked.

"The master is expecting you. In the library."

The house was quiet. Aurélie saw no sign of Dee's wife as she climbed the stairs. She entered the library without knocking and found Dee fast asleep in his favourite chair.

Usually it stood in the window, to take advantage of the natural light and offer a view of the Fleet. Now it stood near the door, beneath a single candle on a tall candelabra. A book lay open on a low table. Aurélie crept closer and thought she detected a faint aroma; the crisp, clear wine of Northern Germany. She smiled; for all the man's sense of destiny, he still found time to appreciate the finer things in life.

Aurélie did not wake him immediately. He'd cleared his desk of its usual paraphernalia. Her heart fluttered when she saw her own profile captured in wax. Matthew had sealed the envelope with the medallion she'd given him. Aurélie took a moment to steady herself – what if it was bad news? She ran her fingertips along the rows and rows of books.

"Something interesting?"

She jumped. "All your books are interesting. You have a weakness for authors with secrets."

Dee laughed. "Authors always pretend to have secrets. It's how they make a living."

"You moved your chair."

"A headache, which grows ferocious in direct sunlight." Dee indicated the desk. "I suggest you begin."

"Walsingham?"

"He'll be here soon."

She caressed the seal before breaking it, while Dee took up his book and continued reading. The last time a letter had come from Matthew, he'd left her to decipher the text alone. He showed no sign of extending the same courtesy now.

Aurélie removed three sheets of paper, already anticipating Matthew's affectionate greeting. He was safe. He hadn't yet found Durant. Aurélie read on with growing alarm, thoughts galloping ahead of her ability to decipher the text.

Elizabeth's enemies were not wasting their time pursuing a fictitious book. It was a plot, greater and more treacherous than anything Walsingham had dreamed of...

Aurélie took a deep breath, forced herself to start again. *Step by step.* Sir Nicholas Bacon had shown her a letter in Norfolk's own hand, in which the duke explained that he'd established an illegal printing press in London, as per the cardinal's instructions, and was ready to begin distribution as soon as he received a copy of the fifth Gospel.

Could Walsingham have forged it? The intelligencer was many things, but Aurélie didn't think he would have gone so far. What then? Two separate plots, with the Guise family sitting at the heart of both?

She turned to Dee. "When do you expect Walsingham? He needs to see this."

"At the moment, I imagine our mutual friend is at Whitehall with Sir Nicholas Bacon. The two of them will be fine-tuning their case."

"He's not coming? You said he was coming."

"Two barristers," continued Dee, "I fear the queen will suffer a veritable torrent of eloquence when they present their case against Norfolk tomorrow."

"Tomorrow?"

He nodded. "I cast the horoscope myself. A propitious day for startling revelations."

Aurélie stared at him. *The chair!* Positioned between her and the door.

"You wrote the letter."

Dee nodded. "But it was your idea. Don't you remember? You stood in this very house and told Walsingham that he needed cast-iron proof in Norfolk's own hand. I only need to see a sample of someone's writing before I can produce a perfect copy. Or, in this instance, an almost perfect copy – good enough to fool Walsingham, but it won't stand up to a proper examination."

"What have you done?"

"A favour for an old friend." He paused, a half-smile on his lips.

Tomorrow! The events played out in Aurélie's mind, figures moving back and forth like puppets. Norfolk would protest his innocence. He would be able to demonstrate that the letter was a forgery. Walsingham, Sir Nicholas and William Cecil were the obvious culprits, driven to seek the death of an innocent man by the unreasoning nature of their religious extremism. They would be destroyed, if not executed then certainly driven from court, stripped of wealth and titles, their wives and children reduced to penury.

Who stood to gain? This couldn't have been orchestrated from abroad; it was too subtle, betrayed such intimate knowledge of the principle players. Who could have got to Dee, as ardent an English patriot as she'd met? Aurélie's brain skipped across the possibilities.

"The Earl of Leicester," she said, "Robert Dudley is an old friend of yours?"

Dee nodded. "I tutored him when he was a boy, a fact which Walsingham should certainly have ferreted out. I can't imagine what Cecil was thinking – Walsingham's too green to play at this level," he chuckled, an old teacher reflecting on the achievements of a former pupil. "Dudley may look like a gypsy adventurer, but he's played with skill and patience."

Aurélie's mind raced. "You also wrote the original letter, persuading Walsingham there was a spy on the Privy Council?"

"As soon as Leicester discovered that Cecil and Walsingham were creating an intelligence network to rival his own. Did they really think he'd let such a threat to his authority go unchallenged?"

"That's what this is? A turf war?"

"Dudley would tell you that Cecil and his supporters are too cautious, putting the country at risk through their reluctance to act decisively. But at heart I believe you're right. A turf war, laced with personal animosity. He still hasn't forgiven Cecil for spreading rumours that he caused his wife's death. Tell me, Aurélie, I'm genuinely curious; what did you think when you first heard of Walsingham's scheme? You're an intelligent woman. You must have recognised how reckless they'd been. A lost Gospel of Jesus Christ, giving Peter and his successors absolute authority over doctrine?"

Aurélie tried to keep her face impassive. Inside, she burned. Dee was right. That had been her reaction exactly, but she'd allowed herself to forget, averted her eyes. Walsingham was a hater. Cecil had told him to find a traitor and Leicester had provided him with one – a secret Catholic whose exposure and execution would act as a rallying call to the faithful.

"You have to let me go." She held up Longstaff's letter. "There's more at stake than you or Leicester realise. If I don't get word to Walsingham, the Privy Council will be torn apart..."

Raising a hand, Dee produced a bell from beneath his robe. The noise brought his manservant.

"Nail the shutters."

Aurélie looked at him in horror. In one fell swoop, Leicester intended to eliminate his most powerful rivals at court – and leave England hopelessly exposed to its enemies in Europe. She launched into a description of the forces currently assembling on the continent.

"If you won't let me go, then at least take Matthew's letter to Leicester. He'll stop Walsingham himself, once he's read it."

Dee's eyes turned cold and hard. "You think I care for their squabbles? Let them fight. Some will fall, others rise."

Aurélie stared in disbelief. Dee ignored her, looking at the bookshelves weighed down with hundreds of tomes.

"In one of the houses given him by Elizabeth, Leicester has discovered a treasure. Nearly two thousand volumes hidden behind a false wall."

He paused while the servant hammered, waiting patiently as the bright sunlight disappeared plank by plank.

"She won't be getting out that way, sir."

Dee nodded in the gloom, lit only by the candle at his shoulder.

"Two thousand volumes, Aurélie," his voice loud now that the hammering had stopped, "I've held them in my hands. I've read the titles." He smiled. "Imagine what I might discover. Proof, perhaps, that this island is the last remaining fragment of Atlantis, the only trace which remained above the waves during the great flood. Leicester has no interest in these books. If I upset his plans now, he'll let them rot.

"Surely you can understand, Aurélie. Whoever wins this bout of petty politicking, it won't change anything. Their game will continue; we're already sunk too deep in error. But the books might help us begin again. There's a new land in the west. Virgin territory where a new Atlantis can be raised, a beacon to draw the poison from our own decayed world. What do the fates of a Walsingham or a Bacon matter when set against such a possibility!"

Aurélie stared at him, speechless. She could only watch as Dee rose to bid her farewell.

"At any rate, I promise you won't be harmed. Sit quietly. There's bread and water in the chest, candles to read by. You'll be released once your friends have committed their folly. My wife and her maidservant have gone into the country for a few days. The house stands alone, as you know, and the folk hereabouts give it a wide berth."

He smiled as he opened the door, letting the servant pass ahead of him onto the landing. "As you know, they hold me for a master of the dark arts."

Aurélie heard the key in the lock. For the count of ten, she simply stood and stared. Madness, every word he'd spoken, and yet so uncomfortably close to her own obsessions. She threw herself at the solid oak door; it wouldn't give in a week, and she had less than a day.

Chapter 31

Jean Rastignac moved with the ease of a man who knew these woods, leading his lackeys and their two prisoners from the narrow track into a wide and blasted clearing.

"This place has a reputation. People say men and women were sacrificed here, before priests came and chased the old gods away."

Looking round, Longstaff could believe it. Why else would nothing grow in the middle of such rich forest? It was as if the earth itself had been poisoned.

Rastignac dismounted, grabbed Longstaff by the elbow and pulled. Hands still bound, the Englishman landed on his shoulder, drawing laughter from the motley crew of lackeys.

"When I was a child," continued the mercenary leader, "my friends and I would challenge each other to come here. It was a test of courage. The very bravest," he raised an immodest finger to his own chest, "would spend a night among the pagan ghosts."

Longstaff followed the line of his outstretched arm, pointing at the treetops a hundred yards away. The clearing was big enough that he could see beyond them, to a distant smudge of smoke against the horizon.

"My home town," said Rastignac. "Years since I was last there, though I'm sure there are plenty who remember me. Simple folk – no university, no secret Huguenots, none of your educated, sceptical men who might ask too many questions. According to reports, my old neighbours have demonstrated their loyalty with unusual enthusiasm ever since Calvin's bastards started making war in France."

Rastignac's men did not hang on their leader's words. Some found shovels and began digging a pit in the centre of the clearing. Other set to work on the carriage, steadily reducing it to firewood. Two of Rastignac's lackeys moved on Longstaff. It was stupid – the number of men had nearly halved since the cardinal's departure, but the odds remained impossible – still, he clasped his bound hands in a double first and struck the first man in the solar plexus then swung behind and began to choke him.

"Release the prophet!"

"Or what?" inquired Rastignac.

Longstaff looked round. The lackeys had all stopped work. Vischer stood with a wheel-lock musket at his shoulder, muzzle trained on Longstaff. "Well?"

"Shoot him," said Rastignac.

"Which one?"

"Don't ask damn fool questions. You know which one."

Vischer pulled the trigger. Longstaff's hostage fell limp in his arms. The rest were on him in seconds. He couldn't fight, curled in a ball, forearms raised to protect his face. The thick leather coat absorbed some of the blows. They forced him down, laid two of the heavy carriage wheels across his back so he was pinned to the ground. It was as much as Longstaff could do to force air into his lungs.

The men returned to work without celebrating their victory or mourning their fallen comrade. Longstaff watched as they shored up the sides of the pit with planks taken from the carriage. One man fashioned a stake from the long axle. Longstaff looked sideways at Vischer. Was the soldier troubled by what he saw? Longstaff did not resist the next time two of Rastignac's men approached, nor when they fastened an iron collar around his neck and chained him to the stake.

His iron leash was three yard's long. Slowly, so as not to provoke his captors, Longstaff shuffled as far as he could towards the pit. It was roughly the length and width of a man. Two of the lackeys climbed in and smoothed the sides with their shovels. They jumped up and down, compressing the earth beneath their feet until it took on the qualities of stone.

*

Aurélie reviewed what she knew of Dee's house; an ancient, rambling pile. Irregular, each floor built by different hands at different times. Could she reach Dee's laboratory across the landing? He kept a store of chemicals there, volatile liquids, explosive powders. None of it any use while she was locked in here, surrounded by books.

Tomorrow the fledgling spy-master Walsingham would bring false accusations of treason against one of the most powerful men in England. Sir Nicholas Bacon would stand beside him. A turn of the wheel and Anne, Anthony and Francis would be stripped of past, present and future.

Aurélie still held Matthew's letter in one hand. There was no sound on the landing. Dee had been right about one thing; the games they played at court were pathetic. Constructing elaborate traps for one another, not to safeguard the realm or the queen, but for the sake of their own careers. They weren't worth saving. And yet they had to be saved.

Stupid, stupid, stupid. However ill-conceived, Walsingham's plan had still uncovered a plot, a combined Franco-Spanish army aimed at the southern beaches of England. If Leicester won and Cecil and Sir Nicholas were expelled from the council, she could imagine how that threat would be met – with mad, ignorant belligerence. And if Leicester lost? The invaders would reach England as Norfolk was being tried and the whole of the North up in arms.

Burn the books? That would get Dee's attention. Could she? Aurélie had seen a library go up in flames before and barely escaped with her life. Others had been less fortunate. She still remembered the smell of burning flesh, burning parchment, the terrified screams.

She paced the room like a caged beast, rattled the window shutters, released a yell of fear when hammering started on the far side. The servant again, nailing them from the outside.

What could she offer him? "Let me go. Cecil will reward you well."

His silence did not surprise her. The endless hammering drove her back from the window. Only now did she register the absence of Dee's book-binding tools. He'd prepared her prison carefully, clearing it of knives, scissors, glue.

Inertia was the enemy of inspiration. *Keep moving!* Aurélie sat at the desk and composed a plain English copy of Matthew's letter. A sheet of good quality paper, she folded it once and slipped it beneath the door.

"Dee," she yelled, "at least read it!"

Had he gone out? Was he hunkering over a bottle of wine in the parlour downstairs, trying to ignore her, too scared to breathe a word.

"At least have the courage to understand what you're risking."

She'd never thought of him as a coward before. It surprised her the label fit so neatly. Too scared to face her. Too scared to do away with her. How could they let her live? With all she knew, above all about Leicester's involvement?

She opened the chest. Just as Dee had promised; a pair of skinny candles, a loaf of bread and a jug of water.

Poison?

She forced the desk drawers, all empty. The candle flickered. Dee hadn't left a tinderbox. Aurélie took one of the sickly yellow candles from the chest, lit it from the milky-white stub of Dee's candle, wrinkled her nose as she watched the wick drown in a pool of spent wax. The candles Dee had left for her stank of cheap tallow. A surge of anger wrapped Aurélie's hands around the tall candlestick; she dragged it to Dee's desk, poured molten wax across the surface. A tiny act of rebellion which did nothing to improve her mood.

One candle – another still in the chest – five or six hours of light. Not enough to see her through until dawn. Aurélie stared at the nailed shutters; how would she even know when the sun rose over London? Was Dee hoping she'd be dead by then? Could he really have poisoned her food? She imagined him in the parlour below, waiting for the thud of her body as it struck the floor.

Aurélie lay on her back – the ceiling hardly visible by the light of the thin flame – and drifted awhile on thoughts of Matthew. How long until the first candle began to gutter? She felt an urge to sleep, let nature take its course, take Dee at his word. She would be released tomorrow, her friends ruined.

Aurélie raised herself on her elbows. *Think!* What would Matthew do? Kick the door down, gut Dee with a swipe of his sword. She didn't have his physical strength. What did she have? The ability to think logically, to ask questions of the shuttered window, the locked door, of Dee, who may or may not have been sitting in the parlour below. She would not eat or drink. She would not burn her jailor's books. What remained?

Secrets.

Carefully, Aurélie broke the final candle in half. Set the smaller piece aside, lit the longer one from the dying flame on Dee's desk and placed it upright in the pool of wax. All of London considered Dee a black magician. Where, then, were his secrets?

*

Longstaff inspected every inch of the chain, searching in vain for a weak link. He did not approach the wooden stake, reluctant to reveal his intentions – how deep was it buried? Given the chance, how long would it take him to dig it out of the earth with just his bare hands? Could Nostredame help?

The lackeys had not deemed it necessary to chain the old man. Longstaff found he could hardly blame them for the oversight. Nostredame sat near the pit, eyes closed, hands folded neatly in his lap, a strange expression on his face, as if he'd already resigned himself to whatever fate the cardinal had planned.

Had fear robbed the old man of his wits? He wouldn't move, didn't look up even when dusk fell and torches were lit in a wide circle around them, did not resist when men seized him by the arms and hauled him to his feet.

"Michel?" Longstaff was amazed to find his own cheeks wet with tears. The lackeys did not have to force Nostredame into the pit. Longstaff screamed at him to run or fight. He wanted to bid the old man farewell, but the words turned to ashes in his mouth. He could only stare as Nostredame lay down, lips moving as if in silent prayer. Longstaff lost sight of him then. He watched the cardinal's men climb out of the pit. They seemed as shocked as Longstaff by Nostredame's complicity in his own terrible fate, until Rastignac broke the spell: "Least he's gentleman enough to make the job an easy one."

The men chuckled as they lowered planks into the pit – half a coffin for the most famous astrologer in Europe.

"Probably thinks it's just so he can have a rest," added Rastignac, tapping a temple with his forefinger.

Two men climbed into the pit, stamping on the planks to fix them in the earth, a finger's breadth above Nostredame's nose.

"No," Longstaff pulled at his chain. The lackeys had done their work too well. He turned his back, listening to clods of earth shovelled over the wooden planks. He glared at Vischer. "At least kill him first."

The German soldier did not reply.

"Then let me kill him, if you lack the stomach. There's no need for such cruelty."

"If he says another word," called Rastignac, "you have my permission to gag him."

Vischer took a step nearer Longstaff, though he was careful to stay outside the range of the chain. "Michel de Nostredame is a false prophet."

"Vischer, please."

"Not another word."

From the remains of the carriage, the cardinal's lackeys built a great bonfire. Longstaff sat on the earth, damp with evening dew, watching in silent horror as they broke open wine-skin after wine-skin. They danced on Nostredame's tomb. One man drew a pentagon in the earth. They filled the points with ash from the fire, then took turns spitting in the centre.

"It has to look right," a voice reached Longstaff from the darkness. Vischer. The soldier sat away to one side, musket on his knees. He gestured: "Burying him alive, the pentagram, this is the second part of the mission Elizabeth gave you – not just to kill him but to acquire his powers through witchcraft."

Longstaff did not reply. The dancing grew wilder, a cloud of dust lifted from the floor of the clearing. He felt it in his eyes, between his teeth, beneath his fingernails. Drying his throat and blurring the edges of the flames.

A man appeared from the eddying cloud.

One more step, thought Longstaff. One step closer and you're mine. Vischer sent the drunken lackey away. The fire began to die. One by one, Rastignac's men tossed their empty wineskins on the embers. They settled down to sleep, until only Longstaff and Vischer were left awake.

"How can you serve men like this?"

The soldier did not reply. Longstaff lay on his back, staring at the stars, trying not to think of Nostredame. Had the sounds of celebration reached him in his living tomb? Had he felt the stamping feet? Longstaff edged nearer the stake. How much air did a man need to survive? The planks had been poorly made, not properly joined. Would air permeate the hard-packed earth and reach the prophet in his tomb?

Vischer shifted quietly in the darkness. "Better not."

"We can still save him."

"I'll wake them, if you move again."

On his side, with his back to Nostredame, Longstaff took Aurélie's medallion in both hands – how she would rage if she knew what was happening here. The cardinal was an educated man, preying on the ignorance of his inferiors, forging a crude idol to draw their hatred – Evangelism, black magic, a virgin queen, an English assassin and prophesies of future glory. Aurélie still hoped people would join a different fight – reason against revelation instead of religion against religion. First, they'd have to throw off greed, fear, envy. Aurélie believed it would happen; Longstaff loved her for it but did not share her faith. The only thing most people could agree on was the need to eliminate people like her, the few golden lights in the darkness.

She knew him, he realised; whatever she heard in the following weeks and months, she would continue to know him. As the hours wore by, and sleep continued to elude him, Longstaff held her in his heart as protection against the ghosts and demons of this haunted place.

*

Aurélie counted eight paces from the window to the back wall, eight and a half from the door to the side wall. Almost a perfect square, or actually a perfect square? It was difficult to be sure; the built-in bookshelves appeared to vary in depth. She rolled back the Turkey carpets and counted the floorboards. Thirteen. Uniform in width, each one fixed in place. She could see where they came to an end at the door. On the far side of the room they disappeared beneath the bookshelves. How many hours had passed? It was hard to be certain, though her body told her she would normally be sleeping by now. She pictured the view from the room's single window, overlooking the garden with its beds of marigold, thyme, isope, rosemary. Then the river Fleet beyond, and steep steps up to the summit of Saffron Hill on the far side.

And the parlour below this library? Aurélie had only sat there once, for less than twenty minutes. Had it been bigger?

One by one, she removed Dee's books from the shelves, trying to make as little noise as possible as she shook each one, hoping something might fall from between the pages, then stacked them in neat piles behind her. Secrets were always found in books; that's what she believed. Aurélie did not know what she was looking for, only that she couldn't give up.

Dee's bookshelves were beautifully fashioned. On hands and knees, Aurélie reached into the depths, tapped her knuckles on the panels. Nothing. As she straightened, hunger uncurled in her stomach like an animal. God, but Matthew would be furious if she got herself killed. She stared across the piles of books at the wall opposite the door. One last chance.

Again, she worked methodically. Left to right, the stacks of searched books grew into a labyrinth behind her. She had to break off to light the second half of the candle. Finally, the shelves were empty, but careful tapping revealed no anomalies. Nothing had floated down from between the pages. Aurélie cupped hands around the candle-stub to protect the precious flame. More in desperation than hope, she dropped to her knees and shuffled alongside the empty shelves.

A glimmer of gold in the darkness. Her fingertips brushed cold metal.

Standing on a pile of books, she looked for a second hinge. The door had been hidden with great cunning. Aurélie fought the urge to rush, searching for the catch while sweat gathered at her armpits and the nape of her neck. She was salivating, no longer with hunger. It was the taste of victory that filled her mouth. A soft click. One narrow section of the bookshelves swung towards her.

The room beyond was small, though it seemed an age before the candle flame cast light enough to see it by; a round table, divided into twelve sections with the waxen seal of Hermes Trisgemistus in the centre. Shapes inscribed on the floor. She'd found Dee's Chamber of Practice, where the outwardly sober scholar performed his incantations and evocations.

Aurélie raised the candle. Had she merely exchanged one prison for another? No. There was a window hidden behind the tapestry. Aurélie craned her neck for a glimpse of stars. Moonlight stirred lazy diamonds on the poorly named Fleet. An almost imperceptible lightening of the sky; dawn was not far off.

Something shifted in the garden. A bird? A breath of wind? Aurélie stood absolutely still. Only her eyes moved, searching the dark silhouettes for anything out of the ordinary.

A grey figure raised its head, a small white face stared up at her. The features were familiar. She nearly said the name aloud. What in God's name? She raised a finger to her lips, signalled with her hands that he should stay where he was. The window was fastened with a simple clasp. It lifted noiselessly.

Where was Dee? Asleep? Pacing restlessly on the ground floor of his home? Aurélie raised a hand: *wait!* She hurried back to the library, soaked a piece of bread in the water Dee had left for her and stuffed it in her pocket. The window faced north-east; soon, the sun would rise, huge on the rooftops. Aurélie assessed the drop, her mind already attempting to betray her with the phantom snap of breaking bones.

She sat on the window sill. Matthew was with her, something he'd told her once about jumping from height: *feet together, toes pointed ten degrees west of north. Knees bent, ten degrees east.*

Suspended in mid-air – *knees bent* – she fell to her right, rolling into the impact. Silence at her back. She crawled to the bushes.

"How did you get here?"

Sir Nicholas Bacon's oldest son. She saw the effort he made to conquer his fear. At least he had the sense to whisper: "Father was at Westminster last night. Mother worried when you didn't come home, but then a messenger arrived. I was at the top of the stairs…"

"I meant, how did you get *here*."

"By boat."

"Where is it?"

"Tied at the bottom of the garden."

She took him by the elbow. Smells reached her. Marigold, thyme, isope, rosemary. They trampled blindly through Dee's herb garden, Aurélie's light shoes soaked with dew. She shivered, her cloak abandoned in Dee's hall. Anthony's boat was little better than a raft, two lengths of elm lashed together with a fraying rope. She felt a sudden burst of admiration for the boy.

He looked back at the house and shuddered. "You described it exactly. I got here all right, but then I didn't know what to do."

She gave him a fierce hug. The small craft rocked alarmingly as they climbed aboard. Aurélie pushed them away from the bank, let the boat drift with the tide though that was the wrong direction, away from York House and Whitehall. Behind them a light appeared in one of the ground floor rooms.

Aurélie could feel the beat of Anthony's heart.

"Go on," she whispered, "you were hiding at the top of the stairs…"

"I never said I was hiding."

"Did anyone see you there?"

"No one looked. I heard the messenger tell mother you'd taken a chill. Nothing serious, but you'd decided to stay overnight at the house of Dr. Dee. Mother was reassured, but I couldn't sleep. Eventually I slipped out, made my way to the

Fleet. I found this boat. No one was looking. I drifted with the tide until I came to the house."

Aurélie looked up at the stars fading in a brightening sky. "Why?"

They turned a bend in the river. Aurélie grabbed the paddle and steered them towards the bank.

"You told us about him. The black magician. About the young woman who goes to his house each day, but she's always careful to leave before nightfall. About the change that comes over him when the moon rises."

Aurélie remembered now. A ghost story to frighten the children, sheets pulled up to their chins, eyes wide with delicious terror. She'd smiled at the time, enjoying the feeling of mischief as she built a tale around the calumnies told about John Dee.

"It was just a story."

He gave her a look of such exasperation she burst out laughing, struggling to control a sudden note of hysteria.

"You brave, mad boy. Your mother's going to kill me."

The boat nudged against the riverbank. They were level with Hockley Fields, where the archers shot their targets. Aurélie had no idea what time Walsingham and Sir Nicholas were scheduled to make their denunciation of Norfolk. The queen was a notoriously late riser. Aurélie had no money for a carriage, no cloak or outdoor shoes. They would have to walk, two hours to reach Whitehall. And then what? In her state, with her accent, would the guards pay her any more attention than a London coachman?

She needed Anne. No one would dare prevent the Lord Chancellor's wife from reaching her husband. Aurélie seized hold of Anthony's hand.

"We have to get you home. I know you're tired. I am, too. But we need to move fast. Understand?"

She dragged the boy in a wide circle around Clerkenwell Green. They hadn't drifted far; the spire of St James's Church was still visible. Aurélie kept her head down. London was a different city at this time of day. Traders in greasy aprons and dirty leggings spat and grumbled as they kicked beggars from their doorways. Night-dwellers – the cut-throats, palliards, whores and pickpockets – had not yet left the streets. Aurélie hardly dared breathe until they left the Clerkenwell Road. The city grew more respectable, which brought new terrors. She knew how she must look, in torn slippers, pulling an exhausted boy. Please God don't let the constables stop her, even a concerned citizen. Any delay might be fatal.

The road forked. Aurélie fought the urge to head for Whitehall. The queen's guards would turn her away. Anne was the fastest route to Sir Nicholas.

The streets grew busier. Anthony stumbled. A terrible weariness dogged Aurélie's own steps. When had she last slept? The two of them fell against the grand door of York House.

Pandemonium. Anne fell on Anthony as if to devour him, shot a look of pure fury at Aurélie – once again, she'd led the children into danger.

Anthony clutched his mother's hand. "Don't. Let her explain." He looked at Aurélie. Francis crashed into her then, wrapping both arms around her legs.

Anne turned to a servant. "Call off the search party. Prepare a bath. We need food, hot drinks and blankets in the parlour." She led them to her private room. Aurélie turned on the threshold.

"Anthony, take Francis upstairs."

"What..."

Aurélie closed the door on the two boys. "Anne, listen to me. Anthony overheard you talking with the messenger last night. He was worried and came to find me. I had no hand in his adventure, except that I might have died but for his courage."

She forced herself to stand straight, though it felt as if every muscle had been hung with weights. "Sir Nicholas has been drawn into a conspiracy. Walsingham is behind it..."

"To unmask the traitor Norfolk. Nicholas has no secrets from me."

"Norfolk is no more a traitor than you. We have to get word to your husband. Now."

Blood drained from Anne's face. "Norfolk is innocent? But Walsingham has a letter in the Duke's own hand."

"A forgery."

"My husband would never… Walsingham?"

Aurélie shook her head. "Leicester's been leading them by the nose since the beginning." She sank into a chair, the last of her strength drained from aching limbs. "You have to warn them."

"I need to dress." Anne hurried to the door, barking orders like a sergeant major.

I need to dress! The sheer, bloody-minded stupidity of it. Even with all her connections, Anne remained a woman; the slightest lapse in propriety would see her delayed a dozen times between here and her husband.

"Have my best dress laid out…

"Take the food and blankets directly to Mistress Longstaff's room…

"Have William sit with the boys. He's not to let them out of his sight…"

Aurélie heard the note of panic in Anne's voice. Thank God; she'd grasped the urgency of the situation.

"Fetch Mistress Longstaff at once if Anthony shows any sign of illness. Otherwise, she's not to be disturbed."

"Aurélie," Anne shook her. "Go to bed."

"Sleep?" objected Aurélie. "There's more…"

Anne cut her off. "I know what needs to be done."

Too tired to argue, Aurélie climbed the stairs to her room and sat at the dressing table. A servant entered with food and drink.

"Shall I draw you a bath, mistress?"

Aurélie reached into her pocket, fingers closing around the soggy remnants of Dee's bread.

"The next time they catch a mouse in the kitchen, have it caged and brought to me here."

Too well-trained to show surprise, the maid merely nodded and continued about her business. Aurélie pulled off her ruined stockings and replaced them with a pair of woollen socks. She lay down on the bed, expecting to lie awake until news came from Whitehall. Her eyes closed of their own accord. Within seconds, she was fast asleep.

Chapter 32

It was nearly dawn when Longstaff finally drifted into restless sleep. He dreamed of Nostredame, falling through layers of foliage, leaves, undergrowth and earth, as if he were an uninvited guest at the prophet's descent into death. When Longstaff woke soon afterwards, roused by Rastignac and his men, he was cold, his skin clammy, and wholly convinced that Nostredame was no longer alive. The sky above his head was blue, the day warm and cloudless, the clearing blurry with dust, small puffs kicked up to join the general haze with every movement. None of the busy, laughing lackeys appeared the worse for wear following their night's carouse.

Rastignac and Vischer stood talking, close enough that Longstaff could hear their conversation.

"We'll be back an hour before sunset. That will give the cardinal sufficient time to reach Catherine's side. My name is well-known in these parts. By the time I'm done with the locals, they'll be up here like a pack of ravening wolves, ready to tear the Englishman apart." He paused. "Don't do anything stupid while we're gone."

"You don't have to worry about me," Vischer sounded offended.

"I'll fire a shot when we're close. Toss him the key and his sword when you hear it."

He raised his voice for Longstaff's benefit. "If he tries to run, put a musket ball in his leg. When you're done, clear off into the forest. I'll let you know when it's safe to come out."

"You're certain this will work?"

"It's what we do," Rastignac grinned as he swung up onto the white charger. "Until this evening, Vischer."

He stood in the stirrups, arm raised above his head – the signal to move out. Longstaff watched them go, then waited until the clearing was silent before turning to look at the prophet's tomb, covered in soot and wine and the scratched lines of a pentagram. He'd grown to like Nostredame and could have wept for him, tears of frustration at the sheer stupid cruelty of it all. Here he was, chained about the neck; he hadn't stopped Leicester's man from shooting an arrow into his shoulder, nor Vischer from torturing him, nor Rastignac from burying Nostredame alive. In that moment, he would happily have killed them all, and the revered Cardinal of Lorraine, as well – him above all. The man who commanded, whose life of privilege and wealth had led to nothing but these ghoulish games of power and influence. The cardinal had no idea of the damage he caused. The common folk looked up to him, aped his methods, and thus the poison spread in ever growing circles.

Vischer swapped his musket for a piece of brushwood, began erasing hoofprints and carriage tracks from the ground, anything which would reveal that a large body of men had been here recently. A good soldier or a victim of his grotesque predicament? The self-appointed task was pointless; if events turned out as Rastignac planned, a mob of murderous peasants would descend on this clearing in a few hours' time, trampling the earth, ending Longstaff's life in a fit of righteous fury.

Vischer looked around, apparently seeking another task.

"Not everything was a lie," said Longstaff. "I was raised in Germany from the age of eight, in Lübeck." He did not look directly at the soldier. "I hated the place. My guardian was a merchant who assumed I'd grow up to follow in his footsteps. There really was a Max Meyer, you know; a humble blacksmith before he became a soldier. I saw him once leading a procession of men along Breite Strasse when I was maybe nine. He looked like a warrior from the old stories, broad smile on his open face, forty armed riders in his train. God but I ached to be one of them."

"I thought the name was familiar," said Vischer,

"I've fought all my life," added Longstaff, "but never in the East. For what it's worth, I'm sorry I lied."

"What happened to him?"

"Meyer? Hansa merchants engaged him to make war on Sweden, then grew jealous and betrayed him to the King of Denmark. That was later."

"Later," agreed Vischer, "when dreams of glory turn to dust. They always do, in the end."

"You've been a soldier long enough. You should know." Longstaff paused. "What you're doing now, it's not soldiering. They mean to start a war."

Vischer cut him off. "I know what you're going to say. Maybe you're right, but a soldier takes an oath, for better or worse, and only knows himself for as long as he keeps it."

Longstaff could have gone on. One look at the man's face told him it was pointless – Vischer would follow his orders to the bitter end.

Time passed. Vischer tossed him a water-skin when the sun was directly overhead. Longstaff drank, then sprayed a portion on the ground, thinking of the nobles who paid children to scatter rose-water where they walked, to lay the dust. Longstaff began to exercise, stretching, lunging, making use of the heavy chain which bound him to the stake. *Toss him the key and his sword.* Rastignac's words. Even a mob might baulk at killing a man in chains and so they'd let him stand and die as if he were free.

"It won't do any good," called Vischer.

"Better idea?"

"You haven't exactly conducted yourself with honour, Matthew Longstaff. You set fire to buildings that are home to women and children."

"I know." The earth was drying out. Soon, the dust would rise again, putting an end to his exercises.

"I'm sorry, too," said Vischer, "for what it's worth."

A thick bank of slate grey cloud arrived an hour later, obscuring the sun and creating a false dusk. Vischer made his pack fast to the saddle of his horse. Longstaff looked towards the gap in the trees through which Rastignac and his men had departed, the same route by which he expected them to reappear. A memory returned to him of walking hand in hand with Aurélie in the woods around Martlesham one clear night, pulling her roughly to the ground when he'd heard the thunder. He'd known what it was, they'd told him when he was a child – the Wild Hunt; Wodan's undead warriors come to collect the souls of the dead. Lie flat, he'd shouted above the terrible noise. *Close your eyes if you want to live.*

The terror passed. When he'd opened one eye, Aurélie was already sitting up, moonlight sparkling in the deep blue eyes.

"Your face, Matthew. Did you really think it was the Old Gods, come to carry us away?"

"I don't see…"

"Geese," she managed before breaking down in giggles. "Migrating geese, a huge skein flying low, thousands beating their wings with a noise like thunder."

Longstaff still wasn't sure she'd been right, though she had a sixth sense for these things. He smiled; a 'sense' was not how she'd describe it – the ability to think, to listen, to read and observe. Once, he'd heard her claim she was without faith. It wasn't true. Aurélie had no time for revelation, but her reverence for the powers of reason was unbounded.

The power of reason had failed Longstaff on this occasion. No trick of the mind would turn the cardinal's lackeys into geese.

Without him, there would be no reason for Aurélie to remain in England. He wasn't foolish enough to think she'd die of grief. Still young, still full of curiosity, still certain she could make this world a better place.

Longstaff prayed the next man would be wise enough to understand her. Aurélie needed to be where life's heart beat with greatest force, not hidden away among peasants and yeoman. For all their good and honest qualities, his neighbours in Suffolk were among the most likely people in the world to confuse curiosity with witchcraft and burn her at the stake.

Chapter 33

A shot sounded in the distance. A dozen ravens exploded from the trees. Vischer was already on his feet.

"My sword," shouted Longstaff, as the first shouts reached them. Vischer approached with the katzbalger in one hand. He buried it point first and unslung his musket in one smooth action.

"You heard the bastard. You run, I'll put a musket ball in your leg. Stand, Longstaff. Face your doom like a soldier."

He produced a key from inside his leather jerkin. "Die with blood on your blade. God knows they deserve it. In a better world, you and I would have fought side by side."

He threw the key in a high arc. Longstaff scrambled to reach it. By the time he turned back, Vischer was gone. The shouts were louder now, growing in number. Longstaff unlocked the iron collar. He knew he was playing straight into the cardinal's hands; a wiser man would have remained in chains, tried to make the mob question the story they'd been told.

Too late for second thoughts. Christ turned the other cheek, not Longstaff. He ran to retrieve his sword. Rastignac had planned it this way; now, the long chain would be one more piece of evidence against him. Longstaff laid it along the ground parallel to the edge of the clearing, one end still attached to the stake.

He took several long strides forward and planted his feet in the dry earth. They came at him with teeth bared, eyes wild with blood-lust. Longstaff cursed. It was Rastignac he wanted, not these poor fools. One came faster than his fellows, long threshing knife waved wildly above his head, mouth open in a terrible scream. Longstaff's instinct was to put him down with the flat of his sword. And then what? Did he expect these bastards to thank him? Would kindness make the others falter? Cruelty might. Longstaff hardened his heart, changed his grip on the katzbalger and swung.

He was just a boy. Fleet of foot, no more than fifteen. Longstaff's aim was true, his strength more than sufficient despite his wounds. The boy's head turned in the air as the body fell to its knees.

Longstaff stood perfectly still, sword held out in front of him, eyes on the onrushing horde. He counted twenty. The men at the rear, who'd already decided to leave the business of killing to their friends, slowed further now. The men at the fore faltered, feeling air at their backs, pulled up in a line twenty paces short of Longstaff, waving knives, scythes and pitchforks above their heads. Longstaff spat; not a single real weapon between them.

"Rastignac," he bellowed, "is this the best you can do?"

Longstaff knelt, one knee resting on the boy's severed head. He grinned at the farmers and small-holders, who took a collective step back. What had Rastignac told them? Had he gone too far with his tales of black magic and devil worship? Some looked back at the treeline, no doubt wondering the same as Longstaff – where were the horsemen? Where was their old neighbour, come to lead them in a holy crusade against the heretic sorcerer?

Rastignac rode out from among the trees on his white horse, flanked on both sides. The mob cheered, shaking their farm tools at Longstaff and shouting curses. Rastignac signalled to two of his men: *bring this farce to an end.*

Longstaff recognised them. On the road from Orléans, he'd assumed they were brothers. Both had the same goose grey eyes. They dressed alike, in black doublets and jerkins with crystal buttons. For a moment, Longstaff was struck by the odd beauty of the scene, each detail grew at frightening speed as the two men spurred their horses. The rabble scattered, cheering even as they dived clear of the flashing hooves. Longstaff turned and ran. A dozen long strides. The timing had to be perfect. He broke right, flung himself down, plunged his sword through the chain's final link. Iron scraped against steel. He used the sword as a lever, lifting the chain to create a tripwire.

A sudden clap of thunder. The horses struck the chain, ripping the sword from Longstaff's grasp. Pain seared his shoulder as he ducked beneath the hooves, blinded by dust. Deafened by the screams of the animals, the furious shouts of their fallen riders. Where were they? Where was his sword. The pain was appalling, Longstaff's vision dimmed. He found the sword, stared stupidly at a jagged edge where there should have been another foot of tempered steel. He forced himself up, broken sword in his weaker hand, drifting through the dust – an avenging angel, bent on murder.

The first lackey, trapped beneath his mount, spat curses through tears of pain. His leather cap had rolled free. Thin hair, lank with sweat. Longstaff kicked the back of his skull, felt bone shatter, saw the face fall slack, eyes enormous with the emptiness of death.

Footsteps behind him. Longstaff saw a ghost in the cloud. The lackey attacked, swinging his sword in a whistling arc. Longstaff let him come, slipped inside a wild slash, buried the broken *katzbalger* in soft flesh, then watched as the man crumpled.

He wanted to throw back his head and howl. He was the ghost, this cloud of dust his dream and kingdom. Only let them come and he would kill from now until Judgement Day.

No one came. In a matter of seconds, the dust would settle and Longstaff lose his cloak of invisibility. They would overwhelm him by force of numbers or kill him from a distance with musket balls. Longstaff could not wait.

He checked the horses. The foreleg on one was bent at a sickening angle. The other appeared to have survived the fall unscathed. Longstaff helped the animal to its feet, sent it running with a slap on the rump, grinning as he imagined the effect – a riderless horse appearing from the dust.

He did not give the first animal a merciful death. He wanted the screams to accompany him on his slow walk, black with dirt, smeared in the blood of his victims. One arm hung useless at his side, the other held a broken sword. A beast from the pits of Hell when he finally emerged from the swirling cloud.

The peasants crossed themselves. Longstaff's teeth flashed white.

"Rastignac," he shouted. "You and me. Let's end it like men."

The mercenary leader leaned back in his saddle and laughed.

"My dear fellow, there is no such thing as you and me. I couldn't have planned this better myself, your name will live on in infamy. No need for any heroics on my part."

Almost without thinking, it seemed, he unhooked the musket from his saddle and put it to his shoulder.

"The black legend of Matthew Longstaff," he called with a smile. Closed one eye and pulled the trigger.

Longstaff moved left. A fraction too late, or Rastignac had anticipated him. The musket ball struck him in the side. In the soft flesh below his ribs.

Longstaff lay on his back, the sky above turned grey. He would not let go of the sword. He felt light-headed. Past pain. Bewildered more than scared at how little strength remained in his legs, how long it took to rise.

He was on his knees, propped against the broken sword, when a horn sounded in the woods. Was this the Wild Hunt, come to claim him at last? Hooves beat their fast tattoo, coming nearer. Longstaff saw Rastignac swivel left and right in the saddle, uncertain who approached. The peasants began to panic – they knew the legends associated with this barren clearing. Some ran. Others dropped to their knees, arms raised, farm tools beside them in the dirt.

Mounted soldiers galloped into the clearing. In royal livery. Longstaff knew he must be dreaming. The pain was making him delirious. He saw old friends. To bid him welcome or farewell? Durant was there, and the insufferable merchant from Paris.

No sign of Aurélie. Only Rastignac. Perhaps the lackey still thought he could win. He spurred the great, white horse. Longstaff watched him come, thundering closer and closer. He feared he would fall if he tried to move, he couldn't bear the thought of being trampled beneath the horse's hooves and so he stood. A single musket shot sounded from the trees on the far side of clearing. The ball struck Rastignac in the stomach. He swayed in the saddle but the horse kept coming.

Longstaff raised a hand: *Stop.* Rastignac ran him down, struck him in the chest and sent him spinning to the ground. Something broke, with the sound of a butcher hacking meat. A *massacre.* Longstaff wanted to laugh, but it was too late. He lay with his head on Nostredame's tomb and watched the white horse slow to a walk. Rastignac's dead body slipped from the saddle, raising a small cloud of dust where it struck the earth.

A hand fell on Longstaff's shoulder. Durant, shouting orders at his men, "Search the trees. Find whoever took that shot."

Vischer, thought Longstaff. It must have been. The German soldier had tried to save his life. He gripped his friend's arm. "Let him go."

He wouldn't be conscious much longer. The pain was suffocating. His hand fell on Nostredame's tomb. He spoke with the last of his strength, already giving himself into oblivion's velvet embrace.

"You have to dig him up."

He drifted into darkness on the Frenchman's oddly chanting voice. A garbled story. Almost a poem, spoken to the beat of a four-fingered hand.

Chapter 34

AURÉLIE

Aurélie was pale, with dark rings around her eyes. Yesterday, she'd hardly been able to lift her arms from the bed. An infection brought on by walking through the damp streets of London in stocking'd feet. Anne had been concerned. Aurélie recalled a stream of physicians, her temperature dangerously high, calves swaddled in a cold compress, but she was healthy, still young, her body perfectly capable of fighting an infection, of feeling embarrassment when she thought of how tenderly Anne had cared for her, sitting at her bedside during the day, rising hourly to change the soaking sheets when her fever broke.

This morning, waking with a clear head for the first time, Aurélie had sent her hostess straight to bed. Now she lay beneath the fresh sheets, feeling restless, her strength returning so fast she could almost feel it happening.

There was a knock at the door. She gave a guilty start, bringing her feet beneath the covers. "Come in."

Sir Nicholas stood in the doorway. Aurélie searched his face for clues. *Had Anne reached him in time?* He was here, she reminded herself, not locked in the Tower.

"Well?"

"May I sit?"

He did not wait for an answer. "The worst few days of my life, and God knows I've lived through harrowing times. Thank you, Aurélie. If it weren't for you, this foolish old man would have laid his own head on the block." Aurélie saw the ghost of a smile. "I'm told Anne was magnificent. Leicester had men stationed all over the palace. They intercepted her. She didn't hesitate, went barrelling right at them, lashing each in turn with that tongue of hers, throwing doors open at random until she found us – Walsingham and I, gathering our documents and straightening our clothes. More than I deserve to have two such guardian angels. The galleries were already full; we'd made sure of that. The palace alive with rumours. Five more minutes and they'd have discovered exactly what matter we wished to bring before her Majesty. With hindsight, we'd have been wiser to seek her out in private, but she's always so willing to forgive her favourites, overlook any mountain of evidence if only a man bends the knee and declares his love." Sir Nicholas looked round. "They told me there was wine?"

"On the dressing table."

She watched him cross the room. He seemed to have lost weight, the heavy doublet sagging at his shoulders.

"We were called a moment later by that ghastly old man with the gouty leg. The longest walk of my life; the way his foot drags, like being escorted by snakes."

Sir Nicholas continued his story at the window. "We made fools of ourselves, of course. Dressed in our best clothes, solemn expressions as we proposed some trifling amendment to fishing rights. Impossible to alter our manner so quickly, somehow – talking about trout in tones appropriate for bringing a charge of high treason. Elizabeth knows me too well to think I'd make sport of her, thank God. We must have resembled a pantomime act, Walsingham and I – one so stout he can hardly climb a flight of stairs, the other a half-starved pup."

Aurélie wanted to laugh, to help Sir Nicholas pass it off as just another day at the English Court. Looking at him, however, she found the story too sad.

"We were spouting gibberish," he continued. "We must have appeared as two floundering whales, judging by the bewildered expressions in the galleries. They were laughing by the end. Only our adversary saw fit to provide us with comfort. The Earl of Leicester was not laughing."

Sir Nicholas found a new perch on the edge of Aurélie's bed.

"Did you never think of telling Elizabeth the truth?"

She watched his eyebrows lift in surprise.

"Inform the queen that her closest advisors occupy their time plotting against one another? She would not thank us for it. Elizabeth takes great pains to keep the players evenly matched, Aurélie. Don't underestimate her. The Spanish have a saying: only the temporary lasts forever. No one thought Elizabeth would survive a year, but she has no intention of going anywhere. She gives the Dutch just enough help to maintain their fight against the Spanish, never enough to win. She engages in endless negotiations for marriage to a French prince, only to keep them from marrying elsewhere. Elizabeth is England, she knows it, everything she does is calculated to ensure her survival."

"What will happen now?"

Sir Nicholas shrugged. "On the surface, things will continue as before. William Cecil and the Earl of Leicester have already met, to congratulate one another on their political acumen…"

"… as if it were a game." Aurélie shook her head in disgust. "Leicester sent a man to murder my husband."

"I have no doubt that Longstaff proved himself equal to the challenge."

Aurélie sat up in bed. "He's discovered more than you realise. It was never about Walsingham's book – Durant was abducted for his skills as a forger, to compose verses that might have been written by Michel de Nostredame."

"Catherine de Medici's pet prophet?"

"She believes every word he writes. The Guise family want her to ally with Spain and declare war on England."

Sir Nicholas rubbed his heavy, grey-blue cheeks. He looked almost too tired to think the implications through. "As we speak, Catherine is on her way to the Pyrenees for a meeting with her son-in-law, King Philip of Spain. Ostensibly, it's an opportunity to spend time with her daughter." He placed a hand on Aurélie's forearm. "Leave it with me. I'll make sure this information reaches the right people."

"And Walsingham?"

Sir Nicholas nodded. "He might be just the man. It was Walsingham who came up with that nonsense about fishing rights. He has a good mind. Cecil and Leicester would both have to agree, of course."

She stared at him. "That's not what I meant. Walsingham is responsible for this whole mess. It was his plan to spread rumours of a lost Gospel in the first place. He was wrong to suspect the Duke of Norfolk, wrong about the reason Durant was abducted, wrong to trust Dee..."

"And yet, if what you've told me is true, Aurélie, then his machinations have uncovered a serious threat against England."

"Blind, stupid luck!" she spluttered.

"A quality people prize," countered Sir Nicholas.

Aurélie couldn't believe her ears. She looked at the caged mouse on the window ledge, dead since feasting on the sodden bread she'd removed from the house in Clerkenwell.

"And Dee?"

Sir Nicholas cleared his throat. "Too well-known, I'm afraid, too many friends in high places."

Aurélie threw herself back on the bed. "So, we all just carry on as if nothing had happened?"

"Not quite." Sir Nicholas cleared his throat. "The Earl of Leicester has a vindictive streak. He can't move against Cecil or me, especially not in light of these latest revelations, but he may regard you as fair game."

"What are you suggesting?"

"A period abroad. A year, two at the most, just until this incident has been forgotten..."

Aurélie shook her head in disbelief. "Walsingham has a glittering career ahead of him and I have to leave the country? What about Durant?"

"Not officially our concern as he's a subject of the French Crown. Unofficially, Walsingham and I stand in your debt. We'll do what we can."

Sir Nicholas took a deep breath. Aurélie could almost hear him telling himself how patient he'd been – he was an important man, too important to waste time smoothing her ruffled feathers.

"Your knowledge of recent events is potentially dangerous to a great many people, but Walsingham would rather have you for a friend than an enemy. He's not incapable of gratitude, you'd do well to think on that rather than rail against aspects of the world which none of us can change."

Aurélie looked past him. She'd risked her life for nothing, except that these intriguers could carry on with their plots. *Aspects of the world which none of us can change?* That wasn't what she believed. Aurélie kept her expression carefully neutral. Personally, she would not miss the house in Suffolk, but she knew what the place meant to her husband.

"I can't speak for Matthew..."

"Of course you can, Aurélie. We both know that."

"He'll take it badly. Exiled for a second time."

"Better to see it as an opportunity for travel abroad..."

"... in the queen's service?"

"And in your absence," Sir Nicholas continued as if she hadn't spoken, "I'll see to the smooth running of the estate."

"I mean it," said Aurélie. "I'll take him away, but we go with official recognition, not like thieves in the night."

He stared at her. "Come on then, spit it out. What is it you want?"

"Anthony Jenkinson."

Everyone in London knew the name. Ivan the Terrible, Suleiman the Magnificent, and the Shah of Persia all knew the name. With no contacts, no previous knowledge of the terrain, its people or their languages – armed, in fact, with nothing but a consignment of kersey cloth – this merchant adventurer had convinced the greatest men in the east that England was a worthy trading partner.

"What about him?"

"I've read your correspondence. I know he wants you to send a diplomatic mission to Constantinople. People with knowledge of the culture, the languages and beliefs. People who know how to look after themselves."

"You and Longstaff?"

"We're qualified."

"Jenkinson won't like it."

"Nonsense."

She lowered her eyes, knowing she wouldn't get what she wanted by provoking him. "Where else would you have us go? I've exhausted my welcome in Italy. France is impossible. There's still a price on Matthew's head in Muscovy. And they burn people like me in Spain, or had you forgotten?"

"Very well," Sir Nicholas shrugged. "How soon can you be ready to leave?"

"So keen to see the back of me?"

"It's not safe for you here, Aurélie."

"I have to find Matthew."

"Nothing easier," said Sir Nicholas. "There's an English merchant who trades out of Bordeaux; a friend of mine who already knows your husband. He'll provide you with everything you need. If you're strong enough, you could be on your way tomorrow."

Awkwardly, he leaned over to plant a kiss on her forehead. "But don't stay away too long. Anne and the boys would never forgive me if you disappeared from our lives indefinitely."

Chapter 35

The lady left alone, to bring about
An era of good fortune. In time, he will
Beg pardon of the Gods, appease the Furies,
Stand in the same river twice, at her side.

The sun fell on Durant's narrow back as he rode the last mile. Even after all these years, every tree on the approach to the old family estate seemed familiar.

He was tired. The months of captivity had taken their toll, and then the last few weeks – starting on the night he'd murdered two men – had felt like a descent into madness. He hardly remembered riding down from the high plateau and the smoking ruins of his cabin. He'd made for the nearest town, in desperate need of new clothes and information. It was there he'd learned that Catherine de Medici was expected in Bordeaux.

He had not forgotten the cardinal's instructions to Vincent: *An assassination, accompanied by sundry effects. Longstaff will play the role of villain, sent by England to murder France's foremost astrologer.*

With no idea of where to look for his friend, Durant had only been able to think that Catherine held the key – get to her, and there might be something he could do for Longstaff. He'd flogged the horse half to death, worrying at how he might win an audience with the most powerful woman in France. A day's ride from overtaking the Royal Progress, it had been pure good fortune he'd crossed paths with Horatio Palavicino and the English ambassador. They'd cleaned him up and somehow arranged a midnight meeting with the Queen Mother. Catherine had been coldly dismissive until he began reciting – poems she'd only received from Nostredame two days earlier. Durant explained the references to his own daughter, his friends. He talked about where he'd been kept and the men who'd held him there. Finally, he remembered to produce the Cardinal of Lorraine's letter. There was no seal or signature, only that single initial – *C* – but Catherine was convinced. Secretly, she put soldiers and horses at his disposal while Palavicino worked his own brand of magic, bribing a man who'd ridden in that morning with the cardinal.

Still, it had been a close-run thing. Longstaff's life had hung in the balance for several days. Durant hadn't left his side on the slow journey to Palavicino's home in Bordeaux, nor afterwards, not until he was sure his friend was out of danger.

Of course, it had to be Bordeaux – the city closest to Durant's childhood home. On his first trip to the local apothecary, he'd recognised the building where his father's lawyer had lived and worked, then recalled a promise he'd made himself at the cabin – to go back, if he survived, and find out what had become of his family estate.

In Montpellier, where he'd studied medicine, he had received regular letters from the estate steward, but that was a decade ago. It wouldn't have surprised Durant if the château had been razed to the ground in the meantime, or sold, or simply fallen into crumbling disrepair. Nothing would have surprised him except the letter he found waiting for him in the lawyer's office.

Dear Gaetan,

If you're finally reading this letter, then Thank God – it's long past time. You can hardly imagine how Matthew and I rejoiced when we heard of your reunion with Laure, how moved we were by your descriptions of the state in which you found her.

Of course, Laure needed to leave Calais, but why Paris? I remembered how you'd spoken of the house near Bordeaux where you were raised and where Laure spent the first five years of her life. When you made no reference to it in your letters, despite my repeated inquiries, I resolved to take matters into my own hands.

I have written to you about Anne Bacon. With her assistance, I wrote to every lawyer's practice in Bordeaux. We found the man your family used and learned the estate was still yours, that it was still standing but sorely in need of funds.

You may not know, but I received a substantial sum of money when Giacomo Vescosi's property was sold in Florence, a portion of which has been made available for the upkeep and improvement of your family home. I hope you will accept this money in the spirit it is given – as a gift – and I hope you can forgive me for interfering in matters which are none of my business.

Aurélie

Postscript: Matthew had no hand any of this. He gives you too much credit as a man of sound judgement.

The old steward had recognised him. The gardens were overgrown and most of the rooms closed up. Upstairs, in the room Durant had shared with his wife, he had to force the shutters open, straining against the tangle of creepers outside. The distant hills looked just as he remembered, draped now in the yellows and greens of spring. He turned and stared at his footprints in the dust.

Everything was the same and everything was different. His wife had died in this room. When Durant had stood here last, there had been a bouquet of flowers on every surface, the bedsheets sown with rosemary and lavender. A kaleidoscope of scents corrupted by the stench of death.

He could not look at the bed. A copy of Horace still lay on his wife's dressing table. He sat and flipped it open to a page marked with a lock of Laure's hair:

Here's what I crave most, son of Latona,
Good health, a sound mind, relish of life,
And an old age that maintains a stylish
Grip on itself, with the lyre beside me.

He couldn't remember – had she read these verses on the pleasures and consolations of old age to torture herself, or as a last message to him? Durant reached inside his pouch for the poems he'd composed during the last days of his captivity. Catherine de Medici had destroyed the originals. Durant had not seen fit to reproduce them all, only these few which he'd written for Laure. Carefully, he placed the pages where she was sure to find them, beside her mother's copy of Horace.

*

Longstaff rested his forehead against the cool glass. His wrists ached where he braced himself against the window-sill, afraid his legs weren't strong enough to support his weight. *Where was he?* He'd woken alone, in darkness, staggered across the room and slipped behind the heavy curtains. Broad daylight – a busy harbour, half a dozen sloops and caravels being loaded, traders running expert hands over barrels, sacks and bales. His eyes on the circling seagulls, Longstaff waited patiently for memories to rise. Durant had been there, in the clearing and on the road as they'd travelled slowly from pothole to pothole in a flat-bed cart. Pain had been his other, constant companion. And dreams – a dungeon, a jailor making eyes at Aurélie. Rage, when he realised how she'd bargained to win a stay of execution for her husband. Images swarmed in Longstaff's mind, of her open mouth, invaded by another man's tongue…

… then he'd felt the prophet's gnarled hand on his forehead. A bitter liquid at his lips. Soothing darkness. An escape from pain into gentle dreams which shifted back and forth to the slow squeak of a wheel – the gap between conscious and unconscious far wider than he'd realised. A road that wound among simple homes and had no end. But the old man was dead: "Rest, Matthew. The road is long..."

Startled by the sound of a door opening, Longstaff peered through a gap in the curtains. Nostredame entered backwards with a basin of water in his hands. The astrologer was limping – another attack of dropsy, no doubt – and paused when he saw the empty bed. It was almost funny, the way he lifted the basin, as if his absent charge might be hiding underneath. Longstaff stepped out from behind the curtain.

"There you are," smiled Nostredame, "up and about already."

"There *you* are," replied Longstaff, "back from the dead."

"Oh, that. How long have you been awake?"

"A few minutes," Longstaff's voice was the whisper of dry leaves. He put out a hand to steady himself against the wall, suddenly aware of a terrible thirst.

"You're white as a ghost." Nostredame gave him water, then helped him back into bed. "Time to change the dressing. Rastignac broke two of your ribs. One punctured a lung. You came within a hair's breadth..."

"How did you do it?" interrupted Longstaff.

"The older you get, the less you need. Sleep, food, drink..."

"Air? I shed tears on your grave, old man."

"I told you my forefathers traded with Moorish Africa. My inheritance included a small library; one book in particular described a way of breathing. I've been doing it for years, you've seen me yourself – my eyesight dims, sounds and smells disappear. After a while, I no longer even know where I am."

Nostredame shrugged. "It's the same trance-like state in which I fashion my prophesies. One simply draws the boundaries and lets the mind run loose within its bony cage, so to speak."

Longstaff's own mind ran loose for a moment, making the sort of intuitive leap he knew Aurélie would enjoy. Under duress, Sir Nicholas Bacon had revealed to Walsingham the details of their journey to the legendary Devil's Library, only withholding the fact that they'd saved a manuscript from the flames – *On Freedom* by the Greek philosopher Epicurus, who had advised his followers not to fear God and not to worry about death.

Walsingham must have sensed this void at the heart of the story. To fill it, he'd invented an opposite work, a Gospel which purportedly concentrated all moral authority in the hands of a single man in Rome – a cage of Man's devising rather than God's.

"I have to find the words, of course," continued the astrologer, "but the images for my prophesies arrive ready-formed. When I was younger, I spent hours each day honing the ability. Just as well – it saved my life."

"Only just, from the look of you."

"Another man would have died in a quarter of the time!" Nostredame stared at him. "You're teasing."

"Just happy to find you among the living."

"It wasn't wholly without cost," conceded Nostredame. "So many hours trapped down there. I saw my birth, Longstaff. I saw myself on the day I took my first steps and on the day I told my first lie. I saw myself again at eight, beaten by a group of children in the town where I grew up. On my wife's deathbed, I saw another me promise to take care of our child, who lay dead of plague in a corner of the room. I became a procession, walking through the years of my life until we crossed into the realm of the dead. We passed a cottage, where the baby left me, scooped into the arms of a beautiful woman. The eight-year old joined a group of boys his own age sitting beneath a tree. I walked across that landscape, and each hurt from my life found a home and a cure. Until there was no one left but me. In a pool of water I saw myself for the first time, the sum of all my wounds. In life, they have been my protection, justifying the multitude of small unkindnesses, the grosser cruelties, distorting my failures so that I'd always seen them as triumphs. For the first time in my life, I was only myself and wildly different from the man I thought I knew."

"And all forgiven?" joked Longstaff awkwardly.

"Nothing is forgiven. Strange things happened in that clearing. I saw my death – a year and two months from today."

Longstaff shivered. The note of longing in the old man's voice was unnatural.

"You're cold," Nostredame interrupted himself with a smile. "You must be wondering where you are."

"Beside the ocean," replied Longstaff, happy to change the subject. He'd already noticed a familiar sense of order in the room. The pillows were unmistakably English. "Bordeaux, at a guess. I remember telling you about Horatio Pavalcino."

The astrologer smiled. "Your trials haven't dulled your wits, then."

"How long?"

"Today is the Second of May."

Two weeks. Longstaff let his head drop back. "You saved my life."

"Not me. I was too weak."

"Durant? I was beginning to think I'd dreamed him."

"His arrival was real enough, thank God."

"Is he here?"

The old man shook his head. "Once you were out of danger, he left to visit his childhood home."

"Then send in Palavicino."

"Not here either."

"What? Have I contracted an infectious disease?"

"Oh, no, there's someone here who wants to see you." Nostredame threw back the curtains and opened the window. He studied the street outside before cupping hands around his mouth and yelling: "He's awake."

He turned to look at his patient. "She wanted to get flowers for your room."

She? Longstaff heard footsteps on the stairs. The door swung open and there she stood, "I told myself I wouldn't…"

She smiled, revealing new worry lines at the corners of her blue eyes.

"Come here."

"I might hurt you."

"Come here."

Pain roared in Longstaff's chest as he held her. It had never been more welcome.

"Nostredame told me about Sparrow. I'm sorry, Matthew."

The prophet cleared his throat. "I'll leave you to it. Don't tire him, young lady."

Aurélie lay with her head on Longstaff's good shoulder. He laughed through his tears, breathing the rich scent of her hair. She'd been twenty-one when he'd seen her first. Years had passed since then – she'd lost her childhood home, her mentor, been forced to start again in a strange land far from the sun-swept hills of Tuscany – but her blue eyes still shone with the same light, her mouth promised the same kindness.

Poor Nostredame, awaiting death with such eagerness.

She lay beside him on the bed.

"What have I missed?" asked Longstaff

"England is safe from invasion, thanks in no small part to you."

He shook his head. "I did nothing, except get myself beaten half to death."

Aurélie told him what had happened in England. Longstaff sighed at the inevitable conclusion.

"And now they'll just carry on as before."

"They think it's a game," agreed Aurélie. "Everyone appears satisfied that this round has been played to an honourable draw. In England, at least. The Cardinal of Lorraine may find his position less comfortable. Catherine is doing everything she can to cut the legs out from underneath him – she's cancelled her meeting with King Philip of Spain and sent orders to young Henri of Guise that he's needed in the east to help keep the borders of Christendom safe."

"It hardly seems enough."

Aurélie burst out laughing. "You sound like me. We're alive, Matthew."

"For the moment."

"And together. Nostredame assures me you'll be yourself in no time." A light blush rose in her cheeks. "Faculties unimpaired."

She saw the look in his eye and laughed. "And Durant is alive…"

"Nostredame said he'd gone home?"

"He's making it ready for Laure."

"For the two of them?"

Aurélie shook her head. "He says the place holds too many memories. He doesn't plan to stay away forever – just until she's had a chance to make it hers."

Longstaff thought for a moment, remembering how the young woman he'd met in Paris had spoken of her childhood home; he hoped it would make her happy.

"Actually," continued Aurélie, "something good does seem to have come from all this – Durant has rediscovered his vocation. He wants to come with us."

"With us?" Longstaff narrowed his eyes. He knew that tone. "To Martlesham?"

Aurélie sounded nervous. "Sir Nicholas wants us to wait before returning. Just until the dust settles."

Longstaff resisted the urge to smile. He did not want to concede defeat before the game was even joined. The wrinkle he loved so well appeared between her eyes – she was ordering her thoughts.

"Where, exactly?" he demanded.

"Sir Nicholas has asked us to travel to Constantinople. As trade envoys."

"You've lost your mind!"

As a boy, he'd dreamed of fighting the Turks, now he was being sent to bargain with them? Secretly, the idea appealed. It was certainly no less ridiculous than any of the other options available to them. He looked at Aurélie, aware she was keeping something from him. He'd find out soon enough.

"It won't be forever," she sounded worried – Longstaff was still doing his best to appear stern and forbidding. "We could be back at Martlesham in less than two years."

Longstaff closed his eyes. They were sending him back into exile while others – men whose reckless stupidity had brought about this crisis in the first place – were rewarded with applause and advancement? Strangely, he felt no bitterness. Perhaps it was the sight of Aurélie after so many weeks apart, but he found it impossible even to trace the threads which had brought him to Bordeaux, with his friend Durant not far away and Aurélie beside him on the bed. He wrapped an arm around her, as tight as his fractured ribs would allow.

It wasn't lethargy or the after-effects of medicine. It was relief. If he was honest, it was love. Nothing changes, he thought happily. Great men play their games, never realising how powerless they are before the circling winds of fate, and the rest of us make do as best we can, turning endlessly in place and mistaking it for progress. *Nothing changes.* That was fine with him, decided Longstaff, for as long as the same heavenly law applied to Aurélie. For as long as she remained always and forever herself.

If you have enjoyed this book, the author would love it if you could leave a review on Amazon, or on the channel through which you purchased this copy.

Also by Tom Pugh

"A gripping, atmospheric debut. I couldn't put it down."

Eve Harris, Booker longlisted author of
'The Marrying of Chani Kaufman'

"Pugh's first novel is a magnificent achievement. Let us hope he returns to enthral us with another very soon."

David Dickinson,
author of the Powerscourt series

The Otiosi? As far as Mathew Longstaff knows, they're just a group of harmless scholars with an eccentric interest in the works of antiquity. When they ask him to travel east, to recover a lost text from Ivan the Terrible's private library, he can't think of anything but the reward – home. A return to England and an end to the long years of exile and warfare.

But the Otiosi are on the trail of a greater prize than Longstaff realises – the legendary 'Devil's Library'. And they are not alone. Gregorio Spina, the Pope's spymaster and Chief

Censor, is obsessed with finding the Library. It's not the accumulated wisdom of centuries he's after – a swamp of lies and heresy in his opinion – but among the filth, like a diamond at the centre of the Devil's black heart, Spina believes that God has placed a treasure, a weapon to defeat the Antichrist and pitch his hordes back into hell.

Only Longstaff, together with the unpredictable physician, Gaetan Durant, can stop Spina using the Library to plunge Europe into a second Dark Ages. The two adventurers fight their way south, from the snowfields of Muscovy to the sun-baked plains of Italy, where an ageing scholar and his beautiful, young protégé hold the final piece of the puzzle. But is it already too late? Can the four of them take on the might of the Roman Church and hope to win?